IN GOD'S HOUSE

About the Author

In 1984, Ray Mouton represented the first Catholic priest charged with sex crimes against children. His subsequent efforts to save children from the Church extended across the United States, working with a canon lawyer in the Vatican Embassy and a bishop holding a secret appointment from the Papal Nunciature. Mouton co-authored a document in 1985 that has since been hailed by the media as the most important document issued in the crisis.

Also by Ray Mouton

PAMPLONA, Running the Bulls, Bars and Barrios
in Fiesta De San Fermin

RAY
MOUTON
IN GOD'S
HOUSE

First published in the UK in 2012 by Head of Zeus, Ltd.

9 7 5 3 1 2 4 6 8

A CIP catalogue record for this book is available from the British Library.

ISBN (HB): 9781908800060
ISBN (TPB): 9781908800077
ISBN (E): 9781908800954

Printed in Germany.

Head of Zeus, Ltd
55 Monmouth Street
London, WC2H 9DG

www.headofzeus.com

This novel is for Scott Anthony Gastal, who changed the course of history when he became the first child to face a bishop in a court of law, testifying bravely before a judge and jury. It is also for all other survivors of clergy abuse, and for those who did not survive but died by suicide. It is for the families of all the children who were abandoned, not by their God but by their Church, as well as the many faithful who placed their trust in priests and bishops and received sacraments from the hands of criminals and men who harbored criminals. And it is for my wife, Melony, without whom neither this novel nor my life would be possible.

*If he were thrown into the sea with a millstone tied to his neck,
he would be far better off than facing the punishment in store
for those who harm these little children's souls.*

Luke 17:2

PART ONE

IN THE BEGINNING

1984

1

THE LAST DAY

8:30 a.m., Wednesday August 22, 1984
Coteau, Louisiana

When I drove away from home that day, headed for the Old Bishop's House, I stopped the car on the gravel lane fronting our property as I always did. I looked back at our house, pond, pool, gazebo, guest cottage, and horses grazing in the pasture. The weather was turning but it was beautiful, peaceful. My eyes skimmed the long run of bamboo and crepe myrtle trees that bordered the driveway. Leaves were blowing from the bent branches and tall stalks of bamboo waved wildly in the gusting winds, the outer bands of a hurricane in the Gulf of Mexico. Somewhere nearby a farmer was burning a field. A light smoke with a strong scent drifted across our land. As I looked over the fields and structures, dark clouds raced across the sky, almost hugging the ground all the way out to the horizon. A storm would blow through in a matter of hours even though the hurricane was making landfall to the west in Texas. I loved rough weather and I loved this place. Now I wish I had lingered longer that last day, for I would never see this place or anything else in life in the same way again.

The tall, skinny, long-legged white bird that came from a big swamp to fish in our pond every day had been wading in the shallows when I'd had coffee on the patio earlier that morning. Our youngest child, five-year-old Sasha, was feeding the ducks in the pond, and in the distance I'd watched my wife, Kate, petting Sasha's horse, Dreamer, while two of our dogs vied for her

2

attention. Our sons, Shelby and Jake, were already off to school, their departure announced by the music of Bruce Springsteen blaring from the huge speakers in Shelby's jeep.

The old Cajun man who took care of the grounds for us, a fellow everyone called Mule because of his phenomenal physical strength and equally stubborn mind, always called our place "Ti Paradis". The acreage was like a paradise carved out under a high ridge in a low basin where the Mississippi River had flowed eons ago.

A journalist covering a law case I was involved in had written that I was a young man who had it all. To some it seemed I had always had it all. It seemed that way to me too. As a kid all I cared about was football. I was a star quarterback on an undefeated, number-one-ranked football team. I had kicked a field goal to win our homecoming game and escorted my girlfriend, the homecoming queen, to the dance. At thirty-six, I had achieved more success than most lawyers my age, had been involved in several high-profile cases and causes and won them all. I believed this great streak of good luck would continue forever. On this morning, no one could have convinced me that one day soon I would lose everything that had ever mattered to me.

The day before, I had received a telephone call from the vicar of finance for the Catholic Diocese of Thiberville, who identified himself as Monsignor Buddy Belair. He invited me to lunch at a residence referred to as the Old Bishop's House, a building no bishop had lived in since the forties. I assumed the purpose of the meeting was to solicit a donation for the drive to retire the debt on the new Catholic high school. The eight-million-dollar drive had been publicized in a number of front-page stories in the local newspaper.

It's always money; they always want money, I thought. You pay a fortune to enroll your kids in their schools, and they immediately make beggars out of them, sending them home to sell raffle tickets or solicit donations.

I had never been inside the Old Bishop's House, and had only been inside the adjacent Saint Stephen's Cathedral for family funerals. In the ancient Saint Augustine Cemetery behind the great church there was a crypt dating from 1847 that had our family name, Chattelrault, carved in stone. It contained the remains of a Civil War general, a governor and others. My family's connection with the diocese was a long one. It was a Chattelrault who donated the land for the cathedral, and Chattelraults had constructed Catholic churches, schools, diocesan offices and a seminary. I had relatives who were priests in the Thiberville diocese and one who was a monsignor in Rome. The Chattelrault family relationship with the Catholic faith was an integral part of my family heritage, something I took for granted, like I took a lot of things for granted that came with being a descendant of the town founder.

As a child I had been devout, serving Mass daily, riding my bike through the dark to be on the altar for early Mass in a nearly empty church. I continued to attend Mass, go to confession and refrain from eating meat on Fridays, and lived as a practicing Catholic until I ran off to a neighboring state at age nineteen and married Kate before a Justice of the Peace. My parish priest explained to Kate and me that we were now barred from receiving the sacraments because we had not been married in a church. In the same conversation, the priest twice refused to marry us in the church, citing our young ages as the reason we were barred from the sacrament of matrimony. He told us that unless we lived platonically we would be outside a state of grace, in fact "living in sin" in the eyes of the Church and God, and we would be in grave danger should we die in this state. It seemed he believed he was the arbiter of who would go to heaven, who would go to hell. If we had not been excommunicated, we were only one step removed, for we had been informed that we were no longer Catholics in good standing with the Church.

The whole of south Louisiana was a Catholic culture and we had our children baptized, later enrolling them in Catholic

4

schools, and occasionally we attended Mass as a family. In what I think was an act of defiance, Kate sometimes took communion. She had gloated when she learned that the priest who had lectured us and basically excommunicated us had impregnated a nun and left the priesthood, presumably to live like us, in a state of sin.

As I watched Kate petting Sasha's horse in the pasture near the barn, I wished nothing bad had ever happened between us. A place in the country had been our dream, but in this paradise we'd built together we sometimes lived separate lives. I knew our marriage was so fragile that almost anything could break it. I felt we would divorce and believed she knew this before I did. We did marry too young, got too much money too fast, and bent all the rules we didn't break. But we loved each other deeply and I knew our love would outlast our marriage, last to the end of our lives. Sensing these were our last days together, I felt I never wanted to leave here, never wanted to leave her.

2

A BISHOP'S BANQUET

Noon, Wednesday August 22, 1984
Old Bishop's House, Thiberville, Louisiana

As I closed the gate and made my way up the walk I heard a
rhythmic creaking sound coming from behind a trellis of
overgrown honeysuckle vines. Climbing the steps to the long,
covered porch fronting the house, I discovered the source of the
noise. A beautiful young woman was seated on an old cypress
swing.

She smiled, stood, and took my hand. "Sister Julianne. I am the
personnel director for the diocese."

"I'm Renon Chattelrault."

"I know you're Renon Chattelrault."

She was young, did not look to be out of her twenties, dressed
in penny loafers, dark blue stockings, a light blue skirt, and a
pastel pink blouse. I tried not to stare at her dark eyes, which
shone when they picked up the sunlight.

"I know. I don't look like a nun. We junked the witch's habit.
Come on. I'll take you into this place priests call the powerhouse."

The man who opened the door introduced himself as
Monsignor Jean-Paul Moroux, the vicar general of the Thiberville
diocese and deputy to Bishop Reynolds. He led the way to the
dining room. From the back, his wobbly gait was like that of a
marionette in the hands of an amateur puppeteer, bouncing and
swaying from side to side. In the dining room, he sat at the head
of the table and placed me on his right. His stature and
commanding presence reminded me of paintings of Napoleon

Bonaparte. His face was nearly hidden by a mane of graying hair hanging over his corrugated brow. Up close, his high, round cheeks were cherubic, but it was his coal-black reptilian eyes that were the dominant feature. The monsignor's soft mouth was fixed in a half-smile of bemusement, like that of a man who knew a lot of secrets and a lot of jokes.

There were several people already seated round the table, and Monsignor Moroux made the introductions. In addition to Sister Julianne, there was the vicar of finance, Monsignor Buddy Belair, and the diocesan lawyer, Jon Bendel. There was also a man wearing a starched shirt and an impressively knotted red tie. I had never learned to knot a tie properly, which Kate always said was proof I was never supposed to be a lawyer. Turning to the man in the tie, the monsignor said, "This is Thomas Quinlan, Archbishop Donnegan's attorney from New Orleans, and next to Tom is Lloyd Lecompte, our diocesan media director."

He gestured towards the big man seated at the far end of the table, who had an even more commanding demeanor than Monsignor Moroux, and added, "I believe we all know Joe Rossi."

We did. Rossi held the sort of political power that could punish enemies as well as reward friends. He raised and contributed enormous sums of money to both political campaigns and Catholic charities, and as a result was an integral part of everything in this part of the state that comprised any part of the power structure.

Moroux made his last introduction. "Finally, this is Renon Chattelrault, who we are all here to speak with."

The confusion I felt was disorienting. *Why were they all here to speak with me?*

I noticed Rossi twisting his napkin in his hands, seemingly impatient for Monsignor Moroux to finish the introductions.

Monsignor Moroux bowed his head and seemed about to offer a blessing for the meal when robust Joe Rossi interrupted the moment and led off with his booming voice. "Renon, the Church has a problem with a priest and the priest needs a lawyer and we want you to represent him."

The silence lasted longer than the sentence. Then Monsignor Jean-Paul Moroux spoke. "It seems our priest has done some things that have the attention of District Attorney Sean Robinette. The DA has asked that we have a lawyer meet with him on behalf of the priest tomorrow morning. We have no such lawyer. The diocese has counsel in Jon. Tom represents the archdiocese. Our priest has no lawyer of his own."

I stayed quiet while a black couple served the salad.

"Renon, let me get to the point." Jon Bendel addressed me directly. "This priest has done some things that may constitute serious crimes. He may well be guilty. But what is certain is the Church, diocese, and Bishop Reynolds are absolutely innocent. If this priest did these things he is accused of, I imagine he will fall on his sword for the good of everyone. I mean... if it comes to that."

Bendel never took his eyes off me. "What we need to know is whether you would agree to represent this priest. And we need to know that you will work closely with us throughout your representation of the priest. This matter potentially has damaging ramifications for the bishop, diocese and archdiocese, and for the Catholic Church, far beyond any ramifications it might have to the priest who would be your client."

"What did this priest do?" I asked.

No one responded.

"What's the priest's name?" I asked.

No one responded.

"What parish is this priest in?"

No response.

Lloyd Lecompte, the diocesan public relations fellow, spoke in a stammer. I wondered what had happened to his voice. I recognized his name. He was a retired radio announcer from the only radio station Thiberville had when I was a kid. "Renon, ya... you... you can... can't talk to the p-p-press." After taking a breath, his speech smoothed out. "Any statement about this case will be drawn up by my office."

I was silent.

Lecompte asked, "Are you related to Monsignor Chattelrault in Rome?"

I nodded. "Yes, I think the monsignor is a cousin or something. Look, I don't want to... Well, I mean... no one will tell me this priest's name or what he has allegedly done or where he lives. No one will tell me anything, and the only legal issue that has been raised thus far is the forfeiture of my first amendment right to freedom of speech. Someone is going to have to say more."

No one spoke.

"What's the secret?" I asked.

Monsignor Moroux wiped his mouth with his napkin and leaned back in his chair. "Well, of course, you are right... it is a secret. The situation is this, Mr. Chattelrault. Some boys have claimed Father did sexual things with them. Father is now away in a treatment facility."

Monsignor Buddy Belair spoke up. "Of course, as soon as we knew what the children were claiming, we sent Father far away from here to get help. The diocese is offering to take care of the children, to pay all their therapy bills, and we are doing this voluntarily."

"How many boys? What ages?" I asked.

"We-ell," Monsignor Moroux drawled, and dragged an extra syllable into the simple word. "There are two sets of boys. They were all about seven to ten years old when these things occurred. The claims of the first set of boys – there were six of them – are settled and those settlements are sealed in the courthouse vault in Bayou Saint John. With the second set... we-ell... originally, all eleven of the children in this second group were represented by one of the lawyers that settled the first batch of claims. Now it seems one of the families, the Rachous, has gone to a new... a different lawyer... and their new lawyer has gone to the district attorney. The district attorney telephoned me and requested a meeting tomorrow morning with legal counsel representing the priest. As I said, there is no such person. We want you for the job."

9

Jon Bendel shifted, leaned toward me and said, "Renon, no priest in the United States has ever been prosecuted in open court before a jury for sex crimes against children. No bishop or diocese has ever been drug into court because of the sex crimes of a priest. And none of that is going to happen here. Not on my watch. We bought the first six claims, sealed the settlements. We buried the cases in the vault of the Bayou Saint John courthouse. And we will buy and bury these eleven claims too."

I was aware that Jonathan Bendel, diocesan counsel, always spoke with that kind of certitude. He could lose a trial and then give an interview to a television reporter on the courthouse steps that convinced the viewing audience he had won.

The main course was served, a small piece of fish and some potatoes and peas.

"What kind of money was paid to settle the first six cases?" I asked.

"Confidential," Jon Bendel said.

"Oh, hell, Jon," Joe Rossi blurted out. Turning to me, he said, "Renon, you got a right to know what we're dealing with. This is kinda like a lawyer–client conference; everything said here stays here. Six kids cost over three and a half million."

Three and a half million, I thought. No way. What the hell did the priest do to those kids that would justify paying millions of dollars in hush money? Maybe they do have more money than God.

"Who's the new lawyer who went to the district attorney?" I asked.

"Kane Chaisson," said Tom Quinlan, the archbishop's lawyer.

Almost everyone in the room would have heard of Kane Chaisson, a formidable and flamboyant lawyer, a force to be reckoned with. I had once heard someone say, "Kane Chaisson would shoot his mother and take bets on which way she would fall." However compliant the first set of lawyers had been with the Church in sealing secretive proceedings, getting paid to keep it all secret, and protecting the diocese from a public scandal, it was sure Kane Chaisson would never play that game.

Rossi almost stood up. "Chaisson – Jazzon. It doesn't matter who that Rachou family has as a lawyer. We can control the district attorney and the press. We just need a lawyer to go to some meetings with the DA on behalf of the priest. A few meetings with the DA and it will all be over with. We elected Sean Robinette as DA and re-elected him three times. He owes us, and Robinette is not about to indict a Catholic priest, embarrass Bishop Reynolds."

Jonathan Bendel said, "Sean Robinette can make this go away if he's talked to right and he will be talked to right."

"What did this priest do with those boys? What kind of sexual acts?" I asked, looking for any kind of factual information.

Jon Bendel was becoming frustrated. "Renon, if you agree to become counsel of record then we can divulge those things to you."

I let my fork drop onto the fish on my plate. "Jon, do you think for a minute I am going to agree to be the lawyer for a man whose name I don't know? A priest who has done things I am in the dark about? And agree that I cannot speak to the press, and have to understand that all the real negotiations with the DA are going to be handled somewhere over my head or behind my back? You really think I am going to agree to this? Who in this room thought I would agree to this? I want to know." Out of the corner of my eye, I saw the nun, Sister Julianne, lean back in her chair. It seemed she was suppressing a grin.

Monsignor Moroux jumped into the breach. "No, no. Not at all. We only want you to know you will have all of us supporting you if you undertake this case. That is why we are all here. The bishop needs your help."

For the first time I realized the bishop was not in the room. As the plates were picked up, a slice of cake was placed before each of us.

"Lemon pound cake," Monsignor Moroux said. "The bishop's favorite. He had it sent over."

Lemon pound cake. The bishop's favorite. The words reverberated in my head. We were discussing one of the bishop's priests sexually molesting seventeen children and his sole contribution was lemon pound cake?

Thomas Quinlan, Archbishop Donnegan's lawyer, took over. "The only wildcard is that Kane Chaisson has filed a motion to unseal his case involving the Rachou boy and the child's parents. Chaisson wants to blow the lid off of this. The hearing is a week from Monday, September 3."

Rossi stood up and laid his napkin on his plate. "Look, Renon is right." Rossi looked straight at me. "You've got a right to know everything. The priest's name is Father Francis Dubois and he was in Amalie near Cypress Bay until last fall, when the bishop removed him. He's obviously some kind of mental defective. We have only two problems. We have to get a lawyer to represent the priest to satisfy the DA and get the criminal thing over with fast. And we have to keep Chaisson's Rachou suit sealed or make sure what the newspaper and television people learn of all this does not reflect badly on the diocese or the bishop because no one in the diocese has done anything wrong. The priest may be guilty, but Bishop Reynolds is innocent."

I spoke softly. "Joe, I don't know who's guilty, who's innocent. But out of curiosity, how are you going to keep the media out of this?"

Rossi lit a cigar and puffed on it several times. Through the smoky haze around his head he said, "Son, even *The New York Times* won't piss on the Pope." Then he turned to the nun. "Sorry, Sister. Forgive my language. Let's eat our cake." He laid his lit cigar on the edge of the dining table and started in on the cake.

I addressed Rossi again. "Something like this can't be kept a secret forever."

"Well," Rossi grumbled, "you get around a lot, Renon. You hear all the gossip around these parts, and you never heard a damned word about any of this until now. We paid for the silence of the families of the six kids involved last year. It's been a damn secret for over a year and it can continue to be a secret till hell freezes over. The Church keeps all our secrets, son, and we can damned well keep theirs."

After the lunch broke up I made my way to the sidewalk across the street from the Old Bishop's House. Joe Rossi caught up to me and grabbed my arm. I had known Rossi since I was a child. As an adult, I came to realize he was among the most powerful men in the state.

Never had I seen such a menacing look on Rossi's face. "Nobody, Renon. Not Kathryn, your wife. Nobody can know what we discussed in that room in there. You talk... talk to anybody, you deal with me first, God second. You understand?"

I just looked at him and at his threat. A moment later he loosened his grip on my arm and let go. I watched him walk to his car and drive away. Alone in the street, I walked to my car, clicking the release on the locks. As I was opening the door, Sister Julianne pedaled her bicycle over. She looked like she belonged on a college campus, not in a room with those men.

"Renon, here's my card. My home number is on the back. You may want to talk with me one day. Don't call my office."

I know my expression telegraphed confusion.

"I think at some point you're going to want to talk to someone. All I can tell you now is this. I'll never lie to you."

Fumbling with the card and jamming it in my coat pocket, I said, "Okaaay. I... I will remember. Sister, can I ask ya... what the hell was Joe Rossi doing in that room?"

"Odd, no? Rossi raises a lot of money for the diocese. The bishop trusts him. What did you think of the meeting?" she asked.

"The lemon pound cake was the best part."

"Yeah, you're right," she laughed. "Cake can't lie."

3

AN ANCIENT PLACE

Pre-dawn, Thursday August 23, 1984
Vatican City, Rome

The tiny birds that roosted in the tall cedars in Vatican City swirled in the blue-black, pre-dawn sky. Local lore had it that these birds picked the thorns from Christ's head on Calvary, and then followed Saint Peter to Rome. Monsignor Jozef Majeski had heard the legend of the birds and thorns, but he had heard stranger things from gypsies near his home village in Poland. He knew superstition was intermingled with most religions.

As a young boy, Jozef had had a calling from Christ. It was a clear voice he heard in his heart. All he ever wanted to be was a simple parish priest. Majeski had little in common with priests in the Vatican who were ambitious careerists.

On the day Jozef's friend was elected Pope, the pontiff's first telephone call had been to Jozef at his country parish in their homeland. His old friend opened by saying, "Jozef, I think we are in real trouble now. Can you come to Rome to be with me?"

"Come to Rome for how long?" Jozef asked.

"Pack everything, Jozef. You will serve this life sentence with me, my friend," the pontiff had said with a trace of laughter in his voice.

The next day Jozef was at the Holy Father's side. He never returned to his homeland except when the pontiff traveled there. No one was closer to the Pope than Jozef. His elegant apartment adjoined the papal quarters.

The pontiff, the man Jozef referred to simply as "my friend," was fast asleep in his own apartment. Jozef sat by an open window, enjoying a cigarette, a French Gitanes made of black tobacco, one of two he allowed himself each day. Late at night, as he sat at this same window, smoking, he sometimes strained to hear music in the distance. He loved jazz, but he could never seem to find the right place to listen to decent music in Rome.

This morning Jozef would risk upsetting his friend in the same way he had done many times before. The evening before he had turned off the alarm clock in the Pope's sleeping chamber and advised the nuns not to bring breakfast until he rang for it. He would let the Pope sleep in. The pontiff would likely not have time to celebrate Mass in his private chapel and Jozef knew his friend would be unhappy about that. But Jozef would simply wave his hand, shrug, and say, as he always did, "God will look past."

The two of them had been at the Pope's summer residence, Castel Gandolfo, the past two weeks, but it had not been a holiday. The pontiff had worked round the clock, as he always did, relentlessly pushing himself without rest, disregarding the abdominal pain that had dogged him ever since the assassination attempt.

Inside the Vatican, the subject of the Pope's health was often discussed among the cardinals, if in coded ways. The Holy Father himself was far more troubled by the tremors in his hands, confiding to Jozef that he worried he had become a caffeine addict. Sister Margarita, a Polish nun who attended to the kitchen, poured cup after cup of powerful espresso for the Pope all day long.

On the previous evening, Majeski and the pontiff had talked late into the night. Though a young man still, the Holy Father drove himself like an old man who believed he was running out of time. He wanted to plan an extensive trip to the forgotten continent, Africa, and there were those in the Curia that opposed the idea. As he went off to his room that night, after a last cup of espresso and a glass of warm milk, he said to his friend in their native language, "Time, Jozef. Tonight we pray for time, that we have enough time."

As tired as he was, the Holy Father had insisted they return to Rome for Sunday, when a rally of thousands of children from over sixty countries was to fill Piazza San Pietro, the big square fronting Saint Peter's Basilica. The children would participate in a Mass and sing in concert before and after the liturgy. All of the countries would have troupes attired in traditional costumes, arranged in one choir. The children would bring traditional altar offerings from their culture.

Jozef had counseled him against returning to Rome because of the heat wave gripping the city. His concern was that the hours on the outdoor altar in high temperatures would pose a danger to the Pope, draining his friend, who was already ailing. But the pontiff could not be persuaded. The Pope would not miss the day of the children.

Jozef knew how unhappy his friend had been in childhood. He had known more death than joy as a child, losing his mother, then his only sibling not long afterwards, and having his father die before he finished school. The Pope had grown old early, forced to give up the things of childhood before he really experienced them. Jozef believed that, above all else, his friend valued and celebrated the innocence and absolute state of grace that exists only in children.

As dawn approached the Holy City and the Pontiff slept, there was not a hint of there being any clergy abuse crisis looming on the horizon. In the past all claims of clergy abuse had always been buried in the Vatican along with other secrets of the church.

4

A SIN OF VANITY

Thursday morning, August 23, 1984
Coteau

I did not return home from the Old Bishop's House for the picnic planned with Sasha and Kate. Instead I rushed to my office to begin researching criminal procedural and sentencing statutes for the case involving Father Dubois. I was particularly interested in the procedural and legal burden involved with a plea of insanity, for my instincts told me this was where the case was headed.

The conference area of my office was littered with files needing my attention: a big case involving a helicopter crash, a client who had been paralyzed as a result of a vehicular accident, a stack of files on criminal defendants, and other cases in which I represented cops, including a police chief. My income was top bracket, but it was all earned as I sometimes worked around the clock.

I had also represented poor clients for no fee, pro bono, and many of them had in fact paid me in whatever way they could. A greens keeper at a municipal golf course brought me sacks of golf balls fished out of water hazards, a hunter turned up with ready-to-cook ducks and venison sausage, a farmer delivered eggs and free-range chickens to Kate at our home. I had once helped a group who wanted to protect a cemetery where their relatives were buried in unmarked graves from being bulldozed. They held a barbecue to raise money for my fees, but when the proceeds fell short of even covering the cost of the event, I reached in my pocket and made up the difference. All cases were the same to me.

I pushed all the current files aside and soon the conference table was covered with criminal procedure volumes and case law, all relating to the priest I'd not met.

I telephoned Kate sometime after dark, offering apologies. She listened, said nothing and hung up.

When I did get home at midnight, I went directly to the guest cottage. I slept there often and had almost lived there at times in the past. The children had been told I stayed in the cottage when I needed to work late. There was some truth to that, but more often than not I stayed there for other reasons.

I was up early Thursday and doing my best to avoid Kate when I heard her bounding up the steps of the cottage. She burst into the living room, wanting an explanation for me missing the picnic with her and little Sasha the previous afternoon. I told her every detail about the luncheon at the Old Bishop's House and the case involving Father Dubois, and how I had spent the preceding afternoon and evening at the office, researching the parameters of such a case, the insanity defense, possible sentences for various offenses, and the limitations of expert testimony.

"Are you crazy, Ren? Really? Are you mad? I think there's something wrong with you if you're even thinking about defending this priest. Jake is barely older than those boys. Sasha is… Christ, let the Church deal with its own problems. I'm sure the bishop knows a lot of lawyers. Why doesn't one of those lawyers defend this priest? I'll tell you why – because they're not crazy, that's why."

"It may not be so simple. Obviously the children are victims, and their families. Every Catholic who has ever received sacraments from this priest is a victim too in a way. Maybe even the bishop and diocese are victims. Hell, for all I know this priest has some serious illness or brain tumor that makes him a victim too. He's got seventeen child victims that I know of. Maybe there's more. And, ya know, Kate, this priest, no matter how horrible he is… he has rights too."

"Hell, Ren, dammit. You're always talking about rights. I think you'd take the Devil's case and argue he has the same rights as God."

I glanced at the floor, not wanting to see her face. "I am flying to Boston to see the priest over the weekend."

"Damn you, Ren, I mean damn you." Kate looked to the side, picked up a small Lalique glass horse figurine and stroked it gently. "You damned well knew I'd invited Sally and Tom and their kids for the day Saturday. You swore you'd be here. Yesterday, Sasha had the picnic basket loaded in one of the little boats; fishing poles and her special bait, that concoction of raw bacon and cooked popcorn. She waited by the pond for you till after dark. She wouldn't come in. She believed you were coming home to picnic like you promised. She's only five so she still believes in a lot of things – Santa Claus, the Easter Bunny, and her daddy."

I reached for her. She pulled away with a lot of strength. "I'm sorry, Kate. I'm a lawyer. This is what I do."

"No. This isn't what ya do. This is what ya are. What you've become."

"Kate, please..."

"Ren, you remember that red rocket ship in the children's park in Baton Rouge? How we used to climb to the top and split a bottle of wine with paper cups when we were first dating in college?"

I nodded.

"Lemme tell ya. I've been on that rocket ship for seventeen years and the ride's getting bumpy. You know, Ren, I've been thinking for a long time... thinking maybe you got a part issued to you the rest of us don't have. Or maybe you're missing a part that the rest of us do have."

I tried to make light of the moment. "Oh, Kate, I have all my parts."

"Really? Ya think? Remember that Mardi Gras in New Orleans when we were on Bourbon Street with the children? When the gunshots started firing, thousands ran for cover. I couldn't squeeze the kids into that souvenir shop. Everybody was running away, except you, Ren. You were running toward the bullets. You're always running toward the bullets."

Kate turned and walked away, heading for the pasture. I watched her from the window in the back door. At first her head was turned to the side, toward a neighbor's bean field. Then her head turned downward toward the ground. I wanted to go to her, but I was already late for a meeting with Monsignor Jean-Paul Moroux at the chancery offices of the Thiberville diocese.

As I drove toward my appointment with Monsignor Moroux, I asked myself why I was drawn to representing this priest. The truth was simple and something I would never want others to know – vanity and money. I knew this would be one of the most celebrated criminal cases in this part of the state, and possibly even more important than that. Jon Bendel had said it would be the first of its kind in the country and in the history of the Church. I knew it would grab the headlines and be the lead story in television news broadcasts.

I wanted this case for the advancement of my professional career, for the notoriety it would bring me as a lawyer. Financially, the case was a criminal defense lawyer's dream. Notorious criminal defendants charged with having committed heinous crimes that command newspaper headlines normally have no money to pay legal fees. This criminal defendant was a priest with a wealthy financial guarantor, a Catholic diocese that could pay like a slot machine.

And there was something else. Maybe Jon Bendel and Joe Rossi were right. Maybe the bishop and everyone else in the diocese were innocent and did not deserve to be smeared by a scandal surrounding this criminal priest. Maybe I could be of real help to the priest and the diocese. For the first time in a long time, I felt like a Catholic.

Diocesan Chancery, Thiberville, Louisiana

Monsignor Jean-Paul Moroux was waiting for me at the angel fountain outside the chancery. No one else was around. The monsignor explained there was a conference in session that most diocesan employees were attending and everyone else was excused from work. We sat on the edge of the fountain and smoked, talking about the weather.

Moroux said, "The meteorologist on Channel 2 says the hurricane is gonna hit across the Texas line. TV weathermen are like fortune tellers. Voodoo priests. The Dominicans used to burn people like that at the stake. Well, actually the Dominicans burned everyone at the stake. TV weather is like TV news, a charade. Maybe all of life is just a series of absurd charades. Everything we do. A charade." He pronounced it "sha-rod".

The ornate office Moroux led me into was furnished with antiques and framed by large windows overlooking the Saint Augustine Cemetery. "This is Bishop Reynolds' office, Mr. Chattelrault. He's rarely here. As vicar general, I play his role most of the time."

The monsignor exhibited a bad tremor in his hands as he signed the financial guarantee I had prepared that made the diocese responsible for fees and expenses Father Dubois would owe me for defending him.

The air-conditioning system was shut down and it was sweltering as the sun beat on the glass. Monsignor Moroux took off his black jacket, revealing a black bib attached to his white collar, which he removed and tossed on the desk. Underneath, he wore a long-sleeved black tee-shirt. He was perspiring heavily. I removed my coat and loosened my tie.

Then the monsignor picked up a thick folder from the floor and handed it to me. "I made this file for you. And I drew a map of the place where Father Francis is, near Deerfield, New Hampshire. These are the complete dossiers on the eleven children with cases pending. The dossiers were prepared by their psychologist, a Doctor Aaron Kennison. There is only one other set in Thiberville. Jon Bendel has it."

I felt the weight of the file as I picked it up from the desk. "If

RAY MOUTON

you don't mind me asking, Monsignor, I'm curious... why was I chosen to defend this priest?"

"Ah, some say the Lord works in mysterious ways." Monsignor Moroux laughed at his own joke. "Joe Rossi picked you. I don't know if the Lord could get more mysterious than working through Joe Rossi."

"What does Joe Rossi have to do with this?"

"Rossi has everything to do with this. In his infinite wisdom, Bishop Reynolds brought Rossi in because it seems our bishop values Joe's judgment. Rossi talked like he knew you well. You know him, right?"

"Oh, yeah, I know him. I played football with the son of a friend of his. Rossi came to our games, some of our practices. And he got me summer jobs through college. Since I've been a lawyer, he's referred some criminal cases to me, usually drug charges against children of prominent families, things I think Rossi could have fixed himself but apparently didn't want to fix. The real money stuff, Rossi always sends to his friend, Jon Bendel."

"There you have it. He did the same thing here. Jonathan Bendel got the diocese as a client and you got the dirty work."

"Who represents the other ten children?"

"A lawyer named Brent Thomas from Bayou Saint John."

I shrugged.

"In the first six cases, I think his clients were his cousins. He had a partner, Ricardo Ponce."

I shrugged again, never having heard of either lawyer.

When the monsignor said, "Have a safe journey," I felt he was dismissing me. He seemed to be the kind of man who was comfortable dismissing people from his presence. As I started down the long, wide, marble and stone hallway, Moroux accompanied me, still attired in only his tee-shirt and black trousers. As we walked, he pushed the sleeves of his tee-shirt above his elbow and wiped his brow with a starched handkerchief.

When we reached the fountain crowned by a stone angel that stood in the plaza between the chancery and the cathedral, I was

22

startled by what I saw. Under the great oak next to Saint Stephen's, a crowd was gathering. There were dogs on leashes, cats in cages, at least one goat, a pet monkey, and a miniature pony wearing a bonnet of flowers.

Making a sweeping gesture, the monsignor said, "Ah, it's called the blessing of the animals. A ceremony begun by a man who was our bishop before you were born. That bishop carried holy water with him so he could bless livestock in the fields. He never learned to drive as he said he feared facing an animal in the road and having to make the ethical choice of killing the animal or swerving and killing humans."

"Bizarre," I said.

"Silly. Some might even say it's sacrilegious. You know we do worse. We bless fishing boats, football fields, sugar cane crops, even oilfield drilling rigs. It's all part of what the bishop's friend and your friend, Joe Rossi, poetically calls the 'smells and bells'."

"The smells...?"

"High Mass with incense. Holy water for a monkey. The smells and bells."

5

NIGHT FLIGHT

Thursday August 23, 1984
Thiberville

Before leaving Thiberville for New Orleans airport, I stopped in at the office of the district attorney, Sean Robinette, for the appointment he had insisted on having with the lawyer representing the priest. Sean and I were friends. He was older by about twenty years and we worked on opposite sides of the street, but we got on well. He was the best poker player I knew. Older lawyers said before he became DA, he supported himself with all-day card games in the law library of his office.

When I walked into his office, he was feeding the fish in the large aquariums that lined a wall of the richly paneled room. I liked it that he was feeding the fish. Over the years I had learned that Sean Robinette busied himself with the fish tanks when he was unsure of his position in a case.

Sean greeted me with a scowl. "So, Bishop Reynolds sent you, Ren. Damn! Bad break. I was kind of hoping for—"

"Hoping for what?"

"Ah, ya know, Ren, someone I can reason with. You're the last guy they should have hired. Your balls are bigger than your brains."

I said nothing.

Sean smiled and shook his head side to side. "Okay, whatta ya want me to say? If you don't have fifty or sixty life sentences in your pocket, go back where you came from."

Sean walked to his desk and touched a thick stack of files that looked pretty much like the material I had just picked up from Monsignor Moroux at the chancery. *The monsignor is wrong,* I thought. *There's more than one set of these files in Thiberville.*

"I got these files from Brent Thomas, a plaintiff lawyer in Bayou Saint John who has ten civil cases pending. I also have the psychological work-ups done by a Doctor Kennison for six kids that Brent Thomas got settlements for last year, as well as the ten cases he has pending. Thomas's settlements on the first six cases were sealed, but it's illegal to withhold evidence of crimes. I got more detailed information on one case from Kane Chaisson, who represents a boy called Rachou – a long, sworn affidavit. Chaisson threatened me, said he'd call a press conference if this priest was not indicted and in jail awaiting trial soon. I told Kane to kiss my ass."

I laughed. "Bet he liked that."

"Hell, he's run against me for this job twice, spent a fortune on those campaigns. Bastard would rather embarrass me than get another wife – and he's had more wives than I can count. You know we've got no use for each other."

"Look, Sean, deal is… I need some time," I said.

"Yeah, that right? Everybody needs something, but me. I have seventeen victims – little kids, victims of this priest, Father Dubois. Seventeen witnesses who're gonna lock your client up for life. Every time that priest raped a kid under twelve, he was drawing into a full house, the big house, mandatory life, no parole or probation. You need a calculator to count the life sentences he's facing."

"I really need some time, Sean."

"Ren, if I gave you till hell freezes over, you'd never come up with a defense for him."

"Maybe there's a valid legal insanity plea—"

Sean cut me off. "For the priest or for you? You're crazy to defend this sick son-of-a-bitch."

"Look, Sean—"

"You gonna file an insanity plea? You know our insanity

statutes and jurisprudence are modeled on the English McNaughton Rule – essentially the only question for the court to address is 'Did the defendant know the difference between right and wrong at the time he committed the offense or offenses?' You gonna argue that a Catholic priest who preached about right and wrong every Sunday from the pulpit didn't know the difference between right and wrong when he sodomized little boys? Fuck me, Renon. That's bullshit and we both know it."

"Sean, look, wait a minute—"

"There's no room to negotiate. When the smoke clears, I think Father Francis Dubois may prove to be the worst child molester in the history of this state. He may be one of the biggest pied pipers in the country. And I'm gonna make him the most decorated piece of shit in the history of this legal jurisdiction."

Robinette walked over to one of the aquariums and began to feed the fish again.

I took my leave, trying to figure out why Sean was feeding his fish, what it was about this case that made him uneasy. The conclusion I reached was that probably the parents of the children were resistant to the idea of their sons testifying in a public criminal trial, which would mean all he had was stacks of paper, no live witnesses to put on the stand in a court trial.

Delta Flight 934, New Orleans to Boston

I tried to work with Doctor Kennison's psychological files on the child victims as soon as the plane took off from New Orleans. The child psychologist's work was detailed. Soon the seat next to me was littered with folders, for I opened one after another, then closed them almost as quickly. I couldn't bear to read the contents of the dossiers. I didn't think anyone could stomach reading the material.

There was a section in each boy's file detailing different kinds of sexual interaction between the priest and the boy, events bearing descriptive titles identifying the location where the criminal acts occurred as well as defining what the criminal acts were:

Places: In the Sacristy, On the Altar, In the Confessional, In the Rectory, In Father's Car, In Father's Camp, In the Boy's Home, In Motels.

Sexual Activity: Viewing Pornography, Group Sex with Boys and Father, Performing Oral Sex on Father, Performing Oral Sex on Other Boys, Performing Sodomy on Other Boys, Being Sodomized by Priest, Masturbating Priest, Priest Ejaculating on Boy's Bodies...

I couldn't finish reading the listing. *My children, my own children*, I thought. *My God, if this had happened to Sasha, Jake or Shelby.* My heart hurt and raced as adrenalin coursed through my veins, and my head ached, throbbed like the pain stabbing my stomach. *A priest, a fucking ordained Catholic priest, had done these things and this monster predator would be my client.*

There were pictures of the children in each file, 5x7 enlargements of school yearbook photographs. Looking at the pictures, I felt I could discern which children were photographed before being sexually abused by Father Dubois and which pictures were taken after the abuse began. Some of the children's eyes were bright like the beautiful eyes of my little girl. In other pictures the children's eyes were blank stares, the child appeared dead.

Through Doctor Kennison, these small voices told a huge story. The psychologist noted in his covering letter that: "All patients whose care is summarized live in a rural area. They were invited to become altar boys by a priest they called 'Father Nicky', a man who had been entertaining (seducing) them with magic shows and puppet plays since they were in kindergarten. They were targeted at age five, almost cultivated to be harvested at the time of their first communion."

I read part of a transcript from a recorded interview with a child named Simeon: "Father Nicky always had guns at his house – his camp. He would point guns at us. He said shooting someone in the eye would kill them fast. It scared me." The same child had talked about all the snakes at Father Nicky's camp, how the priest was not afraid of snakes. And he said sometimes at the camp Father Nicky smelled.

Turning back to Doctor Kennison's covering letter, I read: "An unusual aspect of the scenario that played out at the priest's rectory or home, his fishing camp, and in motel rooms on trips, was the group nature of the sexual victimization. Every week night, Father Nicky had four or five boys stay with him. The ostensible reason was so their parents would not be inconvenienced bringing them to altar-boy practice at six o'clock the following morning. Apparently the trust the parents had in this priest was absolute. On these nights, as detailed in the case histories enclosed, the boys and the priest engaged in every conceivable sexual activity two males can engage in. 'Vile depravity' is too soft a phrase to describe the actions of this predator priest."

A long time passed while I left the folders on the seat. The flight attendant had given me a couple of glasses of ice and a handful of tiny bottles of gin. For a time I stared straight ahead. If I turned at all, I'd see the photographs of the children. I knew there were other pictures. Something I saw in one of the files stated that "Father Nicky took pictures all the time, pictures that come out fast. We were naked as jay birds, but he didn't care."

I didn't want to read any more. I didn't want to know any more. Each of the boys recounted that Father Nicky had said he would have to kill their parents if they ever found out. I had been told by Monsignor Moroux that some of the boys' fathers now wanted to kill not only the priest but the bishop as well.

The last page of one child's file, a kid named Joey, contained this statement in the child's own words: "Sometimes when we were finished with playing with ourselves and Father Nicky, he would bless us sometimes. One time he showed me a picture of

Jesus eating supper with some men. And he said this was how holy men loved each other. He called me his 'holy boy'."

When I put the files away and stared out the window into the black night, something happened that would stay with me for the rest of my life. I saw an image of myself in hell, my face framed in flames, fingers of fire catching my hair, my skin melting away from my skull, nothing but a deep darkness beyond the fire, an abyss never ending in its blackness.

I knew it was just a distorted likeness of my face in the curved aircraft window, my head engulfed by the reflection of the flame from my Zippo cigarette lighter. But it was such a powerful vision that I slowly closed the lighter without touching it to the tobacco. An imprint of the image seemed to burn through my retina into my brain, and there it remained.

Over the years, the image reappeared in other settings: in the glass china cabinet of a dining room when candles were lit on a child's birthday cake, on the surface of a still lake near an Aztec ruin in central Mexico, and in the window of a chocolate shop in a Paris railway station.

In my nightmares, the sequence always opened with my thirty-six-year-old face on fire. Then my face would begin to age, morphing as it melted in the fire, slowly changing until I looked heavier, older, grayer. Ultimately, I appeared ancient, older than I imagined I would be at my death, and I was still on fire. In the nightmare, the fire never completely burned down and I never completely burned up.

6

A LATE-NIGHT ERRAND

Pre-dawn, Friday August 24, 1984
Secret Archives, Diocesan Chancery, Thiberville

For several hours, Sister Julianne pretended to work in her office in the chancery. Finally, sure that the building was empty and she was secure, she had descended the polished wooden stairs to the basement, navigating slowly through the darkness to the room that held the secret archives of the Diocese of Thiberville.

She sat alone at a long table, flashlight in hand, reading a file. It was hot and humid. She had taken a fifteen-mile bike ride in the country before going to the chancery that evening, and now her shorts and halter top stuck to her, and her sweaty palms made watermarks on the pages. She feared turning on the air-conditioning system because the chilling unit for the whole building was located outside Monsignor Moroux's residence – the Old Bishop's House that adjoined the chancery building – and it made a terrible noise, which would probably disturb Moroux and prompt him to investigate.

After Sister Julianne had been in the secret archives for an hour, she heard footsteps upstairs, heels hitting the hard floor of the marble hallway. She turned out the flashlight. Frozen in her chair, she listened intently. The sound of footsteps stopped. Above her in the bishop's office, lights went on. The beam of light coming down the stairwell shone on her like a spotlight. Too terrified to move, the nun remained seated.

Heavy carpeting in the bishop's office absorbed the footfall above her. She could not tell where the person was standing;

whether the person was moving or about to start down the stairs and discover her.

She decided to try and hide. As she got up, in slow motion, the chair made a slight scratching but nearly inaudible noise on the concrete floor. To her it sounded like the howl of a wild animal. She was sure she would be found and she knew she would never be able to explain what she was doing here. She had never been good at making up lies, and she knew no lie could cover or explain what she was doing in this file room well past midnight.

Leaving the files on the table, Sister Julianne crawled underneath the stairwell on her hands and knees. She was wringing wet, perspiration almost cascading from her face and dripping onto the floor. There was no sound above her, only the light shining into the secret archives. Time stopped.

"I know you are here somewhere," the voice above her said.

Though the distance between the bishop's office and the secret archives beneath it was short, she could not immediately recognize the voice.

"I know you are here somewhere!" came the voice again, more loudly this time.

She realized it was Monsignor Jean-Paul Moroux.

Above her hiding space, Monsignor Moroux opened and closed the drawers of a desk and then a credenza until he located what he was looking for – an unfinished wooden mask. "There you are. Found you." With the mask tucked under his arm, he made his way toward the hallway.

The sound of footsteps hitting marble faded then stopped. The big door leading to the Old Bishop's House slammed shut.

Flipping on the flashlight, Sister Julianne searched for the aluminum water bottle she always carried on her bike. It was under the table. She gulped water and considered abandoning her task. Her watch showed 2:15 a.m. She could be finished before the monsignor reappeared after morning Mass at 6:30 a.m.

*

31

By the time the first stream of sunlight reached into the stairwell from the windows in the bishop's office, the basement table was covered with personnel folders. Sister Julianne hurriedly jammed them back into drawers, worrying that some were not properly placed by year or alphabetical order, and that some documents had not been properly re-fastened to the folders. She was flustered by the sight of the overflowing wastepaper basket, filled with copies that had been discarded when the copy machine had jammed during the night. Soon she could find herself trapped in the secret archives.

She stuffed her large camping backpack with the material she had copied in the night, scooped up the trash can and carried it up the stairs with her. Out in the dawn light, she threw the whole can into a large garbage dumpster behind the chancery. Backpack over her shoulders, she raced away on her bike, her heart pounding.

7

THE CONFESSION

Friday August 24, 1984
Saint Martin Catholic Center, Deerfield, New Hampshire

I pulled the chord to open the hotel drapes and believed it was still night. Checking my watch and the alarm clock, I realized the sun should be in the sky. Thunder rumbled near, echoing off the tall buildings of Boston.

I had not slept all night. This would be the most difficult thing I'd tackled, professionally and personally. My hope was that I was not overestimating my ability as a lawyer and my resources as a human being. I felt far from home and as if I had been gone a long time. I ordered breakfast from room service, stared at the food, downed the coffee, and watched the stormy skies through the window of my hotel room.

The cab drive out to the Saint Martin Catholic Center, which was on a rural road south of Deerfield, New Hampshire, took over two hours. The turnpike was crowded with commuters and the taxi was buffeted by winds that rivaled hurricanes we had down in Thiberville near the Gulf of Mexico.

"Ain't s'pose to be no nor'easter this time a year. Gonna blow hard all day and night," the taxi man said.

I asked him to please arrange for a local cab to be waiting at the Saint Martin Center at two in the afternoon, telling him to have the taxi run the meter if he had to wait for me. I did not intend to be in the presence of Father Francis Dominick Dubois any longer than was absolutely necessary.

*

33

The director of the Saint Martin Catholic Center in Deerfield, Sister Mary Bryan, handed me Father Dubois's file. The first document was titled "Final Release Plan: Fr. Francis D. Dubois". Its two pages outlined that Father Francis Dubois was to be released from the treatment facility on the following Monday, in three days. He was to go to Fort Worth, Texas, where he would be employed at a restaurant owned by a man named Orell Lanier, who was described as a "benevolent Catholic businessman".

I perused the entire file. I violently ripped out the release plan. Then I ripped more pages out of the folder, shredding them with my hands, dropping them in the wastepaper basket. My jaw was clenched in anger. Having decided on the long taxi drive that I would be composed this day, would conduct myself as a professional, my first sight of the country-club setting in which Father Dubois had been coddled, and the news that they planned to release him back into society, had set me off.

"Sister, there is nothing in this file about the behavior that brought Father Dubois here for treatment. In the notes I destroyed, Dubois appears like a guest in a resort rather than a patient in a treatment facility. The public would be outraged if they read that."

"We're here to concentrate on the spiritual, not what may concern lay persons."

"Sister, listen to this on page 34: 'Today Father seems tired and depressed, lonely. He needs to be cheered.' Do you understand that no one back home cares how Father felt that day or any other day, that no one wants him to be cheered?" I tore that page from the file as well, crumpled it and let it drop to the floor.

"I think it is important that we are supportive of Father Francis and that he be allowed to begin his life over in Texas. The work of the Church is forgiveness and healing. The work of God is done and he's been forgiven for whatever he has done, and it's our judgment that our work here is finished."

"Sister, no one should ever know that you were on the verge of releasing Father Dubois. No one can ever find out how he was coddled here. You can't imagine how this would play with the families of the child victims, the lawyers who are suing the diocese, the district attorney who will prosecute this priest, and the press."

The nun's eyes watered. I lowered my voice. "If what I think about Father Dubois is true, there will be lawyers and media people crawling all over this place one day. Maybe soon. For his sake, for your sake, for the sake of this center, and for the sake of the Church, it must not appear that he was babied here and that he was being returned to society without any medical treatment having been administered to him."

She nodded.

"Has he been allowed to leave here in his car?"

"Not at night, Mr. Chattelrault. But during the day he is free to come and go as he pleases. The men and women we have here are treated as adults. This is not a place of incarceration. It's a place of reflection."

"Are any of the other residents here child sex abusers?"

"We don't concentrate on what it was that brought them to us, but rather on healing them spiritually and returning them to their ministries and vocations. Our residents have had problems with alcohol, depression, burn-out, taking too many prescription drugs, things like that. A few, like Father Francis, acted inappropriately with children."

"Does anyone on your staff even have any experience or expertise in treating men who have sexually abused children?"

"Not specifically, no. But as I said, the approach in the spiritual life is—"

"It doesn't matter, Sister. Right now I want you to get on the phone and find a place that does have experience treating men like Francis Dubois. And it has to be a place where Father Dubois will be locked up. Not only must he be locked up and have his freedom completely curtailed, he must be locked away to protect him from reporters who are going to be looking for him soon. He has to be locked up for his own protection and to show that the Church has taken serious measures to protect children from him as well."

"Locked up?"

"Locked up… by Monday. He has to be locked up by Monday. Trust me, Sister, if people get a picture of this beautiful place and see how he's living today, how he's free to come and go as he pleases during the day, his problems and the Church's problems will be even larger than they already are. And, Sister – they're people who want to kill him."

Sister Mary Bryan stiffened. "I understand. But do you understand who you are going to meet? Look at this painting he did last week."

She showed me a painting of a small child who seemed to be taking his first steps underneath a large tree, leaning on the tree with one hand. "Father Francis painted this. Look at the face of the child. It's his face. That is how he sees himself – a helpless child, trying to stand on his own, dependent upon me and the staff, leaning on us."

"Sister, I can't be all that concerned about how he sees himself. What I care about right now is how victims, lawyers, prosecutors, press, parishioners and the general public will see him. His only possible defense will be an insanity defense and though I believe he must have been crazy to have done the things he did, everything contained in this file would work against him and against the interests of the Church."

I started for the door.

"Mr. Chattelrault, you must remember… Please, always remember…"

I turned and faced the nun. "Yes?"

"You must remember, Father Francis is a very good person."

It was raining hard when I entered the room where Father Dubois was waiting for me. Windows were ajar and rain was falling on the floor. He made no move to close the windows, but rather sat as still as a statue on an old plaid sofa, legs together, hands in his lap. He looked defenseless, harmless. If he was a grotesque monster, he had a good mask. Looking at him, no one would have believed this priest had done the things listed in Doctor Kennison's files.

"Father, my name is Renon Chattelrault," I said as I latched the windows.

"Hello." There was a long pause. "Jean-Paul... Monsignor Moroux... called last night and told me about you. Please call me Francis."

We shook hands. I noticed how small and ordinary he was, unremarkable in every way, looking neither older nor younger than his forty-six years. He seemed soft except for his hands, which felt like bark off a young tree.

"You spoke to Monsignor Moroux last night?"

"He scared me. Told me I was going to be indicted for crimes."

I opened my oversized briefcase, pulling out files and a portable tape recorder.

"Father, do you want to talk here?"

"Please call me Francis. Will this stuff Monsignor Moroux called me about... will this mess up my release?"

"Francis, you might well be in prison soon for the rest of your life. Yes, I believe this stuff will mess things up for you. You're not going to Fort Worth to work in some restaurant. By Monday night you'll be locked down in a treatment facility where you can be seriously treated and no media or anyone else can get to you."

Dubois looked like he was about to smile when he heard my words. It was more a smirk than a smile. He seemed unfazed by my remark that he might spend the rest of his life in prison. His eerie expression unnerved me and I momentarily lost my concentration.

As I spread the photos of the eleven boys on the coffee table, Sister Mary Bryan entered the room. She put a tray of snacks and a pitcher of lemonade on the table, and sat next to Father Dubois. "Mr. Chattelrault, I think it's best if I am with Father Francis while you question him. For support."

"Sister, the law is that if a third person is present during the communication between a lawyer and his client, then nothing said is protected by the lawyer–client privilege."

"I am not going to subject him to a lawyer's interrogation without anyone on his side."

"I'm on his side, Sister. I may be the only one on his side soon." I looked directly at Father Dubois. "Father, if she remains, I will have to leave. It is not in your best interest to waive the attorney-client privilege and I will not participate in anything not in your best interest."

In the softest, meekest way, Dubois spoke. "I don't want to make anyone mad at me."

I got up and announced, "I'm going to leave the room, let you two talk. When I return… if you are still here, Sister, I'm leaving."

"That will not be necessary." She put a large, flat key on the coffee table. "Lock up when you are done and leave the key with the security guard. Francis, you can call me at home this evening if you want me to sit with you awhile."

As the nun walked out, Dubois picked up the children's pictures and slowly shuffled the photos, smiling serenely as he looked at the children he had sexually abused for years.

"Can I have these pictures?" Dubois asked.

I turned to the windows, looking at the storm rather than Father Dubois. His voice had risen an octave when he asked to keep the pictures. The anger I'd felt on the plane the night before resurfaced and I fought to suppress it, not wanting to give in to my personal feelings. I was a lawyer and I would act like a lawyer.

I ignored the question and set a recorder on the corner of the table.

"Let us go to the first file."

"That would be Robby," Dubois said as he glanced at the photograph in his hand.

I opened Doctor Kennison's dossier on Robby and thumbed to the last page, the index of offenses. "Father, Robby has told Doctor Kennison that you performed anal sex on him approximately forty times. Is that correct?"

"Oh, no," he said. He looked to the window. The rain had frozen to sleet and hailstones.

"That's not true?"

"No. With Robby it could not have been more than maybe twenty-five or thirty times."

"Father Dubois—"

"Please call me Francis."

"Okay, Francis. Each act of sodomy with a child under the age of twelve carries a mandatory life sentence without parole. One time is all the evidence required to convict."

Dubois sat before me like a stone, unmoved, without emotion, showing no reaction. He again gave me the tight smile I had seen earlier, a smirk.

We then began a laborious effort that lasted several hours as we went through each dossier. Hearing the priest recall these things made me feel sick to my stomach.

"Francis, listen carefully. I've got to ask you what may be the most important question I'll ever ask you. I want you to think about the answer carefully."

"Sure." Dubois nonchalantly picked a grape from a bunch in a bowl and popped it in his mouth.

"When you were involved in these sexual acts with these children, or after these sex sessions ended, did you have a sense that what you were doing was wrong?"

Without hesitation, Dubois said, "It wasn't wrong."

"You mean you did not perceive it as being wrong?"

"No. I mean it wasn't wrong."

"You never believed that having anal intercourse", I thumbed through Robby's file, "with a child when he was seven, eight and nine years old, was wrong?"

"It wasn't wrong."

"If it wasn't wrong, Father, what was it?"

"Natural."

"Do you understand that the rest of the world will not see it that way?"

"I tried to keep it secret for that reason."

"It doesn't matter to you that the rest of the world thinks this behavior is wrong?"

"I've always been this way. This is how I am." Turning flippant, he added, "Talk to God. He made you like you are and he made me like I am. Maybe God's a joker."

"If you have always been this way, is it true that you have had sexual relations with boys at every church parish where you were assigned?"

"When Monsignor Moroux called to tell me you were coming here, he said this was only about Our Lady of the Seas in Amalie and that is all I could talk about. I will only talk about Amalie. He told me not to answer any of your questions about anything in any other parishes where I was assigned."

I stood and walked to the window. A large branch had cracked and was hanging loosely from a tall maple. Outdoor furniture was rolling end over end as the wind howled and lightning split the sky. The realization that the monsignor who had signed a contract with me the day before was actively obstructing the investigation I needed to make to formulate a defense of his priest astounded me. My perception that I was working for the diocese was wrong. The diocese was working against me.

I considered shutting the interview down, shutting the defense of Dubois down, flying home and resigning as Dubois's legal counsel. Monsignor Jean-Paul Moroux was sabotaging my defense of Dubois, controlling my client. But if I left now, I knew I would wonder forever what information I could have gained.

"Okay, Francis. I'll take this issue up with Monsignor Moroux, but make no mistake – at some point, we are going to discuss your life before you were assigned to Amalie. Either that or you will have a new lawyer. For now, we will talk only about Amalie."

"Okay."

"Do you understand you hurt these children in Amalie?"

"They were never hurt. I could not hurt anyone. I love those boys. They love me."

"Father, would you be willing to help me – using school yearbooks, altar-boy rosters, things like that – in an attempt to identify every boy you were involved with sexually in Amalie?"

Dubois did not hear me. He was staring at the photographs of the boys.

"Can I have these pictures?"

I was still looking out of the window. The rage welled up again. *This man is sick*, I thought. *Whatever the pathology is, it runs deep.* Rather than feeling I wanted to kill him, I now felt I wanted to know what was wrong with him, what caused him to do these things. And I wanted to find all of his victims and have the diocese offer them anything and everything in the way of professional therapy.

Again I ignored the question about the pictures.

"You're going to prison, Father. The question of how long a prison sentence you will serve will in great measure be influenced by how you and I conduct ourselves between now and the time you are sentenced. It is essential in my view that we identify all the victims. The diocese must reach out to them, offer them help. It's the morally right thing to do. And it's prudent legally."

"I don't understand what you are saying."

"What I am saying is that you must act responsibly to mitigate the damage to these children, to get them expert psychiatric and psychological help from physicians of their choosing."

"This is a lot to—"

"Francis, I know the insanity defense is the only defense available to you. In our state the only test for legal insanity is whether or not you knew the difference between right and wrong at the time of the commission of these offenses. It's not a very good defense because I don't see how I can argue that a man who preached about right and wrong from the pulpit every Sunday did not know the difference between right and wrong. I think if I articulate and argue that defense it may appear I'm insane."

"I don't know what to do."

"Let me explain. If you want me to represent you, it is going to

41

be on certain conditions. First, you have got to understand that no one but the two of us will ever be involved in your case. You must never involve anyone else, discuss any aspect of your case with anyone, except doctors, and you must never lie to the doctors. And you must understand I will never plead you to a life sentence."

"What if that's all they offer? I can promise you, Mr. Chattelrault, if I am to get a life sentence, I will kill myself. I will kill myself. I am not going to be locked up for the rest of my life. I want you to tell me if I am to receive a life sentence, so I have time to kill myself. Can you promise you will tell me, so I can die?"

"Yes, I promise. And I promise I will never lie to you, but I don't want you lying to me. If life without parole is all they offer, then we will go to trial. I don't think it will come to that, but you are going to serve prison time. Make no mistake about that."

Dubois clutched the eleven photos of the boys to his heart.

"When one relies on the insanity defense, the crimes are admitted, so we have nothing to hide about what you did, how many times you did it with how many boys. Monday you will be leaving here for a real psychiatric institution where we can begin to find out what is wrong with you. Tomorrow I can begin formulating and presenting a plan to the diocese and prosecutor wherein you cooperate in identifying each of your victims in Amalie so that help may be made available to them. There is a long roster of victims in the parish of Amalie lined up to testify against you, seventeen that I am aware of so far. There are eleven in this group and a half dozen who have settled claims against the diocese. Adding more names to the list will not make our problems worse. In fact, that might help us strategically. I think an average juror who found out what you did to one kid would want to kill you. If the same juror found out a lot of kids were involved, I think the juror would tend to want to believe you are insane as the only explanation of your behavior. I believe what you did was insane. Hopefully I can give a court expert witnesses whose testimony will support my theory."

"I don't think I understand anything you're saying. What's the best thing I can hope for?"

"If I am to be your lawyer, Father, the best you can hope for is a sentence of twenty years in a prison where you can receive treatment and therapy." I tapped the stack of folders. "Half of these kids claim they were sodomized – they can put you away for life. Only you know how many other potential state witnesses might come forward when this is made public. The minimum sentence I would ever argue for is twenty years. It's enough time to allow the youngest victim to grow well into adulthood before you are free again, and enough time for you to be competently treated so hopefully you are not this way on your release."

"Twenty years?"

"Exactly. And unless you are in agreement with this, there is no need for us to go any further."

"I think I understand."

"I don't think you do understand. If I learned one of my children was a victim of yours, I may well have come here to kill you and I believe I am more restrained than some of the victims' fathers. I don't want your understanding, Father. What I want is your agreement. I want an agreement between the two of us that no one else will be involved in this case, all advice will come from me. And we will fight all the charges and go to trial unless we can get an agreement for you to serve twenty years. If we can get you medical treatment while incarcerated, you will accept the medical care and cooperate with the treatment regime."

"Yes, I understand. I agree."

"You sure you understand? Don't ever give any statement to anyone except a physician unless I am present. Secondly, don't ever lie to a physician about any of this."

I was about to wrap it up and head for the airport. I had noticed an old beat-up station wagon with a taxi sign on the roof idling near the main entrance. Just as I was about to terminate the interview, Dubois laid the photos down and leaned forward, speaking in a stronger voice, with more bass.

"Everybody is gonna find out about me, right?"

I watched as Dubois writhed on the sofa. He appeared to be in pain. It was the first nearly normal reaction I had seen from him. He excused himself to go to the bathroom. The lightning strikes and thunder intensified and the sleet and rain blew horizontally, hitting the wall of the building, rattling the window panes.

When Dubois returned from the men's room, his shirt was wringing wet. "If you wait here, I can go shower. I know the smell is bad. I smell this way when I sweat. I shower all day long. Do you want to wait while I shower?"

"I'm okay," I lied. "Go on, Father."

"Call me Nicky. Please call me Nicky."

It seemed Dubois was trying to run some kind of game on me. I didn't like it, but I let it go. "Okay, Nicky."

I leaned back in the chair, stretched my legs, and stared at Dubois for a long time. Sweat poured out of him like water from a faucet. The stench was almost unbearable.

"I love these children. They love me too. Nobody will want to believe…"

Dubois lifted up his feet and pulled his knees to his chest. He kind of rocked to his right and back to center over and over as tears flooded out of him.

"They're gonna make it out to be vulgar and filthy. It wasn't that way."

"Yes, they will make it out that way, Father."

"Nicky. Call me Nicky. I'm not ugly or dirty, vulgar or filthy."

In a quick motion, he straightened a leg, kicking the recorder off the table. "Confession! That's why you're here, just to get my confession. And then it will be over and everyone can disown me – my Church, my family…"

He collapsed back on the sofa. I righted the recorder.

"What about your family? Do they know why you are here?"

Father Dubois began to really sob.

"My momma… they can't do this to my momma. It's not her

fault I am like I am. I have brothers and sisters, nieces and nephews. They can't do this to them. No one knows. Nobody can know."

"Soon the media will find out, and then everyone will know."

"If you think everyone will know, will you tell my family, my mama, for me? Someone has to tell them. I can't. Please tell them in person when you get home. Don't let 'em find out from anybody else, not from the news people. My mama's name is Iris. Please call her at this number and go see her as soon as you can." He wrote her name and phone number in large script and handed the paper to me.

"What I came to get from you is the truth. I can't prepare a defense in the dark. I know I didn't get the whole truth today, Father."

"I'm Nicky. Call me Nicky."

"Okay. Nicky."

"You want the truth, Mr. Chattelrault? What is the truth? That I'm a filthy, vulgar pervert? Is that the truth? Am I legally insane because I love these boys so much? Does that make me crazy? Can somebody in some clinic kill the side of me that makes me do these things? What's the truth, sir? You tell me."

"The truth is that the lives of a lot of children have been destroyed by your actions and probably their fathers want to kill you. The truth is the whole world is probably going to know about what you have done to these children. That's the truth. I will always tell you the truth. It's not my job to lie to you."

He nodded.

"I have let you control this first interview, but it will not always be this way. Your insistence that I call you Francis and then that I call you Nicky is some kind of game I don't understand. I don't like you running games on me. I don't understand why you did these things and I don't understand why the children did these things with you for such a long time."

"The children did it for the same reason I did it."

I stared at him hard, waiting for his explanation.

"The children did it... because it feels so good."

My head reeled with the deepest disgust I'd ever experienced. Managing to maintain my professional demeanor, I silently wished Father Francis Dominick Dubois were dead, and wondered how the God I believed in could have created this man; how a man would use his Roman collar and other clerical trappings to violate the trust of families, and inflict ritual sexual abuse on boys seven to ten years old.

I quietly gathered up my things, including the photos of the boys. All the while I was packing, the priest never moved. He sat still and stank.

As I started to leave, Father Dubois asked me, "What happened?"

"What do you mean?" I said.

"I mean... who was it? Which boy? Which family got me in this trouble?"

"I don't know. The Church learned what was happening about a year ago – about the time you were sent for treatment, I guess."

"I want to know what happened. If you are my lawyer, can't you find out what happened, how it happened? Can't you?"

"I don't know if we will ever know exactly what happened," I said.

I did not want to hear anything else he might have to say, and I could hardly stand the smell of him. I turned and left.

8

A PRIMITIVE PRESENCE

Friday evening, August 24, 1984
Boston, Massachusetts

Holding my heavy briefcase in two hands above my head, I sprinted out of the Saint Martin Center, ran through the storm to the taxi, opened the door and tossed the case across the back seat. The battered old Chevy wagon was a religious rattletrap. It had a makeshift altar glued to the wide dashboard: little figurines and a scattering of symbols associated with some eastern religious sect were bathed in the soft green glow of a colored bulb in the dome light. There was a trace scent of incense. As I closed the door, the green dome light went out, leaving the altar in silhouette. The words "Free Tibet" were hand-lettered on an envelope taped to the glove box.

The driver wore a turban and a faded red robe. As the car engine sputtered then smoothed out and we started for the road, he looked straight ahead. "Would like to stop for coffee? For something? Before turnpike?" His soft, high-pitched voice was lilting and soothing.

When I got out of the cab under the awning of a gasoline station store and stretched, I realized the rain had let up. The wind was still with us, but its gale force was giving way to gusts. Tapping on the driver's window, I asked whether I could get something for him. He rolled down his window, showed his gentle face for the first time and smiled. "No thank you. Fasting."

We rode in silence to my hotel in Boston. The meter showed a hundred and sixty-five dollars. I handed him two hundred-dollar bills and said, "Thank you."

The driver bowed slightly. "You keep," he said, taking one bill and handing the other back to me. "Too much."

"It's okay. Please." I offered the money again, and the driver bowed again, gently touching my hand, pushing the money away. Then he took a small, light-copper-colored medallion from his pocket, and put it in my hand. "You keep this."

I took the coin.

With his eyes shut tight, the taxi man said, "Go home, sir, go back home."

When I reached my hotel room, I was exhausted. I knew the man in the turban was right. I should go home. A part of me felt like I'd never make it home again.

As I undressed, I emptied my pockets and the copper medallion fell to the desk. I picked up the little coin and examined it. On one side was an intricate design I didn't recognize, and the other side was engraved in a kind of script I'd never seen. I held it tightly in my fist, and walked to the window. The storm had intensified and was raging now. I knew the storm would last a long time.

Fear is the first and last feeling we experience in life. It is the only feeling which occupies every molecule of our being; the only emotion which has its own scent. That night in Boston, I felt fear. I realized my tiredness and the conflicts within me contributed to the feeling, but understanding the origin of one's fear does not make it dissipate.

I now knew Francis Dubois's sins, the details of his crimes. As I stood at the window, I reviewed my interview with Dubois in my mind. I was still unnerved by his apparent comfort, the "oneness" he felt with the horrible crimes he had committed, while still appearing to inhabit the clothes of a priest. Doctor Kennison's covering letter had used the phrase "vile depravity" in describing the perversions of the priest. The heinous nature of his crimes was something I believed was beyond the comprehension of most people. Was it, in fact, evidence of the existence of absolute evil on earth?

I did not believe anyone could understand or provide an explanation of Dubois's behavior. But I knew that if I was to represent this man, I would not only have to understand his behavior, I would also have to explain it to a jury, defend it.

I had lived long enough and experienced enough to know some things have no meaning at all. Nevertheless, tired as I was, I searched for some way to make sense of these things. Until that night, I had never believed in the existence of hell, much less Satan. I had always believed all evil on earth was homemade, handmade, manmade. Now, as I stared into the storm, I began to countenance the possibility that an ageless, graceless, godless force did perhaps walk the earth among us, an Antichrist who was the author of absolute evil, one with many names and disguises.

I had always believed that the frightening and diabolically malevolent creatures that have existed and do exist in the mind of man – terrifying beasts like the werewolves and vampires of Eastern Europe, the zombies of Haiti, the horrifying grotesques represented by the stone gargoyles that adorn great cathedrals, and even Satan himself – were either control devices invented by religions or the products of creative literary and artistic minds. I had always believed that they were no more real than the Satyr or the Minotaur.

I knew that in the distant past writers, painters and sculptors interpreted ancient folk tales told down the centuries. Villagers would invent monstrous villains, mutants and strangers to any known species, often in order to explain crimes committed by their neighbors and kinfolk.

In the enlightened era we live in, we have devised a legal defense of insanity to which courts and society retreat when confronted with acts that cannot be explained rationally or when society cannot accept that a human is capable of such savagery. We use this technical, scientific, medical defense today in place of inventing beasts or invoking possession by a demonic force. It is our way of attempting to reconcile ourselves with that which is irreconcilable.

49

Crimes against children have always been the hardest for any society to deal with. In one mountainous region of what is now Lithuania, a child would disappear from one of several idyllic, walled mountain villages every year in late fall, when the first snow fell, only to be found again during Easter week, lying on the village ramparts, head facing the east, fairly well preserved but missing its heart. Over time a tale evolved about a vicious beast without a heart that had to eat the heart of a child every year in order to survive the winter. Centuries later, a journal was found under the stone floor of an old house that had once belonged to the head of the village in the valley below. The diary recorded all of the murderous deeds he had carried out against children hundreds of years earlier, part of a demented, secret, sacrificial rite in which he buried their hearts near a cave where he believed his angry ancestors still existed, suspended between life and death. The man would keep the children's bodies in a high cave that was sealed by an ice shield through the winter, returning them in advance of Easter so that the bodies could be committed to a family crypt and the souls sent on to the heavens on Resurrection Sunday. Even in the face of that evidence, and despite the detailed confession by the crazed man in his own handwriting, the tale of a heartless beast still persists in the region today and there are lithographs of the imagined monster in the archives of a local museum.

I once read a book entitled *The Animal In Us All*, a historical, anthropological view of atrocities committed by our species against our own; abominations which were committed not in war, but in wickedness. The author recounted a series of macabre acts that were chilling to read. That these acts had happened on all of the continents and island chains defied classifying them in a cultural context. After listing the horrors, he examined the theories which have been offered through the ages to explain man's ability to act in such an inhumane way. One of the theories ascribed responsibility to an Antichrist. The writer accepted the possibility that an Antichrist existed but dismissed the notion that the Antichrist could be responsible for the Holocaust and other savage acts ending in death. He argued that all available writing about the Antichrist made it clear the Antichrist never kills; the Antichrist considers human death a kindness and the Antichrist is not kind enough to kill. Everyone touched by the Antichrist is allowed to live and touch others in the same fiendish way he or she was touched.

Doctor Kennison's covering summary noted that there was a very real danger the child victims might grow to be adult perpetrators of sex abuse. This was cited in addition to a long list of probable and possible problems that might visit victims throughout their lives. He had written: "Because one is a victim of sexual crimes such as these, it does not necessarily follow that the child will himself become a pedophile who will victimize children of approximately the same age. However, medical literature is replete with evidence that almost all adults who sexually molest children were victims of sex abuse when they were children. They do to children what was done to them."

I knew I would not be able to sleep. The raging storm outside mirrored my interior landscape. A single phrase reverberated around my conscious mind. Everyone touched by the Antichrist is allowed to live and touch others in the same fiendish way he or she was touched.

PART TWO

THE SECRETS OF A CHILD

1983–1984

ONE YEAR EARLIER

9

IN A CONSECRATED PLACE

5:40 p.m., Thursday September 8, 1983
Amalie, Cypress Bay, Louisiana

Cheney Falgout spent the afternoon of his tenth birthday on his father's shrimp boat in Cypress Bay. His dad was in the engine well. Cheney was handing him tools. But he was thinking about something he'd read in a storybook at school that week. The story was titled "No Secrets". The hero of the story was a young boy who learned that secrets were like poison and truth was like medicine; secrets could make you sick and truth could make you well. Cheney had felt sick for three years. He wanted to be well again.

Cheney thought about his seventh birthday often. He remembered everything that had happened on the altar that September Monday three years ago, and what had happened after he left the little church with Father Nicky.

Father Francis Dominick Dubois was the only person with keys to the church in Amalie on the shore of Cypress Bay. As he locked the door behind them that day, he had made sure Cheney understood that. The priest had led the way as the two of them climbed the rickety stairs to the belfry. Leaks in the roof had rotted some of the wooden steps and parts of the railing. A long snakeskin lay across the top step. Father Nicky smiled and said, "I think that snake's still in here."

Cheney Falgout was terrified. He had heard ghost stories about the church. The first story was about a man who had hung himself from the rope that rang the church bell and how the bell only rang once as the dead man slammed into the wood siding. The second story was about the bell also. One afternoon it rang so many times that everyone in Amalie and Cypress Bay came running. Just as the crowd gathered outside the church, an old priest appeared on the belfry walk and did a swan dive, his black cassock spreading like the wings of a monstrous vulture. These stories were on Cheney's mind as he stepped over the snakeskin.

When he and Father Dubois emerged onto the walkway around the top of the steeple, the child instinctively breathed deeply, inhaling the salty air, smelling the bay. He looked for the dock on the canal where his father moored his shrimp boat, a big, long hauler. Cheney breathed deep, over and over.

When they were back downstairs in the church, the priest showed Cheney the baptismal fount where he had been christened. Father Nicky allowed him to sit in the clergyman's center cubicle of the old oak-and-pecan-wood confessional. He then guided Cheney round the communion railing to the altar.

As Cheney stood by the altar, his heart raced to be standing so close to God. Father Dubois reached down and lifted the little boy to a sitting position on the altar. He placed the chalice between the boy's legs, and let him touch its gold surface and the jewels set on the side of the cup. Then the priest set the chalice on the floor.

With a hand on the boy's chest, the priest gently pushed him onto his back. Cheney stared at a large crucifix mounted on the wall behind him. Light flooded in through a red, green and blue leaded glass panel on the rear wall high above the sanctuary. From where he lay, the crucifix and everything else looked upside down.

"Now Father must do something very important," the priest said. "It's a physical inspection kind of like at a doctor's office but a little different. You are going to be an altar boy before Christmas. You will be on this altar at Midnight Mass. Everyone will look at you as a holy boy. Father is going to make you a holy boy. What we are doing right now is a secret, a secret that only priests and special boys know. There are lots of secrets you will know that you can never tell anyone, not even your momma and daddy. This will make you feel really good. And after this, Cheney, you will be Father's boy."

Father Dubois unzipped the boy's jeans and removed them. As he was pulling the child's Winnie the Pooh jockey shorts off, the priest unfastened his own pants and let them fall to the floor, pushing his boxer shorts to his knees. The boy shivered and then he felt Father's mouth pushing down between his bare legs.

Cheney had no idea what was going on. He felt cold on the marble altar, scared in his head and icky down there. He had no idea what was happening. He could feel the priest's left hand stroking his face, sometimes running through his hair. He felt the priest's right arm kind of banging against his left leg.

The priest made a noise Cheney had never heard any person make. Then Father Nicky took his mouth away, pulled up his pants and fastened his belt. He helped Cheney dress and lifted him to the floor.

The boy hung his head. He felt like he was going to be sick.

Afterwards, Father Nicky had taken him to Thiberville, forty miles away, where they visited a mall and Cheney got more birthday gifts than he could have dreamed of: a pellet gun and ammo, a tackle box and fishing gear, camouflage clothing, a pirate puppet, and a jam box and a stack of music cassettes.

Over the next three years, everything had escalated in Cheney's relationship with Father Nicky. The gifts got greater and the degradation deepened. Cheney became one of Father Nicky's special boys, a favorite. Once Cheney suffered rectal bleeding and was admitted to the local hospital. The physician diagnosed the cause as a hard stool. Father Nicky visited him every day and brought gifts, once whispering, "Even a doctor cannot know our secrets."

The night before his tenth birthday, Cheney had collected every gift the priest had ever given him and dumped them in the canal where the shrimp boats and tugs were moored.

Now, as Randy Falgout climbed out of the engine well, Cheney grabbed his papa and started crying. The fisherman sat on the deck and pulled his child into his lap. Cheney clung to him, sobbing, "I'm scared, Papa." When he had told enough of his secrets for his papa to have a clear picture, his father wiped the tears and sweat from the child's face.

"Papa, I'm tired. Everything hurts inside."

Randy Falgout picked Cheney up, cradled him like an infant and carried him down a short stairwell to the crew quarters. He put the child in a bottom bunk. Kneeling next to him, he held Cheney's hand until he was in a deep sleep. After watching him sleep for a while, he climbed back to the deck and paced, circling the engine parts that were spread across the planking.

He could hardly think; his emotions overpowered his mind. *How could anyone do this to a child?* His gut burned like fire. He could almost see himself killing the priest. His chest tightened and he began to sweat.

Staring at the sun setting over the gulf, kneeling and holding onto the bow rail, Randy remembered. He remembered that his two older sons had been altar boys at Our Lady of the Seas in Amalie under Father Francis Dubois, the man all the children called Father Nicky.

10

THE SACRAMENTS

11:30 a.m., Friday September 9, 1983
Rectory of Saint Bernadette, Bayou Saint John, Louisiana

The pastor of Saint Bernadette Church in Bayou Saint John, Monsignor Phillip Jules Gaudet, changed the color of his cassocks twice a year. Each year on the day of the autumn equinox he donned black clothing of the kind worn by other priests in the diocese, and on the vernal equinox he switched to the white attire favored by some Mediterranean clerics.

That morning the monsignor was wearing a straw hat with a wide brim, white cassock, white socks and Mexican-made sandals. He stepped gingerly onto the wet lawn, clipped off an orange-colored rose with a long stem, and held it in his gloved hand. Using the clipper, he surgically removed the thorns, then admired the flower and laid it in a basket alongside roses of other hues. Humming the aria *"Nessun dorma"*, Monsignor Phillip Jules Gaudet carefully surveyed the circular bed of roses that dominated the garden between his residence and the Church of Saint Bernadette. Satisfied, he removed his gloves and carried the roses into his home.

Across the street, in the tiny oak-shaded town square, six adults stood in a tight circle around the miniature replica of the cave in Lourdes, France, with its statue of a young girl in brown clothes kneeling before the Virgin Mary.

"We are going in there," Randy Falgout said, nodding towards the rectory. "We have to. Somebody's got to get Father Francis outtahere."

Two of the women were crying. It had been a night without sleep for all of them. After Randy had put Cheney to bed at home, he talked to his two older sons, who broke down and told him about things Father Dubois had done to them. Then Randy called his two sisters about their sons who had served as altar boys in Amalie and they too learned a truth too terrible to believe.

The three couples spent the night on the end of the pier in front of the Falgouts' bayside home. It had been quiet all night, the only sound being the bay lapping against the pilings and, every so often, the sobbing of the women. None of the six could understand how or why such things had happened in their little village, and happened to their children. No one wanted to believe their little boys had been sodomized by a priest who was popular, a man who always had compliments for women not used to receiving them, one who traded talk with the men about fishing, hunting and farming. They felt they were awake in a nightmare, living a horror their minds and hearts could not deal with. Mostly they shut down talking and cried quietly, waiting for the sun, hoping it would all be gone in the light of day.

None of them knew what to do.

Finally, Randy Falgout took control and called the rectory for the parish of Saint Bernadette, demanding an appointment with Monsignor Gaudet. He assumed the monsignor at the big church in Bayou Saint John, a few miles from Father Dubois's parish in Amalie, would be Dubois's boss.

Now, in the town square, they were arguing. Randy's baby sister and her husband were shaking their heads. The man said, "We can't talk to nobody about this. I can't think about it. How can I talk about it?"

"I'll talk," Randy said. "I'll talk."

The couple kept shaking their heads. His younger sister said, "No, no, I just can't."

His other brother-in-law was looking down at his shoes. In a measured tone, he said softly, "Randy, if I see a priest today, I might kill him. My bare hands."

"I want to kill the bastard myself – beat him to death slow like, but we decided," Randy said emphatically. "Last night we decided. First thing, we gotta get him outtahere. We can't get him outtahere by ourselves. That monsignor across the street got to be his supervisor or something. He can get him outtahere."

Randy's wife asked, "How many more boys do you think there are, Randy? How many?"

"I dunno. Maybe every altar boy since Father Dubois came here. We can only do what we can do, honey. We gotta get the bastard outtahere now, today."

The three couples walked up the steps of the rectory. An officious housekeeper opened the front door and led them down a long corridor to an ornate chamber with an old-fashioned stuccoed ceiling and a wall of leaded glass windows. Monsignor Gaudet had his back to them. He was fussing with a spray of roses in a tall crystal vase. He turned around, walked past the couples and handed the vase to the housekeeper. "For the table, Annette."

Addressing Randy, who stood a few feet in front of the others, Monsignor Gaudet said, "My mother is coming for table." He pointed to a black-and-white photograph on the wall. It depicted a young Phillip Jules Gaudet dressed in a sweater, slacks and saddle oxford shoes, standing next to an older woman in a long overcoat; they were in the Piazza San Pietro in Rome, in front of Saint Peter's Basilica. "Mother," he said. "She will arrive punctually with a friend of hers for noon table. We do not have much time. My secretary said one of you had left messages that you had some urgent business with me. Please sit down."

As Randy Falgout started to speak, Monsignor Gaudet raised his hand to silence him. He reached for the small bell on his desk and rang for the housekeeper, who appeared immediately. He asked for iced tea, offering nothing to his guests. Then he sat in a throne-like chair behind his desk, and nodded to Randy.

Randy Falgout's chest tightened as it had on the deck of his shrimp boat the previous afternoon. He wanted to reach across the large desk and strangle Monsignor Gaudet with his Roman collar, but he knew he had to control himself. He knew he had to do whatever it took to get Dubois out of the area before he or his brother-in-law murdered Father Dubois, the man who had sent Randy's youngest son to the hospital with a torn rectum. Randy was surprised by his own voice when the first words he spoke came out smoothly while his insides were screaming.

" It was me who left the messages," he said. "Our children – six little boys –have had all kinds of sexual stuff done to them by Father Dubois in Amalie. We are here to tell you that you best be getting about the business of getting this man out of here now, today, before the sun goes down. I know at least one person who might kill that priest. When word gets out, I think lots of people will want to kill him. He's a sick no good. A no good son-of-a-bitch."

Monsignor Gaudet shook his head side to side. "Please, sir, please..."

"This ain't no time to be worrying about language, Father. We want him out before dark. He even raped our baby. Sent him to the hospital."

All three mothers began crying.

Monsignor Phillip Jules Gaudet turned red in the face, accepted his tea from the housekeeper, sipped, swallowed. "You don't understand, sir," he said. "First, a replacement would have to be found. The chancery in Thiberville takes care of these things. Immediate removal may not be an option."

"Monsignor, I don't think you understand the options. Somebody is going to kill that son-of-a-bitch."

"You should hear what you are saying. And you should know that spreading gossip about a priest is a serious sin against the Church. The most serious sin is a sin against the Church. And this is the worst kind of sin, a mortal sin. We cannot, as Catholics, ever do or say anything that brings scandal to the Church. What you are saying against a priest would indeed bring scandal to the Church. Do you understand me? It is a sin. Nothing is to be said about this outside of this room."

"Father, I think I remember now. You know this priest good. Father Dubois was right here at this church with you before he came to Amalie. It's true, isn't it? You already knew the priest was this way, didn't you? He lived in this place with you, didn't he? You knew what he was when you sent him to our church."

The women dried their eyes with handkerchiefs and fixed their gaze on Monsignor Gaudet.

"Sir, you will not accuse me or interrogate me. I did not send him to you. Vicar General Moroux and Bishop Reynolds make assignments, not I."

Randy looked at his wife and sisters, remembered why he was there, softened his voice. "What are you gonna do, Father? We gotta know."

"Sir, you are overlooking a very important aspect of this matter. If there is any truth to what you are telling me about what Father Francis supposedly did with your children, you are overlooking that there is more than one person involved in this sin. There is the priest – and, of course, there are the boys."

"The boys?" Randy said incredulously. "What about the boys?"

"Sir, we are talking about sin. When two people commit a sexual sin together, both are sinners in the eyes of God."

"You're telling us our boys have sinned?"

Ignoring the question, Monsignor Gaudet said, "Sir... please, please. I do have the solution."

"What?"

"The sacrament. The sacraments are always the solution. If you will bring your children to me, I will hear their confessions. They will receive penance and absolution. Their sins will be forgiven. They will again be in a state of grace."

"What?" Randy Falgout leaned forward, causing the monsignor to flinch and push against the back of his leather chair. "You expect our sons to confess to a priest what another priest did to them? You're not playing with a full deck, Padre."

"I am telling you I will hear the boys' confessions, and give them a penance and absolution. They will again be in a state of grace."

Randy Falgout slammed his closed fist on the top of the monsignor's desk, upending the goblet of iced tea. He turned on his heel and strode toward the door. The others followed him out of the room, down the long corridor, across the town square and into the law office of one of Mrs. Falgout's cousins.

11

AN ECCLESIASTICAL TEMPLE

6:45 a.m., Friday October 14, 1983
Diocesan Chancery, Thiberville

The hairless heads and hollowed eye sockets of twelve dead men stared into the vestibule of the chancery building of the Roman Catholic Diocese of Thiberville, Louisiana. The bronze busts of long-departed popes, mounted on polished marble plinths, stood like sentries around the semicircular stone and glass antechamber that opened to the hallway as wide as a highway. Everything in the building was cold: granite, marble, brick, tile and glass. The hard surfaces made the building an echo chamber, and the slightest sound carried the length of the corridor. It was more like a Pharaoh's tomb than an office building, complete with its own buried sarcophagus – a hidden vault containing the secret archives of the diocese.

Monsignor Jean-Paul Moroux, vicar general of Thiberville, walked the long hall as he did every weekday morning after celebrating the six o'clock Mass at Saint Stephen's Cathedral next door. As always, he was the first person in the building. The echo of his wooden-soled shoes striking the polished marble floor repeated like rifle shots.

After turning on the coffee machine, Moroux pulled the rubber band off the morning newspaper and loaded it onto his hand, cocking his fingers like a pistol. He fired his missile at one of the portraits, hitting a long-dead bishop square on the nose. "Bull's eye," mumbled the monsignor.

Monsignor Moroux was the number-two man in the diocese,

but he had no desire to be bishop. He relished the perceived power he held, but wanted none of the public duties required of a bishop. That made him an oddity, and he knew it.

Ever since Calvary, when men had cast dice at the foot of the cross, gambling for the clothes of Christ, priests had gambled and played politics for the chance to wear the robes of a bishop. But not Monsignor Moroux. In his experience there were three kinds of priests: those who considered themselves to have true vocations, a calling from God; those who became priests because it gave them a prestige that would have otherwise eluded them; and those who viewed the work as a career rather than a vocation and strived for advancement.

The men who believed they had been called to the priesthood by God lived in their higher selves and worked in poor church parishes in unselfish ways. They were few. Most who studied for the priesthood were recruited during the extensive campaigns conducted at Catholic schools around the dioceses, or were pushed into the religious life by their parents, or else were motivated by guilt or other things better worked out in a psychiatric environment.

As Moroux had never had an honest conversation with another priest, he did not know if he was the only empiricist in the priesthood; the only one who believed in nothing. Not the Church, not God, nothing. On occasion he exhibited the rare talent of being both a cynic and a comic at the same time, but few saw those sides of him as he had long ago stopped socializing. He had been apprehended for drunk driving a number of times, and though he never been charged by the police, and had instead completed two different alcohol rehabilitation courses in out-of-state clinics, he had now stopped drinking in public.

Moroux once said he felt knowledge had taken up all the space in his brain that he needed for thinking, and all he had done for the last thirty years was recite knowledge in the place of experiencing and expressing original thought.

He considered himself against literacy, once saying education and technology had polluted civility in its purest form, placing the human equation in a negative balance. The monsignor admired primitive civilizations that were not encumbered by formal education or ritualized religion; he respected people who devised their own superstitions and believed in magic in place of miracles. It was his belief that in such societies no secrets passed into the grave as the elders shared all they had learned with younger tribesman before their demise. In Western civilization, he knew the opposite occurred, that every generation buried their secrets. In his view, ignorance allowed the intellect to breathe whereas knowledge suffocated the mind. Such notions would surely have been considered odd by those who knew him well, but he had never allowed anyone to know him well.

11:50 a.m.

Two young lawyers entered the monsignor's office shoulder to shoulder. On the right was Brent Thomas from Bayou Saint John, a cousin of Mrs. Falgout's. Accompanying him was his former law-school classmate Ricardo Ponce, from Fort Lauderdale, Florida.

Brent Thomas was ingratiating, asking Monsignor Moroux if he remembered that years ago he had taught him religion in the Catholic high school in Bayou Saint John. Moroux pretended to remember but in truth he remembered few people, made it a point not to invest enough of himself in anyone, in case knowing them might constitute a relationship.

Brent Thomas had a smooth, feminine face, dainty features and small hands. Ricardo Ponce looked menacing. He was balding and allowed the few remaining hairs on his skull to grow long. A deep scar ran down the left side of his face from the corner of his eye to his jaw.

Ponce laid a tall stack of legal papers in the center of the desk. "Monsignor, these are legal petitions we are prepared to file on

Monday morning. Supporting documentation for each claim is also included. These lawsuits seek eighteen million dollars from the diocese on behalf of three families. These claims are for six young boys who were ritualistically sexually abused by your priest in the church parish of Amalie, Father Francis Dubois."

Moroux calmly shoved the papers to the side as if they were in his way. "Routinely, Mr. Ponce, I am not involved in the legal affairs of the diocese. I will forward these papers to legal counsel, who will review them."

Ponce remained standing, motioning for Brent Thomas to rise from his chair. Addressing Moroux, Ponce said, "There's nothing routine about this. These cases involve the sexual abuse of six children by a Catholic priest. There are people in Amalie who want to kill both Father Dubois and Bishop Reynolds. All of us have an obligation to attempt to end the violence. We've done our part in coming here. It's up to the diocese now. You have twenty-four hours from now to get Father Dubois the hell out of Amalie."

Ponce reached across Moroux's desk for a memo pad and scribbled a phone number. "This is Brent's telephone number at home. If we don't hear from you by Monday morning at nine, we will file these suits and distribute copies to every newspaper and television station in the state. Then everyone will know about your monster priest."

Outwardly, Moroux remained nonchalant. Inwardly, his heart was racing so fast he feared it would burst. He could not remember ever having had this kind of reaction to anything.

On his way to the door, Ponce stopped and turned toward Moroux, who remained in his chair. "You have until Monday morning to call. Then everyone will know what we know about your priest."

Standing among the bronze pope heads at the end of the hall, Brent Thomas turned to Ricardo Ponce in anger. "Why did you do that? Why did you storm out of there? You didn't give the monsignor a chance to talk. These people are my clients, my kin.

They had never been in a lawyer's office in their lives. They're really uncomfortable about suing. They're family – and you know how hard it was to talk them into suing their Church."

"Yeah, well now they're suing their Church."

"None of them, not Randy or the others, will let us put this on the public record Monday morning, give this to the press, and expose their sons' names and what happened. Christ, we can't file these suits Monday. What the hell are you thinking?"

"I'm thinking the diocese is more afraid of this becoming public than your clients are."

"Suppose you're wrong. Just suppose the good monsignor calls your bluff and tells you to file the suits on Monday. What then?"

"He won't do that. The diocese can't let this stuff hit the press."

"You really were disrespectful to the monsignor."

"Fuck the monsignor."

Monsignor Moroux stared out of the tall, narrow windows and across the huge cemetery. Often he found himself looking at the stone markers crowded close together. Usually the sight soothed him. Not this time.

After the young lawyers left, Monsignor Jean-Paul Moroux did something he had never done before. He locked the office door, as if that would somehow keep out anything else he was not prepared to deal with. He knew he would have to call the bishop and notify the lawyers. He would do that after lunch. First he would remove himself from the chancery and go to his home, next door. He needed a drink. As he stared at the gravestones, he heard the muffled bells in the cathedral tower ring twelve times. Then it was quiet.

12

WASHING OF HANDS

Friday afternoon, October 14, 1983
Old Bishop's House, Thiberville

"Yes. You will take care of this."

That was all Bishop Reynolds could muster over the telephone when Monsignor Moroux finished briefing him on his visit from attorneys Ponce and Thomas.

When Moroux mentioned one of the lawyers said there were people around Amalie who wanted to kill the Bishop, Bishop Reynolds had a long spasmodic coughing episode and rang off.

In turn, Moroux passed the matter over to archdiocesan counsel, Thomas Quinlan, in New Orleans. As he talked with Attorney Quinlan on the phone, spelling out everything as best he could – including the threat of the Monday morning deadline – Moroux sat at the desk in the study of his residence, sipping vodka. As he lit a cigarette, he realized another was burning in the ashtray.

"Jean-Paul, a young lawyer from my office named James Ryburn will be at your office in Thiberville within three hours. Copy every document those lawyers, Ponce and Thomas, gave to you and give them to Ryburn. I need to have the files to know when the offenses occurred, which of our insurance companies have coverage and financial responsibility for the various claims."

Saturday October 15, 1983
New Orleans, Louisiana

Archdiocesan counsel Tom Quinlan moved heaven and earth. Social schedules in the Garden District of New Orleans, dinner reservations in private rooms of French Quarter restaurants, a small soirée at the New Orleans Country Club, golf games, tennis matches and plans to attend the Tulane–Navy football game were all canceled by attorneys who headed some of the most prestigious law firms in the city. These attorneys represented a consortium of insurance companies that had twenty-five million dollars of coverage at risk should the Roman Catholic Diocese of Thiberville be found liable for payouts to victims of clergy sexual abuse.

Most of these insurance lawyers were cynical men with a view of the world no humanist would share. Some were mean to their core. They represented large corporations, institutions and insurance companies against individuals who had been injured by the intentional or negligent actions of their clients. They rarely won a case, for the object of their legal practice was not to have victories in court, but rather to minimize losses to their clients.

In the conference room of Quinlan's office the lawyers quickly established there was no legal precedent that could provide guidance regarding liability issues or the value of such claims as this was the first case of its kind in the country. The Catholic Church had never been sued over the sexual abuse of children by a priest. The overriding concern shared by all counsel was not to do anything that would make it seem like it was open season on the Diocese of Thiberville for claims of this kind. It was their universal silent belief that the six children represented by Brent Thomas and Ricardo Ponce were probably not the only potential plaintiffs who could bring a lawsuit against Father Dubois and the diocese, but maybe only the tip of the proverbial iceberg.

The back-room shuffle among these men of immense egos was fierce. There were arguments about which insurance companies had financial exposure and financial responsibility for which claims. The claims covered different years, and in each of those years the diocese had a different insurance program. Some companies had "first dollar coverage" in some years (where the first money of any claims would be paid from their pockets), but were not even part of the insurance program in other years. In all, the insurance policies were stacked to a total coverage of twenty-five million dollars.

Finally, a lead mule emerged from the pack in the person of Robert Blassingame, of the firm Miller, Sikes, Wilder, Gentry, Donebane and Doise. The insurance company he represented seemed to have the greatest financial exposure.

Blassingame's reputation as a hard-nosed litigator and cold-hearted, clear-headed trial lawyer was legendary. He once excused himself from his own son's funeral wake to appear for a scheduled argument before an appeals court, a matter that could have been postponed by opposing counsel and the court as a matter of respect and courtesy. Blassingame delayed the funeral rather than the court appearance. Nothing was sacred to him except the funds of his corporate insurance clients – from which he extracted exorbitant fees for his services.

The conference lasted through the night. At sunrise, only Tom Quinlan and Robert Blassingame remained in Quinlan's office suite.

Sunday October 16, 1983
New Orleans

Sunday morning the call came to Monsignor Moroux's residence early. Tom Quinlan and Robert Blassingame were both on the line.

"Monsignor, this is Robert Blassingame, lead counsel for the diocesan insurance companies. You have to get that damned priest out of the diocese. I mean today. That's first."

Quinlan said, "Jean-Paul, call those lawyers and tell them we do not want the children injured by a public filing and we will arrange Monday to have a judge sign an order sealing the lawsuits. Okay?"

"We-ell, Tom, I can remove Father Francis and I can call the lawyers. But what about their other demands?" Moroux said.

"Monsignor, this is Robert Blassingame again. You tell them

that serious settlement negotiations will be conducted in your office this Friday at ten a.m."

"The point you have to make with the lawyers, Jean-Paul," Tom Quinlan said, "the point is this. The lawsuits must be sealed and there must be absolute confidentiality or there can be no serious settlement discussions. These lawyers have to control their clients. If their clients talk to anyone about this, there can be no deal."

"Is that it?" Moroux asked.

"You have our authority to buy the cases for four million dollars total," said Blassingame. "I will mail a letter of authority tomorrow. If you cannot negotiate a settlement for that amount, schedule another meeting with them in a week. Monsignor, you will meet alone with the lawyers. You will represent that any funds paid to their clients will come from diocesan coffers, depleting the charitable funds of the diocese, adversely impacting charitable programs. Let 'em know they and their clients are taking money from the Church. At all costs, maintain secrecy."

Monsignor Moroux asked, "Is this legal?"

"Don't worry about it, Monsignor, don't worry. We cannot have those young lawyers smelling out large insurance policies, believing we have the kind of insurance coverage we have. We'll wire money into the diocesan account before you issue a check if you are able to reach a settlement and Tommy Quinlan will prepare the settlement documents and appear at the signing as a Church lawyer. No insurance defense lawyer will be involved for appearance's sake. Got it?"

"Uh-huh. Got it." The monsignor said.

"One other thing, Monsignor," Blassingame said. "Who are these lawyers – these boys – Brent Thomas and Ricardo Ponce?"

"Thomas is from the area around Amalie, down in Bayou Saint John. I think he's a cousin of the families who are suing. All I know about Ponce is what you know. His letterhead has a Fort Lauderdale, Florida address."

When the call ended, Tom Quinlan went to the sideboard and

poured a tall drink for himself. Looking to Blassingame, who nodded his assent, Quinlan topped off a second Scotch, then asked, "Who the hell do you think this Brent Thomas and Ricardo Ponce are, Robert?"

"I don't know, Tommy. I never heard of them. No one is from Fort Lauderdale."

Blassingame downed his Scotch, set the glass on the sideboard and took his leave, pausing at the door to say, "Whoever the sons-of-bitches are, they're going to be rich sons-of-bitches pretty soon."

It was Sunday. Quinlan would attend Mass at Saint Louis Cathedral. Blassingame would go to his law firm's sky box in the Super Dome for the Saints vs Falcons football game.

Tom Quinlan sat at his desk for a long time. In the corner of the office was an Italian bronze sculpture of Lady Justice. He stared at her. He had always understood what the blindfold symbolized as well as the scales of justice held in one hand. He had never given thought to the sword held in her other hand.

13

EXILE TO PURGATORY

Sunday October 16, 1983
South Pass Marsh, Louisiana

On the gulf coast of South Louisiana, the locals called the great floating fields of the marshes 'the lost places'. For years, men had only been able to navigate the area with machines; machines to kill animals and extract oil and gas from beneath the surface. No man ever walked this marshland until a few years ago, when local trappers and oil-field workers in airboats and mud boats began to see a man crawling through the marsh in the distance. No one knew him. They called him the hunter.

The hunter had come to the marsh late that day, about noon, to hunt ducks out of season. The brown, brackish marshes glimmered in the autumn light, and the tall, unrooted marsh meadows swayed in the breeze. Alligators sunned themselves on soggy mounds. Everything in the marsh was moving, nothing had migrated or gone into hibernation. Underfoot, the land was soft silt, soaked by the gentle tides of a salty sea and washed by fresh water fed from bayous. Walking through the black, rancid, chest-high mud required enormous physical strength. As the hunter made his way, big black, blood-sucking mosquitoes covered his face, hands and arms.

The hunter came upon a small pond where a single greenhead mallard floated lazily on the surface. He raised his shotgun and blasted the duck at such close range that he blew it out of the pond. As he reached for what was left of the bird, a huge nutria rat exploded out of the grass and hit the hunter hard enough to shake his balance. The rat's long, orange teeth locked onto his thick hunting vest. In a blinding movement, the hunter drove a knife through the big rat's throat, dropped it to the mud and violently slashed it into unrecognizable shreds.

As the hunter slowly sloshed his way to the earthen levee where he'd parked his car, a thick water moccasin swam toward him. He froze, sinking deeper into the silt until the black snake was level with his face. The snake came straight at him, slid over his shoulder. He smiled as the viper's heavy, hard body rubbed against his neck.

The hunter loved to kill, but he always allowed snakes to live.

Last light
Diocesan Chancery, Thiberville

The hunter had just walked from his church in Amalie to his rectory after evening services when his phone rang and Monsignor Moroux commanded him to come to the chancery in Thiberville immediately.

As Father Dubois pulled his black Chevy Suburban into a parking space near the plaza between the cathedral and chancery, the headlights caught the lone figure of Monsignor Jean-Paul Moroux standing near the angel fountain. He had his back to the street and was staring at the Saint Augustine Cemetery that abutted the land where Saint Stephen's Cathedral stood. Moroux was pondering the proximity of the cemetery to the church and whether this had any effect on weekly donations in the collection plate. In some of the church parishes of the diocese, the cemeteries were far removed from the church. In others, the faithful making their way into the church were confronted with this stark reminder of death in the form of acres of tombstones. He wondered if the face of death made parishioners double down on donations, hedging their bets regarding eternity. Moroux made a mental note to check the per capita donations in church parishes where the cemetery stood next to the church against those where the tombs were far removed.

"Jean-Paul?" Father Dubois spoke softly, hesitantly, as he approached the monsignor.

Standing face to face, Dubois was taller, but both men were small. Deliberately, Moroux extended his hand. Francis Dubois's handshake was damp.

The monsignor asked, "Francis, do you want to talk here? My office? Take a walk?"

Francis Dubois cleared his throat. He did it twice. "It's about my finance reports, isn't it? I know I'm late. Three months, I think. I have no help. Getting everything done, doing it alone is hard—"

Jean-Paul Moroux quietly raised his hand to silence Dubois. "It's not about the reports."

"Well, I want you to know I like Amalie. I hope I'm not being reassigned."

Moroux put his hand on Dubois's shoulder. "Let's walk."

Under the glow of the security lights, they skirted the edge of the graveyard, winding down its stone path to an elaborate, deep green, cast-iron gazebo covering three graves. The two men sat on an iron bench under the gazebo.

"You know, Francis, the three males buried under this gazebo have the exact same name. The old man in the center there was a brilliant inventor. He designed this gazebo when his oldest son was killed, to cover that grave to the left. He knew his wife would come here every day. He wanted to keep the sun off her. A rather extravagant gesture, don't you think?"

"Who was he?" Dubois whispered, feigning interest.

"He was a narcissistic fellow who wanted to live on after death in some way. He didn't believe in an afterlife or in the idea that man has a soul. He wanted his name to survive him so he gave his exact name to two male descendants. First to his oldest son, who

76

was killed in a car accident as a teenager. Then to his first grandson, who also died in childhood. The old man outlived both of his namesakes. He was the last man on earth with his name when he was buried."

Father Dubois said nothing. He didn't know what to say because he had no idea what they were talking about.

Moroux continued, "Well, all that's interesting enough. But what's really significant is that the fellow in the middle was an avowed atheist. That was known to everyone, certainly to all of us. It's against our rules to bury an avowed atheist in hallowed ground. But he was sneaked into this cemetery by the former bishop as a tribute to his financial generosity to the cathedral parish, which he funneled through his wife. She attended early Mass all of her life. Holy Mother Church values a lot of things, Francis."

"Yes," Dubois whispered.

"We don't have to whisper, Francis," Moroux said. Pointing to the graves, he added, "I don't think they will mind. You see, they're all dead."

Dubois nodded nervously. He grabbed a vine growing on the iron latticework of the gazebo, tearing a leaf free.

"One day, Francis, somebody might dig a really big hole and bury this Church."

Father Dubois was beginning to feel dizzy. He was lost. He knew the monsignor had his ways and maybe some understood Moroux's ways, but Dubois was not in that number.

"The point, Francis… You see, the point is that our Church can overlook or look away from many things. We can bury an atheist in the center of our bone-yard. It's a little thing to overlook. Our Church sees nothing it does not want to see."

Dubois was confused. The tension was twisting his insides. Monsignor Moroux did nothing to relieve his anxiety. Rather he dug into the pocket of his windbreaker for a cigarette and pack of matches. For a time he played with the cigarette in his hand. Then he lit it, inhaled deeply and exhaled. Repeating the process again and again, Moroux smoked the whole cigarette without saying anything, and then he flipped the butt, end over end, toward a simple grave outside of the gazebo. When the cigarette butt hit the stone marker, hot ashes scattered like miniature fireworks. A smile spread over Monsignor Jean-Paul Moroux's face and his eyes softened. "That's my brother's grave. He loved to smoke."

Monsignor Moroux turned away from his brother's grave and fixed his black eyes on Dubois. Dubois fingered, twisted, and balled up the ivy leaf in his fist.

"Francis, we have a problem. A problem with little boys."

Father Dubois's hands were clasped between his knees, his whole torso bent forward as he tried to calm the cramps in his stomach. Father Dubois felt he might have to excuse himself to go to a restroom.

"Yes, Francis. We have a problem."

"No!" Dubois said emphatically. "No!"

Moroux murmured softly, "Yes, Francis."

"Who? I've a right, a right to know. It has to be somebody who heard something about the past. Was it a farmer named Weston Courville? He's got a son named Will who has some kind of nervous disorder, mental problems or something, and he lies. He quit going to school."

"No, Francis. I do not believe there is a Courville child involved." Monsignor Moroux checked his memory. He knew there was no Courville family.

"Whoever it is, I can explain. I know I can," Dubois pleaded.

"Not this time, Francis, not this time," Moroux said.

"What's wrong? You don't think it's true, do you? You know me, Jean-Paul. I wouldn't. Not again. I wouldn't..." Dubois's voice trailed off.

"Francis, I told you we have problems. This time they're real problems. It's not like the other times with one boy, two parents. It's more than one boy this time, more than one family."

"Tell me who—"

Moroux interrupted, "I can't tell you who, Francis. I can tell you they have lawyers. This time it's not going to go away. This time you're going to go away."

Father Francis Dubois began to cry. The monsignor offered no consolation.

"Go where, Jean-Paul?"

"You are not to return to Amalie ever again. I've rented a room at the Holiday Inn in Thiberville for tonight. The reservation is under the name John Bosco."

Monsignor Moroux intellectualized everything. He spoke with people, but the only real dialogues he ever had were in his head. He only joked with himself in his mind. He assigned the name Bosco to Dubois because Saint John Bosco, who lived in the late 1800s and was canonized in 1934 by Pope Pius XI, was known as the Pied Piper of Turin because so many young boys followed him through the streets. His special ministry was young boys, disadvantaged street boys. When he was canonized, the Church cited him for employing an education method based on love.

Dubois had no intention of going straight to the hotel. He would first return to the rectory to retrieve his things.

"That's it, Francis. We will announce you are on medical leave. Tomorrow you will go to Alexandria. It's only a couple hours away, but far enough. In Alexandria, there is a room reserved for you at another Holiday Inn. It too is in the name John Bosco. A Catholic psychologist there will contact you. You will see him daily until an appropriate treatment venue is found. In time a reassignment to another diocese will come. You will do God's work again."

"But, but I... I don't... I don't have..."

"Money? There's cash in this envelope."

Dubois made a mental note to remember to remove the thousands of dollars wrapped in tin foil in the bottom of his fish freezer in the utility room of the rectory, money borrowed from the collection plate.

"If you need anything, call me later this evening at my

residence. My private number is on the envelope. Never call the chancery."

"I've got to tell some people in Amalie goodbye."

"It's not a good idea. Don't call or write anyone in Amalie. Never go to Amalie again. The lawyers tell me there are people in Amalie who want to kill you. Maybe the ones who want to kill you are the same ones you think are your friends."

"I have guns, Jean-Paul."

"My God, Francis, just go in peace."

They strolled back to the angel fountain and Moroux handed him the envelope. As Dubois started down the steps toward his car, Moroux called softly, "Francis, do you want to make a confession?"

"What?"

"Do you want me to hear your confession?"

Father Francis Dominick Dubois turned his back to Monsignor Moroux and headed for his car, twice quickening his pace as he went.

14

THE WAGES OF SIN

6:15 a.m., Friday October 21, 1983
Saint Stephen's Cathedral, Diocese of Thiberville

Monsignor Jean-Paul Moroux was hung-over as he walked unsteadily onto the altar of Saint Stephen's Cathedral to celebrate 6 a.m. Mass. He knew each of the fourteen elderly people in the pews, most of whom spent the time in church praying the rosary. He set a land speed record for racing through the liturgy.

In the sacristy, Moroux normally removed and folded his altar clothes carefully, placing them in drawers beneath the high counter. This morning he merely tossed the liturgical vestments on the counter. Pulling a key from his pocket, he unlocked a cabinet and placed the bottle of altar wine on one of its shelves. From the rear of the cabinet, he retrieved a bottle of vodka, unscrewed the cap and poured a shot into a chalice, which he drank in a single gulp, wiping his mouth on the embroidered stole he had worn during Mass.

This was not the first time Moroux had been confronted with accusations of sexual molestation of minors by one of his priests, not even the first time a complaint of this nature had been made against Father Francis Dubois. But it was the first time the children and their parents had employed attorneys. Moroux did not like being told what to do, but today he would follow orders. The entire matter relating to Father Francis Dominick Dubois sexually abusing young boys was now in the hands of a consortium of New Orleans insurance attorneys.

If the families had been paid off in the past, they were paid off with blessings, not money. Diocesan personnel had been assigned to pray with them, pay particular attention to them, give them special treatment, and they had been satisfied. In the past, the offending priest had been moved to a distant parish, and the idea of suing the diocese had never crossed the mind of his devout parishioners. It was always the children of devout parishioners who were the victims, because they were the ones who were encouraged to be altar boys and to get involved in parish youth activities.

This time the families had lawyers. The Church had lawyers. This time it was not about sins, prayers and faith. It was about money.

10:35 a.m.
Diocesan Chancery, Thiberville

Ricardo Ponce had shaved the few remaining strands of hair from his bald head. He fastidiously removed his suit coat, displaying a monogrammed starched shirt, leather braces and a hand-painted silk tie. Pulling a cobalt blue Mont Blanc pen and legal pad from his soft leather case, he purposely avoided shaking hands with Monsignor Moroux.

Ponce bought his clothes with a credit card that had recently been canceled, got his manners from old movies he watched on a cable channel that had been cut off, and was on the verge of having his small sailboat repossessed. An eviction notice had been served on him for nonpayment of rent on his apartment in the marina a week before. The only bill he had kept current was his phone bill, and that was a lucky thing for without it he wouldn't have gotten the call from his old classmate Brent Thomas.

When his cousins had come to his law office in Bayou Saint John and presented him with the facts regarding the sexual abuse of their sons, Brent Thomas knew he was over his head. He was nothing more than a small-time small-town lawyer. He represented the local bank his father-in-law owned and had the odd case for friends he had grown up with. His discomfort at having to bring legal complaints against his Church was genuine, and it robbed him of sleep. As lay ministers, both Thomas and his wife distributed communion at Sunday Mass and often he did readings from the altar. But his qualms were outweighed by his desire to make a large enough legal fee to gain independence from his wife's father, who owned him. So he had called in the hardest-bitten lawyer he knew – Ricardo Ponce.

If Brent Thomas had been a puppy, his tail would have been wagging. He grinned and reached across the huge chancery desk to pump Moroux's hand vigorously and tell him how good it was to see him again.

Monsignor Moroux attempted to size up the two lawyers, an unlikely pair. He believed Thomas was probably dumb, and he knew it would not necessarily follow that Ponce was smart.

"Gentlemen, Father Francis and all of his possessions were removed from Amalie exactly as you requested."

Brent Thomas spoke up. "What about our request that the families meet with the bishop? These families have a right to confront their bishop."

Monsignor Moroux did not remember having heard or read such a request.

Inwardly, Ponce winced. He had not bothered to tell Brent that he cut Brent's pious paragraph from the final draft of their covering letter that accompanied the legal petitions, all the drivel about reconciling the families with their faith, having their shepherd tend to wounded members of his flock. As Ricardo Ponce saw it, this was like everything else in the law, about money and nothing else. After the money was in hand, Brent Thomas could have all the meetings he wanted to have with the bishop.

Ponce jumped in. "What about the settlement offer that is due today?"

"The families have a right to see their bishop," Thomas repeated.

"I want the settlement offer," Ponce said. "Today you are to make a good-faith offer to settle the cases. You told us serious negotiations are to take place this morning. There are six cases and—"

Moroux let a slight smile sneak into the corners of his mouth as he cut Ponce off. "Let me query you, Mr. Ponce. Do you think there is a possible legal conflict of interest in you and Mr. Thomas representing six claimants – in you two deciding which children will receive what amounts? Is your idea that they all receive the same amount or is it your idea that some will receive more than others? The damage to each child cannot be identical, can it? The things described in the legal petitions are uniform to the point of being identical, but Doctor Kennison's reports show great differences in the length and type of relationship each child had with Father Dubois, differences in the damage done to each child. Is not each victim entitled to his own legal counsel to press his claim? Would not the children benefit from each of them having their own legal counsel to represent their interests alone?"

Moroux's remarks were a diversion. He had studied law at the University of Notre Dame for four semesters and he believed Ponce and Thomas could be disciplined for acting as if they, rather than the judiciary, were the arbiters of which child received which amount. But their ethics were of no importance to him. Like the New Orleans lawyers, he was determined that the first court case of this kind would not happen in his diocese. He knew settlement was the only solution, but along the course to compromise he would try to throw the young lawyers off balance.

Ricardo Ponce suddenly said he had a problem with one of his contact lenses. Monsignor Moroux directed him to the public lavatory at the end of the hall rather than the bishop's private restroom. There was nothing wrong with Ponce's contact lens; he just felt rattled and wanted to regroup.

Once in the men's room, Ponce checked the stalls to make sure he was alone. He wished he had a drink or maybe something stronger. Whenever he was away from Fort Lauderdale he missed the juke joints that sold booze on top of the bar and drugs under the counter. As he attempted to calm himself down, his mind turned to his favorite dock bar and to Old Willie, the old man he drank with there. Ponce believed he had learned more from Old Willie, an alcoholic, disbarred lawyer, than he ever learned in law school.

"Lawyering ain't no different from dating a broad," Old Willie had said to him once, "or living with one, or being married up. Think about it. Whenever a couple that is involved sexually comes to different points of view, and they debate or argue over something… think about it. Tell me who wins. Who wins? Who always wins? The woman always wins, and why, son? Why does the woman always win? It's because she has the pussy."

And then he'd got to the heart of it. "In every negotiation you go into in your career, somebody will always have the pussy. When a building contractor is negotiating with a developer about a new shopping mall, somebody has the upper hand – does the contractor need the contract more than the developer needs the shopping mall, or is it the other way around? Is the contractor flush with work or will he go under without closing this deal? Is the developer being squeezed by a bank to break ground or does the developer own the land free and clear? Who's got the pussy? The really good lawyers figure this out before any negotiation begins and act accordingly. Sometimes you will have the pussy, other times the other guy will have the pussy."

Old Willie had made a dramatic pause and then, assuming a serious expression, had concluded, "It's all that matters in the law. Who's got the pussy?"

Ricardo smiled at himself in the mirror, vowed to have reconstructive surgery on the big scar when he collected this legal fee, and thought of Old Willie in the bar back home. In this deal, Ricardo Ponce knew he had the pussy. He represented innocent children who had been sexually abused by a Catholic priest, and he knew the diocese had every motive to pay big money to buy their silence and keep the cases sealed away forever from the public. Ponce knew he was in the driver's seat. He might never again in his career go into negotiations when he had the pussy, but by God, this time he had the pussy and he knew it. No sawed-off, short little monsignor was going to push him around.

When Ponce walked back into the office, he addressed Moroux. "Monsignor, I want you to know there's no conflict of interest, and furthermore, if there were a conflict, it would be of no matter to this diocese, which is hardly in a position to be talking about ethics or moral principles at this point in time."

Brent Thomas visibly shuddered when he heard the words and tone emanating from Ponce, but Moroux did not see him. Brent thought he had been making progress with Monsignor Moroux when Ponce was in the restroom. He had talked about old times at Saint Vincent's Catholic School in Bayou Saint John, when Moroux had been his teacher. Now, Ponce was becoming aggressive, a tactic that was not in Thomas's repertoire.

"We-ell," Moroux drawled, moving to his central concern, prefacing his statement with a lie. "Our financial resources are limited, dedicated to charitable functions of this diocese. Before we would agree to pay any sum to settle these claims we would want your assurance that these are *all* of the claims. That there are no more claims that either of you or any of the families are aware of."

Ponce looked at Thomas and shrugged, saying, "That's it. What about you, Brent?"

Brent nodded. "This is all of them, Monsignor."

As there was no legal precedent to look to, Thomas and Ponce's best guestimate coming into the meeting was that all six cases would settle for a total of somewhere around one hundred thousand each. A total of six hundred thousand dollars would produce a one-third contingency fee of two hundred thousand, a hundred thousand for Ponce and a hundred thousand for Thomas. Neither of them had ever seen that kind of money, nor in their wildest dreams could they have imagined that the settlement brochures containing dossiers prepared by the psychologist would panic seasoned attorneys like Blassingame and Quinlan.

Monsignor Moroux said, "Assuming that your clients execute settlement documents acceptable to our counsel and the settlement remains under seal and is conditioned on the continued silence of your clients, I am prepared to offer a settlement for all six claims in the amount of three million, three hundred thousand dollars."

Neither lawyer needed a calculator to realize that their one-third contingency fee would exceed a million dollars. Ricardo Ponce's heart froze in terror that Brent Thomas would accept the offer before he could bargain for more, but Thomas had been rendered speechless.

They were now playing with winnings. It was liar's poker for high stakes. The monsignor had lied to them, implying the source of the settlement was the collection plate. They had lied to the monsignor on material points.

Ponce had learned from Old Willie that when the talking turned to money, one should always listen. But Moroux said nothing more. There was nothing for Ponce to listen to.

"It's not just about the money," Brent Thomas said. "It's about what Bishop Reynolds did in sending this man to prey on the children of Amalie. The families have a right to meet with the bishop. You haven't addressed this demand of ours."

Ponce felt he was watching an idiot savant. Sheer brilliance was flowing from Brent Thomas's empty brain. Talking that bishop crap again in such a sincere way might be convincing to Monsignor Moroux and might drive the sum of the settlement up.

Monsignor Moroux had only spoken with Bishop Reynolds about this business once. He remembered the bishop's choking coughs as he ended the call, and knew he would never agree to a meeting with the families.

"The bishop very much wants to meet with the families," Moroux lied. Appearing as earnest as possible, he stretched the point. "But I do not think it would be responsible to allow Bishop Reynolds to meet with any party who is presently suing him. When the cases are resolved in court or settled in this office, then Bishop Reynolds will meet with the families."

Ponce stood up, slowly donned his suit jacket, placed the pen in his pocket and touched his smooth, damp scalp, wiping his hand dry on his trousers. He looked down at Moroux and said, "Six hundred thousand per kid. A total of three million, six hundred thousand."

"I don't have that much authority," Moroux lied.

"You can get it."

"Well, maybe—"

"We can finish business now at three point six."

Monsignor Moroux stood. This time Ricardo Ponce thrust his hand toward Jean-Paul Moroux. Moroux grasped Ponce's hand firmly. "Finished business," Ponce said.

"Finished business," Moroux repeated.

The monsignor walked them out and stood at the fountain as the lawyers made their way to a fifteen-year-old Volvo with Florida plates. Moroux pulled out a pack of Camel cigarettes and sat on the edge of the fountain. He rubbed the left side of his neck. He believed the big artery was clogged.

He knew the New Orleans lawyers would be pleased that he had settled the cases under the four million they had authorized, and he knew the bishop would be pleased to know the Dubois situation was resolved. If he had been the kind of man who cared about accomplishment, he would have felt he had achieved something. He was not that kind of man. The soft splash of the fountain was all that broke the silence.

Returning to the office, Jean-Paul Moroux scooped up the files relating to the claims and carried them down the wooden staircase. His hands were full and he could not get to the light switch. From his office above a faint light fell into the dark chamber. Moroux knew the secret archives so well that he did not need more illumination. Taking a key from his pocket, he opened a cabinet drawer and put the material away. It was quieter here than at the fountain. The monsignor sat in a chair at a library table in the gloom, his head in his hands. He stayed in the dark a long time.

15

ALL HALLOWS' EVE

Monday afternoon, October 31, 1983
Amalie, Louisiana

A setting sun was barely visible over tall sugar cane as a parade of masked dwarfs and costumed ghouls sauntered along the rusting iron fence marking the boundary of an ancient burial ground behind Our Lady of the Seas in Amalie. Villagers were cleaning the cemetery and setting flowers on the graves of their ancestors. The line of little trick-or-treaters marched along the old fence in a single file, adult chaperons guarding the perimeter on the highway side. Some of these little children, Dubois's victims, were nearly as dead inside as the corpses entombed inside the old fence.

Amalie had been named for the youngest daughter of one of the original settlers, a child who'd died of a fever shortly after arriving there in 1780. Her grave marker had been changed a number of times over the two hundred years since. These days it was a stone statue mounted on a marble base, a life-size sculpture of a little girl in repose, hands folded in prayer. The only other monument of note in Amalie was the tall smokestack at the abandoned sugar mill on the edge of town, now fitted with a windsock to guide crop-duster pilots. The stack had the word "Catherine" painted vertically on it, the name of the old mill.

Unbeknownst to all but six people in the parish of Amalie, that very morning a set of important legal documents had been signed. The papers were being filed under seal with the clerk of court in Bayou Saint John after business hours. The secret settlement of these six cases would one day become infamous in legal circles as "the Halloween Settlement".

The price of innocence lost had been set at six hundred thousand dollars per child. The Catholic families and their lawyers conspired with the Church to keep the matter secret. Amalie was not changed by the legal settlement for few knew anything about it.

Nothing much had changed in Amalie in over two hundred years. Nothing bad had ever happened there before. Even people who lived forty miles away in Thiberville had never heard of the hamlet. There was never much traffic on the two-lane blacktop that dead-ended in Amalie, except for a few pickup trucks and farm machinery.

As the children made their way on rounds of trick-or-treating, Monsignor Buddy Belair, vicar of finance for the Diocese of Thiberville, accompanied the Bayou Saint John clerk of court, Cyrus Langlanais, on an after-hours errand to lock up the sealed envelope containing the settlement documents in the courthouse vault. Afterwards the two of them dined on enchiladas at a small Mexican place nearby.

Monsignor Buddy Belair ceremoniously announced that Cyrus Langlanais had done a great service for his Church. He would be rewarded by having a seat on the altar for the Red Mass next fall, the special service for members of the legal profession celebrated at the cathedral after the ceremonial opening of court. Hearing this news, the clerk of court fixed on the idea of having his photograph taken with the bishop at the Red Mass, something he could use in future campaign material as the electorate there was wholly Catholic. Then he made a mental count of all the people he would invite to the Red Mass: his parents, siblings, his wife's family, his own children, key political supporters like the sheriff, and the girlfriend he kept in a small apartment in Spanish Town near the state capitol in Baton Rouge.

The Dubois episode was over. It had ended as quietly and secretly as it had begun.

90

16

A LENTEN PENANCE

Monday March 5, 1984, Lundi Gras
Old Bishop's House, Thiberville

Four months had elapsed since the Halloween Settlement. All was quiet in the diocese. The secret was holding. Soon after the lawsuits had been settled and sealed, the bishop celebrated a private Mass at a retreat house for the three families who were involved in the secret settlement. Only four adults appeared. Randy Falgout and his wife no longer considered themselves Catholics. At the end of the Mass, as Bishop Reynolds was leaving the altar, the father of one of the boys shouted, "Bishop, explain how you could send that man to Amalie."

The bishop trembled and stated the obvious. "It was a mistake."

The man shouted, "What happened to Father Dubois? Why didn't anything happen to Father Dubois?"

The bishop had almost tripped as he scurried off the altar to the sacristy.

On the eve of Mardi Gras, an inebriated, tuxedoed Brent Thomas knocked on the door of Moroux's residence. The monsignor opened the door himself.

"I'm supposed to be at the Thiberville Mardi Gras Ball. I left my wife there and…" Thomas paused and pulled at the bow tie that was choking him like a hangman's noose.

Moroux motioned for Thomas to take a chair as he walked to the next room, returning with a lit cigarette.

"Monsignor, there are eleven more cases. Eleven more kids."

Jean-Paul Moroux was thankful he had the cigarette to smoke, something to do with his mouth besides speaking. A long silence passed between them.

Moroux again motioned for Brent Thomas to stay put. He walked into the next room, swallowed a couple of mouthfuls of vodka, wiped his mouth with his sleeve, and returned quickly to Thomas.

"Brent, did you know this back in October?"

Thomas nodded yes. "Yes. Yes, sir. Some of 'em. Not all of 'em."

"We-ell… then you lied to me."

"Yes. No. I could not violate the confidence of my clients. I couldn't talk about these cases back then. I could not be honest with you then."

Monsignor Moroux smoked his cigarette carefully. The only sound in the room was the two men's breathing. Both were exhaling powerfully. The monsignor laid the burning cigarette in a tarnished brass ashtray and stood over Thomas, speaking softly.

"You and your friend, Mr. Ponce—"

Interrupting Moroux, Brent said, "No, Ricardo will not be involved in these cases." Now that Brent knew how to prepare the appropriate legal petitions (by copying Ponce's legal work from the last batch of cases), how to get the dossiers prepared by the treating psychologist, and how to assemble settlement brochures, he saw no reason to hand over half the fee, more than a million dollars, to Ponce. The last time Brent had seen Ricardo, his left cheek had been raw from a procedure designed to erase the scar, and he was growing hair transplants like rows of corn on his skull. Besides, Brent felt he could do better with Monsignor Moroux if Ricardo Ponce was out of the picture. He believed Monsignor Moroux really liked him because he was a devout Catholic.

"Yes, Brent. So you would be expecting… let's see, about six million, six hundred thousand dollars for these eleven cases – six hundred for each child?"

Brent stammered and said weakly, "Yeah. Suppose so."

"Thank you for coming to me. I will get back to you by the end of the week. We have Ash Wednesday in two days, and Lent beginning. Now you should get back to the ball."

Thomas backed out of the door, tripped, lost his balance and almost fell into a hedge.

Moroux closed the door slowly. He turned every lock and fastened every bolt tight against the night. In his study, he filled a tall glass with vodka, and put a recording of Johann Sebastian Bach's Mass in B Minor on the stereo. Moroux did the math. Adding the cost of the Halloween Settlement of three million, six hundred thousand to the price of the new demand for six million, six hundred thousand made him feel tired. The monsignor downed his drink, refilled the glass and raised it as if in a toast to an absent friend.

Tuesday March 6, 1984, Mardi Gras
Old Bishop's House

Diocesan attorney Fredrick Fortier Madison reigned as King of Thiberville's Mardi Gras celebration. Monsignor Moroux turned on his television in time to see King Freddy's float stop at the reviewing stand, where the King toasted his mother, Adele – Bishop Reynolds' bridge-playing, martini-drinking friend. Adele was wearing an old tiara atop a platinum hairpiece, the crown dating from the time she served as Queen following World War II, the wig dating from the early seventies when she got out of bed one morning and most of her dyed, dead hair stayed on the pillow.

Frederick Madison had not even been consulted when the first batch of cases settled. All the legal work was done by the archbishop's lawyer, Thomas Quinlan, and insurance counsel Robert Blassingame. But Fredrick Madison was counsel of record for the Diocese of Thiberville. Moroux believed Freddy Madison was dumber than dirt and knew he was not competent enough to handle the eleven new claims. He had to get Madison out of the way, but only the bishop could fire the King of Mardi Gras.

Monsignor Moroux knew that the insurance companies and their legal counsel were not going to simply hand over another six million, six hundred thousand dollars to settle the eleven new claims without battling the diocese, arguing that when they entered the first settlements in October they had been assured that there were no other claims of this kind.

The first set of claims had been handled by an old boy network in New Orleans. But Thomas Quinlan could only represent one defendant in the civil cases: his client, the archdiocese, so if there were to be battles with the insurance companies, the diocese would require its own legal counsel, a damned good lawyer. Freddy Madison was not a trial lawyer and in Moroux's view he was an exceedingly dumb man who only held the position of Diocesan Attorney because his mother, Adele, played bridge and drank martinis with the bishop.

Ash Wednesday, March 7, 1984
Fairhope, Alabama

Moroux knew that somehow he was going to have to explain to the bishop that the fair-haired son of one of the bishop's only friends, Adele, was not up to the task of tackling these eleven civil suits. He knew he had to confront the bishop in person.

The bishop's small cottage on the northern edge of the Reynolds family compound was situated on a high bluff overlooking Mobile Bay, in Fairhope, Alabama. When Rome overlooked Bishop Reynolds for promotion to Archbishop of New Orleans – despite his family's generosity to the Vatican – Reynolds lost all interest in his career. He removed himself from Thiberville, which he considered a backwater diocese, and spent almost all his time in his family's luxurious compound. Here he played golf, fished, and whiled away the hours devising a refrigeration scheme to ensure that his favorite drink of Scotch and water was constantly at the temperature of a cold mountain stream.

Bishop Reynolds was sporting ashes on his forehead when he greeted Moroux at the door. "Is everything all right, Paul?" Bishop Reynolds said. In all their years of working together, he never called Jean-Paul or anyone else by their given name, but he was usually consistent in using the wrong name he assigned them.

The bishop busied himself slicing lemon pound cake. At the table, Moroux told his bishop about his late-night visit from Brent Thomas. As Moroux talked, the bishop's coarse, unkempt eyebrows danced above his rapidly blinking eyes. "Tell him no. Tell him we won't pay any more. Never." The bishop balled up a ham fist and plopped it on the table with a thud.

Moroux had never seen him so animated, but he had seen him this divorced from reality.

"We need our own legal counsel, a really good lawyer. We're not going to just be up against plaintiff lawyers. I think in this round we may also find ourselves at odds with our own insurance companies, caught in a crossfire. Our insurance lawyers are not just going to keep writing millions in checks without looking for escape clauses in the contracts. They may prefer public trials for these new cases."

"Didn't it go well last time?"

"Right, in the last round, it was all insurance money."

"Who handled this for us in the fall?"

"Tom Quinlan, the archbishop's counsel did all the heavy lifting."

"Good. There you are. He can handle this just as he did the last set of lawsuits."

"I am anticipating that this will not be possible. You see, the archdiocese is a named defendant. This time if the insurers kick, Tom will have to represent only the Archdiocese of New Orleans."

"What's wrong? Doesn't Freddy Madison return phone calls? I'm having dinner with his mother this week to plan the Bishop's Ball. I can talk to her about her son."

"Please trust me. The only problem with Freddy Madison is he's not up to the task, period. We need a better lawyer."

The bishop blew out a gust of breath. "I'm not responsible for this. And if I'm not responsible, then the diocese can't be responsible. I am the diocese." Bishop Reynolds went to the bar and poured a martini for himself, arching his cactus eyebrows to inquire whether Moroux wanted a drink. The monsignor shook his head.

"Bishop, what do you want me to do?"

Bishop Reynolds downed his drink in a gulp. He was guided in his ecclesiastical career by a personal policy of never making a decision that could be traced back to him. Knowing that the papal nuncio in the Vatican Embassy in Washington, DC had been monitoring this situation since before the secret settlements were paid, and knowing this new development would have to be reported to the nuncio, Bishop Reynolds momentarily considered making a decision. But immediately he thought better of it.

"Paul, you are the lawyer among us. You make the decision about what to do, who to hire. And write me a paper on your making that decision."

"We need a lawyer. I don't know where to look and I have little time. I need someone by tomorrow or the next day at the latest. The insurance contracts impose a duty upon us to notify the companies of all claims promptly. I can't put this off. Where do we find a good lawyer?"

Bishop Reynolds was flustered. "You must know someone."

"I don't know a blessed soul," Monsignor Moroux said. He thought that last statement was probably truer than it sounded.

The bishop almost stumbled over his golf putter as the words burst from him. "Call the Bastard."

"The Bastard?"

"Yes, yes, Paul, my good friend – what's his name? You know the guy. The money man. The Bastard."

"Joe Rossi?"

"Exactly."

17

THE BASTARD

7:30 p.m., Thursday March 8, 1984
Old Bishop's House

Joe Rossi had amassed more political power than anyone in Thiberville, maybe as much as anyone in the state. His meaty hands were on everything. His days began in the dark when he had coffee with his lawyer friend Jonathan Bendel in Bendel's mansion. It was in Bendel's kitchen, an hour after he woke, that the rotund Rossi routinely cheated on the diet he vowed to begin every day. Rossi required little sleep. His days always started early and his evenings ended late as he worked the phones in the run-down kitchen of his own beat-up home, eating hot doughnuts delivered by a police cruiser, and chewing the fat with a wide array of contacts.

Born to a short-order waitress and a roughneck in the east Texas oilfield, he had gained a degree in petroleum engineering from Texas A&M and migrated to south Louisiana to strike it rich in the oil and gas play unfolding there in the fifties. He soon learned that everything that was worth anything in Louisiana, including oil and gas concessions, was controlled by the corrupt politics for which the state was famous. He applied himself and soon mastered the art of politics, and his influence and affluence grew.

His oil royalty checks, that he called "post office money", were substantial, but his lifestyle was simple, deceptive. He drove used Lincoln Town Cars and still lived in the small house he'd bought when he sold his first oil deal. Sometimes in winter he walked with a cane to compensate for a bad knee that was the result of a beating he'd received in a teenage gang war. Though he was always garrulous, sometimes outrageous in his personal demeanor, he was a private person. No one knew of the generous scholarships he'd established at Texas colleges for kids whose financial circumstances were much as his had been when a local oilman had paid his way to college.

As a child, he had realized how powerless his family was and for the rest of his life he pursued power, valued power above everything. His high-school sweetheart would not wait for him to finish college, and after she married another man, Joe Rossi had only one love left, a love he remained loyal to – power.

It was evening before Joe Rossi spoke with his answering service and learned that Monsignor Moroux had placed two calls to him. He called Moroux, who asked him for a morning meeting. Rossi insisted their meeting take place immediately.

As Rossi entered the Old Bishop's House, he was wearing house slippers, stained sweat pants and a light blue oxford cloth shirt. Walking straight to the kitchen, he asked loudly, "You got anything to eat?"

Even though Moroux had been around the bombastic Rossi before, he was knocked off balance. The monsignor had a business discussion in mind and already the upper half of Joe Rossi's generous torso had disappeared into his refrigerator.

"This religion ain't got no class in this country, Padre." The grammar was suspiciously unnatural and the voice sounded funny echoing off the inside walls of the refrigerator.

"Ya go to a priest's house in the old country and ya find pasta piled everywhere… fruit, bread, vino. You got some vino, right, Padre? Hell, we can get it out the cathedral, right? What is it you drink on the altar? Should be Italian vino. When I was an altar boy in Port Arthur, we had an old Italian priest who said that Mass don't count, God don't listen, if it's not Italian wine. He said ya can't use French wine 'cause all the French are going to hell."

Monsignor Moroux knew Rossi had been educated in College

Station, Texas, had a master's degree from the prestigious Texas A&M University. The longshoreman's language, the mispronunciation of the simplest words, and the ruffian, uncouth persona Rossi often affected, amused Moroux. He knew it was only an act, maybe something Rossi believed would cause people to underestimate him. But no one who knew Rossi would ever take him lightly.

Rossi loaded a plate with ham, a piece of melon, some cheese, a handful of crackers, a large dill pickle, and an orange. As he filled himself a glass from a large jug of wine, he became calm enough for Monsignor Moroux to brief him. He listened intently, then wiped his brow and face with a paper napkin as if he were sweating.

"Hell, Father, you telling me the insurance companies already coughed up over three and a half mill? I bet that came up about as easy as a fur ball. They only did it because they thought they were buying the whole poker hand. They weren't thinking this punk lawyer Brent Thomas was gonna raise the bet. It might take surgery to get the rest of the money out of these bloodsuckers. There's only one lawyer around here can deal with those Noo Awlins insurance lawyers."

Instead of giving Monsignor Moroux the name of the lawyer, Rossi piled cheese and ham onto a cracker and chewed it up, chasing it with wine. "Ya know, a Noo Awlins lawyer is a different kind of deal than the lawyers we have around here. Dealing with 'em is like dealing with a Noo Yawker whose got manners. Half of 'em in Noo Awlins are homosexual or bisexual too in my opinion, real dandy types. And mean – meaner than a chained dog. And ya know, a chained dog will do just 'bout any damned thing. If things get bad enough, a chained dog will even hang itself without leaving the ground. Those boys in Noo Awlins are like that. But they got nice clothes, nice manners, even if they got no morals."

Monsignor Moroux smiled tightly. "We're not talking about morals, are we? We're talking about law."

Moroux shifted uncomfortably in the chair. He knew Joe

Rossi's close tie to the bishop was a money connection. In fund drives, Rossi raised more money than the Archdiocese of New Orleans. Rossi relished the competition, calling it "oil money versus old money". But this was not a money problem, not yet.

"And who would you recommend, Joe?"

"Jonathan Bendel. Bendel is the only one I'd say to get. He's my best friend. Lots of people say bad things 'bout Bendel, but the two disbarment proceedings were against his law partners, not him. He married three times. The last time when he was caught with a mistress, he married the mistress. That's 'bout as honorable as a lawyer can be around here."

"Is he Catholic?" the monsignor asked.

"Father, you need a good lawyer. Not a good Catholic."

"I don't know, Joe."

Rossi leaned across the table. "Bendel's a warrior. Nobody ever gave Jon nothing. He come into Thiberville hitchhiking. Today he's got the biggest firm that represents everybody who's anybody. He's a damned warrior, I tell ya… and under pressure he's as cool as the other side of the pillow."

Moroux shrugged.

Rossi put his arms up as if a gun were on him. "Hey, Father, the point is this – if you want to hear the point. Jon Bendel knows the game. All law is anymore is a game. Trick or truth."

Moroux sat in silence, wishing he had another option, and Rossi continued, "Ya want me to call Bendel? We could eat shrimp. Together. Tonight. My treat." Rossi bit into a slice of cantaloupe and wiped the juice from his chin with the back of his hand. "A friend of mine just opened a new seafood place."

"No. I'll put in a call to Bendel tomorrow."

"Maybe we oughta start picking up some money. Second collections. Tell 'em it's for some cursed country. We could do some special Masses, High Masses with incense. Give 'em the smells and bells like the old days."

"I know you're joking, Joe. Holy Mother Church may make her share of mistakes, but she does not deal in that kind of chicanery."

"Joking? Who's joking here, Father? We got the best business on earth, the best source of cash there ever was. And it's tax free. Who's joking? Ya gotta be kidding me, Father? I ain't joking about nothing here. We're selling salvation. Everybody's buying that. And we buy back guilt at discount. Everybody's selling that. We own the franchise on forgiveness. Who's joking?"

Rossi laughed heartily. Moroux remained stone-faced.

Rossi continued, "I think we're gonna need to spend some of our own money here. Insurance ain't gonna pick up the ticket for Bendel and other costs you're gonna have. We can pick up some new money, Father. We just gotta call on some heavy hitters, Monsignor, people who have a guilt load. Lots of people around here owe me something, but all of 'em owe God something."

Moroux lit a cigarette and sipped a soda he'd pulled from the refrigerator.

"You know Manning Giroud, Father? The one they call Tee-Man? He's flush and feeling bad. He just had another friction fire."

"Friction fire?"

"Yeah. Ya know. When a big mortgage payment starts rubbing up against an empty bank account there's friction. Throws a spark. Burns the building to the ground. Then the insurance money comes. It's his third friction fire. I can get maybe twenty-five or fifty K outta him myself. Tee-Man Giroud don't want to go to hell."

Moroux smiled and shook his head. Sometimes he had to admit Rossi could be funny.

Rossi lowered his voice and upgraded his grammar. "Now, Father, I wanta be in close on this one all the way. This could get serious. Gotta keep a lid on it, keep it in the pot, cook it down. I wanta stay in the kitchen till we burn it off."

Moroux nodded.

Rossi continued, "Look, I'll see that Jon Bendel is waiting for your call in the morning. That's no problem. But this thing… this thing you talked about tonight. It can be big problems. You did a good thing the way you put a lid on it last time. We can't let da lid come off now that the fire got turned up again."

Moroux nodded. He was surprised to feel comfort in this unholy alliance with Rossi.

"When we get the lid screwed down tight on da pot, then, Father, we got to look at a way to put out this fire for good, the thing that's causing all these problems. Capiche?"

Moroux reached for another cigarette. Rossi too grabbed one from the pack.

"This defective priest? You got him on ice somewhere?"

"Yes."

"You keep that priest on ice, Father. He's gotta disappear. For good." As he stood to leave, Rossi said, "And, Father, you got any more priests round here having sex with children, I don't want to know about it. But you better get their sorry asses as far from this place as possible, and do it tomorrow."

18

ROSSI'S LAWYER

Friday March 9, 1984
Jonathan Bendel's Law Office, Thiberville

Jonathan Bendel charmed the cynical Monsignor Moroux.

Joe Rossi accompanied Moroux to Bendel's law office and walked him through the sprawling, single-story structure that had the white walls and fashionable paintings of a contemporary art gallery. A skylight crowned the conference room where Bendel received Moroux. Its walls were crowded with framed photographs of Jonathan Bendel standing alongside Republican presidents and Democratic governors. Those political photographs had cost Jon Bendel more than all the art in the building. Rossi made the introductions and left.

Monsignor Moroux studied Bendel, a short stocky man with a shock of gray hair. He listened as Jon Bendel made small talk and made the small talk seem interesting. Bendel's calmness and confidence was contagious, his modulated voice soothing.

"Monsignor, it might be of interest to you that I am not a Catholic," Jon Bendel said.

"Mr. Bendel, if a requirement for working for our diocese was that one be a true Catholic, some of our priests might be disqualified." The two of them shared a slight laugh.

Moroux told Bendel the truth about the first six cases, the Halloween Settlement, and the new cases Brent Thomas had mentioned on the eve of Mardi Gras, but he did not tell Bendel the whole truth. As Bendel walked the monsignor to the entrance where Rossi was waiting, he placed his hand on the priest's shoulder. "Send over all the documents. I will see if I can put this matter to bed."

Bayou Saint John

When Brent Thomas returned to his law office in Bayou Saint John after lunch, he was handed a phone message slip with Jon Bendel's name on it. He barricaded himself in his office and dialed the number. He had never spoken to Bendel, never before played at Bendel's level.

"Mr. Bendel, Brent Thomas." Brent waited for Bendel to say, "Please call me Jon," but he did not.

"I represent the Diocese of Thiberville, Brent. Do you have the eleven petitions prepared?"

"Yes, sir." Thomas grimaced at the sound of his voice, addressing Bendel this way. Bendel called him "Brent" and he called Bendel "sir". It was off to a bad start.

"I want the petitions in my office today. I will see that they are filed and sealed in the Bayou Saint John courthouse."

"I can come to see you in an hour."

"I don't have time to see you, Brent. Just drop everything off with our receptionist in a sealed envelope with my name on it."

"Fine. I can do that."

"And I want you to understand you will not have any more contact with Monsignor Moroux or with anyone in the diocese again. Everything will be handled by me."

"I understand."

"Brent, we're both good lawyers and we both know there were fatal flaws in the first set of cases you guys settled last Halloween. These same flaws will exist in these new cases. Had I been involved originally as counsel for the diocese, the settlements would not have happened. Your clients would have received nothing. We both know it is morally wrong to attempt to extort money this way from the Catholic Church for the actions of some demented

104

man they had no control over. Legally, you've got real problems, Brent. Morally, you've got bigger problems. The diocese has done nothing wrong. They have no liability to your clients, and the priest has no assets. In a word, you have nothing."

Brent Thomas was frozen by fear. He missed Ricardo Ponce. It might have been a mistake to cut Ponce out of these cases.

Bendel continued in his mesmerizing voice, "You've got big problems and we both know what they are."

All afternoon, through the night, into the dawn on Saturday, Brent Thomas obsessed over the closing comments of Bendel, wondering what the fatal flaw in his lawsuits was, debating whether he should again call in Ricardo Ponce. Bendel had done more than plant a seed of doubt in the mind of the young, inexperienced lawyer. He had created pervasive fear, a fear of losing that rattled around so loudly inside his head that he worried that others could hear it. Brent Thomas was a man who had a deadly fear of looking bad in anyone's eyes, a man who combed and re-combed his hair five or six times before leaving the house.

Saturday March 10, 1984
New Orleans

Saturday morning, Jon Bendel's pilot flew him to Lakefront Airport in New Orleans. Thomas Quinlan had again hastily arranged a Saturday conference of all insurance counsel. The lawyers who awaited Bendel's arrival at the Quinlan firm well remembered the bad news they had received the last time they convened there on a Saturday.

When Bendel broke the news that there were eleven new cases filed against the diocese, the insurance lawyers went off like Roman candles. All of them were talking at once, stepping on each other's sentences, indignantly insisting that they had received assurances on the day of the Halloween Settlement that there were no other claims outstanding.

It was a rough meeting. At its conclusion, it appeared to Bendel that the diocesan insurers were on the verge of revolt, of assuming an adversarial posture wherein they would allege defenses under the language of the insurance policies in an effort to escape further financial liability.

The price of poker had almost doubled in a matter of months and the obvious worry was that it would continue to escalate. How many more victims could there be? How much more could this cost? There were no answers.

Bendel was the picture of professionalism, remaining unemotional, self-confident, and extremely smooth throughout the meeting. He managed to calm everyone down and the meeting ended with an agreement that all of the lawyers would look over the insurance policies again and stay in touch while Bendel devised a stall tactic to slow the claim train down. The one thing all the lawyers agreed on was that it was in the best interest of everyone that these new lawsuits remain secret until a decision could be made by all parties about how to handle them.

Bendel made his way to his law firm's French Quarter apartment. He called his wife to say he had to stay in the city until Monday, and then he called Tammy Baldwin, a former secretary to a Louisiana governor, who was classified as a consultant on Bendel's law office payroll. Through all of his marriages, Bendel had never been without a mistress. Tammy Baldwin had the most time in grade and rank, having been his companion for five years whenever he was away from Thiberville.

Tammy and Jon spent most of the afternoon and night in bed. A hard rain came and went. Late that night, music drifted up from a nearby bar as Jon and Tammy stood on the balcony of the apartment on Jackson Square. Dressed in earrings and Bendel's starched shirt, Tammy was leaning her back against a wrought-iron railing.

"What are you here for now, working on a weekend?" she asked.

"Some cases involving serious sexual dysfunction."

"Are you a lawyer in these sexual dysfunction cases, honey, or an expert witness?"

They laughed. Bendel said, "There are some kinds of sexual dysfunction that are widely accepted, practiced everywhere, dear, and there are other things that are taboo."

"Like what we do? Taboo?"

"What we do is more like voodoo."

Louisiana, Friday August 10, 1984

From Mardi Gras to hurricane season, things were quiet. Five months later, the secret was still holding. Bendel was stalling Brent Thomas. Brent had trouble even getting a phone call through to Bendel during those months, but he bided his time, deciding not to tell Ricardo Ponce anything about the new cases. He was counting on an announcement from Jonathan Bendel that the settlement documents and checks were ready, at which point he would make a fee of over two million dollars and keep it all for himself. Ponce was sailing off Florida in his new forty-one-foot Morgan, anchoring in Bahamian coves, casting about the Keys, chasing women.

The insurance company lawyers were being a lot tougher this time around, but Jon Bendel was cut from the same cloth as Robert Blassingame, lead counsel for the insurance interests. They had known each other for years and were going to find a way to buy these cases just as the first ones had been bought. Every day that passed without Brent Thomas announcing a new claim led them to believe they were reaching what they referred to as the bottom of the barrel.

Jon Bendel had been in New Orleans so often that Tammy Baldwin was able to redecorate the law firm's flat. They had all but set up house together, and their business arrangement was starting to feel like something else. He had a history of marrying his mistresses, and then taking another in their place, and it seemed history was about to repeat itself.

August crawled onto the coast of Louisiana. Tropical storms

dumped rivers of rain. There were warnings of a big storm to come, a category four or five hurricane, but there were always warnings of big storms to come.

19

FEED & SEED STORE

Noon, Tuesday August 14, 1984
Highway 19, South of Amalie, Louisiana

The Feed & Seed store, south of Amalie, served lunch to the local farmers every Tuesday and Thursday. The fare today was red beans and rice, New Orleans style, made with blue runner beans from nearby Gonzales. All day men drifted in and out of the store, drinking free coffee, discussing crops, equipment, weather, hunting, fishing and local politics.

There was a kind of uniform they wore, consisting of old baseball-style caps with lettering of some kind advertising a diesel tractor manufacturer or other farm implement supplier, and tee-shirts in warm weather or long-sleeved khaki shirts in cooler weather, over faded blue jeans. Some still wore cowboy boots or work boots, but many had switched over to jogging shoes.

Listening to their normal conversation one might think the men of Amalie confused what they did for how they were. If you asked one, "How you doing?" the answer would be along the lines of "Cut four acres of cane yesterday," or "Caught a barrel of redfish on the marsh inlet last night." They were rugged men who took their value and self worth to be a direct reflection of what they accomplished in the face of the elements. For years these were the only things they talked about.

Now a small group of men who met here early every morning had stopped discussing farming, fishing, hunting and trapping. Ever since they had learned their sons had been sexually abused by their pastor, Father Dubois, they talked of nothing else.

Elray "Poppa" Vidros was six foot six inches and 350 pounds. He had always been big and had been called "Poppa" since high school. He was legendary for a feat on the gridiron that happened fifteen years earlier. The Amalie Tigers football team, competing in the smallest classification in the state with only twenty-nine players, had gone undefeated and made it to the state championship. With seconds remaining, their opponents scored and trailed the Tigers by only one point. As they lined up to kick the extra point for the tie, Poppa Vidros began to scream, slapping his taped paws on the helmets of his teammates. They say the look in his eye was more fearsome than the time he beat up four city guys in a mall parking lot in Thiberville. The ball was snapped to the holder and when the play ended a moment later, Poppa Vidros had both the holder and the ball in his arms. Poppa Vidros charged up the field, carrying the player and ball with him, screaming savagely. The tall trophy came home to Amalie where it still stands in a glass case in the school gym next to a faded picture of the legendary team and their mascot, a one-horned cow that wandered onto their practice field every afternoon.

Poppa Vidros might have been the biggest in the group, the one who exhibited the toughest demeanor, a man who would never admit that he cried, yet there had been many times that he had walked behind the barn on his farm. Unable to find release from the distress at what had happened to his son, he wept, sometimes for a long time until he felt even sicker. The fear he had for his boy and how it would affect his life, and the pain he felt about what happened manifested itself in uncontrollable rage.

Wiley Arceneaux was much smaller and quieter than Poppa. He owned the store. He was also the cook. Lately, he had taken to unlocking the store as early as 5 a.m. because he could not sleep anymore, not since he learned what Father Dubois had done to his son. He'd lie in bed at night next to his wife, wide awake for as long as he could stand it, and when he could not take it anymore he'd quietly dress and drive to the Feed & Seed.

On some mornings when Wiley pulled into the oyster-shell

parking lot in front of the frame building, there would be two trucks already in the yard, belonging to Poppa Vidros and Tommy Wesley Rachou. Rachou's wife was seeing a psychologist in Thiberville, but Tommy Wesley had seen no improvement.

When shrimp season was not open somewhere between Brownsville, Texas and Key West, Florida, Randy Falgout was a regular at the gathering. All of them had stood in each other's weddings and been present for the baptism of their children and now they were bonded in a way they could never have imagined. They wanted a Catholic priest dead.

Every day they had the same conversation.

"I am gonna kill him," Poppa said as he broke off a piece of bread. "You can make book on that. Gonna kill that fuck of a priest. Gonna keep my shotgun in my truck till I unload it in his ass."

Wiley paced the sagging porch with a bowl of rice and beans in his hands. "I haven't hardly slept since I heard about all this. I can't talk to Sissy. All she does is cry about it when I talk about it. My boy acts like it didn't happen, but he knows it happened. He wouldn't go to school when it started on Monday... and... sometimes he wets the bed. Nine years old and pissing the bed. What does that mean? What can you do about it? And that piece of shit lawyer Brent Thomas says we can't tell the school what his problems are."

"That damned lawyer," Tommy Rachou said. "Brent Thomas is a piece of shit. Always talking about his faith in the Church. He talked Celeste and me into going to see that monsignor in Bayou Saint John. Then Brent brought us to the chancery in Thiberville to see some shitbird Monsignor Moroux who scared Celeste. She said he looked like a fucking ghost."

Tommy Rachou spat, shook his head, and continued, "That piece of shit lawyer has had our case for over six months and not squat has happened, nothing. I think that chickenshit lawyer wants to go everywhere but to court. I've had enough. I'm switching lawyers. I heard Kane Chaisson in Thiberville has a pair of balls on him. I'm gonna see if he'll take on these fuckin' priests, smoke the Church out of its hiding place, do something for my boy. We see Chaisson tomorrow night. He knows what it's about and told us to come after five when he's closed so he can have all the time he needs."

"Yeah, I'd like to go see that Chaisson fellow too," Wiley Arceneaux said. "But Sissy's scared of the world knowing about what happened to our boy. And that dipshit, Brent Thomas, who is a cousin by her momma or some shit like that, says no one will ever know what happened to our boy if he's handling things. So, I think I'm stuck with him."

Randy Falgout said, "It's my fault. We went to that Thomas fellow and he brought in that dipshit spic from Florida. Thomas is my relation by marriage. All he wanted was me to give him names of more families with altar boys, so he could sign more cases, make more money for doing nothing. All anybody got last year was some money. There weren't no fucking justice. Nothing happened to the bishop. Nothing happened to the fucker, Father Dubois. There weren't no justice done. We was paid off. That little prick of a lawyer Thomas was more interested in kissing the bishop's ass than representing our boys. The Brent Thomas turd was bad enough. And that high-steppin' spic fruit from Florida talked to us like we're stupid."

Tommy Wesley Rachou walked off the porch to the parking lot and dumped his coffee on the crushed oyster shells. "Well, I'm gonna see Chaisson tomorrow and see if I can't shake this thing up. I don't know whose side Brent Thomas is on. I want a lawyer who is on my boy's side."

Randy Falgout looked at Poppa Vidros. "You go ahead. Find that priest. Kill the fucker."

20

THE WARRIOR

Evening, Wednesday August 15, 1984
Kane Chaisson's Law Office, Thiberville

The burly man dwarfed the slight child as he walked him down the hall to where the child's parents were waiting for them. Pointing to the voluptuous, spike-heeled woman seated behind the reception desk, Kane Chaisson said to the nine-year-old, "Donny, this is Misty, my wife. She'll get you a soft drink and show you around – show you all these stuffed animals and tell you about the places where we hunted them. That big bear I shot in Alaska."

The boy was gazing up at the huge bear as Donny's parents, Celeste and Tommy Wesley Rachou, followed Kane Chaisson to his office. There were more animals, including a twelve-foot alligator, mounted on the walls of the lawyer's private office.

"You should be real proud of your son. For two hours we talked – and we talked about everything. I needed to see him alone to know… know whether the child can stand up to the pressure. There's going to be a lot of pressure. The question is can you stand up to it with your son?"

Celeste looked away from Chaisson. Tommy asked, "What do you mean?"

"Mr. Rachou, if you want me to take this case then there are three things you have to understand. First, I am going to see that this priest goes to prison. I will force the district attorney to do this. Secondly, this business of hiding the secret sins of this priest is going to stop. I am going to break the seal on this lawsuit and make this public. The court and press will protect your child's identity, but the world's going to find out what that priest did. I want you to understand this – I am going to give your boy his day in court. We're not going to go to the diocese with our hands out, looking for a check. We're not going to make a deal with those devils dressed like men of God. We're going to court before a jury, where we'll be looking for justice."

"You know the Church… the diocese… bishop and them, Mr. Chaisson? Do you?" Tommy asked.

"Mr. Rachou, I knew what this Church was like a long time ago. When it came time for my older sister to marry, she went to see the rector of the cathedral. We had lived in that parish all of our lives. The priest said they had rules and they followed their rules. He refused permission for her to use the church because my father had not contributed any money to the parish. Papa went to Mass on Sunday, but he was poor and had six children – hardly enough money for food and clothes. I remember her marriage in a dirty room in the old courthouse. They have their own rules and they have always been above the rule of law. With this case, we can show them that the only rule that applies is the rule of law. They preach about sins against God and sins against the Church. I read the Bible. Scripture informs us that in the eyes of Jesus Christ there's no sin greater than a sin against a child. Donny will tell his story—"

"You're saying Donny will have to testify… in public," Tommy Wesley Rachou said.

"Yes," Chaisson said.

Chaisson turned toward Celeste. "Are you sure you can stand up to this?"

"I don't wanna… but I will. I got to."

Tommy leaned forward. "There's ten more boys with cases filed in secret at the courthouse in Bayou Saint John, Mr. Chaisson. I know some of the fathers are real unhappy about the way this is all being kept a secret. Nobody likes to be paid off to keep their trap shut. Could I bring some of them here?"

Chaisson shook his head dramatically. "I'm sorry, Mr. Rachou. This is the only case I can take. I just want to make sure there's no backing out by you or your wife. Somebody has to be strong enough to put this priest in prison. And someone has to be strong enough to let the world know what happened, to take the bishop to court."

"Go ahead. We are not going to crawfish on you."

"Fine. I have a lot of work to do tonight."

As they shook hands, Tommy Rachou said, "Thank you. We appreciate what you are doing for our boy."

"Mr. Rachou, I cannot give back to Donny what was taken from him by this abuse. Nobody can. But what Donny can't get in church, he can get in court."

7:10 a.m. Monday August 20, 1984
Diocesan Chancery, Thiberville

The banging startled Monsignor Moroux. He was on his second cup of coffee, reading the morning paper, ensconced in the bishop's office. As the banging on the front door of the chancery continued, Moroux stared at the cemetery through the picture window, seeking his customary reminder that no matter what the uncertainties of life might be, the end was sure. He often thought about dying, and sometimes believed death might offer the richest experience in life.

When Moroux finally identified the noise – someone hitting and rattling the glass front doors of the chancery building – he thought it might be an old man he saw often, a bum with a dog who slept among the dead out in the cemetery; or perhaps it was someone seeking a handout of money, food or spiritual advice. Whoever it was could wait until 8:30 when his secretary, Lydia, unlocked the building for business.

The knocking continued. Perturbed, Moroux sauntered down the hall, entered the vestibule, and walked into the circle of dead popes. Through the glass door he saw an elderly man dressed in a police uniform.

Unlocking and opening the door, Moroux said in an inquiring way, "Yes?"

The old deputy wore the uniform of the Bayou Saint John sheriff's department and he held a sheaf of papers in his left hand. Extending the handful of papers, he said, "Excuse me, Father. These were my instructions from my boss, that he got from Mr. Chaisson's office. To come here now. Early like this. To serve these papers on you."

Moroux signed the receipt, took the papers and simply said, "Thank you."

After relocking the door, he slowly walked back toward the bishop's office, perusing the papers. Most of them were legal forms in triplicate, indicating that the attached documents were being served on the Diocese of Thiberville and all the other names that appeared as defendants on the original petition. These papers did not involve Brent Thomas, the lawyer Moroux thought was handling the eleven new cases against the Church. The name of the attorney on the documents was Kane Chaisson. The plaintiffs he was apparently representing were listed anonymously because of the court seal, blackened out and replaced with numerical designations: "John Doe #7", and "Parents of John Doe #7".

Moroux knew who Kane Chaisson was and he understood that the last paper in the set of documents in his hands was a court order setting a hearing on September 3 to determine whether the seal should be lifted, making the contents of this lawsuit a matter of public record.

Monsignor Moroux felt nauseated. He walked across to the desk of his secretary, Lydia Domingue, and scribbled a note saying he was ill and would be in his residence. He asked not to be disturbed unless something required his immediate attention. His pace was slow as he navigated the passageway that connected the chancery to the Old Bishop's House. Feeling too weak to walk up the steps to his own bed, he went into a downstairs guest bedroom that he had been in only once before. He pulled off his clothes, stripped down to his shorts and tee-shirt, and slipped beneath the covers. Within a matter of minutes he was sound asleep, dreaming of riding a bike down the center of a red-dirt road bounded by deep green fields. The red-dirt road was peopled by Africans wearing bright clothing. It was a dream he had often, a curious vision in that he had never been to Africa and had never learned to ride a bike.

11:15 a.m.

The phone woke Moroux. Remembering that Joe and Fanny, the husband-and-wife team who acted as housekeepers, cooks and gardeners and whom he sometimes referred to as "servants", were off on Mondays, he picked up the phone. It was his secretary informing him that District Attorney Sean Robinette had just called, saying it was urgent that he speak with the monsignor. Moroux scribbled the DA's phone number on the face of a holy card.

The district attorney was curt. "I have an affidavit of a Donny Rachou furnished by Kane Chaisson that alleges serious crimes against your priest, Father Francis Dubois. I am aware there are at least sixteen other victims. Our information is that six victims have received monetary settlements. My office opened a criminal investigation this morning. We will prosecute the priest. I want a meeting Thursday morning with an attorney who represents this priest. I don't want some diocesan lawyer coming here like in the past to assure me the diocese is taking care of everything. I want to meet with a lawyer who represents Father Dubois."

Monsignor Moroux knew there was no such person. Father Dubois had no attorney of his own. All the monsignor could manage was a mumbled, "I see. Fine."

Moroux's left arm was numb when he hung up. When death did not come after chain-smoking half a pack of unfiltered cigarettes, he pulled himself up from the guest-room sofa and shuffled back to bed, hoping a dream would take him somewhere else.

When Moroux woke again, it was late afternoon. The sun was setting, the chancery office was closed. He walked to the bishop's office, which he used as his own, and looked out at the cemetery for a long time, not knowing what to do about any of the developments of the day.

Unsure what to do about Kane Chaisson filing a motion to unseal one of the civil suits, or about the district attorney's demand for an appointment with a lawyer representing Father Francis Dubois, Moroux made a series of phone calls. Within half an hour his core advisors were assembled in his office; diocesan counsel Jon Bendel, vicar of finance Monsignor Buddy Belair, personnel director Sister Julianne, director of communications Lloyd Lecompte, and lay advisor Joe Rossi.

The question was put on the table by Moroux. Father Dubois now required his own legal counsel: who would they hire?

Joe Rossi immediately took control. "We can get a good lawyer for this mentally defective priest. But I tell ya, 99 per cent of what passes for lawyers around here wouldn't dirty their hands, stain their reputations by representing that pervert. I know one, a good one, who will represent anybody. He's young, but he's good. Let me call Renon Chattelrault for you. No, no… a better idea is to have Monsignor Belair call him for lunch here on Wednesday with all of us. Have the archbishop's lawyer here too. Renon Chattelrault will make that meeting with the district attorney on Thursday. Renon ain't scared of nothin'."

Jon Bendel was cautious. In a hard voice, he addressed Rossi. "Joe, can you control Chattelrault? Sometimes that kid is like a house afire, and he can be like a loose cannon rolling on the deck, playing by his own rules, not giving a damn who he steps on. He's young, but he's a tough son-of-a-bitch to deal with sometimes." Turning toward Sister Julianne, speaking in his smooth velvety voice, Bendel said, "Pardon my language, Sister."

The decision was made. Monsignor Buddy Belair would invite Renon Chattelrault to lunch at the Old Bishop's House.

Moroux walked everyone to the angel fountain. Lloyd Lecompte hurried to his car without saying goodbye. Monsignor Buddy Belair said goodbye to everyone too many times. Sister Julianne pulled out an apple, unlocked her bicycle, and waved farewell as she pedaled away.

That left Joe Rossi, with his hands in his pockets, rocking heel to toe, and Jon Bendel standing ramrod straight, his suit coat folded over an arm crossed in front of his starched white shirt and striped tie.

Moroux sat on the edge of the fountain.

Rossi grabbed a smoke from Moroux's pack and lit it from matches in his own pocket.

Jon Bendel said, "We'll go with Chattelrault, but dammit, Joe, you better be able to control him. We can't have this sick bastard Dubois screwing things up while we buy the silence from the kids and their parents. If this thing becomes public, we're gonna have to get it all over fast. The public will have to understand the diocese could not have prevented these things from happening to those children in Amalie – that all this was brought on by one sick priest alone and he's got to own it, Renon Chattelrault will have to own it. That's right, Monsignor, isn't it?"

Moroux shrugged wearily, and Rossi and Bendel took their leave.

This time of year always brought Jean-Paul Moroux back to his youth. When he was a child, the end of summer was when he was measured for new clothes and fitted with a new pair of shoes. In the fall he sometimes felt as if he was walking back through his life, and his mood then was melancholy, reflective. During the winter, he battled depression. In summer, it was his childhood that dominated his memory. He remembered the way everything was on his family's farm in Acadia Parish when he was a kid, how it all smelled. It made him sad on this night to remember that carefree time, and sadder to miss his mother. He closed off the bank of memories.

Jon Bendel had talked about how innocent the diocese was in all of this. Moroux shook his head slowly, negatively, and frowned. He remembered the murders. He wondered if anyone else would find out about them. He considered going into the secret archives and destroying the file. As his mind focused on the macabre memory, he forgot he had been smoking and the hot ash of his cigarette burned into the flesh of his fingers. The pain pulled him from his trance. Dropping the cigarette to the stone plaza, he plunged his hand into the pool of the fountain.

He thought of his mother again, the way she sang with perfect pitch in that soft voice. No other adult in the Moroux family had ever paid attention to him or any other child. He wished she had not died when he was sixteen, wished that he could go see her again. She was the only person who had ever hugged him or told him she loved him.

Moroux walked slowly toward the Old Bishop's House. His mind was on the murders.

PART THREE

SILENCE SLIPPING AWAY

1984

FOUR DAYS AFTER RENON CHATTELRAULT'S
FIRST VISIT WITH FATHER DUBOIS

21

SUSPICION OF A SISTER

Tuesday August 28, 1984
Diocesan Chancery, Thiberville

Sister Julianne was confused by her phone conversation with Monsignor Moroux. Normally, the monsignor's telephone manner was gruff, held to a few words. Usually, he just said, "Please come to my office now."

But this morning, when she answered the phone, Moroux had been full of cheer. "Good morning, Sister. How are you and how is your world this bright, sunny day?"

"Fine," she said. "Everything is fine."

"Well, I do hope so. Would you have any free time today for a visit with me?"

"Yes, Monsignor. I can walk over now."

"Good, good. I am in the bishop's office. Can I have Lydia make you a coffee or tea?"

"I have my water bottle. I'm okay." A jogger, Sister Julianne always carried a dark blue metallic flask of water with her.

"Good, good then. Come on over at your convenience."

When Sister Julianne walked into the bishop's office, Monsignor Moroux was standing at the window, looking out toward the cemetery. He had his back to her.

"Monsignor?"

"Yes, yes. Come over here, please."

She walked over and stood next to him.

"Do you know what I am doing, Sister?"

"No."

"Pondering. I'm pondering. You ever ponder?" Moroux said.

"I guess so."

"You know what I'm pondering, Sister?"

"No."

"Two things, actually. First there is that dying oak tree on the edge of the old part of the cemetery. You see the one I mean?"

"Un-huh."

"I'm pondering whether I should have it cut down before a hurricane topples it onto the old graves. That would be a pity. Some of those old crypts are beautiful with the sculpture work crowning them."

The monsignor turned almost in slow motion, like a dancer on a music box winding down. "I am pondering about that tree, Sister, and I am pondering about you."

Sister Julianne took a sip from her water bottle.

"Why would I be pondering about you, Sister? Can you tell me?"

She shook her head.

"Come with me. I'll show you."

Moroux led her down the steps into the vault that housed the secret archives. More than a half-dozen file-cabinet drawers were pulled open. "Now do you know?" he asked.

She sipped water again, shook her head, and hoped she was convincing.

"There are only three sets of keys to these file cabinets, Sister – the keys to all the secrets of this diocese. Bishop Reynolds has a set, I have a set, and our personnel director has a set. That would be you, Sister. When was the last time you were down here?"

"About a week ago, I think."

"About a week ago?"

"Yes, sir," she said, then immediately felt stupid for addressing a priest as if he were a cop.

"And what is it you were doing down here? Exactly what?" he asked.

"I was pulling files."

"A lot of files, I think. The drawers are a mess, Sister. I want you to explain what you were doing."

"Sometime, I don't remember the exact details, but I found an error, I think more than one error, on our personnel charts. I think Father Cecil Mosely was shown on my chart as having served in two different church parishes but the whole time he was actually serving full time as Chaplin at Holy Cross Hospital. I thought there could be other errors on the listing. I brought the chart down here and pulled files to see if the information corresponded to what was in the personnel jackets. While I was in the middle of this, I got sick, dizzy, felt like I had the flu and stuck the files back in the drawers and checked out for the day and went home to rest. Maybe I made some mistakes when I put the files back. I was feeling horrible then."

"Interesting, Sister. Some of the fasteners holding documents were undone as well as files being in the wrong places. Why would you have unfastened the documents?"

"I don't remember doing anything like that," she said.

"Let's go upstairs, Sister. It's hot down here."

Once they were in the office, Monsignor Moroux said, "Sister, I want you to return your keys to the secret archives to me now."

"Monsignor, the keys are in my apartment. I'll ride my bike over and retrieve them for you now."

Back in her apartment, Sister Julianne rifled the yellow pages of the phone book, looking for a locksmith shop nearby that could duplicate the keys to the secret archives. She felt she might want to review the files again and was not going to be denied access.

22

WAITING FOR THE GODWIND

Tuesday August 28, 1984
Morgan's Hope, Louisiana

It had only been four days since I first met with Father Francis Dubois in New Hampshire. Now I was fulfilling a request he had made of me. It took several hours to drive to the Dubois family home. It was in the middle of the state – a hilly dry woodland characterized by rises of red dirt and graceless, ramrod straight pine trees. Hardly anyone came here and few ever left. The hills sat as signposts announcing loneliness. Like the sand blown in from the west and waiting to be blown out again on the next gust, the people here were awaiting another wind – the wind from the fire of God's destruction, the Godwind.

The winding two-lane blacktop roads were lined with pre-fabricated metal buildings topped by awkward steeples. Out in front of these gathering places, where self-ordained ministers reigned in this home field of hard-hitting religion, there were portable message signs. Some simply displayed the name of the church, like "Church of the Holy Savior, Lord Jesus Christ". Others carried a message, announcing that the rapture was near, but my favorite proclaimed, "God Don't Gamble, God Don't Ramble. He's Here!"

All the roads off the highway were unpaved, red-dirt tracks leading into piney woods and hollows. The only Catholic church in fifty square miles, the parish of Saint Sebastian was deep in the woods, far from any settlement. There were only seventy-eight Catholic families in the entire area and less than half attended services in the unpainted pine box that passed for a church. On the side of the altar was a life-sized carving of the patron saint of the parish, a nearly naked martyr with nine arrows stuck in his body.

Later Dubois told me that the wood sculpture of Saint Sebastian had been carved by his uncle, John Thomas Dubois. One Saturday afternoon during Francis Dubois's childhood, men from the parish had gathered to drink moonshine whiskey and shoot the arrows into the sculpture. One at a time, the men had taken up the bow and fired at the target. Most missed and the shooting would stop while the children ran to retrieve the arrows from under the pine needles on the forest floor. The young Francis did not know much about the many other branches of Christianity in the area and as he watched the archers he asked his father what the difference was. His papa told him, "Those in them religions don't drink liquor, son. Drinking is against their religion. They make the liquor and sell it to us."

When Francis was a child, on Sundays and holy days a priest would drive up in a white car spattered with reddish mud from the long road leading in from the highway. The priest would hear confessions, say Mass, distribute communion, schedule baptisms and confirmations, and then he would leave. He came in a hurry and left in a hurry. The young Francis Dubois had envied the priest for he was the only one who ever got out of this place.

The Dubois family was poor. Francis's father, Mr. Willifred Dubois, spent his life "farming trees", meaning he clear-cut timber for a rich man from Shreveport whom he had never met. When Francis Dubois was young, there was nothing he was good at in school or on the playground. He helped his father haul trees. When he was not hiding on the far side of the barn roof, paging through the Sears, Roebuck & Co. catalogue, he was in the woods.

Before he was twelve years old, he knew the woods better than anyone except his father and Uncle William James. He could go deeper into the woods than any of the children and most of the adults, and he always found his way back. At an early age, he began to kill. First he killed bugs and birds, then worked his way up to squirrels, raccoons, ducks, deer and wild hogs.

Because Francis Dominick Dubois was not smart, he was teased at school. Because he was the fourth of nine children, he was ignored at home. Because he spent almost all of his time alone in the woods, he knew no one. After a childhood of rejection and isolation, Francis chose a career as a Catholic priest. He was the only Catholic priest ever ordained from the parish of Saint Sebastian.

It would have taken me forever to find the Dubois place in Morgan's Hope had Joe Rossi not been with me. Rossi knew where every place was in Louisiana. It seemed he had explored for oil or gas in every region of the state. I had told Monsignor Jean-Paul Moroux that Father Dubois wanted someone to talk to his family. When Rossi heard I was going, he volunteered to accompany me. Rossi and I would travel on to New Orleans later that night after meeting with the Dubois family. There was a morning meeting scheduled in the city with the archbishop and every lawyer involved in the eleven civil suits.

Iris Dubois, Francis's mom, had been quiet when I called her early that morning. The conversation was short and she asked no questions when I told her I would be coming that evening on behalf of her son, Father Francis, whom I had visited with over the weekend. I advised Mrs. Dubois that I would want to talk with her, her husband and as many of her children as possible.

The light was fading fast in the red hills when we reached Morgan's Hope. Rossi and I had stopped talking ten miles back. Pickup trucks and old cars crowded the small clearing in front of the Dubois home, a frame building balanced on short concrete piers. A rusting glider and a galvanized tub sat on the unpainted pine slats of the front porch.

Heavy footsteps shook the house. Through the rusted screen I could make out a short, rotund female figure doing a kind of a waddle walk, wiping her hands on her apron as she approached.

"My, my... I'm Iris. So happy ya'll made it. Ya'll come in. I was just making coffee. Coming all the way from Thiberville, that's a big trip. We went there one time. For Easter, I think."

I realized she was nervous and was going to jabber until I stopped her. "Thank you, Mrs. Dubois."

The living room was small enough to be mistaken for a foyer. One wall was adorned with a large faded photograph of Father Francis Dubois on the day he was ordained. An amateur oil painting, an attempt to copy the photograph, was on the opposite wall. There were no other pictures or paintings in the room.

Iris Dubois waved at the pictures with her dish rag. "It's Nicky," she said. "My, my, what a day that one was. That's the day the bishop made Nicky a priest. Thought I was gonna pass out. Jus' from bein' proud. It felt like a sin to be so proud."

From the small entrance room, Iris Dubois led Rossi and me to our left, through a passageway connecting the house to the kitchen. The kitchen was larger than the rest of the house. The long table would accommodate a dinner for at least twenty. The room was crowded.

"Say your names again," Iris said, motioning to us.

After I spoke my name and Rossi's, Iris went around the room introducing Father Dubois's brothers, his sisters and their spouses, and finally her husband. Dubois's dad was dressed in work clothes which were clean but stained by pine sap from the trees he cut and the motor oil of the engines he worked on.

"We have a good gumbo and some red beans, fresh okra and—"

"No, thank you," I said. Rossi and I took our seats at the head of the table. "We've already had something to eat," I fibbed. "Why don't you just have a seat?"

A long silence followed. I faced the family, mentally counting fifteen people in the room besides Rossi and myself. I knew it was not the entire family. A few siblings were missing.

"I have some very sad news. Sad news I need to tell you, about your son, about your brother."

I paused, in part because I was not sure I could go on. As the moment arrived, I was fully conscious of the weight of what I had to say, a weight so heavy it could crush the heart of anyone who loved Francis Dubois. I knew my visit would alter the lives of these people forever. This was the hardest thing I had ever had to do and I had no idea how to do it. I realized the monsignor or bishop should have come. This was a job for a priest.

"Your son, your brother. Father Dubois. Nicky. He is going to be indicted soon by the district attorney in Thiberville. He could be charged with hundreds of crimes. The criminal charges will involve allegations that... that while he was in Amalie at Our Lady of the Seas... that... that he sexually molested a large number of young boys... very young altar boys."

Iris Dubois stared stoically at something across the room. She seemed to have shut down. I thought she wasn't listening, but then she spoke.

"My, oh my... God. The children. Mr. Renon, the children. Who is taking care of the little children? Are they hurt? Did they get hurt? Oh no... little children..."

"Yes ma'am. Doctors are taking care of the children."

"The bishop? Does the bishop know?"

"Yes, ma'am."

"Nicky did this to children?"

She put her head in her hands. It was as if she had not cried over anything in her whole life and all those tears had been saved up and were rushing out now.

One of the men seated at my left grinned inappropriately, and I assumed there was something wrong with him. He wore a New Orleans Saints sweatshirt and appeared to be about the same age as his brother, the priest.

"Did Nicky do this? Is it true? Did he?"

I didn't see who asked the questions. As my eyes searched the room, a pudgy blond female about thirty-five years old kind of raised her hand.

"I'm Houston's wife, Glenda. Did Nicky do these things? Is he guilty?"

Looking at her, I answered the question as best I could without violating the confidence of my client, while trying at the same time to remain truthful. "At this point it is not my intention to argue that he is not guilty of the charges. We will argue that he was very sick, legally insane, at the time these alleged acts occurred."

"When will this happen?" asked a man wearing a ball cap and suspenders over a worn tee-shirt.

"I don't know. There are also civil lawsuits filed against your brother and the diocese. It could be a long time before there are trials. But I am pretty sure all this will come out in the press quite soon. From now on there could be reporters around here."

Five or six people asked questions simultaneously.

"Do we have to talk to them?"

"What do we say?"

"Will Nicky be able to come here again?"

"What do you think will happen to Nicky?"

"What can we do to help Nicky?"

"Is the bishop on Nicky's side?"

I motioned for a little quiet and did my best to field the queries. "The bishop has hired me, and the bishop is paying for Nicky's medical care now. The Church is paying for the care of the children. I just saw Nicky the other day and he's okay. He has been moved to a more secure place and the press will not be able to harass him where he is. I think what you can do to help Nicky is to continue to do what you've always done. If you used to write him, keep doing that. I have his new address. Just act the same and let him know he has your love and support. And remember you do not have to talk to the media at all. Just be polite and say that you do not want to talk, and walk away—"

Rossi cut in on me with a booming command. "Do not – I repeat – do not speak to anyone in the media about anything at all. No one in the press is on your son's side, your brother's side. Do not for a minute make the mistake of saying anything to the press."

Everyone nodded, almost in relief.

"Do you think he is going to jail?" It was the feisty pudgy blond again, Glenda, Houston's wife.

"Yes, ma'am, I do."

The one Iris had identified as the oldest brother, Russell, spoke softly. "What is the worst we should prepare for?"

"The worst for your brother is that he could receive a series of multiple life sentences and spend the rest of his life in prison. And that could happen. These are very serious charges."

A voice from my right asked, "Do you think he's crazy?"

"I don't know. It may be he was deranged then because of some organic or chemical problem in his brain. That's why we will argue he was legally insane. Hopefully we will end up with some kind of sentence where he can continue to receive medical treatment in prison. The point is that, in my judgment, he is going to go to prison. The only questions I have are how long he will be in prison, where he will serve his sentence, whether he will get medical care in prison, and what kind of treatment he might receive, if any. The psychological tests and brain scans are just now being ordered up. I will seek out the best experts in the country in this field and hopefully be able to mount a credible defense on the issue of his mental condition."

"Who sent you up here?" I could hardly make out the male speaker who had his chair propped against the wall in a dark corner. The man's mustache all but covered his mouth and he sounded like he had a speech impediment.

"Your brother asked me to come here. Monsignor Moroux wanted me to come. The monsignor specifically asked me to tell you that he and Bishop Reynolds will do anything your family needs."

A soft female voice echoed itself, "I don' believe. I don' believe." It was the voice of Iris Dubois, muffled by a dishtowel held against her mouth. Iris walked us to the porch, reciting the phrase like a mantra. The last thing I heard in Morgan's Hope was the priest's mother mumbling, "I jus' don' believe."

23

THE COMMON GOOD

1 a.m., Wednesday August 29, 1984
New Orleans

Rossi insisted we open the doors between our adjoining rooms in the Monteleone Hotel on Royal Street in the French Quarter of New Orleans. It was after midnight. I heard him ordering cheeseburgers, ice cream and soft drinks on the phone.

When room service knocked, he hollered, "Hey Ren, I'm on a call. Get the door. Pay him. Tip good. One of the burgers and Cokes is for you."

When Rossi came into my room, I had not touched the cheeseburger. I was working on a legal pad, trying to make an outline of a plan I hoped to be able to unveil for the archbishop, bishop, their legal counsel and the insurance lawyers in the morning.

"Look here, Renon. I been wanting to say something all day, but we had to do that thing up at Morgan's Hope."

Rossi was dressed in baggy boxer shorts, dark dress socks, an old fashioned undershirt and a large holy medal around his neck. He had a bowl of ice cream in one hand, and a Coke in the other, and a burger balanced on the glass of Coke. He set the ice-cream bowl on the bed opposite mine. When he sat on the bed, some of the ice cream dripped onto the covers. Rossi stared at the mess a moment and chose to ignore it.

I pushed the pad aside and laid the pen on it. "Shoot."

"You plead the sick priest to life in prison and the problem is gone. You do it before that Kane Chaisson prick has his argument to make his lawsuit public, before anything at all happens, before the public knows anything. You do this thing, plead the priest to life in prison, and the problems will begin to go away. The first thing the media will find out is that this mental defective took his medicine. Big story maybe, but a one-day story, a two-day story, not much really. It's in the best interest of the priest, his own family, the kids and their families, the diocese, the bishop, everyone in Amalie and Thiberville, every Catholic everywhere. You can end this damned thing before it begins."

"I don't see it that—"

"End it before it starts. And a good end, Renon. People will be sick to hear what the priest allegedly did, but none of the details you told me about in the files of the psychologist will come out. People will feel sorry for the children and their families, and the bishop, and everyone who had to deal with this – even you."

"No, Joe. Not a chance I would plead him guilty at this stage. Forget it."

Rossi almost roared. "Listen, dammit! This shit has to end before it begins. Jon Bendel's a damned good lawyer and he's been at it a lot longer than you. Jon's got a big office full of lawyers. One whole area ain't nothing but tits and typewriters."

"Your point being?"

"Jon said his people researched it, the whole country, every damned jurisdiction, and there has never been a public civil and criminal mess involving a priest and a diocese like the one that could happen here. Don't you think there is a reason there was never a mess like the one that's fixing to happen here? It's because smart people stopped it before it got started."

"Francis Dubois is entitled to a defense," I said.

"Entitled? He ain't entitled to shit. That's what he's entitled to. Not shit. What about the families and children down there in Amalie? Do they count? What are they entitled to, Renon? You gonna put thousands of people through pain and a crisis of faith for this monster of a motherfucker – so he can get a trial for things we all know he's guilty of? What the fuck?"

"Look, Joe, I can't stomach Dubois or what he did. The whole business makes me sick. The things that man did are monstrous. But I'm his lawyer, ya know. All the DA would accept today in a guilty plea would be a life sentence. I really think if Dubois believes he has to serve a life sentence, he'll kill himself. I believe that would happen. I think my obligation to my client, at a minimum, is to not participate in a plan that I think may end his life."

"So this priest kills himself. So what? Your obligation as a human being is to the common good, Renon. Dubois ain't no kind of human being. The first time he used his Roman collar to molest a child, he forfeited his right to be considered a human being."

"I need to get some sleep."

"In the morning, you tell the archbishop and everyone in that room you are going to plead him to life in prison. Then you call the DA and arrange a court date for next week, then the diocese will release a statement to the media, then you tell your client he's gonna serve life. And if he kills himself—"

"You can talk a hundred years, Joe. The answer will be no. Dubois is obviously a very sick man. Probably he deserves to be incarcerated for a long time. I think that will happen. But he damned well deserves treatment for the way he is, for whatever makes him this way. It is Dubois's interests I represent, only his interests."

"If you have your way, there will be the torture and agony of a long drawn-out legal mess with all the media crap around it. You have the power to end this ordeal for the priest, for the priest's fine family we saw in Morgan's Hope tonight, for the little kids and their families in Amalie, for all the people of Thiberville, and for all the good priests of the diocese, for the innocent bishop and all the innocent priests – for the greater good, Renon."

I got up, went into the bathroom, wet a hand towel, turned the shower on hot, closed the door and returned to the bedroom. I wiped up the ice cream off the bed cover.

Rossi lit the cigarette he had been holding, choked on the smoke, and choked on whatever curse was coming out of him. I quickly stripped, opened the door of the bathroom, which was now filled with steam, readjusted the water temperature, and stepped into the shower.

Rossi stormed into the steam-filled bathroom, screaming above the noise of the shower. "Can you hear me? I'm saying it will all be on your head, Renon Chattelrault, all on your head, and you'll be finished. Do you really think you can walk around town after defending a cocksucker like this? Do you? Do you? You gotta act for the common good."

From inside the shower stall, I shouted back, "I told you, Joe. He's entitled to a defense."

Rossi climbed into the shower with me, wearing his undershirt, boxer shorts and socks. When his cigarette got soaked he tossed it to the bottom of the bathtub. When he got soaked, he screamed, "I heard ya. I already told you what he's entitled to. Not shit."

I stepped out of the shower, toweled off and pulled on sweat pants.

If I had not known Joe Rossi all of my life, I might have thought he was crazy. But having known him, and having worked political campaigns with him, having represented clients in cases Rossi had an interest in, having done favors for him, and having spent weekends at his duck camp, I knew Rossi was just crazy like a fox, as sly as a fox and far more dangerous. If only he had been the buffoon he sometimes pretended to be.

Rossi followed me to the bedroom. "Now look what you done, goddammit. Only pair of socks I got with me."

I laughed. "Look in the mirror, Joe. Your comb-over collapsed. You look like some kind of cartoon."

"Yeah? Fuck you, Ren."

Rossi picked up what was left of my cheeseburger and took a huge bite. As he approached the door to our adjoining rooms, he spoke with food in his mouth. "Ya know, I love ya, kid. Really. If I had a son, I'd want you. Ever since I used to watch you play football on Friday nights. You're a great guy in some ways, and other ways you're just plain fucked up. You oughta pray over this. Don't you fucking pray, you son-of-a-bitch?"

"No."

"You don't pray?"

"Seems like begging to me. I talk with God."

"Well, goddammit, talk to your God tonight. If I can't get no sense in ya, maybe your God can."

Rossi looked over his shoulder again. "Ask God what's right."

"I already know what's right, Joe. And I don't think God listens in on fucked-up conversations like this. People who talk about killing others or having them kill themselves – for the common good or for any other reason."

Later I heard Rossi on the phone talking to Jon Bendel. He was speaking in a low tone, but the combination of his booming voice and the crack in the door allowed me to hear him. "We screwed the pooch, Jon. Fucked up. We told him we wanted him to represent the priest and that's what the son-of-a-bitch is doing."

There was a pause and then I heard Rossi say, "So, yeah, it was my fuck-up to get him involved in this shit. You gotta get him uninvolved in the Dubois deal. Fire his fucking ass off the case before he brings the cathedral down on our heads."

24

ALL THE KING'S MEN

Wednesday August 29, 1984
New Orleans

I had been asleep three hours when the phone started ringing. As I picked up the handset, I switched on a lamp and looked at my watch. 6:05 a.m. My voice cracked out a hoarse "Hello".

"Mr. Chattelrault, I am sorry to wake you up. You said we could reach you here. It's early, I know, but I got work at the plant over in Texas and I gotta go in a minute."

"Yes. Who is this?"

"This is Walt."

There was a pause. It seemed neither of us was going to talk.

"Walter… Walt Dubois. I was at Momma and Daddy's house last night. I had a Saints shirt on."

"Yes, I remember you." I remembered his grin when I described what his brother had done to the altar boys.

"Well, last night you never said the word. The word for what Nicky is. The word is pedophile. That is what he is. He's a pedophile."

"Ooo-kaaay," I said slowly.

"I'm a pedophile too, Mr. Chattelrault. Same as Nicky."

I lowered my voice, not wanting to rouse the snoring mass of man that was Joe Rossi in the next room. "Walt, why are you telling me this?"

"I thought ya needed to know. Nicky knows. I don't want what he's done to get me in trouble. Can I get drug into this?"

The obvious struck me hard like a hatchet. "Walt, did you and

137

your brother ever share… you know…" I stopped talking and held my breath for the answer.

"No. Never. Nicky and I don't even like each other. I can't stand him. Ever since he went off to the seminary, he believes he's better than all of us. Ya know the truth? He's worse. He's worse than me, worse than everybody."

"Who else knows this about you, Walt?"

"Nobody who would tell. A psychologist in Shreveport knows. My two ex-wives know."

"You told them?"

"No, one of them caught me with her son. The other one's two sons told on me."

"Look, Walt, we both have places to go this morning. Don't tell anybody about this. Don't even tell anyone you spoke with me about it. I am kind of busy these days. But I will get back up to Morgan's Hope to talk to you. And for Christ's sake—"

"I know. I ain't touched no kid in a long time, but I know what you don't know."

"And?"

"Lemme tell ya. You can't do nothing for Nicky. Nobody can do nothing for me and I ain't even as bad as Nicky."

"Okay, Walt. Stay in touch."

"Yes, sir. Thanks for talking to me."

I rang off, opened the drapes and watched barge traffic on the Mississippi River. It was too difficult to process what I had just heard, so I stored it. It seemed important to me that two of the Dubois siblings were afflicted in the same way.

I had breakfast brought to the room before I woke Rossi. Joe grumbled and moaned that I'd kept him up all night and then he attacked his breakfast and raided mine. I asked if he knew the directions to the place where the meeting was being held that morning.

"Saint John Major Seminary? Yeah. It's the Louisiana priest factory. Your boy, Dubois, woulda come through there. Ya know, I was gonna be a priest once upon a time."

"You? A priest?"

"Yeah. I gave up on being a priest – thought it would bore me. See, a priest just hears the exact same laundry list of shit all the time. I got too short a temper to listen to people whine and whimper and want assurance that God is on their side. Hell, son, the truth is that God ain't on everybody's side. Ain't that obvious?"

While Rossi polished off both breakfasts, I struggled with my tie for the third time in front of the mirror. The tie didn't look bad, but it didn't look quite right either.

As we approached the seminary, Rossi said, "I wanna bring some melons back to Thiberville." He made me pull over at a roadside fruit-and-vegetable stand on the curb of a big boulevard in front of the seminary compound. Joe was looking at all the produce, picking out things and handing them to me. The proprietor wore a faded and frayed New Orleans Saints football cap.

"Like the Saints?" Joe asked.

"What can I tell ya? Used to be we only had two things could break our hearts down here – the weather and our children. Then we got the Saints."

"You had this stand long?"

"I was working with my old man here back when I was a kid and shoulda been in school. Back when we sold real produce. See this melon you got here? Everyone knows God don't let these melons grow at this time of year nowhere. But now they got these big sheds that cover acres of ground. And they control the temperature, soil composition, light, moisture, every damned thing in those places. They can trick a plant into thinking it's in moonlight at noon and that it's summer when it's winter."

"Well, the strawberries look great," I said. "Could you put the strawberries in a separate bag?"

"I'll sack it anyway you want."

"You been here all these years?"

"Yep. Like I says, my old man was here before. Used to be free here 'cause it's a public easement and ya just make a little donation to whoever is mayor. But the last archbishop, that Yankee prick from Noo Yawk they brought in here, tried to charge me rent. Everything's different than before."

"Yeah?"

"Yeah," he said. "I've known every sum-bitch come through this seminary the last sixty years, known every archbishop since before the one who became a cardinal and went to Chicago. He was the best one. He had that girlfriend, remember dat? He got in lots of trouble for giving her a bunch of money. She was a sweetheart, sweet as you please. They used to get their produce here. I could always tell when the old boy had knocked off a piece. You know you can tell by looking at a man if he's had any lately. Like, take your friend here," he punched Rossi's fat tummy and laughed. "I can tell this guy ain't had none since at least Mardi Gras, maybe longer."

I laughed. Rossi furrowed his brow and opened his mouth to make a smart retort, but the man cut in.

"It's all changed now," the man said. "When I was a kid, my old man let me play football with the priests and seminarians right there on the big grass lawn. It's bigger than a football field. They used to play ball out there all the time. Rough games with scratches, bruises and blood. And there was a gym inside with a boxing ring where they used to pound the crap out of each other. No more. Not for thirty years now. The only thing that's ever on that big lawn now is a lawnmower. All the boxing stuff, weights and all that is gone from the gym. Some seminarian told me they painted the gym, floored it with carpet, changed the lights, and put backgammon tables in there now. What the hell is a backgammon table?"

Rossi walked toward my car. Over his shoulder, he said, "Pay the man, Renon."

The meeting room in Saint John Seminary resembled the great hall of a Rhine castle I once saw. It was two stories tall with a vaulted ceiling. Heavy dark-wood panels were inlaid at eye level with depictions of pastoral scenes. In one corner near leaded glass windows, there was a collection of antique crucifixes.

Rossi and I were minutes late. Seats had been reserved for us at one end of the long oak table next to Jonathan Bendel, the diocesan lawyer for Thiberville, Monsignor Moroux, and Bishop Reynolds, a short, heavy-set man in a black suit and roman collar, with a crucifix on a long chain around his neck. It was the first time I had seen him in person but there was no time for introductions.

At the other end of the table was Archbishop Donnegan, dressed similarly to Reynolds. I recognized him from newspaper photographs. Flanking the table were a dozen other men, some in clerical garb, some in suits. Every lawyer involved in the eleven civil suits filed against the archbishop, his archdiocese, Bishop Reynolds and his Thiberville diocese, named and unnamed monsignors, and others who had supervised Father Dubois in his career was here. The suits were wearing nice ties. The only one of them I recognized was Thomas Quinlan, the archbishop's lawyer, and for the first few moments we were there, Quinlan seemed to be in charge. He introduced me and Rossi to the group, saying, "Renon just spent a few days with Father Dubois, and maybe we should give him the floor to begin."

I felt nervous and said nothing, kind of hoping someone would take my turn. I wanted a feel for the room before I moved forward with the plan I had outlined in the hotel.

A bald man at the far end of the table addressed me. He had his spectacles propped on his forehead so that they reflected light from the ceiling chandeliers and made him look like a four-eyed monster.

"Renon," he began. "My name is Robert Blassingame, of Miller, Sikes, Wilder, Gentry, Donebane and Doise. I don't know that it is a good idea that we hear from you at all. I don't even know if it is a good idea that you are in this room. There are many different interests represented here, which include the archdiocese, the Diocese of Thiberville, and a consortium of insurance companies who had policies in play during the period covered by the plaintiff's claims. I don't think your client's interests are aligned with any of ours."

"My client is willing for me to share the truth with you about his conduct and he is also willing to work with me to identify every victim—"

Interrupting, a short, skinny man stood and picked up his briefcase, saying, "I am going to leave because I don't want to know what the priest said. I don't think any of the counsel representing insurance interests ought to be in this kind of discussion at this stage."

"I'm telling you that I have information which may define or delineate the exposure your various clients may have in these cases."

Jon Bendel made a motion indicating I should stop talking. He leaned over and quietly said, "Renon, step outside with me." To the room, Bendel said, "Give us a moment, please."

Outside in the hallway, Jon Bendel took a long drink from a water fountain. "Shit, the chemicals they put in the water in New Orleans are probably worse than the poison they're trying to get out of it." He shifted to me. "Get off that crap about identifying the priest's victims. Quinlan was an idiot to ask you to talk. We're supposed to be discussing Chaisson's motion to try to make his Rachou case public. Nothing else."

Once we were back in the room, I looked at Mr. Blassingame with his glasses propped on his forehead, and addressed him. "I am not concerned with what any of you want to hear. I am telling you that there is an obligation all of us in this room have – a moral obligation – to reach out to all the Dubois victims we can find. We're talking about the Catholic Church, not some soulless corporation."

Blassingame exploded. "We are not in the business of issuing invitations to people to sue us. That's that."

Quinlan raised his hand to silence me as I started to speak again. I stopped. Quinlan spoke. "Let's discuss what we are here to discuss: Kane Chaisson's motion to unseal the Rachou suit."

Next to me, Bendel scrawled four words on his legal pad: "Son-of-a-bitch". He tore the sheet from the pad, showed it to me, and then neatly folded it before placing it in the side pocket of his coat. For a moment I thought Bendel was referring to Blassingame and I concurred with his opinion. Then something made me realize the reference was to me.

I spoke out of turn again on the subject of Chaisson's motion. "What is there to discuss about the motion to break the seal? No law in this state or any other state allows a plaintiff or defendant, acting alone or in concert, to keep public documents out of the public record. The public records doctrine is one of the strongest legal precepts we have. If anything, I think we should all be talking about preparing statements to release to the media before the suit is unsealed by the court on Monday. A kind of pre-emptive strike, getting our word out first, maybe a public letter by the bishop to be read at Masses this Sunday, released to the media and then—"

Apparently Blassingame had been elected captain or something, as he was the only one who spoke, and he interrupted me again. "I don't think this issue even applies to your interests, to your client, and thus I see no reason for you to be addressing anything."

I charged at Blassingame. "Whether or not it becomes public knowledge that my client committed thousands of criminal acts against more than a dozen children is indeed material to his interests. Father Dubois can go to prison for life. I don't want any of this to be public knowledge any more than any of you do, but I know that it will be made public. A freshman law student would know this. There is no authority anywhere that would allow a court to rule differently."

Jon Bendel cleared his throat. "I have information that Kane Chaisson's Rachou case is being reassigned to a new judge today. I have reason to believe the new judge will be empathetic with our position."

They fixed a frigging judge! I thought. *Jeeezus Christ, they fixed a judge.*

Blassingame smiled broadly. "That's good work, Jon. I don't know how you do things down there in Thiberville, but that's what we count on you for."

Archbishop Donnegan turned to his lawyer, Tommy Quinlan, and asked, "Is there anything more to discuss?"

"No, Excellency."

The archbishop stood and said, "I thank you all for coming. May the Holy Spirit keep us all safe and guide the court to render justice on Monday, and keep this lawsuit sealed, avoiding scandal to Holy Mother Church."

25

LUNCH AT ANTOINE'S

Wednesday August 29, 1984
New Orleans

A circular table in a private room at Antoine's was set for Bishop Reynolds, Monsignor Moroux, Jon Bendel, Joe Rossi, and me. The bishop was eating a dozen oysters with different sauces and hardly looked up as Rossi and I entered the room. If the group had been talking before we arrived, they stopped as soon as we sat down.

"You need to try the oysters," Bishop Reynolds said.

I turned to a waiter. "Vodka rocks."

Menus were passed around the table.

Monsignor Moroux spoke for the bishop. "Renon, the bishop has been asked to file a more detailed supplemental report with the papal nuncio in Washington, Archbishop Carlo Verriano. The canon lawyer in the nunciature in DC, Father Desmond McDougall, is calling me every day. I must include something about the status of the criminal case. What can you tell us from your visit with Father Francis?"

The waiter set my drink before me. Lighting a cigarette and taking a long drink of vodka, I considered what I would say. I decided to skip a report on Father Dubois's state of mind, which I knew no one was really interested in, and get straight to what I wanted to know.

"There was an area I did not cover in my discussion with Father Dubois. He absolutely refused to talk to me about anything other than what happened in his last church parish, Our Lady of the Seas in Amalie. He said that you, Monsignor Moroux, ordered him not to talk about anything but Amalie. You hire me one day to represent your priest. The next day you act to sabotage my defense of Dubois, to keep me from getting important factual information from my client. I want to talk about what happened in the parishes he was assigned to before Amalie."

Jon Bendel stood and addressed me. "Renon, I hate to keep asking you to step out of rooms with me, but I feel we need to confer in private."

"That's fine, Jon. I don't mind you asking. But I am not stepping out of any more rooms with you. We're all on the same side, aren't we?"

Jon spoke smoothly in his patented pacifying tone as he sat down. "Of course, I did not mean to offend you by asking to speak privately. I did not want to bore the others with lawyer talk. That's all. However, I am going to now tell Bishop Reynolds and Monsignor Moroux that I do not want them discussing anything with you relating to what knowledge anyone within the diocese may have had at any time – what they could have known, may have known, or should have known about the activities of Father Dubois in Amalie or anywhere else."

I nodded my understanding. Then I addressed the bishop directly. "Bishop, the law is clear, unmistakably clear. Kane Chaisson's Rachou suit is going to be made public next Monday. There is no authority in the law that supports the argument that a civil lawsuit should remain a secret from the public."

Bendel said, "And what do you suggest we should do about this?"

"I think it is imperative that all of us prepare pre-emptive strikes and deliver public statements to the media Sunday morning in advance of Chaisson's hearing on Monday. The diocese could issue a letter from the bishop to be read from the pulpit at all Masses and released to the media, and I could issue a short written statement confirming that Dubois is confined, not free, and that he is undergoing medical treatment and is not simply on leave. That would assure everyone he is no longer a threat to their child or any child, and it would lay groundwork for his insanity defense. We must define the issues ourselves. We cannot wait for Kane Chaisson to define these things in the public mind."

Bishop Reynolds looked at Monsignor Moroux and Moroux looked at Bendel, but it was Joe Rossi who handled the response.

Rossi said, "Don't be so sure that we cannot keep a lid on this in court and in the media, Renon. We've got a good judge on the case now."

"If we don't believe that all of this is going to be public... Well, I mean, of course this will all be public," I said. "It's just a matter of time. If this local judge rules for the diocese, an appeals court will force the trial court to break the seal and make it all public. I'd like to see the diocese and Dubois get some footing before Chaisson starts shooting at us in the press."

I drained my glass and let the vodka race through my veins, soothe my sagging spirits. I continued, "I'll go back up to see Father Dubois if I have to. I want to know the answer to the basic question of who knew what about Father Dubois's actions and when did they know it. The whole world is going to know the answer one day, and I think you hiding it from me is nonsensical. If we are not going to cooperate with each other, then what are we doing here today?"

"Having lunch," the bishop said flatly. "My treat." His eyes remained on the food he was devouring. Already I felt the bishop disliked me, but he did not seem to like anyone else at the table either. "This is my favorite restaurant," the bishop said, "and I wanted you all here today. The bisque is exceptional and I recommend the grilled pompano with crabmeat topping. These people understand that a fish is to be baked, grilled, or fried. There is nothing fancy, no pretensions. This is where we hosted a dinner for the Holy Father – in the Rex Room. They have everything you could want here except lemon pound cake. You fellows don't have to talk law or argue. We ought to just have lunch."

The bishop reminisced some about his childhood in New Orleans and how Antoine's was never open on Sundays and how right that was, that all businesses should be closed on Sunday. After the meal, when coffee was served, Rossi asked the waiter to close the door and leave the silver pot of coffee on the table. The bishop asked that a bottle of cognac and glasses be brought.

Joe Rossi spoke first. "We have something really important to talk about and I think this is the time. Bishop?"

Cued, Bishop Reynolds began. "I have done nothing wrong, Renon. Nor has Monsignor Moroux or any of the other priests of the diocese. I don't deserve this."

Now, for the first time, I looked properly at the bishop. I stared into his distorted, oversized face with its milky eyes sunk into flabby, splotched flesh. His eyebrows looked like thorns.

"No, sir, I did nothing wrong. This man… this Father… uhhh, Father…"

"Dubois," I volunteered.

"Yes, uhhh Dubois… He has a duty. He has a duty to me, his bishop, to Holy Mother Church. We cannot allow him to disgrace the priesthood, the Church, our diocese or my office. No, sir. I will not have it. We cannot allow the sick actions of one disturbed man to bring scandal to the diocese and Church."

Monsignor Jean-Paul Moroux gave me an inappropriate half-smile and advised, "As I said, I must file a supplemental report with the canon lawyer for our papal nuncio in Washington. In this report I will need to present the problems in more detail, and I will also need to present the solutions as well. It seems our papal nuncio and the Vatican have never seen a situation quite like this one where already millions have been paid, more millions are being sought, and both criminal and civil cases are involved, not to mention the threat of a widespread public scandal."

Moroux stopped talking when the waiter returned with the bottle of cognac and tray of balloon glasses. As soon as he had gone, Moroux continued.

"Is Father Francis ready to acknowledge, admit and atone for his sins, and accept his punishment?" Monsignor Moroux asked.

I remained silent.

Bendel placed his napkin on the table, reached for the coffee pot and poured, looking at his cup as he spoke. "Is this man ready to plead guilty to whatever Sean Robinette charges him with and accept whatever sentence the court gives him? This is the only solution – to use your phrase, the only effective, pre-emptive strike. It will be clear to all who are concerned that the priest is a sick criminal who has accepted his punishment and the bishop and diocese have done nothing wrong. That Father Dubois alone is guilty."

"Was I hired to represent this priest or was I hired to convince this priest to throw himself on his sword, to use your phrase from our first lunch, to spare embarrassment to the bishop, avoid a scandal to the Church?"

Bendel almost shouted, "Don't go putting words in my mouth or anyone else's mouth."

"It's what you said at the Old Bishop's House a week ago, Jon. Fall on his sword."

Joe Rossi pushed away from the table. "Are we going to have to fire you?"

"You can't fire me, Joe. Read my letter of employment that Monsignor Moroux signed. The diocese is not my client." Looking at Bendel, "I have no attorney–client relationship with the diocese, Jon. The diocese is only the financial guarantor of my fee agreement with Father Dubois. The diocese is liable for payment of my expenses and fees. Father Dubois is the only one who can fire me and I don't think he's going to do that."

Bendel stood. "Your Excellency, I will get the check. This lunch is over."

Outside the front door, I pulled Rossi's suitcase out of my car and put it on the sidewalk, telling the doorman to be on the lookout for a short, fat guy and to hand him his luggage. I drove off alone, headed for my home, Coteau.

26

GUILTY KNOWLEDGE

Thursday August 30, 1984
Stalder Institute, New Jersey

I was beginning to feel like I lived in airports. I was back in the east again, in the lobby of the Stalder Institute, a psychiatric facility on the outskirts of Morristown, New Jersey. I had Francis Dubois move here a week ago, after his time in Saint Martin's in Deerfield. A slight, handsome man identified himself as Father Francis Dubois's physician and walked me to his small office.

"Doctor Dobson, I really only want answers to a few questions. Father Dubois has told me he will kill himself if he is sentenced to life in prison. Do you believe this?"

The doctor looked through the patient file.

"Well, let me ask you a question, Mr. Chattelrault. Are we talking about an abstract hypothetical here or is this the actual scenario we are dealing with? Is he going to receive a life sentence from the court?"

"Were he to plead guilty to the crimes the grand jury will charge him with, he would receive multiple life sentences."

"So he has been charged with nothing yet?"

"Well, the exact list of his charges will be determined by a Grand Jury – a group of ordinary citizens chosen from the voter roll. They will hear the testimony of the children, and, guided on matters of law by the DA, will return an indictment charging Father Dubois with a laundry list of serious crimes, many of which are likely to carry life sentences."

"So would you advise him to plead guilty to a life sentence, before going to trial?"

"No. Even though a life sentence may well be the result of a trial, the process has a lengthy pre-trial phase, as there are motions both the defense and prosecution can raise. My hope is that I will be able to return Dubois here for treatment while he awaits the trial itself, and that could be a year or even longer."

"What is the best possible result your client might hope for, in your opinion? Realistically?"

"Realistically, I think he will end up in prison for the remainder of his life. If some miracle occurs between now and the trial date, then maybe I can strike a plea bargain with the District Attorney that would allow him to serve time in a clinical environment like this rather than a penal institution where he would never be treated for the condition that afflicts him."

"So you're asking me whether, if forced to accept a life sentence immediately, the patient will commit suicide? In my opinion?"

I nodded. "Yes, that's my question."

"Well, if forced to answer the question you put to me, if I had to answer it in one word, it would be the same answer I gave the monsignor."

"The monsignor?"

"Yes. You are not the first person I've spoken with about this." Doctor Dobson flipped back four or five pages in the file. "Yes, yes. Just after Father Dubois was admitted, we got a call the same day from a monsignor in his diocese. He called about the financial responsibility forms and we discussed the patient's condition. I cannot make out the monsignor's name – Morrow, I think it is."

"You told Monsignor Moroux what you've told me?"

"Yes, that would be right. I told him basically what I told you. I got a clearance from the patient to discuss him with his superior. I told Morrow the patient was on suicide watch and was talking about ending his life if he had to go to prison for the rest of his life."

"And... so, you believe he will kill himself?"

"One never knows about suicide. But in a word, I'd say, yes. And I feel he is resourceful enough to accomplish that in any setting, even in here."

"You know that just from him being here a few days?"

"He had an extreme paranoid episode that began shortly after he was admitted and it's just beginning to abate this morning. He believed he'd been tricked into locking himself up here and would never be free again. He kept saying you were paid by the diocese to make him disappear. We let him use the phones. He told us he had talked to a powerful judge and everything was going to be okay. He was that delusional."

"So, you think—"

"He's heavily medicated. The emotional and mental strain on such a shame-based personality where there really is no true self present, no integrated personality, poses a real risk of suicide. These factors are counter-balanced perhaps by the fact that he is such a narcissistic personality, if a borderline personality at that; thus destroying himself may prove difficult to impossible. But he is totally removed now from an environment where he can access his addiction – children. We are considering administering the drug Depo-Provera, which will lower his testosterone level. I believe he will begin attempting to take his life the day he is told he is to serve a life sentence, the day it dawns on him that he will forever be denied access to his addiction."

I didn't understand the jargon, and asked him to restate in language I could understand.

"It's tough to explain in a few words, but a shame-based personality is normally associated with a lack of nurturing as a child which manifests itself in feeling unlovable and worthless. Defense mechanisms are developed, including exuding false self confidence or attaining a position in life where people look up to you, but feelings of shame prevail – and that is not the same as guilt. We feel guilt about what we do – and a healthy person feels guilt when they act outside their value system. Shame is about what we feel we are. Obviously, it's easier for one who feels worthless to take his life than it is for one who feels real self-worth."

"So how does that connect to a borderline personality disorder?"

"BPD is also a condition where one feels worthless inside and fundamentally flawed. It's my belief that some BPD people act in ways that are fundamentally flawed, as some sort of validation of themselves. Many tend to have love–hate relationships or no relationships at all with peers. Addiction is common, gambling, drinking, drugs, sex. And suicidal behavior is a prominent symptom of BPD."

"You told this to Monsignor Moroux?"

"No, no. Not nearly in this detail. I informed him that his priest was on a suicide watch here and I believed he would kill himself if he became convinced he would be forced to serve the rest of his life in prison."

"Doctor Dobson, before I leave for Louisiana, I will drop off a document for you with Father Dubois's signature to the effect that no personnel at this hospital are authorized to speak with anyone except me about any aspect of Father Dubois's condition or care, and specifically no one associated with the Catholic Church will be permitted access to Dubois or any information pertaining to him. Only his family and I may speak with him on the phone or visit him in person, or someone I authorize, or someone he authorizes who is not associated with the Church."

With a lackadaisical manner, almost yawning, Doctor Dobson closed the file and asked, "Is that it?"

"One more thing, if you would. In layman's terms I can understand, could you tell me Francis Dubois's diagnosis and prognosis?"

"Your client is a fixated, ego-syntonic pedophile; garden variety, if you will. We see a lot of them. In layman's language, we apply the term pedophile to an adult who has sex with pre-pubescent children, kids without any secondary sexual characteristics such as pubic hair, hair under their arms, stuff like that. In the case of little girls, an absence of developing breasts would be important to a pedophile. To be fixated means to be focused on victims within an age range of approximately three years generally. Could be four to seven years of age, or six to nine years, et cetera. To be ego-syntonic means the perpetrator or patient, depending on whether it's the law or medical profession viewing the pedophile, has no response of conscience, regret, remorse, guilt or other appropriate response to their behavior which might provide a motive or desire in them to want to change or alter the behavioral pattern of their life."

"Is there a cure, Doctor?"

"That's for another discussion."

"In a word, is there hope?"

"In a word? Well... no. There is no hope of a cure for a pedophile."

"Doctor, have you treated other priests for the same condition?"

"That would be confidential."

A staff orderly escorted me from Doctor Dobson's office, along a maze of corridors through a series of locked double doors to the unit where Father Dubois was on a suicide watch. It was a comfortable ward, different to what I'd expected.

Dubois was in a lounge area, wearing jeans, a tee-shirt and jogging shoes, appearing younger and more relaxed than when we first met. He actually looked like a different person from the man I had met in New Hampshire one week earlier. Even his hair was combed differently, and his posture was relaxed.

"Hi, Renon Chattelrault," Dubois said casually as he glanced up from a magazine. "You want a Coke or something? There's a machine down the hall. I have money at the nurses' station."

"Maybe later. How're ya feeling?"

"Great." Dubois grinned. "Been pilled up pretty good since I got here. At the other place in New Hampshire there were no doctors, no prescriptions. Here I am taking all kinds of drugs. A guy down the hall calls them worry pills because he says if you got a worry and you take these pills you not only stop worrying, you can't even remember what it was you were worrying about. But I can remember pretty good. I spoke with my mom. She liked you."

"That's good."

"So, what brings you here so soon?"

I felt grateful to find him in this frame of mind, even if it were drug induced. "We have some things to talk about. The first thing will be the hardest."

"What's that?"

"We have a new problem. The diocese, everyone involved in that end of things, sees you as both the problem and the solution."

"What do you mean?"

"This is going to break wide open soon, probably Monday when the Rachou boy's lawsuit is unsealed and the media gets it. The Church wants to convince the world when this all breaks loose that you're the whole problem – only you; that the problem begins and ends with you. Maybe the problem does begin and end with you. I'm here to find out."

"I'm confused."

"The solution to the problem, as they see it, would be for you to immediately disappear into a faraway prison for the rest of your natural life, never to be heard from again, or just plain disappear, period. It's not easy to come here and talk this way to you, but you gotta know what we're up against."

Dubois put his head in his hands. He stayed that way for a few minutes. I sat quietly.

"This scares me. A lot of people take comfort in the Church. But it can be a scary place if you are on the inside as a priest. It's not just people like me who find themselves locked inside the walls of the Church who are scared. On the inside it can be a house of horrors."

You're hardly in a place to speak about horrors, I thought. The man speaking those words was not the Father Francis Dubois I had been introduced to only six days earlier at the Saint Martin Center. A dramatic personality shift had transpired. I wondered if the medication could account for the change, or if, in fact, the man could change his personality at will. It was not just that this person in front of me was well spoken, thoughtful, objective, but that he was also calm, assured. The erratic figure I'd confronted in New Hampshire had clearly been attempting to manipulate me as he shifted from being Father to Francis and then Nicky. Was this another attempt to manipulate me? How many more personalities could Dubois show me?

I said, "Only one thing is clear to me."

"What's clear?"

"What's clear to me is that the diocese knows some things about you that they want no one else to know. About whether you were involved with children in other church parishes before you were assigned to Amalie. They threatened to fire me when I asked them about these things. They can't fire me. Only you can fire me. They don't want me to know, but I am going to know because you are going to tell me right now."

Dubois rose, walked to a window and stared through the bars into the early evening sky. When he turned toward me, he asked me if I wanted to smoke. "I remember you smoke quite a bit. There's a room past the nurses' station. The one with the pool table. Let's go there."

Dubois started talking as soon as we walked into the smoking room. "I made a promise to Monsignor Moroux when he visited me in New Hampshire. He was with the archbishop's lawyer, a Mr. Finlan or Quinlan or something. What they said made sense to me. The lawyer and Jean-Paul said what I was being accused of in Amalie was bad enough, but if anyone ever found out there were other boys before, then they would not be able to save me. I promised them I would never talk about the other times, the other boys. Moroux made me promise again on the phone the night before I met you."

"Look," I said. "Look straight at me."

Dubois was very intent as he looked at me, more focused than I had ever seen him.

"As long as Monsignor Moroux and the Church lawyers have no problems of their own, they can screw with us. If they have problems of their own, they will be busy fighting to save their own asses. Once they're in the deep end with us, they gotta swim too. And I think the new lawyer for the Rachou family, Kane Chaisson, is about to put their collective asses in a sling. I have to know the truth about whether they have any real problems themselves."

"Problems?"

"When did the Catholic Church first know about your problem, your proclivity to have sex with little boys? Now, Father, if you are going to lie to me about this or anything else, just let me leave."

"I won't lie."

"Then tell me. When did the Church first know about your problem?"

"There were complaints from an orphanage in New Orleans when I worked there one summer while I was at Saint John Seminary. The rector then was a Monsignor Billadeaux who belonged to the Diocese of Thiberville. He questioned me and counseled me about this and said something would be placed in my file."

"When was this?"

"Over twenty years ago."

"Before you were a priest?"

"Oh yes, before ordination. And another summer when I was a seminarian helping out in a New Orleans church parish, I got involved with an altar boy, a kid from a broken home. His mom told the pastor about it. My work was terminated in the parish. Again Monsignor Billadeaux questioned me and counseled me."

"Twice before ordination, before you even became a priest?"

Dubois nodded.

"What did Monsignor Billadeaux ask you?"

"Well, I think he just said 'Is it true?' or something like that and I said 'Yes'."

"What was the monsignor's counsel?"

"I don't remember the first time because I was so nervous. I really liked the orphanage job and didn't want to lose it. But the second time he talked to me about it, he advised that I consider having what he called a 'particular friendship' with another seminarian. That was the monsignor's suggested solution."

"A particular friendship?"

"I knew what he meant. It's code in seminary. Means having a fuck buddy. You know, pairing off with another seminarian for sex. But I'm not gay, Renon, no matter what anyone thinks. I'm not queer. A lot of priests are queers, but I'm not. And I didn't want a particular friendship with some faggot seminarian."

I was at a loss for words. Dubois was summoned by a nurse to take his medication. I welcomed the break and racked pool balls, broke and started taking aim at the stripes. Dubois wandered in as I missed my fourth consecutive shot. We continued to talk and I continued to miss.

"Were there any other times in the seminary when your superiors became aware of your sexual activity with boys?"

"No. Not really. I was always having sex with boys, but not getting caught. But they knew how I was."

"When was the next time your superiors or supervisors were confronted by your sexual conduct with children?"

"The first year I was a priest in the Diocese of Thiberville. In the first parish I was assigned to. A nice young couple came to the pastor and complained about me. Their son was seven. The funny thing is nothing much had really happened yet with their son. I had touched him through his clothes, I think. Maybe we took a shower together, but no real sex stuff had happened yet. But there were a lot of other boys there I was having sex with in that first parish, kids who never said anything to their parents. Just last year one of them asked me to go back to that parish and perform his wedding ceremony."

I put the pool cue down. "What did the pastor do that first time?"

"He called the vicar general, a man named Darnell. He's dead now. Darnell must have told the bishop because I had to see the bishop that time."

"Bishop Reynolds?"

"No. He wasn't the bishop then."

"Okay... and what happened with the bishop?"

"I knelt in front of him. He asked if I was sorry. I said yes. The bishop blessed me and told me to make a good act of contrition and remember my body is a temple."

"That's it?"

"That's the way it was every time, except one time when Bishop Reynolds or Monsignor Moroux sent me to a psychologist in Thiberville, who I saw two times. The doctor told me that I did these things because of the stress and he said I should take up some hobbies like golf and tennis."

"Every time? How many times were there?"

"Well, before Amalie I was in six... seven other parishes and each time I was transferred because some boy said something to his parents and they brought it to my pastor or to the chancery directly."

"Every one of those complaints was known to the chancery?"

"Yeah, right. The vicar general, Jean-Paul, dealt with these things just like he did this time."

"Were they recorded?"

"That's what I was told once by Jean-Paul. He said all this was kept in something they call the secret archives."

"You're telling me that before you were assigned to the parish in Amalie there had been six, seven, or more occasions when you were in the seminary and later as a priest when pastors, the vicar general and the bishop would have been aware of complaints about you having sex with children, complaints you admitted were true each time?"

"Un-huh, they knew everything about me, how I was, what I had done."

I was physically exhausted. A week with no sleep was taking its toll all at once. I knew I could not go back to the airport and fly back to my life. I told Dubois I needed to make some phone calls. He brought me to the nurses' station and a nurse showed me to an oversized telephone booth.

Fishing a card out of my pocket, I phoned the limo driver and asked him to buy a bag of ice and a bottle of vodka, and to sink the bottle in the ice.

Then I called my secretary, Monique, in Thiberville. I asked her to book me into the Park Lane Hotel in Manhattan and to reschedule my return flight to Thiberville for Monday. I needed the weekend to myself, somewhere anonymous.

"Mo, if Kate calls you about me, tell her where I am," I instructed Monique.

"You're not going to call Kate yourself? Christ, you don't pay me enough."

After my conversation with Dubois, I didn't want to talk to Kate or anyone else about anything for a long time. While Dubois appeared to be calm, I felt I was unraveling.

When I walked back to the room where Dubois was, he was staring out of a window with iron bars on the outside. "Do they have windows in prison?"

I ignored his question, pushing on to finish my interview. "What was the assignment you had before being transferred to Amalie?"

"I was an associate pastor in Bayou Saint John under Monsignor Gaudet – Father Gaudet. I don't think he had made monsignor then," Dubois said.

"So, before Amalie, you were at Bayou Saint John?"

"I was also appointed chaplain to the Boy Scouts for our diocese."

"Chaplain to the Boy Scouts?"

"Yes, and Cub Scouts. It seems stupid now, doesn't it?"

"It should have seemed stupid then. How did you become chaplain?"

"Bishop Reynolds appointed me with a letter."

"I guess you were caught with Scouts."

"Only once, I think. A Cub Scout. But I had boys in Bayou Saint John too. With Monsignor Gaudet, I never knew what he knew. Monsignor Gaudet was a little whacko. He made me listen to opera on Sunday afternoons. He wanted to find someone who he could have conversations with in Latin. Nobody speaks Latin. He and I hated each other. He must have wanted me to go away, so I was given the church at Amalie as my own."

"Did you meet with the bishop when the parents of the Cub Scout complained?"

"Yes."

"Did the bishop bless you again?"

"No."

"What did he do?"

"He only told me I was being assigned to Amalie as pastor."

"Was there anyone else assigned to Amalie – any other priest, anyone you reported to, anyone who was supervising you – who would know what was going on there besides you?"

"No. I was alone. I was alone except when the boys came over to the house I lived in."

"And the bishop and vicar general of the diocese were aware that you had had sexual relations with children in every place you were assigned to before Amalie? You sure?"

"The bishop and the vicar general knew I had been having sexual relations with children at every assignment, even before I was ordained as a priest. But every time there was a problem, you know, the bishop or Monsignor Moroux would send me somewhere else – to another church parish far away from the one where I got in trouble. Then there would be problems at the new place I was sent to, but nothing like this."

"You had sex with boys at every assignment you had as a priest?"

"I had sex with boys almost every day I was a priest."

27

BLOODY PUPPETS

Thursday August 30, 1984
Doctor Kennison's Office, Thiberville

Everyone called him "Little Will" and said it as one word, "Lilwill".
Little Will Courville would have won a contest for the cutest and
most lovable boy in the diocese. His mom, Hattie, kept his dark
black hair long so that it curled. His eyes were dark and his skin
coloring was like that of an Egyptian. He was a beautiful boy.

Will was in Doctor Aaron Kennison's office, sitting up straight
against the back of a sofa. His feet barely reached the end of the
seat cushion. Every time he came to this doctor's office he felt
sleepy.

Like most of the boys who were Dubois's victims, Will did not
open up much to child psychologist Doctor Aaron Kennison or
social worker Sharon Cassidy. During five months of therapy, the
closest Will had come to discussing his relationship with Father
Dubois was to mumble "Unhuh" to leading questions posed by
the doctor. When asked if he liked Father Nicky, he always said
"Unhuh", and when asked if he was afraid of Father Nicky, he also
said "Unhuh". He said "Unhuh" to everything.

In twenty appointments over five months, Doctor Kennison
had failed to elicit any information, emotion, or expression of
feeling from Will about his experience with Father Dubois. Two
other boys, who cried through sessions and avoided eye contact,
had told Doctor Kennison of the activities they, Will, and others
had observed and participated in during their weekly sleepover at
the Our Lady of the Seas rectory in Amalie. The boys had said

162

Will was Father Dubois's favorite and got the most attention.

The boys were in the doctor's office every week. And now they were also going to the offices of the District Attorney, and the office of their own attorney, Brent Thomas. The DA's staff were preparing the boys to give grand jury testimony in the criminal case against Father Dubois. Their own lawyer, Brent Thomas, was worried that with Chaisson trying to make one lawsuit public all the other cases might end up going to trial in open court. So Thomas was trying to gently prepare the parents and children to be questioned under oath by Church insurance lawyers. The pressure on the kids was intensifying.

Sharon Cassidy had twice before tried leaving Will in the primary-colored playroom of the psychologist's suite, retreating behind the one-way mirror to watch how he interacted with the toys. Both times Will had ignored all of the toys, curled up in a corner of the room in a fetal position, and slept until the session was over.

Today Ms. Cassidy brought Will into the playroom again, sat on the floor with him and tried to talk with him about what was going on in his life. He was not responsive. She asked him to please paint a picture or as many pictures as he wanted that showed how he felt today. She set out the water-based paints, brushes and a stack of blank canvases on the floor before Will. Then she demonstrated how to mix the paints if he wanted something other than red, yellow or blue.

Retiring to the alcove behind the one-way glass, she set up the video recorder and settled in to observe. Will picked up the largest brush and touched it to his face, smiling as the bristles tickled his cheek. Ms. Cassidy was relieved. The last time she had left one of the other boys from the group alone in the playroom, he had done nothing with the toys or paints, but rather had pulled down his short pants and attempted to masturbate while crying and praying half of the "Our Father", before banging on the door to be let out.

Will wandered the perimeter of the room, its bright green shelves packed with toys. He fingered some of the action figures, chose a racing car, wound it up and set it running. When a second car failed to work, Will picked it up and carefully set it back on the shelf.

On a bottom shelf, Will found three small, hand-carved wooden elf puppets. He carefully untangled the strings on two of them, and tried to make the figures move. Then he brought them to the center of the room and set them down on a blank canvas. Picking up a jar, he poured red paint over the wooden puppets and dripped the residue onto the canvas.

Will stood and put all three control sticks in his left hand. Ms. Cassidy glanced at Will's file and noted he was right handed. She made a note that he was not using his dominant hand. As Will awkwardly jangled the controls, the strings became hopelessly entangled into a single cord, leaving the three puppets suspended and welded together. Will stood still with the puppets dangling from his grip. Then he violently shook his hand several times and the elves clacked against each other. Red paint dripped off the puppets and splattered across the canvas.

Brent Thomas's Law Office, Bayou Saint John

While some of the children were in Doctor Kennison's office in Thiberville for their weekly appointments, five sets of parents sat around a conference-room table in Brent Thomas's law office in Bayou Saint John. These parents had gotten along well as neighbors for years, but today the tension in the room was as strong as the silence of the ten people who sat quietly and stiffly. Most of these people had always felt it was a sin to sue their Church. All believed they were harming their children by dragging them through this legal process.

Kane Chaisson was turning into Brent Thomas's worst nightmare. Wiley Arceneaux, owner of the Feed & Seed store, had stopped Brent Thomas on the street and told him, "If it wasn't for my wife

Sissy being your relation, I'd be leaving you to go with Tommy Rachou to that Chaisson fella myself. You better start acting like some kinda lawyer and quit acting like the ugly girl at the dance."

The Chaisson motion to break the seal on the Rachou case against the diocese, alleging negligent supervision against the bishop, was set for a court hearing on Monday. There was no question that Chaisson's sole aim was to blow the lid off of things. Brent's clients were scared their claims would become public too. Some were talking about forgetting the whole thing, rather than having what happened to their sons become public knowledge.

Earlier in the week, Brent Thomas had finally got through to Jon Bendel on the phone for the first time since the Rachou family had fired Thomas and brought in Kane Chaisson instead. Brent asked Jon Bendel directly, "What does Chaisson running the Rachou case out from under me mean for my other ten cases?"

"If Chaisson forces us to try the Rachou case, I am going to advise the diocese and insurance lawyers that we should go to public trial with all of your ten cases as well. If we have to go to trial against Chaisson, we'll have nothing to lose by trying your cases. The damage would already be done by Chaisson." Jon Bendel was lying, but he was convincing.

Brent Thomas believed him. As he listened to Bendel, he worried he might throw up on the handset. Thomas had tried to go it alone with this new batch of cases. He had not called Fort Lauderdale and advised Ricardo Ponce of the existence of this potential two million dollar fee. But Thomas had never tried a case in court. Once he had even lost an uncontested divorce because he did the paperwork wrong and the judge threw the case out.

He knew what he had to do, and he knew what it would cost him both maritally and financially, for his wife Cindy would find it hard to forgive him for bringing Ricardo Ponce back in for a full share of the fee. Brent knew she hated Ponce – and she loved money. After hanging up from the upsetting phone call with Jon Bendel, Brent had finally broken down and called Fort Lauderdale, Florida.

Ricardo Ponce was in Thomas's private office as the families waited in the conference room. Today, Ponce would meet these parents, tomorrow he would meet the other five sets of parents.

"This isn't going to go like the first set of cases, Brent. You know this, don't you? The diocese and its insurance companies are not going to keep handing out millions like candy. We are going to have to do some real work for the money this round. You let the Rachou family get away to Kane Chaisson. Chaisson put the district attorney and a criminal prosecution by the district attorney in the mix. It's all changed. We are going to have to argue the law to stay in court and prove facts to win."

Brent nodded his head repeatedly as if to say "I know, I know, I know already".

Now for the first time since he arrived that morning, Ponce let anger flash in his face. "You filed these new cases without me. You thought you could go the distance alone. You were cutting me out of a million dollars in legal fees. But you couldn't handle it. So, now here I am."

Thomas thought Ponce was going to hit him. Instead, Ponce pulled a thick legal document from his tan leather valise and continued. "Before I do one thing more, you are going to sign this contract giving me 65 per cent of the first million in fees, and 60 per cent of everything above that. And full control of the cases."

"I don't think—"

Ponce stood. "Sign it, Brent, or I'm leaving. You tried to fuck me over. We both know that. After all the money I made you last round, you tried to fuck me. You can't go it alone. We both know that too. Don't even try to run a bluff by me."

Affixing his signature to the document, Brent said, "Ricardo, be delicate with these people in the conference room. They're as good as the people we represented last time, fine people. None of them has ever been in a lawsuit before. Some of them feel guilty about suing the Church. None of them like the idea that their kids may have to give testimony before a grand jury or give sworn testimony to Church lawyers in depositions, and they are all terrified that their children may have to testify in court at public trials in the civil cases and criminal prosecutions. The boys are shutting down all around, cooperating with no one, not even Doctor Kennison, and with most of them their behavior at home is out of control. All of these parents thought these cases would be like the cases their neighbors or cousins had where the kids went to see a doctor, we did some legal work, and the checks cleared. You are going to have to explain what is different this time. You're going to have to keep them from leaving our representation for another lawyer, or keep them from picking up their marbles and going home."

After Ricardo was introduced to the parents, he went through his usual production of removing his coat, exposing his expensive tie, cufflinks and braces.

"Tell me what's on your mind," Ponce said, addressing the group of parents.

A man wearing a baseball cap with the John Deere tractor company logo on it spoke up in a gruff voice, pushing his cap onto the crown of his head. "I'm saying we should forget the whole thing. Our boy is gonna be all right. If he didn't have to come here or go to the doctor's or the district attorney's office, he'd be fine, is what I think. The kind of person I am is… I believe bad things happen sometimes and we gotta just get through the bad times, and I don't think I'm helping my boy by putting him through all this. He cries for no reason. He's scared of everything, he won't sleep in the dark unless the overhead light is on in his room. And I don't think it's 'cause of what happened with that priest fellow but 'cause of what's happening to him now, what we're putting him through. If he was old enough, he might sue all of us too."

The mood in the room seemed to signal a silent assent, an agreement by the other parents that the fellow in the cap was right in all he said.

When Ponce looked at the faces of these people, he did not see the suffering. All he saw was the millions of dollars in legal fees these five families represented, of which 65 per cent was to be his.

"Yes, sir," Ponce began. "What your sons have been asked to endure is unconscionable. What you, as parents, have been asked to endure is beyond my comprehension."

Ricardo Ponce stood and began to pace. "When I was a boy we lived in a really poor barrio in Mexico. My aunt lived next door and she had a cold-water drip and that was our only water source. My parents always had two jobs and sometimes I had to help them at their jobs, and I had to go to school. My father stole books from the houses of the rich people whose gardens he worked in. He couldn't read, so he never knew what he was stealing. He made me read the books out loud to him. I resented my parents. I think I hated the things they made me do. I don't think I ever noticed what my mother and father did for me – not until later, a lot later."

Ponce stopped pacing and stared at the floor for a long time, beginning the close with his eyes downcast, his voice cracking. "Today my parents are my heroes. Before they died, they got to see how all the reading helped me, and for the last years of their lives I was able to make it so they had no jobs at all. They had the strength to do what was right for me when I was a boy. Now I know this."

Ponce paused for a long time, looked away, bit his lip and pushed back on emotions that seemed to be rising within him. "I know when your sons look back on what you did for them, how you supported them through such a hard time, how you gave them the strength to put this maniac priest in prison forever, how you forced the Church to change its policies and procedures... when your sons realize how many little boys you saved from this Father Dubois and from other priests like him, you will be their heroes forever."

Ponce sat down at the head of the table again. Remaining emotional, he said, "What you are doing today is something only God could ask you to do, not something I could ask you to do. I ask you to pray about this. Remember, it is your Church that has abandoned you, not your God. Remember that if we quit, what we are saying is that Father Dubois is more important than your sons; that Bishop Reynolds is more important than your sons. We must never forget that there is no one on this earth more important than your sons."

A lady asked, "Will my Stevie ever have to talk or give testimony or whatever in public?"

"I give you my solemn word on this – on my father's grave. None of the boys will ever have to appear in open court in either a criminal or civil proceeding. And they will not have to go to see a doctor anymore either after the cases are settled."

"You swear our boys won't have to go to court?" the man in the cap asked.

"On my father's grave," Ricardo Ponce said.

When the meeting broke up, Brent and Ricardo went to a Mexican restaurant around the corner from Thomas's office. Casa Grande had sombreros on brick walls and Herb Alpert music in the background. They sat in a booth with frozen mugs of draft beer in front of them, the ice sliding down the sides and making puddles on the red plastic tablecloth.

"Why do you eat here?" Ricardo asked Brent. "Mexican food is loser food. I only eat Mexican when I lose a case. You could jinx the whole deal for us by eating frijoles."

Ignoring Ricardo, Brent went to the top of his agenda. "How could you tell them their kids will not have to continue to see a doctor, Ricardo? Christ, I think one of the mistakes we made with the first group was not setting aside money for medical treatment in the settlement, money that could be used only for that purpose. Don't you think these kids need serious long-term therapy and treatment regimes?"

Ponce sipped a beer and shrugged. "I'm a lawyer, not a doctor. I don't know what they need. Sometimes I think the way that guy in the cap thinks. I think sometimes the kids just need to get through this. If they don't want any more therapy, it's no skin off my back. I just want enough medical documentation to support large monetary settlements in these cases."

"And how could you… how could you promise them their kids would never testify in open court in a criminal or civil trial? You don't know that."

"Nobody knows that. It's what they needed to hear today, so I said it." Ponce drained a third of his beer, retrieved a monogrammed handkerchief from his pocket and blotted his lips.

"Jesus, Ricardo. You were in there swearing on your father's grave."

"My father's grave?" Ricardo glanced at his Cartier watch. "About now I imagine Dad is on the seventh or eighth tee at the Coral Reef Country Club. He lives along the sixth fairway. He's a retired orthopedic surgeon in Miami. He's never seen Mexico. Like me, he hates Mexican food. Jesus, we're Puerto Rican, third generation south Florida. My old man cut me off in college because he found a kilo of pot in the trunk of my car, but he's a good guy. You'd like him. He'd like you. Bet you never smoked grass in your whole life."

Brent Thomas sadly shook his head.

"Damnit, Brent," Ponce said. "We spent three years getting drunk together in law school. There's nothing we don't know about each other. If we play to our strengths in this, we can get more money than we ever dreamed of. You can build a mansion for your wife. I can load up some boat whores and cruise the Caribbean. This is our shot, man, this is our fucking shot. So just relax, can't you? We got through this morning. We're gonna get through the other parents tomorrow. This time around, though, I'm going to have to be better at what I do and I wish you would do more of what you do so well."

"What do you mean?"

"Find some more cases, Brent, some more boys this priest sexually abused. I'd bet all the money we've made and the money we're gonna make that this fucking piece-of-shit priest diddled

every boy who came within spitting distance of him. Dig 'em up.
They're out there somewhere. Tell ya what, Brent – if you can get
some more clients signed up, we'll go fifty-fifty on those legal fees.
Ten more kids would be another million for you, another million
for me. You must have used the first families to get to these
families. Do it again. Get us some more cases. I can handle the
guns. Just get me the ammunition."

"Don't you even care about the children? About them getting
medical treatment? Don't you care about reconciling these
families to their faith, the only religion their families have ever
had for generations? Don't you care about what's right?"

Ricardo Ponce looked at Brent Thomas quizzically. He stood
up and laid a crisp twenty-dollar bill on the table. "You care,
Brent. No one is paying me to care."

28

LIGHT AND DARK

Monday September 3, 1984
Park Lane Hotel, New York City

Only a tiny sliver of light showed through the heavy blackout drapes when the wake-up call came from the hotel switchboard. I had no idea where I was. I stumbled across the room and ran into thick draperies. Pulling them apart, I saw the night lights of a big city. As my eyes began to focus, I realized I was overlooking Central Park in New York City. Disoriented, still exhausted, I fell back on the bed.

The last thing I remembered was walking across the hotel lobby three nights earlier. It was late and the limo had driven me in from New Jersey. I'd had a garment bag over my arm, briefcase in one hand, half-empty vodka bottle in the other. The elevator was mirrored and I had hardly recognized myself in the dimly lit reflection.

Now, as I forced myself up and toward the bathroom, I bumped into two room-service carts and was pleased to know I had eaten, done something besides sleep all weekend. Under the shower, I wondered what had happened to me. It was as if the events of the last week had overloaded the wiring in my body, blown the circuits. I must have collapsed here after seeing Francis Dubois at the Stalder Institute on Thursday and not left the room all weekend.

Now I needed to face the world again, get back to Thiberville.

Old Bishop's House

From New York I flew via Houston, Texas and landed in Thiberville about 10 a.m. I went directly to the Old Bishop's House, where I found Monsignor Jean-Paul Moroux, Thomas Quinlan, and Monsignor Buddy Belair huddled around a television set, watching a video clip of Kane Chaisson. His bald head filled the screen.

It was obvious to me that, despite my recommendation, no pre-emptive statement had been issued by the bishop on Sunday. Thus, the first the public heard about any of this was an articulate accuser's assault.

As I stared at the screen, the camera pulled back to reveal that Kane Chaisson had given this statement in front of Saint Stephen's Cathedral – a few steps from where we now sat. The bells were ringing in the background; he had clearly timed his Sunday morning announcement advisedly. It was classic Chaisson as he railed against the Church. "Both the Bible and the Constitution of our country make a boy equal to a bishop – equal in the eyes of God, equal in the eyes of the law. My client wants me to break the secret seal Church lawyers put on his case tomorrow. The public, especially Catholics, have a right to know that the bishop was responsible for the worst kind of vicious, violent, repugnant, immoral horrors perpetrated on an innocent child at the hands of a Catholic priest."

If Chaisson had been able to ring the chimes once more when he concluded his statement, he would have, but the statement alone was dramatic enough. The piece ended with a long shot showing the high steeple of our landmark church.

I whistled. "Where and when did this air?"

The archbishop's lawyer, Tom Quinlan, said, "Channel 2. Five, six and ten last night. And early this morning, I understand. That's it for Chaisson. The judge is going to put a sock in his mouth just about now. Bendel's filed for a gag order on all counsel as well as an order barring the press from being present in the

173

courtroom for the hearing this morning. Joe Rossi's close to the judge. There shouldn't be a problem."

Switching off the video recorder and television, Quinlan continued, "Jon Bendel and Joe Rossi got to the *Thiberville Register* late last night and there wasn't a word about this in the paper this morning. But I understand that a lot of media are down at the Bayou Saint John courthouse right now."

I was impressed that Kane Chaisson had managed to seize the moral high ground from the Catholic Church, not an easy thing to do in these parts.

10:30 a.m.
Courtroom, Bayou Saint John

Concluding his argument to Judge Amos Simon, Jon Bendel said, "In the final analysis, Your Honor, it is the position of my clients, the Catholic Diocese of Thiberville and Bishop Reynolds, that we seek only what is in the interest of the young boy who is the plaintiff in this legal action. We are asking the court to exercise its discretionary power to protect this child of a tender age, to ensure his identity is shielded from the media and the public. We request that, firstly, you close all legal proceedings relating to this lawsuit to the media, barring the press; and, secondly, that you order that the seal of secrecy remain in place, which will forever protect the young child from having his identity publicly revealed. Finally, we ask that your order extend to commanding all legal counsel to refrain from commenting to the press. Thank you."

Bendel was not in his chair before Chaisson was on his feet, his voice booming. "Your Honor, I've no words to address the arrogance of the diocese and bishop. They come before you today, represented by Jonathan Bendel, and pretend to care for my client, a child of nine. Yet they showed no concern for him over three long, torturous years when he was being sodomized by their priest. It's a little late for them to assume a pious stance in this matter. The only secrets Mr. Bendel seeks to preserve are the dark secrets of a bishop and his diocese. If there is something that someone has to hide from the world, it is not my client. The press has a right, in fact a duty, to inform the public of the secrets Mr. Bendel's clients want to keep hidden away in a vault in this courthouse. We respectfully request that you deny the motion of Mr. Bendel in all parts."

Judge Amos Simon poured himself a glass of water, took a swallow, and began. "The court admonishes all representatives of the media to respect and protect the privacy of the party to this litigation who is of a tender age. Should the child's name be mentioned by any media organization, a contempt citation will be issued for the arrest of any reporter who violates the order of this court. As regards the motion Mr. Bendel filed on behalf of his clients to bar the press, to keep the lawsuit sealed, and to place a gag order on the lawyers involved in this litigation, the court denies the motion in all parts."

Noon
Old Bishop's House

A delivery from a seafood restaurant was spread on the table. As Moroux set a pitcher of tea and cans of soft drinks at one end of the table, he apologized that his help had the day off. Sister Julianne and Joe Rossi had arrived. We were waiting on Jon Bendel to return from the Bayou Saint John courthouse.

Twice I was pulled aside. First, Monsignor Moroux motioned for me to join him in the kitchen, where he asked if I could come by later that day. I told him I had a late-afternoon meeting with District Attorney Sean Robinette. "Come tonight then," he said. "I will be here in the residence or in my office. This back door will be unlocked."

As I left the kitchen, Joe Rossi grabbed my arm and guided me to the back porch. Rossi blew his nose into a handkerchief. "Funny,

Renon. You leaving my luggage on the sidewalk in front of Antoine's like that Wednesday. Real funny. Everyone was headed back to Thiberville before I realized I was stuck in Noo Awlins. I ended up in Bendel's love-nest apartment in the French Quarter with a window air conditioner blowing on my head all night. Caught a damned cold. But I'm gonna forgive you."

"Hey, Joe, I didn't apologize."

"Look, Renon, so we don't see all this stuff eye to eye, but we're all in it to the end. Trust me, son, you don't want to fight this one without friends. And you don't wanta fight with me. I'm the last person I'd want as an enemy."

The porch door opened behind Rossi. Jon Bendel motioned for us to come inside. He was pulling off his coat and loosening his tie. The unflappable Jonathan Bendel looked rattled.

Turning to look straight at Joe Rossi, Bendel said, "Joe, your good friend Judge Amos Simon caved in like a cardboard suitcase. You said he would hold, but he folded. He denied the gag order, refused to bar the press, and he unsealed the Rachou lawsuit. We lost on all counts."

Monsignor Belair blurted out his shock. "Kane Chaisson won?"

Bendel looked at Belair like he was an idiot child. "Right. The Rachou suit against the diocese is no longer sealed. It is open to the press and the public. The clerks are burning up a copy machine down at the Bayou Saint John courthouse right now, making copies of the Rachou file for the press."

"Shit," Rossi said, then nodded to the nun. "Sorry ma'am."

Bendel poured a glass of tea. "The good judge was so shook up he let Kane Chaisson run wild when the hearing started. Chaisson first filed a two-hundred-page supplemental brief into the record that probably traced the public records doctrine back to the time of ancient Greek civilization, maybe to the time of hieroglyphics. Then Chaisson's oral argument danced back and forth between the constitution and the Bible. He was good. The son-of-a-gun is a powerful orator when he gets a head of steam."

The diocesan spokesman, Lloyd Lecompte, rushed into the room in a sweat, literally wringing wet with perspiration. "Did you see the noon news on Channel 2? Did anyone see it?"

No one spoke.

Lecompte dropped video cassettes on the table. "It's on all the channels. But Channel 2 was the worst. The reporter read directly from Chaisson's lawsuit. It seemed like he was reading for a half hour. The paragraphs he concentrated on were allegations of negligent supervision on the part of Bishop Reynolds. And... and he said a subpoena was filed in the record by Chaisson moments after the hearing, a subpoena which seeks the production of the personnel files of Father Francis Dubois. He named him – he actually said his name. And though he didn't name others, he said thirty-one other priests' personnel files were also being subpoenaed by Chaisson."

Rossi stood and addressed Monsignor Moroux. "I gotta get to that station manager at Channel 2, unscrew his head and pour some sense into him."

Lecompte tried to get the floor back. "I think we have to issue a statement. We ought to read it at my office across town and keep the cathedral out of the picture. It was horrible what Chaisson did last night – using the cathedral as a backdrop for an attack on the bishop and the diocese. Horrible. We need to work on the statement now, I think."

Tom Quinlan cleared his throat loudly. "Mr. Lecompte, why don't you use the monsignor's office and begin working on the statement. We'll join you later. Right now I think we need a meeting of just counsel with Monsignor Moroux."

Turning to Moroux, he asked, "May we use the bishop's office?"

Quinlan, Bendel and Moroux rose and started out of the room, running into Rossi, who marched by, announcing, "I'm going to see those sons-of-bitches at the TV stations." This time Rossi did not apologize to the nun for his language. He just grabbed a handful of fried shrimp, wrapped them in a paper napkin and headed for the door.

Tom Quinlan turned around and said, "Renon, why don't you join us?"

As we moved through the hall connecting the residence to the chancery, the lights were out in the windowless passageway. We walked into the dark.

Once we were seated in the bishop's office overlooking the Saint Augustine Cemetery, Tom Quinlan said, "Renon, we have to know now. Is there any chance, any chance at all that you can get Father Dubois to do the right thing and plead guilty now? Right now? This week? End this?"

I shook my head. Quinlan just stared at me. Bendel sighed, blowing the air from his lungs. Quinlan grunted once, cleared his throat and turned to Monsignor Moroux. "Monsignor, Kane Chaisson just gave us a great gift by running his mouth on TV. We have an opportunity to do some clerical housekeeping. Before the sun comes up tomorrow, we need you to go through all the personnel files of active priests in the secret archives and purge any material that could cause scandal to the Church."

I kept my eyes on Monsignor Moroux. It seemed that life was draining out of him. His body was limp.

"Here's the thing, Monsignor," Quinlan said, "and I'm confident both Jon and Renon will concur. You see, if you receive a court order commanding you to produce a document, then you must comply and hand over the document described in the subpoena. However, if the document does not exist at the time the subpoena arrives, then you cannot very well hand it over, can you? Because it simply does not exist."

Jon Bendel caught Quinlan's drift. "Monsignor, these personnel files that Chaisson is subpoenaing... we don't know the names of the thirty-one priests yet, and we will not know that until the subpoena arrives. So, the personnel files of all active priests will have to be purged."

"I don't understand," Monsignor Moroux said.

As was his habit, Quinlan cleared his throat again, albeit softly this time. "Monsignor, we are talking about sanitizing the personnel files. We have an obligation to protect innocent priests and their reputations. And Church law imposes an obligation on one in your position, on all of us, to do whatever is necessary to protect the Church from scandal."

"You're saying I should cull all the personnel records," the monsignor said, "and remove any unfavorable or damaging material? I cannot do that. I won't. We have to maintain these records. The next bishop, my successor as vicar general, and all future administrators of this diocese will need access to the information in these files in order to evaluate priests and plan assignments. I will not do what you ask."

Quinlan was composed and condescending. "Monsignor, as a matter of policy, we have many of our corporate clients shred tons of material on an ongoing basis to avoid documents falling into the wrong hands and being misinterpreted in litigation. It is standard strategy in corporate litigation. You have to make the other guy prove their case. You don't prove it for them."

Monsignor Moroux shifted in his chair, sitting more upright. "I will not do this. Jon can fight this in court for us. I will refuse to turn over the files of men who are not involved in this case. I will not destroy any part of any record pertaining to any priest. I am not giving the court anything but the records for Father Francis."

Quinlan shook his head. "Jean-Paul, we're old friends and I have immense respect for the reverence in which you hold the secret archives of this diocese as well as your resolve not to turn over the files. But we're going to have one of our priests in prison soon. We don't need two of our priests in jail. You may well go to jail yourself for contempt of court if you defy the order to produce subpoenaed documents. The judge might even jail the bishop as well. We cannot let any damaging information out of our possession."

"How could the files of thirty-one other priests be relevant to a case involving just Father Francis?" Moroux asked.

The monsignor was looking directly at me. It seemed he wanted to hear from me. "Monsignor, hypothetically, if a situation existed where this diocese – people like yourself in the chancery, even the bishop – knew about Dubois's problem with little boys before the first complaints from Amalie came in, if there had been similar situations in other parishes and the response of Dubois's superiors had been inadequate – so inadequate as to constitute negligence – then Chaisson scores big in court. And if Chaisson can show through the use of these other priests' files, and testimony, that there have been other priests in the diocese with similar sexual problems, and that the method of handling their problems and Dubois was so similar as to be identical, he will say that there exists a pervasive pattern of neglect and disregard for the welfare of children in this diocese. If he can argue that priests who are known sexual predators have been assigned and reassigned to places where they have access to children, then Chaisson raises the stakes so high that it's really winner take all. A monetary verdict from a jury could be monumental, astronomical."

"Then, Renon, you're saying you agree that I have to – as they say – 'sanitize personnel files'."

In one of the worst moments of my life I responded, "Yes, sir." I knew I had violated every ethical, moral and legal standard I had ever believed in and had sworn to uphold. I was so exhausted, completely drained, that I just gave into the two strong willed lawyers who were advocating that Monsignor Moroux destroy material that might be the subject of a court subpoena.

Quinlan said, "Monsignor, Kane Chaisson is taking a broad swing at the Church, trying to knock it out. When we finish with a little clerical housekeeping, Chaisson is going to hit nothing but air. He'll be shadow boxing."

29

WHISKEY RIVER

Monday afternoon, September 3, 1984
The Levee Bar, Whiskey River, Louisiana

District Attorney Sean Robinette was in jeans, a plaid shirt and cowboy boots, standing at the end of a pier off the backside of the Levee Bar, tossing pieces of bread to fish circling under the pilings. I stopped at the bar and picked up a long-neck beer before walking to the deck to greet him.

"I think you need a hook to catch fish," I said.

Without turning around, Sean said, "Sometimes a net is better."

When Sean did face me, he did not extend his hand. Professional and personal formalities were not part of our relationship.

"Wow, ya look like shit, Ren! What happened to you?"

"Just tired, Sean. Beat to hell."

Sean moved to sit on a high stool as did I. He chucked all the bread to a school of bream below.

We had battled hard more than once and our friendship had stayed strong. He would take me fishing and make me do all the work on his boat, always promising some favor in return that never materialized. Once we sent a jury out at mid-morning on a case that required a unanimous vote for a verdict either way. As we sat in Sean's office at noon, he punched his speakerphone and dialed the bailiff's office. "Let's see what the jury ordered for lunch," he said.

A deputy picked up the phone and told us, "We got an order for eleven cheeseburgers, eleven fries and eleven Cokes."

Sean laughed. "You've won. Got a hung jury. One of those jurors is so mad at the others that he or she will not even eat. You know something is wrong when I gotta have twelve to win but you only need one to keep from losing."

I knew Sean liked me as much as I liked him. We respected each other, and I believed that somehow we could get through the Dubois case with our relationship intact.

He caught me off guard a bit when he cut to the chase quickly.

"I am giving you notice that I'm going to grand jury. It will be this week or next. The next couple days, I hope. You're not going to make me extradite him, are you? I don't want any John Wayne crap like what happened in the Baton Rouge airport. I'm going to get him for life sentences, but there isn't going to be any parent shooting him in an airport. He's gonna die of old age in prison."

I understood the reference. The prosecutor in Baton Rouge had recently refused to file criminal charges against a man who murdered a pedophile who had abused his son. The shooting happened at the airport while TV news cameras were filming the criminal's return to Louisiana in the custody of policeman. The Baton Rouge DA's action in that case made it open season on child molesters in Louisiana.

"Okay, Sean. No extradition. No media circuses. I'll bring him back. You tell me in advance. I'll go get him and bring him back the day after the indictment comes down and we can arraign him then."

"Will you be ready to plead him guilty at arraignment?"

"To what?"

"To life."

"Look, you need twelve jurors to get him. All I need is one juror who won't order lunch. If I hang the jury, then we will be doing it all again, having a new trial. How many times you want to do this? Of course I'm not going to plead him out to life. For now, I'm going to plead insanity. We'll go to trial before I throw him away for life."

"Ren, you can tell your colleagues, Jon Bendel and Joe Rossi, that I don't want any more phone messages from them. I won't even take a call from the Pope about this Father Dubois business. I asked to see a lawyer who represents Dubois. They sent you. I'll deal with you and no one else."

I just nodded. I was exhausted.

Sean switched gears again and doubled back on me. "I've talked to the kids."

I stared at the sunset.

"I know you know, Ren. You know what happened. Out of the priest's mouth it might sound awful, but when you hear the boys tell it, it twists your guts."

I had nothing to say, but my guts were twisting too.

"Fold your hand, Ren."

I smiled and shook my head, and touched his arm as I turned to leave. "I never fold. I always ante-up, make the bet until the last card is played on the poker table. You know that."

"Living that way is going to be the end of you one day."

The sun was sinking toward the water line and the sky glowed over the swamp as I made my way back down the levee to my car. Just hearing Sean talk about the kids was all it took to twist my guts.

30

NO ONE'S INNOCENT

Monday evening, September 3, 1984
Diocesan Chancery, Thiberville

Between the cathedral and the chancery, street lamps flickered and illuminated an old bearded fellow walking near the angel fountain, carrying a sleeping bag and a rucksack, heading in the direction of the Saint Augustine Cemetery behind the great church. He stopped at the fountain, put his belongings on the ground, cupped his hands and splashed water on his face. After shaking the water off, he whistled and a shaggy puppy came running out of the cemetery, wagging its tail and jumping up on the man's leg. He stroked the dog and then the two of them sauntered off toward the tombs.

I waited a moment and then walked onto the plaza, past the fountain, trying to see where the drifter had gone. As I reached the edge of the graveyard, I saw Monsignor Jean-Paul Moroux through a large window in the bishop's office. There was only lamp light in the room. Moroux was backlit, hunched over, looking like a gargoyle in profile, his shaggy hair hanging over his face like a mane.

The door to the kitchen of the Old Bishop's House was unlocked. From there I made my way along the dark corridor connecting the house to the chancery. When I reached the doorway of the bishop's office, I saw Moroux standing over a large plastic trash can. The noise from its paper-shredding machine blocked out everything else. High, neat stacks of files covered the bishop's desk, the leather sofa and part of the carpeted floor. I stood watching Moroux, waiting for him to take a break, not wanting to startle him. He was wearing dark shoes, dark socks, black trousers and a white sleeveless tee-shirt. There was a tattoo on his upper left forearm, a shield or coat of arms.

Moroux caught me staring. He turned off the shredder and slapped the machine, saying, "A gift from Tommy Quinlan, delivered this afternoon. Top of the line, I think."

He realized I was not looking at the machine, but at his arm. He touched the tattoo, smiled and said, "An African shield. Mountain tribe. Got it near the Sorbonne when I was studying in Paris. I was on a three-year scholarship to study philosophy. Spent it all studying African art, culture and history. Got drunk and tattooed. Yes, I've been drunk and tattooed in Paris."

I must have looked surprised, if not shocked. Moroux's hair was a lot longer than I had realized and it hung down over his face, almost covering his eyes until he pulled it away.

He laughed. "Yes, Renon. In Paris I listened to jazz and lived a student's life. Almost stayed there, the way all of us almost do something in life we should have done."

"You really studied in France?"

"I studied everywhere. The old bishop who was here believed in education and he had more than enough priests without me. There used to be so many priests that the average church parish had two, the larger parishes three. The old bishop sent me anywhere I wanted. I studied in Rome and Ireland too. In Ireland, I collected some blackthorn walking sticks and downed pints; in Paris, it was Armagnac, jazz and tattoos. Rome was… Rome was… a place without a soul. I got nothing from Italy. It's a belligerent country, so proud of wonderful things that happened hundreds of years ago in the arts that they haven't painted a building since. In Ireland, they educate with a Socratic discourse. In Paris, everything is in the libraries rather than the professors' heads. In Rome, everything is hidden, nothing is learned – maybe nothing is known."

I took a seat and, pointing to the stacks of files, said, "Are any of these men innocent?"

"No one's innocent. It's all about degrees of guilt, isn't it? Guilt and shame. No one's been innocent since Eden. We're all guilty and we feel our guilt and shame in proportion to degrees of discovery, what others learn about us. The more others know of our sins, character defects or failings, the greater our guilt and shame. We're strange creatures, no? It does not seem to matter to us that God knows everything we've done. We respond more strongly to what fallible humans know and think of us. Isn't that what I'm doing tonight? Eliminating any chance that the guilt and shame recorded in these files will be discovered by other fallible human beings?"

"I don't know what you're doing or what you're destroying."

"No, you don't. I am the only person who will ever know what was in these files. Our bishop only reads golf magazines. When I die, a lot of people's guilt and shame will die with me."

Moroux took a hit from his newly lit cigarette and resumed shredding files.

I stepped out to the receptionist's desk and dialed home. "Hi, Kate."

"God, where are you? Where have you been? I know, I know... I could have found you by calling Mo. The days of me having to talk to a secretary to find my husband are over, Ren. Did you forget it was your birthday yesterday?"

"No. No, Kate. My birth—" I couldn't finish the word. I shakily sat in the secretary's swivel chair. Kate must have heard my hard breathing.

"Ren, you okay?"

"My birthday? I didn't even remember my own birthday?"

"The kids had balloons, presents, cards, cake. Your dad was here with pictures of you from birthdays long ago. Sasha refused to go to her room last night. She slept on the sofa with your gifts, waiting for you to come home. Are you still out of town? There was something on TV about the priest stuff last night and again today. Kane Chaisson was on."

I felt a wave of nausea rolling through me. I had always loved my birthday, especially after the kids got old enough to give me silly gifts. "My birthday? How old am I?"

"The kids were really upset. Sasha was furious. It's not funny."

I knew it was not funny. All I could say was, "Later. I'll be home later. I'm at the chancery. It might be late."

"Good. I want to talk to you. We need to talk, Ren."

"Yeah. Me too. I want to talk. Kids okay?"

"Other than being upset over you missing your birthday yesterday, they're great. Everyone's fine, but I'm worried about you."

"Well, the phone's not good."

"No. I'll see you later. I do love you, Ren."

"Uh huh. Me too."

I'm now thirty-seven, or am I thirty-six? I thought. I was so tired. Just this morning I had woken up in New York. That seemed ages ago.

The sound of the shredder stopped. Moroux walked over, took a chair and grabbed the pack of smokes.

"Monsignor, when I drove up I saw an old man going into the cemetery. To sleep, I think."

"With a dog?"

"Right."

"Every night he's there. For months now. They say he was a priest somewhere once. They say he carries a breviary, a book priests read every day."

"An ex-priest?"

"There's no such thing as an ex-priest in canon law."

"I want to talk about Dubois," I said. "I'm going to tell you straight out that the things I said today when we were talking with Quinlan and Bendel about sanitizing these files were not hypothetical, Monsignor. I now know that Dubois was having sex with little boys dating back to the seminary and that people in this chancery, including you, have had knowledge of his criminal behavior from the beginning. Over twenty years."

Moroux walked around the desk and sat heavily in the bishop's chair. I could hardly see him over the stacks of files on the desk.

"Is all that other stuff about Father Francis going to come out in this case? Isn't this case just about Amalie?"

"Sooner or later – sooner, I'd bet – you and others are going to be ordered by a court to give sworn testimony in depositions, to tell the truth about everything."

Moroux coughed. "The truth about Amalie and Father Francis's time there will not be any problem. Of course, I will answer everything truthfully about that. What I don't understand is how the scope of inquiry can be this broad, how it can go beyond Amalie, into his past as a priest of this diocese. What Father Francis did in Amalie ought to be the sole issue, right?"

"What you and the bishop and others knew or should have known about Dubois before you assigned him to Amalie, and what you and others in the chancery did or did not do to prevent injury to those children in Amalie, will clearly be relevant in the Rachou case. My bet is Chaisson will get all of that into evidence easily. It seems to me, from what I learned from Father Dubois, that your negligence and that of Bishop Reynolds is the kind of negligence the law calls willful and wanton – criminal."

"Well…"

"May I have a copy of Dubois's file?"

"I'm sorry. Jon Bendel specifically told me no one could look at these files."

"I don't want Dubois's file sanitized – shredded. I don't want you removing anything from Dubois's file, Monsignor. Can you promise you will keep his file intact?"

Moroux nodded his head, slowly. "I will remove nothing. I will not even look at his file. You're his attorney. I will follow your instructions. I'm sorry I cannot let you look at the file now."

"This just gets crazier every day. The diocese wants me to represent him, but I cannot see his personnel file."

"That is how it is. But let me ask you about something we didn't cover this afternoon that has been bothering me since I pulled all the records from the secret archives. It's bothered me all evening."

"What's that, Monsignor?"

"We-ell, suppose I am ever put in a position where I am asked if I destroyed documents. What do I say?"

I was too tired to think. I shrugged.

"Lie? Do I?"

I shrugged again, then I said, "Quinlan and Bendel weighed in that what you are doing tonight is not illegal. I don't know. Morally, this is obviously way across the line. Is it technically obstruction of justice? Even if it's technically legal, no one would ever understand a monsignor shredding evidence under subpoena."

As Moroux walked me to my car, he brushed his hair straight back over his head and I could see his full face again and the obvious pain in his eyes. When I was in the car with the motor running, Moroux was still standing next to my car door. I pushed a button and the window came down.

Moroux sighed. "Renon. The reason I asked to see you this evening is this... Well, you see, I have to be involved in this. I have no choice. I've been involved a long time. I must do these things, but you don't have to be involved. I think things may get very bad. If there is such a thing as karma, then what is going to be visited on the diocese, maybe the entire Church, is not something I would wish on anyone. You did not cause any of this and you don't have to be part of it. I wanted to kind of give you permission to withdraw before anyone knows you are involved. We could find another lawyer for Father Francis."

"You'd find a lawyer who would tell Dubois to plead guilty to a life sentence so he'd kill himself?"

"No. I swear I would not let that happen. I just wanted to offer you a chance to… you know, to take your leave of the proceedings before they begin. You can go quietly now. Once it starts, I don't think it will be quiet again for a long time."

"Thank you. I will remember you offered this. I believe I'm gonna go the distance."

31

PORCH TALK

Midnight, Monday September 3, 1984
Coteau

Winding along the country road on the way home, I had the windows down and the moon roof open. I could hardly stay awake. I could not reconcile the conflicts within me; I could barely even identify them. Since becoming involved in the case, I had spent a lot of time thinking about doing the right thing, even arguing with others about what was right, and now I believed I had witnessed or participated in an act that by any other name amounted to obstruction of justice.

The house was quiet. Purple and gold crepe paper draped the kitchen, the colors of my team, the LSU Tigers. An uncut sheet cake was set out on the den table. I looked at the cake and candles. I saw gouge marks in the cake that I knew could be matched to Sasha's little fist.

Kate was in the den thumbing through gift catalogues.

"Have you slept? You have dark circles under your eyes again."

"I slept all weekend, I think. I'm just really tired. It's been a long week. I must have over a hundred phone messages at the office and I worry that everything is coming unhinged there. I'm just kinda overloaded."

"Can we go outside to talk?" she asked.

"Sure."

I went to the refrigerator and got two long-neck beers. I cradled them under one arm as we held hands all the way out to the guest cottage.

When we reached the cottage, Kate turned on some of the landscape lights, including the green light I had had an electrician install on the far bank of the pond. We settled in rocking chairs on the porch.

"Ren, I'm worried about you."

I nodded. "I feel like I am drowning and I have a long way to swim. Something is really wrong in the diocese, I think, and I don't think anyone's going to try to do the right thing. Someone has to get it right for the children somehow."

Kate stood up. "You missed your birthday, Ren. You forgot your own birthday! What does that tell you? It tells me you're coming apart fast. You gotta get away from this stuff."

I said nothing.

"Sasha was so hurt, so disappointed, she acted out her anger. She beat up the cake – pounded it with her little fists. She thought she was mad, Ren, but she was scared and hurt. She slept on the sofa with your gifts so you would wake her up when you came in. I carried her to bed in the middle of the night. She woke up this morning and when... when you weren't here, she said she was scared something happened to you."

There was a long silence. I couldn't think of anything to say.

"Ren, I really think our marriage has been over for some time. It doesn't matter how it died – I killed it, you killed it. It doesn't matter who killed it. The marriage is dead. If we stay in this, one or both of us is going to die emotionally."

"I've been here a lot this summer, Kate. I'm here right now."

"No you aren't. You're never here. I bet you even money that right now, at this minute, you're thinking about some law thing. Yeah, you're thinking about some law thing. I know it. It's sad, Renon. People should not be sad so much. I really can't take it anymore."

She kicked a flower pot off the porch into the shallows of the pond.

"No, Kate."

She wiped her tears with her shirttail and said, "I will stay as long as I can. I really love you so much my heart hurts, my throat's raw, and I wish I could stay for—"

She was finished talking about this. I always knew when she was finished. I was relieved that she stopped as suddenly as she had started. Kate took my hand and walked me into the guest cottage, guiding me to the bed.

"Let's talk, Ren. Tell me."

"Children," I said. "God, I don't even know how many children, Kate. You wouldn't even want to know the things done to them. I know some of their names, but I think there are a lot of children whose names I don't know, will never know. I've never felt like this. I don't know what I can do. But I can't walk away."

I told her everything from the lunch at the Old Bishop's House to my essentially agreeing that Monsignor Moroux lie under oath about having destroyed evidence. When I finished, there was a faint light in the sky.

Kate sat up on the bed, cross-legged. She addressed me like I was a child. "Ren, don't you see? There's not just one. The diocese has a nest of perverted priests. That's what I think they are covering up."

"What?"

"They have a nest. I think that is what they all know that you don't know. They would not be expending all this money and energy if Dubois was the only one. Having one pervert couldn't hurt them."

"You think the diocese has a bunch of guys like Dubois?"

"Well, yeah. That's what I think."

"Kate, I'm so tired."

"I know, Ren, I know."

"Tell me you will stay with me till this is over. Can you tell me that?"

"No, Ren. I love you, but I can't tell you I will stay another day. We wore this marriage out a long time ago. I'm as sorry as you are."

"Just till this is over, Kate. Just—"

"Ren, I will stay as long as I can, okay? That's all I can promise you."

She lay down and held me in her arms. "Try to sleep a little. I'll wake you in a couple hours. Okay?"

I liked feeling her heart beating close to mine, hearing her breathe.

32

POLICING THE PRIESTS

Friday morning, September 7, 1984
Jacques' Café, Thiberville

Johnny Wilcox, a retired state trooper and the best private investigator I knew, had picked up a copy of the subpoena list containing the priests' names from my secretary, Mo, at my office Thursday afternoon. He set a meeting for 7:30 the following morning at what he referred to as his office – Jacques' Café, a downtown eatery.

The diner was crowded. I had never gotten there early enough to find out what time they opened. The owner, Tee-Possum Reaux, Little Possum, tasted everything and his huge girth attested to that. Everyone called him Possum, just as they had his father, because he always seemed asleep, even when standing behind the register.

I sat across from Wilcox. We were served by the waitress everyone called Turtle, an ancient black woman who moved slowly. It was useless to specify a breakfast order with Turtle. She would not write it down because she couldn't write, and she wouldn't remember it because she didn't try to remember. She just told the kitchen to give her whatever came to her mind.

"I've got the list, Ren. What d'you want me to do with it?"

"I want you to dig up anything and everything you can on these thirty-one priests. Skip the first name, Father Francis Dubois."

"And I would be looking for what exactly? Stealing from the collection plate?"

"Sexual abuse of children."

"Oh, that," Johnny said with an exaggerated air of nonchalance. "Just that? And just exactly how am I supposed to find that kind of information? Ask the priests? Ask the kids in the neighborhood parishes?"

"Johnny, if I knew how to do this, I'd do it myself. All I can say is that I know less than a handful of priests – just the ones who are or have been in parishes where my kids go to school. And every single one of them is on that list."

"Look, I'm not going to bullshit you, Renon. I don't think I am going to turn up anything. I don't see how I can. I don't know why I'd do this thing. I think it is useless and I'd just be wasting your money."

"Why don't you look at it this way, Johnny. You will be getting paid, getting a little closer to that new bass boat you talk about all the time."

"Speaking of that, my boat's hooked to my truck around the corner. I'm on my way to fish the Atchafalaya Basin from here."

"What do you do with all those fish you catch?"

"Throw 'em back. Same as I do with the people I catch. When I was a cop, I kept the people I caught, locked 'em up, and I kept fish too. Now, I throw everything back. If I kept the fish I caught, there would be no fish left."

"You ever use bacon and popcorn as bait?

"No. Why?"

"I heard it was good bait. My daughter says it's magic bait."

Johnny Wilcox nodded slowly. "Popcorn and bacon."

"Okay. Let's eat whatever Turtle wants us to eat," I said.

"Whatever Turtle wants..."

The Palms, Thiberville

When I left Wilcox, I drove to an old house filled with memories. The house had once belonged to my grandfather. Now my father lived there alone. I knew my father could have seen the television interview with Kane Chaisson, and I knew that soon my name would be tied to Father Dubois in the media. It was time to talk to him.

As I approached The Palms, as the old estate was always called, I felt apprehensive. My father was a better man than most men I knew, and he was a man of faith. Like many sons of aging fathers, my feelings about him were mixed with sadness and regret about what might have been. My father had miraculously managed to hang onto his goodness, a lot of his naiveté, and even some of his innocence well into his eighties. If I could not imagine Father Dubois doing the things he had done, I was certain my father would never grasp these things.

The long driveway had once been lined with sixteen palms, which my grandfather always believed had been brought in from Cuba. My father thought they were grown on a farm in Pensacola, Florida. I remembered the tall palms. For the rest of my life I would love palm trees and love places where palms grew naturally. They did not grow naturally in Thiberville. Disease killed some of the palms and others were knocked down by hurricanes. As I turned into the drive, I noticed that the last palm seemed to be doing well.

I let myself into the house and wandered through the maze of downstairs rooms. My father's hearing was all but gone and I did not want to shout, nor did I want to walk up and startle him. As I slowly made my way to the glassed-in back porch, I heard him speaking French in a soft voice.

He was across the room when I saw him, sitting in a rocking chair. His eyes were closed and he was unaware of my presence. In his first language, French, the only language he knew as a young boy, he was reciting his rosary, a mantra for a man grown old.

What could I tell him? What could I say to him?

Every morning he went to Mass and communion. Since he'd moved to The Palms, he walked to Mass at Saint Stephen's

Cathedral. He even went to Mass on mornings when he was sick, leaving his bed to pray in the place where he had invested all of his faith. I knew there were a lot of people like him in the diocese. In a way, I believed my father and the faithful laity were going to become collateral victims when they learned the truth about their bishop and the monsignor, about how they had consciously sacrificed children to save themselves and their Church from scandal. I wanted to talk to him before he found these things out from the media. But as I watched my father pray the rosary in French, I lost whatever words I had prepared to tell him about the Dubois situation. There was no way to explain.

When we were children, he would gather us every night to pray as a family. My mother would read from the Bible and my father would lead us in the rosary. When I was confirmed, he gave me a sterling silver rosary. I still had the rosary, in its small cloth pouch in a drawer at home. It had been years since I had seen the rosary and I imagined the silver beads were tarnished. I no longer had any idea of how to recite the rosary.

Now I really wanted to say the rosary, to pray the rosary with my father. Instead, I slowly backed out of the doorway without interrupting him, made my way through the great room and let myself out. Once in the drive, I walked over to the last palm and put my hand on the tree. Closing my eyes, I imagined I could still hear him, slowly rocking in his chair, praying the rosary in French.

PART FOUR

THE PROCEEDINGS BEGIN

33

THE BELL SOUNDS

Tuesday morning, September 11, 1984
Coteau

The call came early. When I heard the voice on the phone, my heart raced. It was District Attorney Sean Robinette.

"Ren, I can't wait. The kids and their parents have been through enough. I've got to get them through the grand jury. We will meet late this afternoon – at a rural schoolhouse, to make the children more comfortable and to avoid the possibility of some reporter hanging around the courthouse discovering us. I will have an indictment before the ten o'clock news tonight."

"What will you release to the media?"

"You know me. Name, rank and serial number. I won't tell the press anything. My office will release a written statement listing the counts of the indictment. We will advise that you are Father Dubois's counsel and that you have agreed to waive extradition and return the defendant voluntarily to this jurisdiction so he can be formally arraigned."

"O-kaaay, I'll go get him."

"You should get out of town this morning. Or you're gonna have a lot of company, a planeload of media going with you. You have my numbers. Stay in touch. We'll work out his return. Don't come home until we talk. Got it?"

"Wait," I said. "Sean, what do you expect the indictment to be?"

"Enough to make sure he's never in a place where he can do anything like this again."

"I'll leave this morning. Call you tomorrow."
"You be careful, Ren. You and that priest."

By the time we hung up, I was wide awake. Both Sean and I knew exactly what he was alluding to when he signed off. There were already rumors of people around Bayou Saint John who planned to murder Dubois. Sean did not want some vigilante act to end Dubois's life.

In the kitchen, there was coffee. I called my secretary. Mo was huffing and puffing as she paced on her treadmill. In short order, she had flights and a hotel booked for me. To avoid being traced and found, I was not going anywhere near the Stalder Institute. I was going back into Manhattan and would stay there until everything was in place to bring Dubois home.

"Call me tonight. And Ren..."
"Yeah, Mo?"
"Watch your back."

Tuesday night
New York City

Mo was waiting for my call from New York.
"Hey," I said.
"Hey back."
"You got it, Mo?"
"I got it. It was the lead story at ten. According to the news, the indictment contains three counts that carry mandatory life sentences, twenty counts than run up to twenty-five years each – then I lost track of the other counts. Channel 2 did say Father Dubois was in a lock-down facility. I don't know where they got that. They said that you were representing him, and that the district attorney expected extradition would be waived and Dubois would return this week to be arraigned."

"Okay. They won't find me. I worked it out at the desk with a hundred-dollar tip and I'm registered in this hotel under the name Richard Starkey."

"Okay, Ringo. You be safe."

I turned out the lamp and sat in the dark next to the window, looking down on Central Park from my thirty-fourth-story perch. I was moving into uncharted waters, and would be going farther from home than I had ever been, to places I had never wanted to see.

I wanted to call Kate, but she knew me too well, knew my voice too well. She would hear fear in my voice. I never wanted anyone to know I was scared of anything. I pulled the nun's card out of my wallet and turned it over to where Sister Julianne had written her home phone number. I thought about calling her. Instead, I dialed room service for a bottle of vodka.

Looking at the lights of the city and relative darkness in Central Park, I remembered I had been here just over a week ago, in this same hotel with this same view. It seemed like years ago. Everything was moving fast and at the same time everything seemed to be fading fast to a distant memory. The night sky was like a blank canvas. I could have painted any image I wanted in my mind but nothing came to me.

Wednesday September 12, 1984

My early-morning call to the Stalder Institute presented unexpected problems. When I advised the nursing supervisor on Dubois's wing that I would be picking up Father Dubois and accompanying him to Louisiana, I was told he was not allowed to go anywhere.

"What do you mean you will not allow him to leave? He is checked in on a voluntary basis. There is no court order to hold him."

"Sir, I have my orders from the director. Just as I was coming on duty last night, the patient received a phone call and learned that there had been television news about criminal charges against him in Louisiana. He said the caller told him he was going to prison for life. He totally destabilized. He is on suicide watch again with one-on-one supervision around the clock."

"Who in the hell called him and told him that?" I asked.

"Let me get the phone log and check."

I waited a few minutes for the supervisor to come back on the phone. "Here, I have it. Walter Dubois. A brother."

Dubois's pedophile brother, the one who hated him. The one who'd worn the Saints jersey and had choked back a laugh when I broke the news to the family about their son and brother. The one who'd phoned me.

"Ma'am, if he does not voluntarily return to Louisiana, there will be a court hearing up there in New Jersey to extradite him. Going through that hearing will do more damage to him than going back home with me. The last child molester extradited to Louisiana was gunned down in the Baton Rouge airport while he was in police custody. We don't want to go through an extradition hearing we can't win and travel with the media surrounding us."

"All I can tell you to do is to put in a call to Doctor Dobson after nine this morning, or maybe the director of the Institute, Clay David. But I don't think they will release a person who is on suicide watch. If he did kill himself because of this, someone could sue us for negligence. It would be unprofessional and irresponsible – actually malpractice – and would create huge legal issues if such a patient were allowed to walk out."

Understanding I would get nowhere in this call, I signed off politely and quickly dialed another number.

Sean answered on the second ring.

"Sean, you awake?"

"Yeah, but it's kind of early for you, isn't it?"

"Well, I'm up and I have a problem."

"Your problems are just beginning."

I recounted the conversation I'd had with the nursing

supervisor and asked Sean to give me some time to try to work things out.

"I'm not your problem. The media will be looking for him this morning. They're not gonna stop until they find him. You better tell those people at the diocese not to disclose his location. Otherwise—"

"The diocese won't talk to reporters."

"I will hold this info tight. What airport will you both be flying out of?"

"Philadelphia. And we will be flying tomorrow. You can book that, Sean. I will do what I have to do to get him out of the place he's in and we'll be heading back tomorrow."

"Okay."

As I was about to ring off, thinking of Sean having to handle all those children in a grand jury setting, I said, "I don't envy you for what you had to do yesterday."

"I don't envy you for what you have to do today," he said.

The rest of Wednesday blurred. I spent the whole day on the phone. When I finally got through to the Stalder Institute's lawyers, they were tough. After exploring every possible option, I had Mo send them my financials via a telecopier to substantiate that I was worth more than any claim that could be made by a relative in the event Dubois killed himself after we walked out of the institution. I took full legal and financial responsibility, agreeing to indemnify the Stalder Institute in the event Dubois died by suicide as a result of being released into my custody.

It wasn't suicide that concerned me. It was homicide. Someone might be lying in wait for him when we arrived in Louisiana.

I called Sean Robinette to confirm that Dubois and I would be coming home the next day. Sean said, "Good. I need to confirm some things. Tomorrow two detectives from Bayou Saint John are going to meet you. Their names are Wade Melancon and Samuel Delcambre. They're good guys. I picked them myself. They will meet you at Philadelphia airport at the US Air check-in counter any time after noon. Renon, don't go freelancing or improvising on me. Don't you leave Philadelphia until you hook up with detectives Melancon and Delcambre."

"Detectives are meeting us? For what, Sean? Why?"

"Just to help you come home, Ren."

"How will I know these guys?"

"They know you."

I ordered a car and driver to take me down to Jersey, where I visited with Director Clay David at the Stalder Institute, signed legal documents accepting responsibility for Dubois, and received permission to take him back to Louisiana the next day.

In a nearby Holiday Inn, I tried to sleep. It was a pointless exercise. That evening in the motel restaurant, I finally had a meal. A burger and a Coke float.

34

DEATH THREATS

Thursday September 13, 1984
Philadelphia – Thiberville

Detectives Melancon and Delcambre were good guys. They were polite and deferential to the priest, explaining that they were only in Philadelphia to escort us home. We made our way down the concourse to the boarding area. I accompanied Detective Melancon to the counter for check-in.

We were not going direct to Louisiana. Later, I learned the media had all Louisiana airports staked out. The plane we were boarding was flying to Houston Intercontinental. When the detective laid the four ticket folders on the counter, I realized that Dubois and I were not ticketed in our own names. Dubois was flying under the name Sean Robinette, and in some twisted private joke, Sean had me ticketed in the name of Eloi Labat, a judge I despised, and who would be presiding over the trial.

When we boarded the plane, Dubois took a window seat and looked out at the sky. It turned to night shortly after we took off and Dubois stared into the darkness the whole way to Texas. On his lap he held the parcel of new clothes we'd bought in a mall on the way to the airport. I'd picked out a suit, shoes, socks, a tie and two shirts for him. The colors were earth tones. I knew there was no way to make this man acceptable, even presentable to the public, but I hoped he would appear sincere. On no account was I going to allow the DA or the sheriff to parade him through a courtroom dressed in an orange jail jumpsuit, or worse, have Dubois insult the world by dressing as a priest.

In Houston, we followed the detectives through the airport and took a shuttle van to a small hotel on the outskirts of the airport property, where Dubois and I were put in the back of an unmarked police unit. Melancon drove and Delcambre gave directions. It was after 2 a.m. when we approached the Louisiana boundary with Texas at a place called Orange.

Detective Melancon swung the car off the Interstate and into the parking lot of an all-night diner. He parked the cruiser near some garbage dumpsters. Inside the diner, Delcambre picked a booth toward the rear, directing Dubois and me to sit with our backs to the door. Delcambre, Melancon and I ordered full breakfasts. Dubois passed. Said he wasn't hungry. He asked for a coffee and one of my cigarettes. While we ate, the detectives talked with Dubois about duck hunting.

Back at the car, the detectives pulled guns and ammunition from the trunk and locked and loaded the weapons. They put the guns in the front of the car and Dubois and I took our places in the back.

As we crossed the Sabine River into Louisiana, the car was doing nearly a hundred miles an hour, bouncing over the uneven marshland road. "Sorry. We gotta beat daylight into Thiberville," Melancon said. We exited the Interstate at a closed service station in Pont Soileau, twenty-five miles out of Thiberville. Melancon went to a pay phone. I followed him. He poured quarters into the phone, dialed, and instantly said, "Yes, Mr. Robinette. We're in Pont Soileau now."

It was just after four in the morning and Sean had obviously been waiting for Melancon's call.

"I got it," Melancon said into the phone. "The bridge. Bridge is open. Bridge is closed." Hanging up the receiver, fishing out his change from the coin return slot, Melancon turned to me and said, "It's a code we have. Let's go. They're waiting to catch us in Thiberville."

When we turned off at the first Thiberville exit, we were the only car on the wide avenue as we traveled the first hundred yards. Then we began to get company – another unmarked unit pulled in front of us, a second came up behind us, and one flanked us on our left. I assumed they were also armed. No one in our car spoke.

At the university football stadium, the convoy turned left toward the Thiberville courthouse. Melancon made a radio call, identifying himself as SO, or sheriff's office, unit one, calling base.

"This is SO Base, come back," the voice said. It was Sean Robinette's voice. He was handling the dispatch desk at the sheriff's office at 4:30 a.m. I was too tired to even try to figure out what Sean was doing on the police radio at this hour.

"This is SO One," Melancon repeated. "Is the bridge to Baton Rouge open?"

Robinette came right back. "SO One, there's traffic on the bridge. Repeat. Traffic on the bridge."

Before Robinette finished speaking, our whole caravan took a drastic left turn, heading away from the courthouse. As Delcambre gunned the powerful engine, Melancon almost dove over the seat, grabbing me and pushing me to the floor, Dubois on top of me. We stayed there, feeling the car careening wildly through the streets of Thiberville.

The radio crackled again, and Sean Robinette's voice said, "SO One. SO One. Bridge open. No traffic. Bridge open. Close fast."

Melancon said, "SO One to Base. Roger that. Closing fast."

As the car made a sharp right-hand turn and accelerated, Melancon shouted toward the back of the car, "Stay down!"

Other than the sound of the motor racing, the only noise was metal slamming on metal as Melancon made ready the guns on the floorboard in front of his seat.

The car stopped so suddenly it felt like a crash. As the police unit rocked on its strong suspension, all four doors opened at once and there was a lot of shouting. I was pulled from the back seat first and found myself in the grasp of four or five cops. I got a glimpse of others with shotguns pointed toward the street, but only a glimpse. The cops were running with me in their arms. My feet did not touch the floor until we were in an elevator. "Sorry, Mr. Chattelrault," said one of the young deputies, whose face I recognized, "DA Robinette's orders."

The elevator stopped on the top floor, the jail. The young deputy led me to a small office and asked me to wait for Mr. Robinette. He gestured to the coffee pot. I poured a cup, deciding to drink it black, something I had never done before.

Father Dubois was equally disheveled when he joined me in the office. He was trembling. Neither of us spoke. We both knew something was seriously wrong.

When Sean walked in, he was wearing a tight-fitting tee-shirt that identified him as a policeman, blue jeans, cowboy boots, and a pistol snapped into a holster on his hip. He offered both Dubois and me cigarettes from his pack. Dubois took one with a shaking hand. When Robinette handed him a lighter, he had difficulty getting the flame to the cigarette. Dubois studied the Zippo with a flight of ducks engraved on it, then returned it to Sean, saying, "Thank you, Mr. Robinette. That is a beautiful lighter."

Sean handed the lighter back to him. "You keep it."

The DA was not the only official awake early that morning. It was not even 5 a.m. and I saw the sheriff in the hallway. I was confused, but too tired to think.

"Let's go ahead and get the pictures, fingerprints and booking entry done," Sheriff Crozier said. We followed him into the hall.

The pictures took an instant. As they began printing Dubois's left hand, a deputy shouted, "Man on elevator!"

No one touched Dubois but four deputies immediately grabbed me, lifted me off my feet, and hustled me back to the office, slamming the door shut behind us. There was coffee all over me. I grabbed some paper napkins and sat in a metal chair, blotting my shirt. The deputies left.

From the hallway I heard a shout, "It's the doughnut man on the elevator. All clear."

Sean walked into the little office a moment later. I was still dabbing my shirt.

"Sean, if you don't mind, if it's not a lot of trouble, would you mind telling me just exactly what the fuck is going on here?"

"It seems some people want to kill you, Ren."

"Me? Who? Who wants to kill me?"

"I don't know. There have been death threats phoned into Mo at your office. Two threats against you came into my switchboard, one downstairs in the sheriff's office, and the *Thiberville Register* and Channel 2 got calls telling them to watch you die. I only know it's not been the same voice on every call."

"I see."

"That's why you came in as you did, at this time when everyone is sleeping. We decided not to tell you about it until now. There was nothing you could do from where you were. A good cop from narcotics has been covering your office and Mo. We have uniformed guys at your home. They are outside, not inside. And I have some good men assigned to you when you walk out of this building. They will shadow you."

"Somebody wants to kill *me*?"

"My guess is some people want to kill your client. I imagine they don't think they can get to the priest since he's in custody and has police protecting him. The news people made it sound like the bishop has hired some hot-shot, high-priced, asshole defense lawyer to try to get his priest off scot-free, so I guess they want to kill the lawyer if they can't get to the priest. So, they're gonna kill you, Ren. I think that's about the size of it."

Sean was standing. I was seated. First, I looked at the floor for awhile and then I looked up at him. "You blame them, Sean?"

A deputy escorted Dubois into the office and Sean and I stopped talking. It was explained to Dubois that he would have an isolated cell in the jail infirmary, far away from the other inmates. I was assured that after his luggage had been searched, the clothes we had bought in the mall would be brought to him.

The arraignment was set for 10 a.m. I told Dubois I would be back upstairs with him before then and would ride the back elevator from the jail to the courtroom with him. Sean then took me down to the fourth floor, where the courtrooms were. Under the battery of fluorescent lights, I saw two large metal detectors.

"I had these set up so we can screen anyone trying to gain entrance to the courtroom. Realizing you might make some kind of complaint about this, or preserve some objection on the court record about this somehow prejudicing your client, I want you to concur with the procedure, agree in writing before the arraignment."

"I'm tired, Sean. I haven't slept in two nights. Shit, I don't think I've really slept for a long time. I don't understand what you are saying."

"What I am saying is that there are some cases where convictions have been overturned, convictions of organized crime figures, because of the elaborate security procedures put in place for those cases. Appeals courts have ruled that such procedures may have sent a message to jurors that their lives were in danger, influencing them to vote one way or another."

"Hell, I'm not worried about any of that. But I do want you to have these things torn down and removed, placed out of sight, before the courthouse opens for business."

"You want me to tear them down?"

"Right. Get rid of them."

"Why? Why do you want them down?"

"Because I think whoever made those death threats against me is going to be here this morning. If it appears we are afraid of them, it will empower them. They will get stronger. If we don't appear scared, I think they will go away."

"You're taking a risk I don't want you to take."

"It's my call. You said it's my call. May be the last time I am in charge of anything in this case, and I want these things gone."

"You're sure?"

"A shooter doesn't call and a caller doesn't shoot. If someone

211

was going to kill me, they would just kill me. There would be no advance warning."

Sean brushed his hair back and let all his breath out. "A shooter doesn't call and a caller doesn't shoot? You're gonna gamble your life on that?"

"Right. And I don't want any cops at my house. I don't want police riding around with me either. I appreciate what you've done, but please pull 'em off."

Sean nodded. "You aren't scared of the Devil, are you?"

"The Devil? Yeah, you bet your ass. I'm plenty scared of the Devil."

35

INNOCENT BYSTANDERS

Friday morning, September 14, 1984
Coteau

Kate was standing in the kitchen when I walked in at first light. She crossed the room quickly and took a swing at me. I grabbed her arm and held off the blow.

"You crazy fucker. Look what you've done to us now. Cops are everywhere, all over our land."

"Kate…"

"I told the chief cop to clear off our land. He said the DA ordered this. I called Sean Robinette and told him to go to hell. Some spook of a monsignor called yesterday to see if we were okay. Okay from what? I didn't sleep all night. There were police flashlights everywhere on the property. I locked up the dogs in the house 'cause they were going crazy. Sasha's horse freaked and almost ran itself to death in the corral. This is the last fucking time I stay up all night because I am married to Renon Chattelrault. This is the last night I'll be married to Renon Chattelrault. Why are there cops everywhere? Nobody will tell me. Does someone want to hurt me or our children?"

"No, no. They don't want to hurt you or the kids. Someone said they want to kill me."

"Oh, that's great. Some son-of-a-bitch is going to kill you in front of our kids."

" Kate…"

"You brought all this into our lives. I told ya, dammit. I told you to quit this stuff. This is the Church's crap. You're just somebody to stand between the public and the bishop to obscure the truth."

"I'm home…"

"Fuck you! Look what you brought home with you."

When I tried to pull her to me, to hug her, she jerked away.

"I told you in the little house the other night that I'd stay as long as I could. This is it. E – N – D. The fucking end."

"Everybody's fine now, Kate."

"No. Everybody is not fine, dammit. Nobody is fine. Wednesday, Jake got picked on at school. Kids were screaming at him, attacking him in the playground, saying that his father is a pervert. Some kids fought with him."

"Jake got beat up?"

"No. Jake did not get beat up. Jake kicked their asses. Who won the fight is not the point. Don't you get anything? Winning is not always the point, dammit."

"I know, I know."

"It doesn't matter. Wednesday night, Jake announced he was not going back to school. He did not go yesterday and I doubt I can get him to go today. When all this was discussed Wednesday night, Sasha refused to go to pre-school. Shelby even had a tough time at Saint Paul's with his classmates, but it was only verbal."

"I'll talk to the children this morning."

"Damn right you're gonna talk to the children this morning. Damn straight."

Kate walked over and poured a cup of mocha. She looked at me from across the room. "I'm gonna let the kids sleep a bit longer. You can clean up. It looks like you have mud all over you."

"It's just coffee. Spilled coffee. That's all."

The children were at the breakfast table. Sasha was still clutching her stuffed Disco Duck under one arm while she ate cereal. I hugged them and kissed them all on the cheek.

"Guys, I'm going to talk to you about what is going on in our lives. I was dumb to think this stuff would not affect your lives. I believed it would only affect me."

Shelby was stoic. "It's not so bad. We talked about it in class some. Nobody understands why anybody would defend this priest for what he did. I don't get it."

"The people at your school aren't alone, ya know," I replied. "My dad and others are gonna have questions too, I think. The United States is better than some other places in many ways. Other places are better in some ways. But one thing we have is a good justice system, a constitution. We're all equal in the eyes of our law, even a really sick guy like this priest. And I think he might be real sick."

"Constitution?" Jake said.

"It makes us different than communists."

"Does the Father have a consti-rution, Papa?" five-year-old Sasha asked.

"Yes, he has what lawyers call constitutional protections. This is one of the things that make us different from communist countries."

"I know all that," Shelby challenged me, "but tell me why you are doing this? I want to hear your reasons from you."

"First, I believe this man is very sick. I hope to find out what made him do the things he's charged with. And I hope we get a chance to have him treated medically to cure or arrest whatever his sickness is. He has been abandoned by everyone but his family and they are in no position to help him. Secondly, I really do believe all of us are equal under the Constitution, and I believe we all have rights that need to be protected and asserted on our behalf, which only a lawyer can do for us. Finally, I believe if I do my job right, maybe some good can come out of this. For the children – the little kids he hurt. I want to do something for the children who were hurt."

Jake seemed more relaxed. He raised his hand like he was in class. "What about the cops in the driveway and at the stables? Do we need police to protect us?"

"They're leaving today. Mr. Robinette sent them here so you would feel safe while I was bringing the priest home."

"I like 'em. They're really nice. When I was fishing yesterday, one of 'em put worms on my hook, yucky worms," Sasha said.

"Well, I'm sorry, Sasha. I know how you like to have servants, but your worm hooker is leaving today."

Turning to Jake, I said, "I'm going to the Bears football game at four today and I want to see you play. I know the rule. If you are not in school today, then you cannot play in the game."

Jake nodded.

"And you, Sasha, will you be in school today?"

"Whatever Jake does."

"Okay, you guys get ready for school," I said.

"Can you help the little kids he hurt?" Sasha asked.

"I really hope so."

36

THE ARRAIGNMENT

Friday September 14, 1984
Thiberville Parish Courthouse

When I got to Dubois's cell, he was dressed in his new suit. He was sitting on the bunk. I took a seat next to him.

"You okay?" I asked.

"Somebody… a guard, I guess it had to be… somebody told the prisoners I was in here. They screamed at me from down the hall for a long time. Just after we got here. They talked about things they were going to do to me tonight."

"Nothing will happen, Father. No one can get to you. They're just hollering."

"Everyone feels this way about me, don't they?"

I was not going to lie. "There have been threats on my life. Some people saying they are going to kill me because they can't get to you. So, yeah, I think there are people who would like to do you harm. They're all in shock. They just learned about what happened in Amalie. It's going to be my job to make them understand you are sick."

"I don't think it will matter."

"Maybe not. All we can do is what we can do. The first thing I am going to do is to try to get you out of here and back up to the Stalder Institute so you can begin a real treatment regime. I think DA Robinette would like you out of here too and Judge Labat will do anything the DA tells him to do."

A warden came to tell me I had a conference call in the office with Mr. Robinette and Judge Labat. The jail was just waking up and as I made my way to the office it was hard to keep focused above the din of breakfast carts squeaking across the hall, utensils banging, and prisoners shouting incomprehensible slang. The jailer closed the office door so I could hear. The call was brief. Sean did almost all the talking. We wrote a script for Dubois's arraignment.

"Ren, there are going to be more plainclothes cops in the courtroom than spectators," Sean said.

"Okay. Call when it's time for us to go down."

The warden gave me a phone book and I found the number for Saint Joseph's Elementary School. Kate had dropped Jake off at the front door of the school that morning, then parked and waited in the Principal's office. She intended to wait through the morning recess to see how he fared in the playground, but that wasn't necessary. When I got through to her on the phone, she said she was just about to dial my office and leave a message.

"Jake's homeroom teacher came to the office after first hour to give me a report. She said the first thing they did today was current events, and Jake's hand was waving in the air. When she called on him, Jake went up to the front of the room, faced the class and said, "That priest who molested those children in Amalie. My dad is his lawyer. The priest is really sick. There is something wrong with the priest that made him do these things. He has a right to have a lawyer because this is the United States. My dad is not going to quit being his lawyer. If it was not for guys like my dad, we would all be communists."

"Well, it's good that he's okay, if a little confused."

Kate laughed. "I feel better. You going to the office after court?"

"No. I want to see Jake's football game this afternoon and Shelby's tonight, so I'm coming home to nap first so I can stay awake for the games."

"I'm coming to court," she said.

"You never come to court."

"I wanna… for the children, Ren. If something happens to you…"

"It's gonna be all right, Kate. They have a lot of security. I'll see you at home. Look, I better go. I'm on the jail phone."

"Oh good. Right here at the end of everything, you got your one call from jail and you called me. I knew if I waited long enough..."

"That's right. My one call from jail was to you. Don't ever forget it."

The air in the elevator was stale. It was warm, but my hands felt cold. Earlier Dubois had asked whether there was danger of a shooting in the courtroom. I told him there would be a lot of armed plain-clothed policemen and a fair number of uniformed deputies in the courtroom as a precaution. As the elevator began its descent, Father Dubois reached into his pocket and pulled out a rosary. "If anything happens in the courtroom, give this to my mother."

I nodded and took the rosary.

We exited the lift into a small, closed-off room outside the courtrooms. "When we get into court," Dubois said, "I want to stand between you and the audience, in case..."

I tried not to show my surprise, and ushered him in.

One of the doors opened and the deputies started moving Dubois and me briskly into Judge Labat's court. I walked behind Dubois, scanning the crowd, curious to see if anyone from the diocese was attending the court proceeding. At first, I thought no one had come and then in the back row I saw Sister Julianne. She wore an expression of curiosity. When our eyes met, she smiled slightly.

Sean Robinette was on his feet when we walked in and before we were in our places he said, "Your Honor, in the matter of criminal docket numbers 4561 et seq.—"

Following the script, I cut Sean off and said, "The defendant waives a formal reading of the indictment and to all counts enters pleas of not guilty and not guilty by reason of insanity, requesting time within which to file motions."

Judge Labat spoke last. "So ordered. Bail set at five hundred thousand dollars."

I nodded to the bailiffs and we were behind the closed door and back in the elevator before anyone had time to realize what had happened or that the proceeding had ended. The arraignment was finished. The legal issues between the State of Louisiana and Father Francis Dominick Dubois were formally joined.

By pre-arrangement, the elevator went to the ground floor before taking Dubois to the jail on the top floor. I wanted to get away as quickly as I could, to beat the pack of journalists who I knew would be crowding onto the public elevators and running down the stairwell. But as I exited the elevator and hustled toward my car, I was body blocked.

Joe Rossi stood shoulder to shoulder with Jon Bendel. Rossi grabbed my shoulders to stop me in place. "You have any idea what you did up there? Goddammit! How many fucking times I told you – guilty, guilty, guilty. Plead the fucker guilty. Get this shit over with," Rossi said.

Smoothly, Jon Bendel spoke in a lower, more modulated tone. "You and your client. Neither one of you amount to one single penny poker chip in this game. You're going to change his plea. Do you hear me? Can you listen to reason?"

"Now!" Rossi screamed in a higher-pitched voice than I knew he had. "Now! Right fucking now! You go up to Sean's office and do some papers and plead this fucking Dubroc—"

"Dubois," I said. "His name is Dubois. Father Francis Dominick Dubois. Why can't any of you remember his name?"

"Do you understand what you are doing?" Bendel asked.

"Things happen when people get in the way of this kind of power, son," Rossi said. "I don't want nothing to ever happen to you. You're playing against real power. Fold your fucking hand, son," Rossi said.

I looked at Bendel, then Rossi, addressing both of them. "Fuck you!"

I took Rossi's hands off of me. I walked toward my car.

Coteau

At noon, I lay under the covers in our bed, hoping for sleep so I could enjoy the boys' football games that afternoon and evening. Kate walked into the room, sat on the bed, pushed my hair back and said, "I made a list last night and I'm going to get onto things Monday, to move you out of here soon. I will find a great place and make it really nice."

"I know it will be nice, but I'll be alone."

"We have to talk about this, Ren."

"God, I'm whipped, Kate."

"I know this is not a good time to talk to you about this, but there's never a good time with you."

"But…"

"Look, Ren, I know you don't have time to even change your shirt these days. I will find a nice place you can rent, furnish it well, and I'll move your stuff there. You can do whatever legal papers you want. I trust you. And with the kids, I want no restrictions. I want you to be with them whenever your schedule allows time for them. You might actually see more of them under this arrangement."

"Why, Kate?"

"Because… because I love you so. I don't want that love to ever die. And it will die if I stay with you."

"Maybe if I was not so tired, that would make sense."

She started to speak again. I put my finger to her lips. "No more, Kate, no more."

"What's the word they say in Mexico that means forever?"

"*Siempre.*"

She kissed my forehead and said, "*Siempre*, Ren, *siempre.*"

37

THE STAR CHAMBER

Wednesday September 19, 1984
New Orleans

Never once had I read a newspaper account or viewed a news broadcast about an event I was personally involved in that had been wholly accurate. I had little respect for journalism generally and had encountered some journalists who were plain dumb. This was not the case with Zeb Jackson, a well-educated, crusading writer who worked independently as a freelance investigative journalist in an era when there was a shrinking market for in-depth reporting. Dealing with a smart journalist is like dealing with the Devil. They always want everything from you and offer nothing in return.

Zeb Jackson was cooking breakfast for me in his second-story French Quarter apartment. As I looked down on Royal Street from the balcony, Zeb shouted from the kitchen, "I would have bought you breakfast at Brennan's, Renon, but I'm waiting on checks. That's what it will say on my tombstone – 'Here lies Zeb Jackson, freelance journalist, who died waiting on a check'. It's the life and death of a freelance writer. They have deadlines to file stories, but there's never a deadline for issuing the check. Hell, this breakfast is probably better than Brennan's anyway."

Phone messages from journalists started piling up on Mo's desk right after the first Dubois news story broke. Zeb called seven times in one day. I ignored other calls, and I wasn't sure why I returned his message or agreed to meet with him. Zeb had dated my younger sister when they were both at Tulane University ten years ago, and it had been that long since I had seen or heard from him. There was that, the fact that I knew him, and there was my belief that the media was very much a "monkey see, monkey do" operation. A strong, well-reasoned report on a major story would be parroted by others too lazy to do the hard work themselves. Thus I had an interest in confiding enough to one journalist off the record to influence his reporting in a way that favored my case. In a word, I wanted to use Zeb Jackson, to convince him of something I myself was not convinced of, that Francis Dubois was legally insane. At the same time, I doubted anyone had ever successfully used Zeb Jackson.

Below the balcony, street musicians were staking out prime spots, and jugglers and painted human mannequins were setting up shop. A fortune teller was arguing loudly with a policeman about a city ordinance that outlawed the crystal-ball crowd; in this bastion of voodoo, they had overrun the French Quarter like locusts. For a moment I thought about visiting Old Harry, my favorite fortune teller, in his alley shop. With Zeb, I decided that, in this opening gambit of what might be a long-running game, I'd play it like the painted mannequins in the street and say nothing.

We ate breakfast from a rickety table. As Zeb poured coffee, he said, "I only know what I read in the paper. That wasn't much. What I want to know straight up, Renon, is this. Is there a story in this Father Dubois stuff?"

"No," I said. "I don't think there's a story. I think there's a book. My sense is it's going to be that big a story before it's over."

"You think it would be worth my going down to Thiberville for a few days?"

"You might want to move to Thiberville."

"That big, eh?"

"Yeah, Zeb."

"What can you tell me about it?"

"Nothing."

"Hell, to get anyone to assign the article – and I have to get the piece assigned in order to have expenses covered – I have to pitch the story. Tell an editor something."

"Tell him what you know already from the press reports. If he or she is not a moron, they will know there's gotta be fire when there's this much smoke."

Zeb stopped eating and poured more coffee. "Renon, from here, from what I read, it looks like there's one really sick priest down there. That's it. Case closed."

"It looks that way to a lot of people. Maybe it's supposed to look that way."

"Will you help me?"

"No."

"You won't help me?"

"No. You can tell me things, ask me questions. I won't volunteer anything, but I will confirm when your information is correct."

After we finished eating, Zeb walked me down to the street, and thanked me for coming. I thanked him for breakfast and gave him my unlisted home phone number.

"I'll see you in Thiberville," Zeb said.

"And next time I will take you to Brennan's and we'll compare cuisine," I said.

From Zeb's bohemian quarters I moved to the elegant high floor of Tom Quinlan's law offices. All of the principal players that had been present at the meeting at Saint John Major Seminary were assembled again in Quinlan's conference room that morning – all except Archbishop Donnegan, Bishop Reynolds, Monsignor Moroux and Joe Rossi. Most of the New Orleans-based insurance lawyers had brought young associates with them. Quinlan introduced James Ryburn, an associate in his firm, who looked like he was too young to have finished high school.

This meeting of all legal counsel had been called by Robert Blassingame. The stated issues on the agenda were: what to do about the subpoena Kane Chaisson had issued for the priests' personnel files, and what to do about the notices for depositions that Chaisson had issued, notices to take the sworn testimony of Father Dubois, Monsignor Gaudet of Bayou Saint John, Monsignor Moroux, and Bishop Reynolds.

Blassingame opened. "The personnel files. Jon, you want to give us a status report?"

Jon Bendel drew a line across his legal pad. "Clean. Not a sentence of damaging material. All those files were sanitized, any damaging information destroyed."

I saw Quinlan's young associate, James Ryburn, actually gulp air and visibly flinch when he heard Bendel flatly admit material had been removed from the subpoenaed files and destroyed.

"The question," Blassingame said, "the question is, even though the files are clean, do we want Chaisson to get a look at them – to have any kind of victory?"

His question was rhetorical, and he continued uninterrupted. "The files clearly have no relevance to the Rachou case. Maybe it is not a good idea to have plaintiff lawyers poking around in our secret archives. If we give in to Chaisson, we'd have to give the same stuff to Ponce and Thomas and any other lawyers who might file lawsuits. We should refuse to produce the files. Let the judge decide."

"I do not see how our judge could let him have a look at those files," Bendel said.

Blassingame pushed his reading glasses to his forehead. "I seem to recall that you were also sure your judge was not going to allow the last hearing to be in open court or allow the seal on the Rachou case to be broken. Are you as sure about this, Jon?"

Bendel bristled. Tom Quinlan, ever the gravelly voiced diplomat, verbally stepped in to separate Bendel and Blassingame, and suggested a compromise. "We could offer the court alternatives. File a motion to quash Chaisson's subpoena for the files, and in the alternative suggest that only the judge review the files and determine whether they are relevant to the Rachou lawsuit."

Looking directly at Blassingame, I said, "The solution to the files situation, to the entire Rachou case and the other cases that

Ponce and Thomas have, is all one and the same. Enter a stipulation of liability on behalf of the diocese. Admit the obvious – the diocese is legally and factually responsible for their negligent supervision of Father Dubois."

Blassingame's glasses fell from his forehead to his nose. "It's not your place to plan legal strategy for our clients. It's our money in play."

"Christ," I said. "If you stipulate the diocese is liable, which they obviously are, you stop all the depositions and other legal discovery in their tracks. No more subpoenas, no depositions of diocesan officials, no diocesan documents. Announce to the court and public that the diocese is doing the right thing morally and legally. Then the Rachou trial will not be about what the bishop did or didn't do. It will simply be about what Dubois did, and involve the testimony of the psychologist who treated the child and an independent psychologist appointed by the court to examine the child. And all the jury will decide is the extent of the injuries and how much money the child gets. In that scenario, the bishop wears a white hat and rides a white horse, and the payout will not be inflated by the jury's inflamed anger at the diocese. You guys with insurance on the line would probably make a huge saving."

Blassingame pulled his glasses off and spun them across the table where they fell into James Ryburn's lap. "None of this is any of your business, Renon. Your client does not have one penny at stake here. We stand to lose millions. I'll be damned if I even understand what the hell you are doing in these meetings."

I was seated closer to Blassingame than I had been at the meeting in the seminary and I was distracted just looking at him. His scalp was completely bald and his head had knots, lumps, and markings like liver spots. A cheap toupee would have been easier to look at than his skull. When he took his glasses off, his eyes seemed to lose all focus. He looked like a blind man. But there was something else that kept me staring at him. He had not only lost all the hair on his head. Blassingame had no eyebrows.

Recovering, I responded. "My client is a named defendant in all the lawsuits. We are all on the same side, want the same result."

"I don't think so. My client's writing the checks. You are not in our area of mutual interest."

"I tried to tell you last time we met that Father Dubois has agreed to identify all his victims and I feel that the diocese has a moral obligation to reach out to those victims, and—"

"Shut it down, Chattelrault," Blassingame shouted.

"Look, Bobby." At the very mention of someone calling him "Bobby", Robert Blassingame turned purplish red. "I'm not one of your flunkies. You're not going to talk to me this way."

Blassingame seemed to be rising out of his chair. I was about to stand, hoping for a shot at him, when Tom Quinlan stepped in again to referee and send us back to our corners. "Okay, fellows. There is a lot at stake here. We all want the same result. Let's move to the next item on the agenda. We have these notices of depositions set for next Thursday, the 27th, at Chaisson's office. He wants to take the depositions, statements under oath, of Bishop Reynolds, Monsignor Moroux and Monsignor Gaudet, and, of course, Father Dubois."

Blassingame said, "There's nothing we can do but prepare our witnesses. You will do that, Jon, right? And Chattelrault, you will prepare this Dubois fellow, right? We will instruct our clients not to answer anything that does not deal with the Amalie situation directly." Looking at me, Blassingame said, "And I don't want Dubois to say a damned thing. Let him assert his Fifth Amendment constitutional right not to incriminate himself, assert his right on every question, answer not a single question after he gives his name."

"We both know the law does not allow Dubois to assert his Fifth Amendment right not to incriminate himself in a civil case," I said.

"I do not want Dubois talking under oath or any other way."

"One moment you say we have no common interest. The next moment you are trying to run my defense of Dubois. I'll call the shots in my case."

"I apologize," Blassingame offered insincerely. "I want what is in Dubois's best interest," he lied.

A woman from Quinlan's office produced a tray of coffees and a pitcher of water and glasses. Some of the attorneys helped themselves. Robert Blassingame and I never broke eye contact.

Tom Quinlan said, "There is a point here that may be of some controversy that Robert needs to talk about."

Everyone turned to look in Blassingame's direction. "I issued a notice this morning to take the depositions on the same day Chaisson wants to take the sworn testimony of the bishop and monsignors. My notice is to take the sworn testimony of Celeste Rachou, Tommy Wesley Rachou, and Donny Rachou. I will question each of them under oath."

"What?" Bendel asked. Jon sounded smooth but I think he was as ruffled as I was by this news.

Blassingame folded his glasses and stuck them in his top pocket. "Chaisson made the kid's case public. He wants the kid treated like any other litigant in Louisiana. Well, I am going to give the Rachou kid the same treatment any other litigant gets. The kid is gonna put up or shut up. And I don't think a nine-year-old can step up, so then Chaisson is going to have to draw down. And we'll settle Chaisson's Rachou case, buy it just like we bought the first six, the same way we're gonna buy the ten cases Ponce and Thomas have."

Tom Quinlan's associate, James Ryburn, swiveled in his chair and seemed about to bolt from the room. It was apparent to me that this young lawyer was upset.

"Let me make sure I understand," I said. "You are going to cross-examine a nine-year-old boy who was sodomized by a Catholic priest since he was six?"

"And I'm going to cross-examine his parents, Celeste and Tommy Wesley Rachou. The negligence of the parents in this case is something the court is going to hear about. What kind of parent entrusts a child that young to spend nights at the home of a priest who is not a family member?"

"Devout Catholic parents," I offered.

Blassingame threw his file into a briefcase and snapped it shut. "Some people may not have the stomach for this case," he said pointedly, clearly meaning me. "This kid, this Donny Rachou, damned well knew what he was doing was wrong too. And he is going to give me that under cross-examination. The kid is not free from fault and neither are his parents. I'm going to prove that."

"Prove that to who?" I asked. "Who in the hell will you ever convince? Dubois is a sick son-of-a-bitch, but there's some sick sum-bitches in this room too," I said.

Blassingame stood. "This meeting is over."

Young James Ryburn was the first one out of the room, rushing. I lingered. As Blassingame was walking past me, he stopped. "You know, sometimes I really think we ought to lock you and Dubois out of our house."

"Fine with me, Bobby. You want a war, you can have one."

"You threatening me? The diocese that hired you? You threatening us?"

"You go after that Rachou kid and I'm gonna go after you."

"You be there next week. I'm going after all three – mother, father and child."

38

MOTHER, FATHER, AND CHILD

Thursday September 27, 1984
Kane Chaisson's Law Office, Thiberville

Well over a half-million dollars' worth of luxury cars bearing New Orleans license plates were parked against the Chaisson building when I arrived. There was a television truck in the corner of the lot. I knew the TV cameraman. Our paths had crossed often. He was setting up a tripod on the roof of the truck. "Billy," I shouted. "Don't you guys travel in a pack? Where's the rest of the jackals?"

"At the courthouse for the load-in shot. Got four possible shots today. Dubois getting in the car at the jail, getting out here, getting in here, and getting out at the jail. I heard network wants some footage fed to them."

Inside, a young lady guided me to a conference room with an adjacent room big enough to square dance in. The Church lawyers were sitting or standing in the conference area as the court reporter unwound cable and set microphones on the teak table.

I saw the Rachou family huddled in a corner of the big room. I walked straight to them and put my hand out. Without hesitation, Tommy Wesley Rachou took my hand and nodded. His wife, Celeste, nervously smiled, while the boy, Donny, stared at his shoes.

To the parents I said, "My name is Renon Chattelrault. I am the lawyer for Father Dubois."

Celeste Rachou stiffened visibly.

"We're all gonna get through this somehow, Mrs. Rachou. I've got children about the same age as Donny."

Mrs. Rachou looked real hard at me. "But you don't know."

"No, ma'am. I don't know. I will never know."

Trying to remember the Rachou dossier, I said, "Donny, you look like a baseball player to me."

The boy reached around to his back pocket and pulled out a ball cap. "I got my cap with me. That's my team. The Redbirds." The cap was a knock-off of the Saint Louis Cardinals logo.

I took the cap from Donny and inspected it. "Well, I'm happy it's not a Yankee cap."

The boy grinned.

"Donny, I know Mr. Chaisson told you what was going to happen today. Some men are going to ask you some questions. I wanted to say hello because I don't have any questions for you. I won't be asking you anything. And I will believe everything you say because I know you're gonna tell the truth."

"That's good," said Tommy Wesley Rachou. His voice was deep and did not seem to go with his slight frame.

Turning back to the boy, I asked, "Are you an infielder?"

"Yes, sir. Shortstop and second base. We were in the playoffs this summer. I hit a home run under the legs of an outfielder. It rolled in a water ditch and he was scared to put his hand in the water."

"A home run is a home run, Donny."

Celeste Rachou looked at her watch. "Do these things start on time?"

"The notice said ten o'clock, but it's not gonna be ten until Mr. Chaisson decides it's ten."

A door to the parking lot opened and a handsome young man walked in wearing pressed jeans, casual loafers, and a polo shirt under a raw silk sport coat. All three Rachous turned to him, and Donny smiled broadly.

"Aaron Kennison," he said as he put his hand out.

"Renon Chattelrault."

Looking down at Donny, Doctor Kennison said, "Good, you remembered your lucky cap. I wore my lucky socks."

Donny smiled again.

The door banged open from the parking lot and the black suits entered with the subtlety of a coal train, the bishop leading Monsignors Moroux, Belair and Gaudet. The bishop glanced at the Rachou family with an expression of disgust. Tommy Wesley Rachou gave the bishop a steady stare as he passed by. The anger in Celeste Rachou's eyes was violent. Donny kind of trembled and Doctor Kennison touched Donny's hair, calming him.

Kane Chaisson entered the conference room like an enraged bull entering a bullfighting arena. Intimidation was his game and even in his seventies he remained an imposing bear of a man. Though blessed with a fine head of hair, he had decided to start shaving his skull clean in his thirties because he believed it made him look uglier, scarier. He had multiple chins, huge ears, and hanging jowls. Everything about his huge head was as fleshy as his bear-sized palms and long fat fingers. Local lawyers had told me he wore a corset to contain his girth and that all his teeth were false – when prepared for bed he was a pitiful, overweight, toothless tiger, apparently. But that's not how he was when he was performing publicly.

The two gladiators, Chaisson and Blassingame, faced off from opposite ends of a highly polished teakwood table. They were flanked on both sides by diocesan and insurance lawyers, and clerics. Chaisson was calm and controlled while Blassingame was fidgeting with papers in a file. Even before it had begun, it appeared it was advantage Chaisson.

In a booming voice, he announced, "Donny Rachou has school today in Amalie, so I request we allow his deposition to proceed first."

I could almost feel the surprise among Bendel and the New Orleans crew. They were expecting Kane Chaisson to file some kind of psychological report with the court in an attempt to postpone the boy's deposition for medical reasons related to his emotional and mental state. Here he was offering the boy's sworn testimony first.

Chaisson escorted Donny to a chair at the end of the table, next to the court reporter. Then he seated Donny's parents along the wall and pulled up a chair next to Donny for Doctor Kennison. "Gentlemen, these are Donny's parents, Celeste and Tommy Wesley. And this gentleman is Doctor Aaron Kennison, Donny's treating psychologist. Considering the age of the deponent, I assume there is no objection to their presence."

Robert Blassingame motioned to the court reporter to turn the recording device on. "I am Robert Blassingame, lead counsel for the parties listed in our responsive pleadings. Of course, we have no objection to the presence of the young man's parents. For the record, we object strenuously to the presence of Doctor Kennison. No one advised us the doctor would be present and we are caught by surprise. The doctor is not a party to this suit, has no right to be here. Unless we are to be provided the opportunity to question Doctor Kennison to learn why his presence is required in his opinion, and question Doctor Kennison at the same time about his treatment of Donny Rachou, then I feel it is inappropriate for him to be here, and I feel that these depositions should be canceled and all costs associated with these depositions, including the travel of counsel from New Orleans this morning, should be assessed against Mr. Chaisson's interest."

The child was flanked by legal counsel on one side and his doctor on the other. The baseball cap was in his hands. He fidgeted in the chair. Doctor Kennison reached over and whispered to him. He nodded and pulled the cap on backwards, blond bangs covering his forehead. Kennison whispered a second time and Donny looked under the table while Aaron Kennison pulled up his jeans an inch, showing Donny his lucky socks. These were their signals, and the child relaxed, took a drink of water, and seemed less nervous than everyone else around the crowded table.

Chaisson's voice boomed in response to Blassingame's speech. "Mr. Blassingame, I commend your formidable intellect, for it takes a brilliant mind to embrace two completely opposing ideas at the same time. On the one hand, you argue that you want Doctor Kennison removed from this room because you were unaware that he would be here this morning and find yourself unprepared for his very presence. On the other hand, you argue that you are fully prepared to take the sworn testimony of Doctor Kennison. This kind of logic confuses a simple mind like mine. What does not confuse me is this: these depositions are going to go forward today, with or without you. If you remove yourself and the witnesses I have subpoenaed, I am confident the court will issue sanctions, fines and costs against you. And I, Mr. Blassingame, will release to the press the statement you just made in the record, and will advise the public through the media that it is the diocese and bishop's position that this nine-year-old boy should not have his treating psychologist available to him while he is interrogated by grown men who ought to have the decency not to question him in the first place."

Blassingame pushed his glasses to his forehead. "Fine, counsel. This is your home field and we will play by your rules. However, my objection to the presence of Doctor Kennison shall be considered to be a continuing objection throughout the course of this day, without the necessity of my raising it again."

The court reporter administered the oath to the young boy and he swore to tell the truth, "So help me God." The sworn testimony of Donny Rachou was underway.

"Donny, my name is Robert Blassingame. It is necessary for me to talk to you this morning. Is that okay with you?"

"Yes, sir." Donny glanced at Doctor Kennison, who smiled warmly.

"Is that your name? Donny? Or is it Donald?"

"Donald. Donald Wesley Rachou."

"How old are you?"

"Almost ten."

"Almost ten. That's pretty old, isn't it?"

"I dunno. My sister's fourteen."

"But you are not old enough to be a lawyer, are you, Donny?"

Donny Rachou giggled. "No, sir. And I don't want to be no lawyer."

"Well, what I mean, Donny, is this. There are a lot of legal papers in this case and, of course, I know you did not write the legal papers. It is true that you have not read any of the legal papers either, have you?"

"No."

"And if you are almost ten, you are not old enough to be a doctor yet either?"

Again, Donny giggled. "No, sir. And I don't wanna be no doctor."

"There are some medical papers, some reports, in this case and, of course, I know you did not write the medical reports. It is true that you have not read any of the medical reports either?"

"No."

"Well, good. We are not going to talk about legal papers or medical reports. We are going to talk about you. Tell me about yourself."

Donny looked at Doctor Kennison, who smiled.

"There's not too much to say." Donny shrugged. "I'm only nine. I love my momma, my daddy, my sister, my dog and my horse. I don't like my sister's dog because it chases my horse."

"Donny, would you say your dog behaves better than your sister's dog?"

"Yes, sir."

"Your dog does things right and your sister's dog does things wrong?"

"Unhuh."

"Would you say that you know the difference between right and wrong?"

"Unhuh."

"Was that a 'yes', Donny?"

"Yes, sir."

"The things that happened with you and Father Dubois,

Donny. We're not going to talk about those things exactly. But I want you to think about those things. Do you think those things were right or wrong?"

"Wrong."

"And when you were doing those things, you knew those things were wrong, didn't you?"

"I suppose."

"You love your mommy and daddy."

"I do."

"And you have always loved your mommy and daddy, haven't you?"

"Yes, sir."

"How often did your mommy and daddy let you sleep over at Father's house?"

"About every week. I went there after school on Wednesdays, before altar-boy practice the next day. My group, we went on Wednesday. After school."

"And how old were you when you started to sleep at Father's house?"

"I dunno. I was little when it started."

"Did you ever tell your parents what was going on at Father's house?"

"No, sir. Not till Daddy talked to me one night after he heard something from my friend's daddy."

"Before the night your daddy talked to you – before – did your parents ever ask you what you did at Father's house?"

"No, sir."

"Did you like Father Nicky?"

"Sometimes a little bit."

"When did you like him?"

"When he was nice and gave me things and good snacks."

"Was he nice to you a lot of the time?"

"I suppose."

"Donny, someone told me you are a star baseball player. Is that true?"

The boy giggled. "I don't know. I play on a good team. The Redbirds. We did good this year."

"Was this your best baseball season?"

"Yes, sir."

"And when you leave here today, you are going to school?"

"Yes, sir."

"Who is your teacher?"

"I have three teachers and a coach."

"How was your report card?"

"We get the first one next week."

"Do you think it will be a good report card?"

"Not math."

Suddenly the outside door slammed open and two deputies rushed in, almost carrying Father Dubois between them. Dubois's face looked like a rubber mask. He was handcuffed behind his back, leaning forward, his hair hanging in his face.

"NO! NO! NO!" Donny screamed.

Celeste Rachou rushed to her son, grabbing him. Scooping him in her arms, her husband at her side, they cast expressions of terror in Kane Chaisson's direction. Chaisson was out of his seat, opening a door to his office suite, motioning them to follow. As they walked behind Chaisson, both parents were holding their son in their arms. I could not tell if Donny was shaking or in seizure.

To the court reporter, Robert Blassingame stupidly said, "There will be no more questions of the witness."

I got up and walked to the deputies and Dubois, motioning for them to follow me to a file room. I signaled them to remove the cuffs and allow Dubois to sit in a chair. "I'll be back," I told Dubois.

Blassingame asked the court reporter to step out of the conference room so he could speak in private to me, the Church lawyers and the clerics.

Blassingame said, "The kid did not lay a glove on us. If Dubois says nothing, we're going to get out of this day clean. We're gonna dismiss the parents today and reserve our right to take their testimony at a later date. Does anyone disagree?"

Quinlan said, "Good job, Robert. You're right. The kid is doing well now with baseball, school, everything. He seems fine. He knew what he did was wrong. This could not have gone better. The kid is fine, no real long-term damage."

I thought Quinlan was crazy. "The boy's fine? Did all of you somehow miss what happened when the boy saw Father Dubois?"

Blassingame said, "None of that is on the record. The last thing on the record is the kid saying his report card is going to be pretty good and me saying I had no more questions. There's no video here, only the transcription of what was spoken."

I stared at him in disbelief. Blassingame removed his glasses to wipe them with a handkerchief. "I told you these kids cannot step up under pressure. If I get this kid in a courtroom, I'll gut him. Jesus Christ, his parents never once asked what was going on with Dubois, and he knew what he was doing was wrong. This is a red-letter day, gentlemen."

I looked around the room. Neither the monsignors, the bishop nor the other lawyers were making eye contact with me. Tom Quinlan's young law associate, James Ryburn, was the only one looking at me, eyes wide, with an expression I could not interpret.

As Chaisson re-entered the room, he spoke to Blassingame as if he was the only person there. "Doctor Kennison has taken Donny and his parents to his office. He felt it best to remove him from this building while Father Dubois is here. The Rachou parents can return later to be deposed."

Blassingame responded, "I will make a statement in the record that I am releasing both Mr. and Mrs. Rachou, and reserving our right to take their testimony at a later date."

"I will have them notified at Doctor Kennison's that they are released for today. Now, get Dubois. He's first," Chaisson said.

When I opened the door to the file room, I motioned for the deputies to leave. Dubois was obviously heavily drugged. As I approached him, he almost fell out of the chair. He was coming toward me, having forgotten to stand first.

"You okay?"

He shook his head.

"What's the matter?"

"Doctor Sonnier at the jail asked if I was nervous. He gave me two pills."

"Shit. What kind of pills?"

Dubois shrugged.

"Father, don't ever take drugs from Doc Sonnier again. He's not fit to be a vet. Doc only has the jail job because his daughter married the sheriff's son. They use pills up there to knock out violent guys twice your size."

"Can we change this to another day, Renon? I feel like I'm gonna be sick. My head, my stomach. My mind is spinning around."

"No. No way. We gotta get you through this thing and get you back up to the Stalder Institute in New Jersey."

Dubois took some labored breaths and I asked, "Do you remember our plan?"

He nodded.

"Sure?"

He nodded again.

"Let's go."

39

DEALING WITH THE DEVIL

Thursday September 27, 1984
Kane Chaisson's Law Office, Thiberville

I held Francis Dubois's arm and guided him to the witness chair. I sat to his left. The court reporter administered the oath. Then Kane Chaisson began. "Father Dubois, my name is Kane Chaisson. I represent Donny Rachou and his parents. Let me begin by asking you, what is your full name?"

"Father Francis Dominick Dubois. Blaize is my confirmation name."

"Where do you live?"

"In jail... I don't know how to answer."

"Well let me ask you where you were living before you were incarcerated in the Thiberville parish correctional facility. Where was that?"

I put my hand in front of Dubois the way one throws his hand in front of a child in the passenger seat when braking a car suddenly. "I instruct my client to refuse to answer that question in the interest of his own security and the security of other patients at the facility where he was residing before being incarcerated. For the record, I am willing to make this statement under oath that would be sealed if it takes that to satisfy Mr. Chaisson. I have visited the treatment facility. It is located in a distant state and is at least as secure as the Thiberville correctional facility."

Chaisson ignored me. "Father, it is true, is it not, that your most recent assignment in the Diocese of Thiberville was at a parish known as Our Lady of the Seas in Amalie, Louisiana?"

I leaned over to Dubois and whispered in his ear, "Now. Every question."

Dubois nodded and said flatly, "Under the advice of counsel I invoke my Fifth Amendment right against self-incrimination and refuse to answer the question."

At the other end of the table, Robert Blassingame leaned away from the table, tossing his pen onto his blank legal pad, obviously satisfied that his instructions were being followed to a T. Kane Chaisson was going to get no evidence at all from Father Dubois.

Chaisson said, "Father, it is true, is it not, that you are acquainted with a young man named Donald Wesley Rachou – or Donny?"

"Under the advice of counsel I invoke my—"

"That's fine, Father. You don't have to go on. I understand. This is not about you, Father. It's about your lawyer, who has given you unsound legal advice. For the record, Madame Reporter, I am going to recess this deposition and attempt to get the judge on the phone for a ruling on the untenable, obstructionist position Mr. Chattelrault has assumed in these proceedings. The law is clear and has been clear for ages. The Fifth Amendment privilege against self-incrimination Father Dubois seeks to avail himself of is an individual right that is only available to a defendant in a criminal proceeding. The principle has no bearing on a civil proceeding such as this." Kane Chaisson stood. "Now, this deposition will stand in recess while I attempt to reach a judge for a ruling."

Robert Blassingame stood at the moment Chaisson stood. "This deposition will not stand in recess, Mr. Chaisson. You have no authority to act unilaterally to recess this matter. That would require the consent of all counsel. I speak for the others gathered here when I tell you that we stand united in our opposition to your attempt to recess the deposition. Either you continue until you have no further questions or we will assume you have no further questions and this deposition will be ended."

Chaisson looked like he was going to whip Blassingame's bony ass. "Frankly, Mr. Blassingame, I don't give a good damn what you or your co-counsel think. The only person I care about is little Donny Rachou. I am going to my office and I invite Mr. Chattelrault to accompany me."

I leaned over to Father Dubois and told him to stay put. Then I walked behind Chaisson to his private office, a room that could have been an upscale taxidermist's shop, an immense chamber that looked like the staging area for Noah's Ark.

Chaisson pulled off his suit coat and tossed it on a chair, loosened his tie, and said, "Okay, Renon. We know each other. You are way too good a lawyer to be playing games out there. What the fuck are you doing? A judge will never let Dubois get away with not answering my questions."

"What's a judge gonna do to him? Put him in jail? He's in jail already and probably headed to prison for life. You have no leverage here, Kane. Calm down, listen. I know what you want. And there is something I want."

"What is it I want, Renon?"

"You want Dubois to break down, to get his confession. You want to be the man who broke him down."

Chaisson nodded. "Fucking right, son. I want the truth. I know the truth, but I gotta get the truth from him."

"You can have it all, but you have to give me what I want."

"And what the fuck does Renon Chattelrault want?"

"We want to be left the fuck alone. I have a deal with the DA and Judge Labat. Neither of them wants Dubois around while waiting for his trials. After this deposition is finished, I can move Dubois back to the treatment facility and keep him there until the trials."

"That has nothing to do with me."

"Well, it does. First, it's in the interest of your client. You saw what happened to the kid when he saw Dubois. He'd be better off knowing the priest was a long way away. Also, you can make my good friend, our DA, do circus tricks. The media will broadcast anything you say because you are the only one talking. When I move Dubois back to treatment, one comment from you about how

Dubois is being given special treatment, and there will be an uproar caused by the media and from the people down around Amalie and Bayou Saint John. The DA and Judge Labat will shit themselves and haul Dubois's ass back to the Thiberville jail overnight."

"So, what the fuck are you asking me to do?"

"Simple. We give you what you want this morning. In fact, if you ask the right questions and go beyond Amalie, you're gonna get a lot more than you are expecting to get."

"Okay."

"The one proviso is that we will run aground again if you try to ask Dubois one question about the diocese, those monsignors in there or the bishop. The nuthouse Dubois is in costs twelve grand a month. And I'm not cheap, and they are paying the freight for all medical and legal expenses. You will get what you need about the diocese from the monsignors and the bishop. And Dubois is not the right witness anyway. A man like Dubois has no credibility and you don't want to find yourself vouching for his honesty about the diocese and what they knew, when they knew it, what they did and what they failed to do."

"I have no problem with that. He would not be privy to the decisions the diocese made about him anyway, whatever discussions were had. But, Renon, you're still not telling me what you want from me."

"You agree you will never ever mention Dubois's name again after today. Not anywhere under any circumstance, except in questioning witnesses about him in legal proceedings. Leave us alone. Dubois's net worth is less than a nickel. You can battle with us, but the war you have to win is against the diocese. That's where the money is. If you have to bang someone in the press, beat up on the bishop. Dubois and I get a pass from you, a permanent pass. He goes back to the treatment facility and you make no statement at all about him going back to the facility, getting special treatment, or anything else about him."

"You think it matters what I say?"

"Hell, yes. You spook my good friend, Sean Robinette, like

nobody else. If you start raising hell about Dubois getting special privileges, I know our DA, Robinette, will yank his ass back in jail. No more treatment."

Chaisson stuck his hand out. We shook. I stood gazing at the walls of his office and though I was appalled by the gallery of dead animals hanging there, I acted like I was impressed.

Chaisson made a sweeping gesture toward some of his trophies. "Shot a big animal on every fucking continent, caught a big fish off every coast. Killed and caught everything there is to kill or catch except a whale. I'm looking for a charter right now that will take me on a whale hunt."

Chaisson re-entered the conference room, tie loosened and askew, looking more like the street fighter he was in his heart than the lawyer he was in his head.

The deposition resumed as I whispered to Dubois, "Okay. It's okay now."

"Now, Father Dubois, let's get down to it. Did you have sex with young boys in every assignment you ever had in the Diocese of Thiberville?"

Chaisson was testing me early, out of the chute, with his first question, going for the whole game.

"Yes, sir. That is the truth. I had sex with boys when I was in the seminary too."

Blassingame bolted from his chair and charged toward me, shouting, "Now, this deposition will stand in recess. Defense counsel will confer among themselves."

William Chaisson grinned from ear to ear and said, "Well, Mr. Blassingame, I ought to cite the age-old case of 'Goose versus Gander' – what's good for the goose, is good for the gander. A few minutes ago you went on record that no one has a unilateral right to recess this deposition and now you want to recess it yourself. Having better manners than you, I grant your request."

Chaisson motioned to the court reporter to follow him to his office, leaving the rest of us in the conference room.

"Let's go outside, gentlemen," Blassingame said.

"You bet," I said.

In single file we headed for the door with me in the lead. I swung it open to the light, stepping into the parking lot. The first person I saw was Zeb Jackson, leaning against a wall, reporter's pad in his hand. Television cameras and a couple of still photographers rushed toward us. Behind me I heard Robert Blassingame mutter, "Jeeezus Christ. Get back inside."

Jon Bendel stumbled and fell on his face on the carpeted floor as we pushed our way back through the door. I waved to Zeb and turned around to walk in.

All of the lawyers were crammed into the small file room that had held Dubois earlier. More than half of them were talking at the same time. When I stepped in, the talking stopped.

Blassingame said, "I've had enough of your shit. Last week in New Orleans you agreed your client would take the Fifth. You started off right today, keeping your word. You spend five minutes with Chaisson and you cave in. What? Are you scared of Chaisson?"

"No, Bobby. I am not scared of Chaisson. Are you?"

Blassingame leaned forward, grimacing. "I'm not scared of anything."

"Every one of you would be scared to death of the truth, if you knew what the hell the truth was."

Blassingame said, "We are in this together. We have a strategy."

"We, Bobby? We? What's this 'we' business? You are the only one who ever talks for all these other people and all you ever tell me is that you want to throw me out of the room."

"We cannot allow what is about to happen in there happen. How can it possibly be in the interest of your client to testify to these crimes?"

"Our plea in the criminal case is not guilty by reason of insanity. We are not going to contest the facts alleged in the criminal charges. We will only argue and try to prove he was criminally insane at the time he committed the crimes. The more acts of sexual molestation that are in the court records, the crazier Dubois looks."

"Shit," Blassingame said. Turning to Jonathan Bendel, he asked, "Can you talk some sense into him, Jon?"

With that, Blassingame led all the others out of the room, leaving me alone with Bendel.

Smoothly and softly, Bendel said, "Renon, I have looked at the contract you signed with Monsignor Moroux. According to the diocesan corporate charter, I believe we can fire you."

"Maybe you can fire me, but you're not gonna fuck me," I said, turning my back to him and walking away.

In his wildest dreams, Kane Chaisson could never have imagined the kind of deposition he would get from Father Francis Dominick Dubois. They talked about Donny Rachou in detail and Dubois admitted every allegation in the Rachou legal petition and even increased some of the numbers contained in the psychological dossier. Dubois also admitted to having had sex with a large number of victims, a number so large that he had lost count. He agreed it was probably over two hundred, maybe a lot more.

When the deposition ended, as if playing poker with Blassingame and company, Chaisson made the same move Blassingame had made earlier in passing up the chance to depose the Rachou parents, reserving his right to do so later. In the record, Chaisson made an identical reservation regarding the right to later take the sworn testimony of the monsignors and the bishop.

As Chaisson advised Dubois he was free to leave, Dubois turned to me and said, "Please ride back with me." I nodded and went outside to tell the cops to bring the car to the door. As I was walking back in, all the lawyers and clerics filed by me in silence, avoiding me, except for young James Ryburn from Quinlan's office, who nodded, almost smiled, and said, "See ya."

Dubois and I were hustled to the police cruiser by two deputies.

From the jail, I walked to my office. As I strolled in, Mo followed me to my desk.

"Gimme the scoop. How were the depositions?"

"Piece of cake, Mo, piece of cake."

40

THE BAG MAN

Friday morning, September 28, 1984
Coteau

Kate and I were on the patio. I knew she wanted to tell the children we were divorcing and she wanted to do it on Saturday. I didn't want to talk to the children about this and I didn't want to talk about talking to the children about this. Nothing but pleasantries had been exchanged between the two of us for two weeks. She had completed the arrangements that would have us living apart, decorating a townhouse in Thiberville for me to live in. In the old days, I would have started raising arguments against divorce, trying to convince her to change her mind. This time I knew she was right.

Mildred, our housekeeper, had set out a tray with coffee, juice and pastries she'd heated in a frying pan with butter. She brought a phone to the table. I took the call and Kate waved and walked toward the horses.

"Renon, this is Zeb. Did you see yourself on the national TV news programs last night?"

"Nope. Could you tell which one of us was the criminal?"

"With both of you in suits it wasn't easy."

"What you got?" I asked.

"I'm pushing up against a deadline. I have a deal with the weekly here in Thiberville, *The Courier,* and they have a strange print cycle. It hits the stands on Wednesday, but our stories have to be in by Friday, edited before Sunday night. Can I ask you some questions?"

"Shoot."

"First, the subpoena list for the priests' personnel records. The Chaisson subpoena. Can you tell me what you know about those priests?"

"Don't know. I've only met a couple of them. Can't help you."

"Can you tell me what the bishop knew about complaints made against Father Dubois before he was sent to Our Lady of the Seas in Amalie? I don't even live here and already I'm hearing rumors about Dubois in other church parishes. It's secondary stuff. No one related to a victim is talking, but others are, and the talk is strong. But it's just talk so far."

I laughed. "Why don't you ask the bishop, Zeb?"

"Right. Like he's gonna be talking to me. By the way, the diocese has a congenital idiot as director of media relations, Lloyd Lecompte. I called him and he lectured me on my obligation as a Catholic not to bring scandal to the Church. How does he know I'm a Catholic anyway?"

"He just assumes it. Almost everyone here is. Lecompte may be an idiot, but he's got control right now. He's got the local TV stations and the daily, *The Thiberville Register*, under control. You might find you are the only person not playing by his rules."

"What are you telling me, Renon? The rest of the media is fixed here? You saw the trucks and people at Chaisson's law office yesterday."

"Right. They were all there. And I bet Chaisson came out after we left and held court for whoever would listen."

"Yeah, he was out there for half an hour. Afterwards, he talked to me inside for over an hour."

"Zeb, I am willing to bet you that breakfast at Brennan's that *The Thiberville Register* has next to nothing in this morning's edition; nothing about the bishop, and nothing of Chaisson for sure. My wife, Kate, saw the Channel 2 news last night and said they had film of Dubois leaving the jail with deputies around him, and the two of us getting in the cop car to leave Chaisson's office, and maybe a one-minute voice-over about the priest being deposed. They had no pictures of the bishop or monsignors at Chaisson's office. They had nothing of Chaisson's press conference. This is Catholic country, the bishop's king and everyone else is a pawn."

Zeb rattled through a long list of questions. I couldn't have helped him even if I'd wanted to. He seemed to know a lot more than I knew or he was close to knowing a lot more. After twenty minutes, I saw Joe Rossi's car coming up the drive and rang off.

Mildred escorted Joe Rossi to the patio. Rossi hit his head on a low branch of the big cedar tree near the brick walk. He hit it hard enough to draw a bit of blood.

Plopping in a chair and grabbing a pastry from the tray, Rossi breathed deep and leaned toward me. "Jon Bendel told me about the dust-up yesterday at Chaisson's office. I think you are going to get your ass fired off this case. Jon tells me the diocese's corporate papers specify that although the bishop and the vicar general are authorized to enter into a contract calling for the payment of a sum in excess of ten thousand dollars, the contract only becomes binding after a majority vote from the lay diocesan financial advisory committee. Your agreement never went before the board. So, the contract with you is in violation of the diocesan rules. Jon can cancel it. They can fire you."

"Wrong again, Joe. First, as I told you before, Dubois is my client and only Dubois can fire me. Now you say Bendel can cancel my contract where the diocese guarantees my fees and expenses. Wrong. I have not sent the diocese any invoice for professional services yet, so we don't know if the contract with me is in excess of ten thousand dollars, do we? This is just Bendel's bullshit and you don't need to drive all the way out here to carry messages for him."

"Renon, you know I like you. I always have. You've been like a son to me at times. But you're crazy. You know that too, don't you? I don't know what you think you're doing."

"Listen to me a minute. By last night, Dubois had honored every outstanding subpoena. Ponce and Thomas passed on taking testimony from him. I have an agreement with the DA and Judge

Labat to have two deputies accompany Dubois back to the treatment center. It is in the interest of virtually everyone, especially the diocese, to get him out of here as soon as possible, as far away as possible. I know the bishop wants him out of sight, out of mind. You want him out of here, and Bendel, and—"

"Yeah, right, so let's get him out of here. What's the problem?"

"The problem is I need the diocese to front a half-million-dollar bond by tonight. That takes 10 per cent in cash, fifty grand. You're tight with that thief that runs Best Bonds. Can you get him to put up a bond for that amount? He's Catholic, right?"

"Gimme a phone."

I gave him the phone and went in search of Kate. I didn't find her.

When I got back to Joe Rossi, he was on his second pastry. With food in his mouth, Joe said, "Frank says it's gonna take fifty thousand, but if it's in cash it won't hit the books. No record. No one in the media will know the diocese put up all that cash for Dubois's bond."

"Really? You and Jon Bendel gonna get the lay financial advisory board to sign off on this deal? A fifty-thousand-dollar cash, under-the-table payment into the pockets of a greaseball wanna-be Mafioso bondsman – on behalf of a priest charged with raping children? Will the lay advisory board sign off on that?"

"I'll get the money from Jean-Paul Moroux and I'll deliver the cash to Frank at Best Bonds. I'll have the bond form at your office at three o'clock. But you gotta promise you're gonna quit freelancing. We all have Dubois's best interest in mind, but we have a greater obligation…"

"I know, Joe, I know. The common good."

"You double-crossed some powerful people yesterday for that powerless prick Dubois. If you went on a search-and-destroy mission across this state, you could not find anyone as powerless as this prick Dubois or anyone as powerful as the people you're fucking with. Shit, son, we can make a monkey governor – done that twice. It's just plain stupid to fuck with us, Renon. And you're not a stupid guy. Maybe you're playing way over your head, maybe we drafted you into a league you can't play in. The stakes here are high."

"I thought you said I was stupid awhile ago. Now you say I'm not stupid."

"No. I never said you were stupid. Crazy. I said you were crazy."

7 a.m., Friday, September 28, 1984
Jacques' Cafe

I went to Jacques' Café for a follow-up with cop-turned-private-investigator Johnny Wilcox. Usually with Wilcox, I'd wait for him to finish a job and report to me. This time I called the interim meeting. I wanted a progress report.

Wilcox got right to it. "I hear from some old retired city cops that over twenty years ago the esteemed vicar general of the Thiberville diocese, Monsignor Jean-Paul Moroux, was picked up at the bus station here, in the men's room. He offered five dollars to an undercover vice cop named Dauterive for a blow job. I don't know if he wanted to blow the cop or wanted the cop to blow him."

"Doesn't sound like he's in Dubois's class. It's not kids we're talking about here. My first response is, bizarre as it sounds, who cares? But exactly how do you know this?"

"I know people. An ex-dispatcher here told me. Then I found Dauterive. Actually, this Dauterive guy is still sort of a cop. Now he's with the sheriff's department in Lake Charles, where he lives with his daughter and works part time as a courtroom bailiff. He barely remembers the incident. Can't remember which way the good monsignor wanted the oral sex. There was no arrest, no report. He says he thinks the priest was pretty much dead drunk at the time and a police supervisor drove him home. I also have unconfirmed information that Moroux has been treated several times for alcoholism somewhere way out of state."

"That's interesting. You got anything else?"

"Not much, Renon. I told you it would be damned near impossible to get anything."

Wilcox took the list out of the pocket of his windbreaker and handed it to me. "The guys I circled are just priests who were moved within two years of the time they were posted in a parish. I have a source in the diocese who tells me quick moves like these transfers can be suspicious, but it may mean nothing. The ones I marked with asterisks, and I think there are twelve or thirteen on this list, are well known to the police as homosexuals who frequent that bar, The Daisy Chain, down by the underpass. Two asterisks, like the ones next to Moroux's name, indicate priests who have had encounters with police in bus stations, rest areas and the like, but no charges. Record wise, the whole list is clean. No criminal charges or civil suits against any of them."

I counted the names circled and those with asterisks. The total was twenty-four. Twenty-four out of thirty-one. "That's it, Johnny? All you got?"

"Pretty much. There is a name that is not on this list. I bumped into this information when I was poking at the woodpile. There is a Father O. D. Ellison. I've picked up information from two people, former cops, that this priest murdered two boys while he was assigned to a parish in Willow Springs. What they knew was sketchy, but both parties said they thought the priest killed two brothers. That church parish now belongs to the Diocese of Providence, but at the time it was part of the Thiberville diocese. I hear the priest is now in a monastery on the Kansas plains somewhere. Ellison was not on the list, so I did not pursue it. You want me to follow that trail?"

"Follow that trail to the end, Johnny."

Friday morning,
Chattelrault Law Office, Thiberville

Zeb Jackson was waiting for me when I got to the office. We sat at the conference table and he had coffee. Zeb handed me the typescript of the article he planned to submit to his editor, and asked what I thought. I read it quickly.

"Not much. I don't think much of it. It's not anything. What the hell is it supposed to accomplish?"

"I'm not going to lie to you. It's cold out there. Everyone is talking but no one is talking for the record. People can only give me rumors and gossip."

"So you have nothing."

"Exactly. This cover piece is just top-water bait. Maybe it will bring some fish, some victims, to us and we'll be able to develop stories. Maybe it will bring the big fish off the bottom, the diocese, to the surface, attacking us. If neither one of those things happens, I expect to be back in New Orleans soon, permanently. There's a story here, but I am not sure anyone will ever get it. I'm trawling now, just skimming the surface, hoping something takes the bait. I know this weekly newspaper is not going to do any more unless there is some major movement in the next few days. I think the editor is a born-again charismatic Catholic, whatever that is."

"Well, don't worry about it. Even if you go back to New Orleans, I suspect you will be back. I think this story has a long way to go."

Zeb had not been gone from my office ten minutes when Rossi burst in unannounced, sporting a Band-Aid on his forehead. He was sweating. Sweating and pacing. "I tried to tell you, Renon. I tried to talk reason."

I was behind my desk. "Christ, Joe, don't you have a life? You want to tell me why you're here?"

"Tell you? Goddamn right, I'll tell you. On the way from your house, when I am trying to get back to work, get back to my life, my car phone goes off. Damned thing sounds like a bomb when it rings. It's Jon Bendel calling about that piece-of-shit weekly newspaper I wouldn't wipe my dog's ass with. This prick reporter called Jon's office all day Wednesday and tried to button-hole him yesterday at Chaisson's office. Bendel put a tail on him. And where the fuck did he go? He came here. That's where."

I smiled. "You have a car phone? And a dog?"

"Funny, huh? Everything's a fucking joke to you. You have no idea. You have no idea how much trouble we have gone to, what we have done to keep the media away from this Dubois thing. Now we find you entertaining a reporter in your office. We can sure as hell fire you now. We got ya. Conflict of interest, call it what you want. You are working against the interest of the people who are paying you."

"I'm lost, Joe. You got me doing what exactly? Having coffee with a man who has not published a word and is asking questions of everyone who is involved, including your buddy, Jon Bendel?"

"It's the teaching of the Church to avoid scandal to the Church. It is the obligation of every Catholic. Nobody who is bringing scandal to the Church is going to be employed by the Church. Talking to a reporter about this shit is causing scandal to the Church."

Rossi wheeled around, a maneuver that was not easy with his girth, and he almost fell over in the process. At the door, he paused, looked back at me and shook his head.

41

LOSS

Friday afternoon, September 28, 1984
Chattelrault Law Office, Thiberville

Monsignor Jean-Paul Moroux had spoken with my secretary, Monique, a few days earlier and requested a Friday afternoon meeting with me at the chancery. I now had Mo call him to advise him that I would not come to the chancery. He was told he could see me in my office at 2:30 p.m. and he was prompt.

I greeted him warmly. "Monsignor, it's good to see you."

We shook hands and he settled in a client chair. I sat next to him in the other client chair.

"Well, Renon, I actually have been told by Jon Bendel it might be wise if I did not speak with you anymore. Twice I've been told that. But there are other considerations. There are things within the Church and Church structure that have nothing to do with these civil law cases. This is a Church matter I come to you about. I am here to give you this name and address."

He handed me a piece of diocesan stationery. In type in the center of the page was:

Fr. Matthew Patterson, M. D.
Hope House
Williams Crossing, Virginia

In Moroux's handwriting were notations of the street address and two telephone numbers.

"I would like for you to call this Father Matthew Patterson and visit with him in person. Apparently Father Patterson is an eminent psychiatrist as well as a priest. He founded Hope House and treats priests, nuns and people in religious orders for a lot of different things there. I believe it would be in the best interest of everyone for Father Patterson to do an evaluation of Father Francis, maybe take over his treatment. At all costs, I would like for you to travel to meet Father Patterson as soon as possible."

"Monsignor, I cannot do this. If Father Dubois is evaluated and treated by this priest, then Father Patterson could be called as a witness in the criminal trial. No matter how sympathetic this Father Patterson might be to the insanity defense I will rely upon, how do you think it would look to a jury, to the press, to the public? A priest defending a priest? It cannot get much worse than that. There is no need for me to even call him."

"Well, this really matters. The requests that you go to see Father Patterson have become demands. They come from a Father Desmond McDougall, a canon lawyer at the papal nunciature in Washington, DC, which, as you know, is also the Vatican Embassy. Father McDougall is a prominent faculty member at Catholic University Law School, an author, a redactor of the revised code of canon law. He is the man who vets the shortlist of potential bishops and cardinals in the United States. His influence in the American Church and Rome is great. I need to grant his requests – demands. And he's demanding you travel to Hope House. All I can do is ask you again. I have done that."

Friday night
Thiberville

The old, abandoned college football stadium was only a block from the family home where I grew up. When I was a kid, I'd sneak out at night and run to the field, crawl under the chain-link fence, and climb to the top of a light standard above the press box.

I would spend almost all night up there. In those days it was the tallest structure in Thiberville.

Tonight I waited until it was late before leaving my office and stopped at a package liquor store for a bottle of Pouilly Fuissé. The clerk used a corkscrew, re-corked the bottle and gave me a plastic cup. I drove to the old stadium. Parking my car near the old baseball diamond next to the stadium, I walked along the bamboo-lined centerfield fence and crawled through the hole that I had made when I was twelve years old.

I made my way around the cinder track that ringed the football field and was pockmarked as a result of neglect. Walking across the end zone of the grassy field to the concrete-and-brick bleachers stand, I climbed a wooden ladder to the roof of the old press box, now home to hundreds of cooing pigeons. From there I went up a steel ladder to reach the top of the huge lights, where there was a railed platform approximately five by ten feet in size.

I had never told anyone, not even my best friends, about this place. It might have been the only secret I ever kept. When I was a kid, going to this place was a great adventure; it was risky and the payoff was a rush. As a child I came here when I was happy. As an adult I used it as a place of refuge when I was troubled.

I had always loved the night. I loved being alone in the night. There was no place I had ever known where I could be more alone.

As I climbed the rusting steel ladder, I dropped the cup. Once I was on the decking, I pulled the cork and tossed it toward the field, watching it drop on a fifty-yard-line seat just below the press box. I looked down on the field far below. I had once played in an important high school game on this university field. The goalposts I had kicked footballs through were gone. We came close to victory that rainy night. I was run out of bounds at the two-yard line as the clock ran out. When I was tackled, I was pushed into a mud puddle. I thought it was the mouthful of mud that left the taste in my mouth, but that bad taste did not go away for a long time. It was the taste of defeat. I had the same taste in my mouth now.

On the railing was a faded tie of mine. I had knotted it around the steel strut on a night ten years earlier when I'd decided I was never going to wear ties again or do any more work that required a costume of any kind. By the next morning, I had found myself again dressing in a suit and tie. Now, once again, I pulled off the tie I was wearing and tied it next to the other one.

The view into the darkness was beautiful. In daylight, Thiberville was shrouded by the spreading branches of live oak trees that never lost their leaves. Almost all the lights of Thiberville were below the tree canopy; in some directions it was like looking at lights under a blanket. There was only a faint hint of civilization, the things one was aware of at street level. Off to the east the brightly lighted towers of a power plant were shrouded by a white vapor spewing from the tall stacks and falling back to the ground in the still, heavy air.

The town was asleep. More than a hundred thousand people in Thiberville knew nothing of the truth about the diocese that was tormenting me.

My clothes were moist from sweating during the climb and the high humidity. As a child, I used to wonder how it could be so hot at night when the sun was not shining.

I set the wine bottle on the platform and watched as clouds obscured the stars. Looking back at the football field, I thought again of that rainy night long ago, and of the other Friday nights we had played on the freshly cut grass. Even then, winning had always been everything to me. In those football years, there were only two times we lost. As a lawyer, I had lost only one trial. I could count every loss in my life.

My first loss was when I was six. I saw my puppy run over by a car. The feeling I had when I buried him was the same feeling I had whenever I lost anyone or anything. But never had my heart ached like it did tonight. Losing Kate and the children made me more aware of my heart than ever before and my heart felt like it really could break.

Without my family, what else was there in my life? I had a bishop and a monsignor averting their gazes from a priest who defiled little kids. Unable to do anything for the child victims, I was losing there too.

And I was also feeling the loss of my faith.

As an altar boy, I had been happy serving Mass. I had felt I belonged to something that was about God and goodness. It was the Church that made me want to be good when I was young. Now, as I sipped dry white wine, I felt the enormity of the loss of my faith, a faith I was unaware of until it was lost.

Maybe I had always been what some call a "cultural Catholic", one baptized and raised in a Catholic community. The only God I had known was a God given to me, explained to me by religion teachers in the twelve years I attended a Catholic school. Sure, I questioned a lot of things as I grew older – like eating no meat on Fridays, or confessing sin to a mortal man – but I had faith in God and the Church, and had always believed both to be one and the same: a repository of goodness.

I'm certain I once believed priests were superior spiritually to lay persons. Tonight I knew I believed none of that. Now that I had knowledge of what the Church was really like on the inside, I knew my faith would have to be deaf, dumb and blind for me to continue to believe in this institution made of mortal men, some whose sins were worse than those who confessed their sins to them.

My hatred of losing, the very taste loss left in my mouth, was probably the core force of my being, the reason behind almost everything I did. It wasn't an epiphany, but an insight I'd never had. As I looked over a town asleep and down on an overgrown, abandoned sports field, somewhere deep inside I realized that I was losing everything that mattered to me. I worried I was losing myself. The taste in my mouth was not something wine could wash away.

Saturday morning, September 29, 1984
Coteau

On Saturday morning, we told our children that we were separating and that I would be living in a townhouse in the city that Kate had fixed up for me. We told them the family house would eventually be sold and that they would move somewhere else with Kate. Actually, Kate was the one who did all the talking. As she announced that we were separating, Sasha broke in two before our eyes. She began crying, sobbing, screaming "No, No, No", and hyperventilating to the point where she could not catch her breath. It took a half-hour to calm her. The boys were quiet. Shelby looked away, through a window, and Jake hung his head, staring at his jiggling legs. When the conversation ended, the boys left. They went to Shelby's jeep and drove away. Sasha walked out in the pasture and sat down in a field of wild flowers.

That afternoon we received a phone call from our friend who ran the country grocery store up the road. He said that Sasha had walked in with her little bank of coins and tried to buy lottery tickets. It was against the law to sell lotto tickets to a child. When Kate went to pick Sasha up at the store, she told Kate she was trying to win enough money to buy her house and keep it.

42

IMMACULATE DECEPTION

Saturday morning, December 8, 1984
Saint Stephen's Cathedral, Thiberville

The rain and freezing December temperatures caused all the leaves of the cathedral's live oak to become encased in ice. The bells in the steeple competed with loud claps of thunder, sounding out like dull drums banging in the sky. The thunder and bells reverberated in Monsignor Jean-Paul Moroux's skull, which had been hollowed out by a tall bottle of Russian vodka the night before.

The previous evening Moroux had locked the weather outside and stayed in his home. He'd sat in front of the fireplace with a glass in hand and a bottle of vodka and bucket of ice on the sideboard. When the fire faltered, the monsignor walked over to the Nativity set with its large straw figures. He burned the shepherd and then tossed in the lambs to keep the flames going.

In between shots of vodka, Moroux whittled away at his latest African mask, using his small woodcarver's knife and occasionally applying his special woodburning tool. Carving African masks was the only endeavor that fulfilled him – and something he kept secret from everyone else. Usually he carved and burned the masks at a workbench in the attic of the Old Bishop's House, but it had been too cold to work up there on Friday night.

The monsignor loved the beauty of African faces. In his Paris university years, he had come across a lot of Africans in the cafés he frequented, something he had never experienced at the backwoods Acadia Parish farm of his childhood, and he had some African photography books. The masks he made varied from the

261

warlike to the ceremonial, though none were lifelike. The current face was a funeral mask, exaggerated and angular.

In the early hours of Saturday morning, Moroux polished off the last of the vodka. Sucking the blood from a knife-wound to his finger, he used his free hand to rake wood shavings from the top of his desk, dumping them in the wastepaper basket. He gently placed the mask out of view, in the well of his desk.

In Saint Stephen's at the Saturday service, amid the sounds of the church bells, thunder and soaring organ music, Monsignor Moroux unsteadily followed in the footsteps of an altar boy carrying a crucifix. Every priest from the diocese was there. In procession, they entered the cathedral from the sacristy and slowly made their way down the center aisle and around to a side altar furnished with a statue of the Virgin Mary and a life-sized Nativity set. Even Bishop Reynolds was present. The priests of the Thiberville diocese were celebrating a feast day, a highlight of the liturgical calendar, which some still called "A Holy Day of Obligation"; a day commemorating one of the miracles in the Catholic faith. This was the Feast of the Immaculate Conception.

In this season of Advent, as Catholics around the world celebrated the anticipation of the coming of Christ, the Diocese of Thiberville went on the offensive in a public relations battle. The expensive and intensive four-tiered media campaign had been the idea of Joe Rossi.

A few days before the Feast of the Immaculate Conception, Rossi had convened a meeting that even included Bishop Reynolds. Rossi held the floor. "This is our season. We got everything to sell and we gotta sell it. Sell the smells, sell the bells. The smells and bells."

Rossi paced the room, almost dancing as he shifted his hefty girth from one side to the other. "Look," he said, "one little pipsqueak named Zeb-a-dee-dooh-dah got him a little typewriter and that trashy little weekly paper is treating him like he's one of those reporters who brought down the Nixon presidency. We gotta bury that stuff. Now is the season. It's our time of year."

Archdiocesan legal counsel, Tom Quinlan, had brought in a top advertising firm from New Orleans to mount a television, newspaper, radio and direct mail campaign. It was a campaign designed to make everyone feel good about the diocese, to remind them of the good works of Catholic charities.

When the advertising agency had showed them rough footage for a preview, Rossi had almost had a heart attack. Halfway through watching the video tape, he flipped on the lights and fumbled with the remote control. He could never figure out how to shut down the monitor, so this time he just pulled the plug out of the wall.

The young people with the agency were aghast. Joe said, "I'm gonna pull the plug on all of you, on the whole damned project. What you got here in this film is lots of pictures of priests. We can't have no priests in the film. We're not gonna show priests in television commercials. You hear that? You got that? No priests. You can show churches, altars, schools, hospitals, homeless shelters, soup kitchens, the Church doing good things, whatever – you don't need to show no priests in the pictures. Lay people, the faithful, good loyal Catholics. No priests. Now ya'll come back next week with film to show us that got no priests."

After the agency people left, Rossi had mumbled to himself and the room, "Who knows if any of the priests in the film are gonna end up having jail mug shots like Dubois one day? Who knows anymore? We ain't gonna be picturing priests. I don't want to make a hero of somebody who could bite us on the ass. Priests are our problem."

Priests were their problem. It was no longer one priest. Nobody knew how many other priests would be exposed, but already things seemed to be approaching critical mass.

Zeb Jackson had been running wide open for a couple of months, writing big stories nearly every week. He had the cover story in *The Courier* four times in eight weeks.

Everytime Zeb's editor gave him the cover of *The Courier* it was because his article was unmasking and naming yet another pedophile priest in the diocese. The growing list of diocesan priests who were sexual predators was shocking enough, but the interviews with their victims were horrifying to read. Each cover story ended the same way with an offensive, insulting comment issued to *The Courier* in writing by Lloyd Lecompte, diocesan media director, "The diocese does not wish to comment on allegations raised by Mr. Jackson. Yours in Christ, Lloyd Lecompte."

By Christmas week, Daryl Dessiré, publisher of the large-circulation daily *The Thiberville Register*, was outpacing even the paid media campaign of the diocese, regularly firing his big guns. The *Register* ran full-page stories accusing *The Courier* of being a haven for a yellow journalist, scandal monger and, worst of all in those parts, an outsider from New Orleans who wanted to hurt the Thiberville community in order to promote himself.

Not satisfied with their attacks on journalist Zeb Jackson and on the weekly he wrote for, the *Register* ran a Sunday page-one editorial attacking me as being an obstructionist who was causing pain to the good people of Thiberville, Bayou Saint John and Amalie by prolonging the inevitable finding of guilt against Father Dubois. The unsigned piece stated it was in my power to honor the children, Church and community by bringing an end to this. It was vintage Joe Rossi dressed up in the prose of Jon Bendel. As Bendel was the attorney for both the newspaper and its publisher, he had complete control over the content of stories relating to the diocese and Father Francis Dubois.

The main thrust of the offensive launched by the *Register* was in a series of stories and editorials headlined "Church Not On Trial", which repeatedly asserted that there was no proof in the public record of wrongdoing by the bishop or his vicars. This was true. There was no proof in the public record of wrongdoing by the bishop or his vicars.

43

A LADY FRIEND

Saturday evening, December 8, 1984
Sister Julianne's Apartment, Thiberville

It had been months since anyone associated with the diocese had spoken with me. If the lawyers were having meetings, I was locked out. I decided it was time to call Sister Julianne, the nun who had given me her card on the day of the lunch at the Old Bishop's House. There were things I wanted to know the truth about, and she had said she would never lie to me. I left a message on her home phone Friday and received a return call Saturday morning.

"Can we talk?" I asked.

"Sure. How about tonight about six?" she said.

"Tonight's okay?"

"I'll have to break a date – with Bogart. I was gonna watch *Casablanca* and *The Barefoot Contessa* again."

The address was near the cathedral, an old, well-kept Victorian home. On the porch I found four mailboxes and buzzers. Three of the mailboxes had names on them and the other had a small toy fat nun in traditional habit taped to it. I rang the nun's buzzer and immediately heard her coming down the steps. When Sister Julianne opened the door she was wearing sweat pants and a tee-shirt with lettering that said "My Way Is the Highway".

"You're here," she said.

I followed her upstairs to a comfortable flat filled with books, photographs and some paintings. The old gas heaters warmed the apartment, gave off a blue flame and fogged the windows. "I didn't know nuns had apartments."

"We do. Priests have regular houses now. A lot has changed."

"The art's great," I said, motioning to the crowded walls.

"The paintings are cheap ones I find in flea markets. I took most of the photos a long time ago during summers in Europe. I love Europe."

I pointed to a photo of a handsome, athletic young man with a bottle of champagne in one hand and sunglasses propped on his forehead. She picked up the picture and smiled at it. "He's probably one reason I'm a nun. We wanted to marry, but he was killed in a car accident in our senior year at college. This was taken in Switzerland one summer when we traveled together. We camped out a lot, shared our dreams."

She offered me water, tea, a soft drink, a beer or what she called "really cheap wine". I took the soft drink, and so did she.

"I'm glad I don't gamble. I would have bet you would never take me up on my invitation to talk."

"Sister—"

"You don't have to call me Sister if I don't have to call you Mister. How about Julie and Renon?"

"Just Ren is fine. What kind of religious order are you in?"

"I belong to an order of administrators. It's what we do. What I do for the diocese is what we do for dioceses, hospitals, Catholic charities and other organizations around the world, including relief agencies working in places like Africa, Latin America and developing countries."

"Thiberville is Third World in some ways," I said.

"You're right. After Tommy was killed, I buried myself in schoolwork, finishing with a double major in management and economics, then an MBA. Along the way I studied with two nuns in this order. I looked their situation over, and decided to become one of them."

"Why?"

"Don't you know that I've asked myself that a whole lot of times. It's silly, I think, but the lack of money appealed to me. Tommy and I were both non-materialistic. We hoped to never own much in the

way of possessions. We were idealistic and wanted to work for
organizations like the Peace Corps our whole lives, to try to make
a small but positive contribution to humanity. Maybe make a few
lives better. I thought if I joined the order, I would end up in Africa.
Both of the nuns I studied with had worked in Africa."

"And?"

"Obviously, I did not get to go to Africa. I was sent to Thiberville
when the diocese made a request to our order for a personnel
director. That was four years ago, a century ago it seems."

"What do you do as personnel director?"

"I insulate Monsignor Moroux from the complaining,
whimpering and whining priests who don't like their assignments.
A lot of priests here are elitist and only want to be in the big parishes
where rich parishioners can dote on them and spoil them. It's like
sucking up to rich Catholics is a special ministry here. Priests want
to be in parishes where they are pampered by old ladies whose
maids bring them meals and feted by old men who take them
golfing and fishing. Some rich parishioners take priests golfing in
Florida, even gambling in Las Vegas. There's a lot of money in
Thiberville, but I'm not telling you anything you don't know."

"You're between Monsignor Moroux and his priests?"

"Right. The policy is that no personnel complaints of any kind
can be made direct to the vicar general, Moroux, and no one ever
gets an audience with His Excellency, Bishop Reynolds, who I
think I've met only three times. Our ghost of a bishop is known to
many of us as 'Casper' – you know, after the cartoon. No one ever
sees him except on the altar on important holy days. He hangs out
all the time on some bay in Alabama where his wealthy New
Orleans family has a compound. He is a ghost, but way too ugly
to be called Casper."

I laughed.

"It's a weird place. The vicar general has a closed-door policy.
No one can approach Monsignor Moroux about anything. All the
complaints come to me. I alone have the responsibility for hearing
all complaints, but I have no authority to address a complaint. I

have no authority to do anything but write a one-paragraph summary of the complaint for Monsignor Moroux to peruse and ignore."

"Sounds bizarre."

"It's the way this diocese works, probably many dioceses. Bishops are the sole authority in their fiefdom, and a diocese is a fiefdom. What bishops do is delegate responsibility, but they never delegate authority. Even our vicar general is like a eunuch in terms of authority. Moroux has a lot of responsibility, but no authority."

"I want to know some things."

"Ask whatever you wish, Ren. I can tell ya that this case with Father Dubois was long overdue. I knew it had to happen and I believe things are going to get a whole lot worse. Tell me what you want to know."

In detail, I laid out everything I had learned since I'd met her on the swing at the Old Bishop's House months earlier, everything I had experienced, everything I thought and felt about what I had learned. I even told her about the night that Monsignor Moroux had sanitized and shredded the priests' personnel files, confessing that I thought I might have been an accomplice in obstructing justice. And I told her about Kate's theory that the diocese had a nest of perverted priests, something I was beginning to believe was true now that Zeb Jackson had named other priests who had molested children. It took me a long time to finish telling her all that I knew. I believed I was running no risk for I was already persona non grata with everyone else in the diocese. And if she was with them, one more enemy would make no difference.

When I finished talking, she brought me another Coke. I pulled out a pack of cigarettes and motioned to the balcony. She grabbed the pack from my hands and said, "Don't you know these things can kill you?"

Then she laughed, pulled one out, extracted a lighter from her pocket and pulled an ashtray from behind her stereo. "We can smoke right here, Ren. We'll die together."

I said, "Since that luncheon at the Old Bishop's House I've

obviously had no ally, been alone. Those I thought were going to be my allies have acted as enemies since the first day, literally the day after I signed on to represent Dubois and flew to New Hampshire to see him. I guess I am looking for an ally in you."

"Whoa! Hey, I may not be the ally you're looking for. I'm probably not as brave as you hope I am. If I spoke my mind or if it were known I was assisting you in finding out the truth, or even having this visit with you, I think I'd be gone tomorrow, fired. They can replace me overnight. They don't even need to replace me. They can just outlaw all complaints, which is the way I think it was before they hired me to listen to priests vent."

"And you want to stay?"

"No. I didn't say that. We're going to tell the truth to each other, right? Well, I don't want to stay here or stay in the religious order either. I'd like to be married one day. I am not a lesbian, Renon, never even experimented with it. I have a gay brother and gay friends I'm really proud of, people who are healthy and comfortable with their sexual orientation. Inside the Church, it's different – a lot of nuns and priests are gay and hiding behind robes and cassocks, pretending to be something unnatural that no one can be, a sexless being."

I nodded. "I know most of the priests I've met are either gay or missing a good chance."

"Probably the priests you're talking about are gay. It's twisted and this kind of sexual suppression overflows into everything in the institution. A lot of people in the religious life sublimate their natural sex drives and end up acting them out in ways that are pathological, positively evil. The sexless priest or nun – it's the first lie. This is the least healthy place I've been and I just don't fit here. I've finally gotten over or maybe I've just gotten through losing Tommy, and I want to live again. So, I will be leaving Thiberville and leaving the order. But I'd like to decide when that happens, rather than being forced out of Thiberville for cooperating with you. I think I am willing to run the risk of giving you some information, but I want as much cover as you can give me."

"I really need to know what is in Father Dubois's file. I don't know if it was sanitized by Moroux. He would not even let me see my own client's file. He had orders from Jon Bendel. Can you tell me what's in Dubois's file?"

"I can show you." She got up, went into the next room and returned with a huge folder bound by oversized rubber bands. "This is a copy of the complete personnel file of Father Francis Dominick Dubois. Consider it a gift. Do with it what you wish. I'd rather not be named as the source. If you have to do that, I'd like some warning, so I can make plans like packing, gassing up my car, and heading for the highway."

As I pulled the individual files from the folder, she said, "Reading this will take some time. I am going to drive over to the university indoor track and go for a run. On my way back I will pick up some health food. I'll be gone a couple of hours. We'll talk over dinner."

I read every line in the file. The documents bore out everything Dubois had told me at the Stalder Institute. There was documentary proof of every horrific thing he had done. If Dubois had been damned by the accounts the children gave to Doctor Kennison, his personnel file damned the prefect of the seminary, Bishop Reynolds, Monsignor Moroux, and every priest who had been complicit in covering up his crimes for decades. I kept returning to something Dubois and I had not talked about, his seminary academic records.

Finally, I heard Julie pounding up the steps. The door flew open and a perspiring beauty carrying two pizzas crossed the threshold. She went to the kitchen, picked up two beers, grabbed a towel from her bathroom, wiped her face and draped it over her shoulder. "Here, my new friend. Health food – pizza."

"How far do you run?" I asked.

"About six miles. It's what you do when you don't have sex," she said.

"Have you read his file?" I asked.

"Yep. When Father Dubois was first sent away to New Hampshire, I went into the archives one night. Copied it, brought it home and read it. Just before the time you tell me Moroux shredded damaging information in the personnel records, I went back into the secret archives. I went back in to make sure Dubois's file had not been updated and I found that document where he was suspended from performing sacraments or acting as a priest. So, it's up to date. Every document is in the file."

I fumbled for the right words to pose my question. "Reading over Dubois's transcripts from the minor and major seminaries, it seems to me that he failed academically every year, yet he was always promoted to the next level. Can that be right? He was either an awful student or plain stupid."

"Probably both. My guess would be both."

"And... and there is a letter from the rector at Saint John Seminary, this Monsignor Billadeaux, in the file that is carefully drafted. It's a letter to the man who was bishop here then, recommending against the ordination of Dubois. The letter mentions Dubois's unnatural affinity for young boys. I mean, it's there. It's in black and white. Before he was even ordained. They knew about his sexual activities with boys when they made him a priest."

"Right. Probably happened a lot of times with other priests."

"Well, how... how?"

"Well, you've got to understand, Renon, this Church does not operate like any other institution on earth. In canon law, no one in any diocese has any authority over anything except the bishop. No one is over the bishop. The Pope couldn't pick our bishop out of a lineup. Every bishop wants to look good in Rome's eyes and there are not many things Rome notices, but I think maybe they do notice the number of vocations a diocese has, the number of new priests ordained that year, the number of men in seminary who are to be assigned to the diocese upon ordination – that and finances. I think maybe the Vatican notes those things."

"And?"

"And that's how a Dubois happens. The number of priests a diocese has is important for a lot of reasons."

"That's how he got here. But how did he stay here? How did the first bishop and that vicar general then, Monsignor Darnell – or Bishop Reynolds and Monsignor Moroux – allow him to stay here when he kept sexually abusing boys every place they sent him? He should have gone to prison twenty years ago."

"This place is what is known in our Church as a benevolent diocese, meaning that out of our bishop's goodness we will ordain men or accept transfers of priests who some other dioceses might deem unfit. There is a high tolerance here for conduct that would not be tolerated anywhere."

"It's an outrageous concept."

"It's worse than outrageous. There are no words for it. I attend conferences of diocesan personnel directors. I've had conversations with some who are really distressed about the caliber and character of priests in their diocese. They are also in benevolent dioceses."

"What a phrase! Benevolent diocese!"

"Right. A priest who has had a string of drunk-driving problems or other alcohol issues is dried out in a treatment center and shipped to a benevolent diocese. It's the same with a priest who has impregnated a parishioner and has to find a new home. Men with all kinds of afflictions, addictions and flaws find a new home in a benevolent diocese."

"A benevolent diocese? And this extends to harboring criminal child abusers?"

"Right. And your wife is right. Father Dubois is far from the only one here. I don't know what that guy Jackson and *The Courier* will ultimately uncover, but your wife is right. What did your wife call it?"

"Kate called it a nest – a nest of perverted priests."

"She's right. I have knowledge of others like Dubois. There are fifteen I am aware of, and another ten I suspect. I think somewhere over 10 per cent of our priests are either sexually abusing teenagers or little children. I can't bear to think about it. I feel so powerless sometimes. "

"Do you have their files? The fifteen?"

She nodded. "When you need those files, I'll give them to you. Eat your pizza, Ren. It's getting cold."

During dinner we talked about the history of Thiberville and the surrounding settlements, a place founded by my ancestors that she knew a whole lot more about than I did.

She went to the French doors leading to the balcony and struggled with the shutter latch that was too tall for her tiny, taut, runner's stature. I went over to help her. As I unlatched the hardware our bodies touched. She looked up at me with the clearest dark eyes I had ever seen. With my right hand, I smoothed away a wayward lock of her sweaty hair. Then I quickly withdrew. "Sorry." The moment was awkward and I did not know how we were going to get out of it.

She laughed hard. "It's okay. I'm not going to break if you touch me."

She walked me to my car, carrying the Dubois file under her arm. She handed the file to me and said, "Good luck. And, hey, call me if you have to use the file. Give me some warning – ya know, to pack up and get outtahere."

I nodded. "This has to be the worst diocese in the country," I said.

Julie was standing under a streetlight, momentarily lost in a serious thought. I waited for her to speak. She shrugged. "It's all so secretive, Ren. It would not surprise me if every diocese in the world is exactly like this one. But I cannot imagine anyone would ever know that."

Christmas Eve, 1984
Julie's Apartment

I saw Julie again on Christmas Eve. Kate was skiing with the children in Breckenridge, Colorado, and my dad was visiting my sister in Florida.

I had been frozen out by all of the Church lawyers and the diocese. I only talked about Dubois and the growing number of priest scandals with Julie, who had become a phone friend. Over the previous two weeks we had talked on the phone nearly every night. She was my only window into the workings of the diocese. And she was honest.

I knew Julie had stopped attending Mass. One night on the phone she made a reference to "our Church".

I said, "It's not my Church anymore."

Julie said, "I don't know if I've quit the Church, but I've quit going to church."

Knowing she would be home on that freezing Christmas Eve, I brought a new bicycle to the porch of her apartment building. A big bow was tied to the handlebars. I rang the doorbell, raced around the house to the alley where my car was parked, and drove away. Two blocks later, my car phone rang.

"How did Santa know I needed a new bike? You can't be far away. Come back. I'll fix us some breakfast."

When I was settled in her small living room, she handed me a wrapped package. "Yeah, I had this gift for you. I just didn't know if I should give you something."

I pulled the wrapper off. It was a book on the life of Saint Ignatius Loyola.

"You might be surprised by this man's life," she said.

"Thanks. I'll read it."

"Okay. Now, that's the good part. The bad part is I lied. I don't have any breakfast. I have one egg, a few suspect pieces of bread. I have leftover pizza from last night. I can heat it."

"Julie, dear, do you eat anything besides pizza?"

"Sure. Apples."

44

A PECULIAR PRIEST

Wednesday evening, January 16, 1985
Rectory of Saint Bernadette, Bayou Saint John

Jon Bendel was whispering into the phone.

"You gotta speak up, Jon," I said. "It's your phone or my car phone. I can't hear."

He coughed. "Let me get to another phone. I'll call you back in a minute."

I was on my way to Coteau. Kate had invited me for dinner with the kids. I always felt good when driving toward Coteau.

Bendel rang again. Still speaking in low tones, he said, "Look, I have my hands full over here at the chancery trying to prepare the bishop for his deposition. It could take all night the way it's going. I really need your help."

"In preparing the bishop?"

"No. I'd not wish that on anyone. Monsignor Moroux tells me this Monsignor Gaudet down in Bayou Saint John is resistant to the idea of attending the depositions at Chaisson's office tomorrow, actually refusing to testify. I can't get down there. I've had Monsignor Moroux call him to tell him to expect you this evening at seven o'clock."

"For what?"

"Standard preparation for a deposition. Explain what will take place in the depositions tomorrow."

"He's not my client. He's your client."

"Please do this. I think this monsignor just needs to understand, needs to have the legal process of a deposition explained to him. It can't be that difficult."

My line went dead.

After Bendel hung up, I pulled into a parking lot fenced with crushed beer cans. A tin sign advertised the long, rickety shack as being "Razor Leblanc's Bar, Barbershop, Pool Emporium, Grocery Store & Marrying Parlor".

The phone was still in my hand. I was torn between calling Bendel back to cancel on Monsignor Gaudet or calling Kate to cancel on dinner with her and the children.

I hadn't spoken to Bendel, or any of the other Church lawyers, in weeks. Now he was offering me the chance to talk to one of the priests who had supervised Dubois. It might be the only such chance I would ever have.

The lady who responded to the doorbell at the rectory wore a stiff, starched uniform that made a slight cracking noise when she moved. The house smelled like The Palms, where my father lived. It was of that same vintage, built of the same materials and closed up for as many years. As I followed the lady down a long hall, I heard music. The maid carefully opened the carved wooden French doors to the monsignor's study. The sound of opera filled the room.

Monsignor Phillip Jules Gaudet was seated in a wingback chair, wearing a black cassock with large pearl buttons. He had a long red scarf draped around his neck. He raised the index finger of his right hand to his lips, signaling me to remain silent, and motioned with the downturned palm of his left hand for me to take a seat. The record ended. For a moment the needle bounced on the vinyl, making a scratching sound, while the man in black seemed to swoon in reverie, eyes closed. When he stood and turned off the stereo, a clock began to chime seven.

"Ah, the hour is now seven, the hour you were expected. My timing was perfect. You were more than punctual. This is an unusual trait in the era we live in."

He was not going to shake my hand. "Do you have legal papers or something for me?"

"No. I was asked to help prepare you for your deposition tomorrow."

"Oh, that? Well, I am not going to do that. I was in that lawyer Chaisson's office one time back in September. I am not going to subject myself to that man's questions. I spoke with Mother an hour ago. We agree I should not have my name involved in such tawdry business. But I have prepared table for both of us now. Normally, I have table at six thirty. Tonight I made an exception to extend hospitality to you."

It took a moment for me to realize that what the monsignor was calling "table" was what the rest of us called dinner.

"Thank you, but I'm not hungry. Monsignor, we do have work to do."

The monsignor became very agitated. In a petulant tone, he said, "Table. I will have table. I always have table." His outburst could not have been more childlike if he had stomped his feet.

When we were seated in the dining room, Monsignor Gaudet folded his hands carefully and prayed in Latin. The prayer lasted an interminably long time. When he finished praying, he crossed himself, reached for a small bell and shook it. The lady in the stiff white uniform appeared with finger bowls and napkins that were as starched as the clothes she wore. The monsignor rang the little bell for each course. The sherbet served to cleanse our palates was the only thing that had any flavor. Table took exactly one hour.

What we talked about at table was his mother. I heard about her illnesses and ailments, and learned that since he had been a priest his mother had faithfully attended his Sunday-morning Mass every week.

"My mother lives in Cathedral Parish in Thiberville. By all rights I should be rector of the cathedral. Then my dear old mother could see me every day. Instead, I am exiled to this inglorious outpost."

Once we were back in the room with leaded glass windows that he referred to as his library, I realized the shelves were filled with music albums, all operas.

"What is it you want to discuss?"

I decided not to talk about the deposition he had informed me he would not attend. I would save that for later. There were other things I needed to know about my client.

"Monsignor, Father Francis Dubois was assigned to this parish as your assistant—"

He cut me off. "They now call them associates, not assistants. But I would never have associated with this man by choice. Nor was he of any real assistance. The man could not relate to anyone older than ten. He is a pederast, pure and simple."

"Did you know this about him when he lived in this rectory? That he was, as you say, a pederast?"

"Young man, every priest in this diocese knows Father Dubois is a pederast."

"Yes. That's true today. That is not the question. The question is: did you know Dubois was a pederast when he lived in this rectory?"

"It does not matter when one came to know this or how one came to know this. I know this man is a pederast. This is my knowledge."

"And this will be your testimony tomorrow in Thiberville when you give your deposition?"

"Young man, I told you. I am not going to involve myself in these proceedings."

"Monsignor, perhaps you should read the document the sheriff's deputy delivered to you. It is not an invitation or a request. It's a court order. A judge has ordered you to appear at the offices of Kane Chaisson on Caffery Boulevard in Thiberville at ten tomorrow morning."

"I am not going."

"If you do not appear, Mr. Chaisson will hold up the proceedings until he has an arrest warrant issued for you."

The monsignor asked me to please leave the room and said he would send Annette, who I presumed to be the housekeeper-cook, to bring me back to him when he was ready. I welcomed the chance to go outside and smoke. As I was closing the library door behind me, I heard him dialing the phone.

When Annette came for me, I realized I had been on the porch for nearly twenty minutes. The monsignor was patting perspiration from his forehead with a folded handkerchief when I entered the room. "So, tell me, young man. What exactly happens at these depositions?"

"A deposition is the giving of testimony under oath. All of the lawyers in this case, and that would mean lawyers representing all of the parties who have been sued – Father Dubois, the archdiocese, the diocese, Bishop Reynolds, Monsignor Moroux, Monsignor Belair, and you—"

"What do you mean? I have never been sued by anyone over anything."

"Monsignor, if you read the paper, the subpoena the deputy brought, you will see the caption of the suit names you as one of the defendants."

"Who is my lawyer? Don't I need a lawyer if I have been sued? Mother has property."

"You are represented as are all of the officials of the diocese by Jonathan Bendel, and there are lawyers representing the many insurance companies who insure the diocese. There is no chance any of your property or your mother's property will be at risk."

"What happens tomorrow?"

"All of the lawyers and a court reporter, as well as any parties to the lawsuit, will assemble in a conference room in Mr. Chaisson's office. No one else will be admitted. It is certain there will be some press people outside of the building, and I want to start by addressing that. Television cameras and still photographers for newspapers will be there. Whatever footage they take will last forever and may be broadcast many times over. What a person does on a television tape or in a still photograph can inadvertently create an impression very different from what the person intends. So it is important not to smile like this is something you are making light of. Not to frown like you are disapproving. Not to show any reaction or emotion. Not to do anything cute."

"I have never done anything cute in my entire life."

"I don't imagine you have."

"What happens inside the building?"

"Once the court reporter swears you in, places you under oath, you will be questioned by Mr. Chaisson, who represents a boy called Donny Rachou and his parents. Mr. Chaisson may ask you questions for as long as he wishes and you are compelled by court order to testify truthfully."

"So, I will tell them Father Dubois is a pederast. Case closed."

"Monsignor, again I ask you to separate what you know today from what you knew when Dubois lived here. Did you know he was a pederast when he lived in this rectory?"

"You cannot separate and compartmentalize what you know. I know the man is a pederast. Didn't everyone in the diocese know this from the beginning? And I know he is a cretin as well, but I will not say that part."

"Please do skip that part."

"There is another thing…"

"Yes?"

"I become nervous and confused when I am asked to answer questions. I always think I don't know the answer. I try to avoid anyone who might have a question unless it is a question about our religion, doctrine, faith, sacraments."

"You will know the answers to all the questions you will hear tomorrow."

"All I know is this is the Roman Catholic Church and no one in the world, not this Mr. Chaisson or anyone else has the right to ask anything of a Catholic priest."

"Tomorrow you will be asked questions. No one can stop this."

"I could make a mess of things."

This could turn out to be the biggest understatement I ever heard, I thought. Aloud, I said, "Monsignor, you are going to be asked if you had problems with Dubois and boys when he lived here. I want to know the truth."

"I did move him from a ground-floor bedroom to a bedroom on the second floor."

"Why was that?"

"Little boys were crawling in the window at night. They broke some of the rose bushes Mother and I had transplanted from her garden."

"Did you ever tell anyone about the little boys crawling in the windows?"

"No. And I certainly am not going to tell Mr. Chaisson tomorrow."

"You have to tell the truth."

"This Chaisson fellow sounds like an unjust aggressor against Holy Mother Church. One of the most sacred precepts of the priesthood is to avoid all scandal to the Church. I will not scandalize Holy Mother Church."

45

CHURCH ON TRIAL

9 a.m., Thursday January 17, 1985
Kane Chaisson's Law Office, Thiberville

The television vans were at Chaisson's office when I arrived. The lawyers' luxury cars were not in sight. They had parked at the rear of the building and used a service entrance to avoid being filmed. When I entered Chaisson's conference room, only the Church officials and their legal counsel were there. When they saw me, everyone shut up.

Thomas Quinlan pulled me into the adjoining room. "I have been appointed to ask you to leave. These depositions do not concern Father Dubois's criminal case and your involvement in the civil cases is meaningless. Your client has no assets. It's our money, our assets, our asses that are hung out here."

"My client is a named defendant. I received a notice for this deposition. I am going to do my job whether all those assholes in that room want me here or not."

"I am asking you again to take your leave."

As I was about to answer, Kane Chaisson walked in another door and said, "Court reporter is ready, gentlemen. Shall we proceed? I will start with Monsignor Phillip Gaudet."

We moved back into the room. I took a seat next to Tommy Quinlan. Bendel was to my right and Blassingame sat at the head of the table, opposite the witness at the other end. After Monsignor Gaudet took the oath from the court reporter, Blassingame cleared his throat and began. "Ms. Court Reporter, are we on the record?"

The reporter nodded, and Blassingame pulled the microphone closer to him. "We object to the taking of this deposition on grounds of relevancy and materiality. We are prepared to place into the record a sworn affidavit of Bishop Reynolds to the effect that Monsignor Gaudet has never been assigned to the Catholic parish of Our Lady of the Seas in Amalie, Louisiana. That he has never celebrated Mass there or had any connection with the church parish in Amalie. Because the petition of Donny Rachou prepared by Kane Chaisson alleges acts that occurred only in Amalie – things Monsignor Gaudet could have no knowledge of – there is nothing Monsignor Gaudet could offer this morning that would be of any value to the litigation before the court."

I noticed Blassingame was not as articulate as he usually was.

Kane Chaisson responded, "Thank you, Mr. Blassingame. We will note that your objection is a continuing objection to the entirety of this proceeding." Turning his attention to the witness, he said, "Now, Monsignor, for the record, please state your full name."

"Monsignor Phillip Jules Gaudet."

"You understand that you are under oath to tell the truth?"

"I do."

"And isn't it true that the things Mr. Blassingame just said are not the truth, for the truth is that you in fact received complaints about Father Francis Dubois from parishioners in Amalie on at least three occasions, including Mr. and Mrs. Tommy Wesley Rachou?"

"Yes, I met Mr. and Mrs. Rachou, but that was in my residence, the rectory in Bayou Saint John, not in Amalie. I have never had any involvement in the affairs of Our Lady of the Seas Parish in Amalie."

"When you met Mr. and Mrs. Rachou, were they alone or were they with others?"

"One time, two or three couples came to complain about Father Francis. But the Rachous came alone, I think. "

"And did the Rachous tell you that Father Francis Dominick Dubois had been sexually abusing their son, Donny, in Amalie?"

Monsignor Gaudet hesitated, looked around the room as if, maybe, someone might give him the right answer or stop Chaisson from following this line of questioning.

"What did these parents tell you, Monsignor?"

"What I recall is that they described things they said Father Dubois had done, which would have made him a pederast by any definition."

"What advice did you give them?"

Blassingame was quick to interject. "We object on the basis that whatever Monsignor Gaudet might have said to the parents would have been said in his role as a priest and thus be protected by the privilege—"

"What privilege?" Chaisson bellowed. "There is no privilege. We are not talking about a confession. We're talking about a conversation."

Blassingame nodded at the priest to continue.

"Well, I believe I told them what I am sure I told other parents who came to complain about Father Dubois – that if they would bring their son to me for confession… if their son made a good confession and received absolution, then their son would again be in a state of grace, his sins forgiven."

"You thought the solution was for the child to make an act of confession?"

"That was the solution, sir. The sacrament. The sacraments are always the solution. This is about sin, penance and absolution, the sacrament of penance. What is now referred to as reconciliation by some people."

Monsignor Gaudet appeared to have completed his answer when he blurted out, "Sir, I fail to understand how you or anyone else outside of the Church has any right to ask me…" His voice trailed off and the monsignor stared into space, focusing on a blank wall opposite him.

"Did you tell them that you would report this to anyone?"

"No." He was still staring at the wall, away from Chaisson. "I would never talk about the internal workings of the diocese with a lay person. That day it was none of their business how the Church dealt with its priest. Today I do not believe it is any of your business."

"Did you in fact report this to anyone?"

Monsignor Phillip Jules Gaudet turned and faced Kane Chaisson. "Yes. On this occasion, I am sure that very day, I telephoned our vicar general at the chancery in Thiberville – Monsignor Jean-Paul Moroux."

"Do you remember what you said to Monsignor Moroux?"

"Not really. Probably I said something like, 'Father Francis is at it again. There is another family complaining.'"

"Another? You knew this Rachou boy was not the first boy Father Dubois had done these kinds of things with because these things had been reported to you by other parents, right?"

"Yes, I guess."

"Father Dubois was assigned to your church in Bayou Saint John before he became pastor in Amalie, correct?"

"Yes, for two years he lived in my rectory. But I did not ask for him."

"Would it be right to say he was sexually involved with children in your parish?"

"No, sir," the monsignor answered indignantly. "I did not receive a complaint of the kind we're talking about here. In my rectory, I know he was not sleeping with little boys. I moved him upstairs to keep little boys from climbing in his bedroom window."

"Boys were climbing in his bedroom window?"

"I think it happened only that once and I caught them. They trampled rose bushes under the window. The next morning I moved him because I could not have that. I could not have young boys climbing in the window of a priest's bedroom, could I? And trampling young rose bushes."

"I ask you to assume Father Dubois has admitted to having sex with boys in your rectory. Would you believe that is true?"

"I don't know that I would believe anything Father Dubois has said to anyone about anything, and I would be surprised if anyone in this room believed anything he said."

Kane Chaisson pulled a Bible out of a briefcase and placed it on the table.

"Monsignor, I purchased this copy of the Bible at the Catholic Bookstore on Robert E. Lee Boulevard here in Thiberville. Is this the same version of the Bible that you read?"

Monsignor Gaudet took the Bible in his hands. "Yes."

"Do you know that scripture says that anyone who harms a child should have a millstone tied around his neck and be thrown into the sea?"

"I don't know that you've got the exact wording, but that's the gist of it. Yes."

"Being guided by this, if you were faced today with parents complaining about their child being sexually abused by a priest – Monsignor, I want you to think about this – would you respond differently than the way you responded when you received complaints from the parents of Donny Rachou? Would you go to the police and advise the parents to go to the police?"

"It would be a serious sin to do anything different from what I did."

"Why?" asked Chaisson.

"It would bring scandal to Holy Mother Church. Do you not understand this?"

"No, I don't."

"I am a priest, part of the Roman Catholic Church. Police are part of the secular world, Mr. Chaisson, and have no place in Church affairs, and in my opinion, neither do you. I do not believe you have any business asking these questions of me. Dubois was not my charge. I am not responsible for anything that man did and neither is anyone else in the diocese. He is an adult with free will."

"He sexually abused young children."

"Priests are people and there are all kinds of people and all kinds of priests, even pederasts like Father Dubois, I suppose. It was not my business what Father Dubois did in his own time as long as he did his job. My concern when he was an associate at my parish was in Father Dubois, the priest. Francis Dubois, the pederast, was not and is not my concern."

Kane Chaisson quietly said, "Thank you."

46

A FATAL MISTAKE

1:30 p.m., Thursday January 17, 1985
Kane Chaisson's Law Office, Thiberville

When everyone returned from lunch, Monsignor Moroux came over to me and handed me a letter. The letter was dated the same day. It was curt.

> *Again I am advising that it is critically important in the view of the diocese for the medical welfare of your client and his pastoral care that you immediately travel to consult with Father Matthew Patterson at Hope House in Williams Crossing, Virginia. I expect you will make travel arrangements today to see Father Patterson.*

Beneath the two sentences were the address and phone numbers for Hope House in Virginia.

Moroux said, "I've been urgently requested again. As I told you, it's really a demand by the papal nuncio's canon lawyer."

"And this papal guy is...?"

"This papal guy, as you refer to him, is the Pope's personal representative to the United States, the Vatican ambassador."

I put the letter in my pocket and walked into the conference room, taking a seat next to young James Ryburn, Tom Quinlan's gopher. Ryburn touched my arm and gave me a strange look that seemed almost like a slight gesture of solidarity.

I think everyone in the room was expecting Chaisson to call Monsignor Moroux as his next witness. But Chaisson asked the bishop to take the witness chair.

First, Kane Chaisson reminded the bishop that the court had issued an order for him to produce all documents in the possession of the diocese relating to Father Francis D. Dubois. "Your Excellency, do you have the documents the court ordered you to produce today?"

The bishop had a foul expression on his face. "What documents are you talking—"

"The personnel file of Father Francis Dominick Dubois."

"Ahh, ahh…" the bishop mumbled.

Monsignor Moroux reached inside a briefcase and handed the subpoenaed file to the bishop.

"Is this the complete personnel file of Father Francis Dubois?" Chaisson asked.

The bishop looked plaintively at Monsignor Moroux.

There was a copy of the complete personnel file of Father Dubois in the trunk of my car, Julie's copy. I had stopped by Julie's the night before and talked with her about the possible necessity of my producing the file at the deposition in the event the diocese produced a sanitized version. She had heard me out, nodded, and said, "Do what you have to do."

Chaisson was calm, deliberate. "Bishop, I ask again. Is this the complete personnel file of Father Francis Dubois?"

Moroux nodded at the bishop and Bishop Reynolds mumbled, "Yes."

Kane Chaisson announced that in the interest of saving time for everyone involved, he would recess the deposition for a few moments to review the contents of the file. No one objected.

I stood and started for the door to have a cigarette outside and shoot the breeze with some of the media guys, pretty much the only people on Chaisson's property who were still talking to me. Moroux caught up with me before I reached the door. "Please call Father Patterson today and make arrangements to meet with him. Maybe the nunciature will leave me alone then."

"I'll do this for you, Monsignor, but I want you to stop Rossi and Bendel from threatening to fire me every time they have some nightmare that I'm sabotaging the diocese. Bendel and Rossi blame me for the bad press the diocese is getting. I have not ever told Zeb Jackson or *The Courier* one thing that was published in any article. Whenever I read those articles, it's always news to me. Maybe all of you knew about those other priests *The Courier* named, but I never heard of any of them. I have enough to do in trying to defend Dubois without fighting with Rossi, Bendel and Blassingame all the time."

"You know there is not much I can do," Moroux said.

As the bishop's deposition resumed, Kane Chaisson placed the Dubois file in front of him and said, "I make a motion to have the entire Dubois file copied by the court reporter and attached to this deposition, labeled as Rachou One, and filed with the deposition in the record of this litigation."

No one spoke. I wondered if it was the real file or the sanitized version.

Kane Chaisson continued, "Then, without opposition, the personnel file of Father Francis Dubois produced this date by the bishop in response to the subpoena issued to him, is hereby made a permanent part of the record of this proceeding. Bishop, I want to give you an opportunity to review every document in this file and I want you to take as much time as you need to do this."

The bishop put on thick, black-framed eye glasses and began to read the file. Some documents he seemed to read closely, but the majority of the papers he seemed to scan. Then the bishop nodded toward Chaisson in a belligerent manner.

"Bishop, I know you are a busy man. We could go through each one of these documents one by one, and we would be here until the cows come home. I think all of us who have ever lived on a farm know that the cows never come home. What I am going to do is attempt to ask you about the things in Dubois's file in more of a summary fashion, but at any time, if you prefer, we will revert to going through the papers in the file page by page. Is this okay with you to proceed in this manner?"

"Yes."

"Bishop, if I read this file correctly – and I want you to correct me if at any time you believe I have made an error in my understanding of these documents – if I read this file correctly, Father Francis Dubois was twice caught sexually molesting young boys while he was in the major seminary. If I have this right, the rector of the seminary, Monsignor Billadeaux, opposed his ordination as a priest in a letter addressed to the former Bishop of Thiberville. In this letter the seminary director, Monsignor Billadeaux, stated that Francis Dubois had an unnatural affinity for young boys... Bear with me, Bishop."

Kane Chaisson flipped through pages of notes he had made on the Dubois file, and continued. "Nevertheless, Dubois was accepted for ordination and then in all of the parishes he was assigned to, including the parish in Amalie, he had to be removed because of complaints that he was sexually involved with young boys. And on one of the occasions when you removed Father Dubois from a church parish, you made Father Dubois chaplain to the Cub Scouts and Boy Scouts—"

Blassingame stood and shouted an interruption. "I object to the question as it is a compound question, and I instruct Bishop Reynolds not to answer. On behalf of all counsel at this table, I object to the attachment of the Dubois personnel file to the deposition of the bishop in that it has not been properly authenticated by all of the persons who prepared documents that may have been placed in that file, documents which may or may not be true and accurate. This Monsignor Billadeaux you refer to is someone I have never heard of, and no one but that Monsignor Billadeaux knows what he meant by the comments he made in the document you refer to. The likelihood is that all the other documents contain no more than inadmissible hearsay, and few, if any, of the documents are notarized and therefore self-proving, and none of us can cross-examine pieces of paper. Finally, I am calling a recess to this deposition so that I may confer with my client and co-counsel."

Kane Chaisson could not suppress his grin. Perhaps I was the most surprised person in the room. It seemed Monsignor Moroux had kept his word to me. The Dubois file had not been tampered with.

I spoke up. "Mr. Blassingame misspoke himself when he held himself out to be speaking for all counsel at this table. I have no objection to the entire personnel file of Father Dubois being attached to the deposition of Bishop Reynolds and I am legal counsel to Father Dubois. As the document was produced by the bishop in response to a subpoena issued to him, I believe our evidentiary law provides that the bishop has vouched for the authenticity and accuracy of the information contained in the file."

"Thank you," Chaisson said. "Now we will stand in recess as long as Mr. Blassingame wishes. Have someone get me in my office when you are prepared to resume. While you are all on break, you might call your offices and your homes and advise of a change in plans. Because, when we resume, Mr. Blassingame, I intend to review the Dubois file page by page, paragraph by paragraph, line by line, word by word with the bishop. Looks like we will be here until the cows come home."

After Chaisson and the court reporter left the room, Blassingame turned to me, "I would like you to leave the room, Renon."

"Nope, Bobby. I'm not going anywhere. Get a court order to remove me, if you can, but on my own I am not going anywhere."

Turning to Monsignor Moroux, Blassingame fixed him in an accusatory stare. "It was my understanding that there was no damaging information that existed in any of the files Chaisson subpoenaed. I thought all the damaging documents were purged, shredded, destroyed."

Blassingame then turned on Jon Bendel. "We had two conversations about this and you assured me the files were clean. Now we find ourselves ambushed by this. I want an explanation."

Monsignor Moroux's expression never changed. He pointed to

me. "Father Francis is his client and he instructed me that the personnel file of Father Francis was to remain intact. The other thirty-one priests named on Chaisson's subpoena list had no involvement in this and no legal representation. Presumably they are represented by Mr. Bendel and yourself as the two of you represent the diocesan interests. Father Francis is represented by Mr. Chattelrault and I followed the dictates of Father Francis's legal counsel in this matter."

Blassingame looked at me, grimaced and said, "Do you realize what you have done to your bishop? Your diocese?"

I said, "He's not my bishop. This is not my diocese. The bishop has not answered the question on the table. You have it in your power to stop all of this now. Call the insurance companies and enter a joint stipulation of liability. Then you will stop any introduction in court of any evidence about what the bishop knew or did not know. If you let this go on today, you will sink the diocese, Bobby. You'll be able to blame me or whoever else you wish, but the diocese will sink faster than the *Titanic* and it's you who is in the wheelhouse, not me."

"I'm not having a discussion with you, Chattelrault," Blassingame said, as he headed in the direction of Kane Chaisson's office.

Forty minutes later, the two men returned. They had made a deal. The depositions would be suspended, and a stipulation of liability would be filed. Chaisson and Blassingame made a joint entry into the court reporter's record to the effect that the Diocese of Thiberville was admitting liability in the case. Blassingame added a lot of self-serving verbiage that this was being done to spare the child and his family any unnecessary pain in the legal proceedings.

Everyone filed out of Chaisson's law office. It seemed the worst was over for the diocese as the public would never know what the bishop had known about Father Dubois and when he had known it.

47

A DOUBLE-CROSS

7 a.m., Friday January 18, 1985
Coteau

Mo made my reservations for Washington, DC and spoke with
Father Patterson's office at Hope House in Virginia in the suburbs
of Washington. A meeting was set for Saturday morning. As I
packed, I got a call from Zeb. He shouted, "Bishop Covers Up
Priest's Crimes For Decades!"

"What?"

"That's the headline in the Baton Rouge paper this morning.
Check out New Orleans – 'Bishop Moves Child-Abuser Priest
Parish To Parish'. The story is not out of the state yet, but it will
be running on the wire for the first time today. Naturally, *The
Thiberville Register* did not run anything at all this morning. But
the story is out there now. It's clear what role the bishop played.
It's also clear Father Dubois was abusing kids before ordination
and in every parish he served in. Christ, Monsignor Gaudet's
appalling attitude toward victims is unbelievable. It's all beginning
to come into focus now. It's not just a sicko priest story anymore.
There's a sicko monsignor and a sicko bishop in the mix."

"What the hell happened? How did the story get out? The
depositions weren't even supposed to be filed with the court."

"Well, between us... but I don't think it matters if it stays
between us, because by noon probably everybody will know.
When all of you left Chaisson's office, he had an informal press
conference and he passed out business cards for the court reporter.
The court reporter had everything printed and copied by ten last

night. He sold all of us copies of Monsignor Gaudet's deposition, the partial deposition of Bishop Reynolds and the personnel file of your client that was attached to the bishop's deposition. I stayed up half the night reading. All that stuff and the proposed stipulation of liability agreement between Chaisson and Blassingame is damning for the diocese."

All I could say was, "That's good." I was running late for my meeting with Johnny Wilcox and rang off. As I drove out of the driveway I thought about it and all I could think was *That's good.*

8 a.m.
Jacques' Café

Turtle was humming a spiritual song when she put coffee in front of us. Wilcox looked at the coffee and said, "Now, Turtle, just suppose I had wanted juice instead of coffee this morning? What would you have done?"

"Me? Honey, I woulda just changed yo mind."

When Turtle went off to decide what we wanted for breakfast and load it onto a tray, I asked Wilcox, "What ya got, Johnny?"

"I got two dead kids. Brothers. In a parish in Willow Springs. First kid supposedly committed suicide in 1971. The brother supposedly died in a bicycle accident a few weeks later, a one-bicycle accident at that. Ever heard of a fatal one-bicycle accident?"

I shook my head.

"This Father O. D. Ellison disappeared shortly after the second death. He was treated in two places and then he was in a monastery in Kansas for almost ten years. Now he lives in a home for retired priests just south of Sarasota, Florida."

"Break it down."

"First kid is supposed to have killed himself in the rectory of Ellison's church while Ellison was away from the property. The priest told police that the boy was upset about school, his friends calling him names at school because he liked all the things girls liked and didn't like anything the boys liked. The kid was only nine and allegedly distraught about being called a sissy and kids calling him 'BobbaLou' rather than Bobby. Ellison said he had to go visit a sick parishioner in the local hospital and he left the boy in the small chapel in the residence and told him to pray until he returned. The cops found it checked out that the priest gave communion to a patient in the hospital that afternoon. Since they confirmed his story, no one with the local police suspected the priest of having killed the boy. Almost no one in Willow Springs suspects that it was murder to this day. Only a couple of retired deputies believe it was murder. They could only whisper about it because he was a priest. Suicide was impossible."

"Meaning what?"

Before he could answer, Turtle delivered a fabulous breakfast for both of us, better than we would have ordered for ourselves.

"The sheriff's office had photographs. A fellow who was a state trooper with me when I was a rookie is the sheriff's top administrator up there. It took him damn near a week to find the pictures in a file box stored in the basement of the sheriff's office. I have photocopies of the pictures with me, but I don't think you want to see a kid hanging while you're eating."

"Did you see the scene?"

"You bet. Rang the rectory doorbell and a big fat black woman answered. I asked for the pastor and she said he was at a meeting at the diocese offices in Providence. When I told her I was a building inspector for the Diocese of Providence and I needed to inspect the property, she let me in and made me coffee. I asked if any changes had been made to the rectory since it used to be in the Diocese of Thiberville in the seventies and she said, 'No suh, I been here since President Kennedy came through here making votes 'bout 1960. There is nothing ever changed here except some paint.'"

"So you saw the scene?"

"Renon, the scene doesn't tell you anything the pictures don't tell you. It would have been virtually impossible for this boy to have situated the rope over the rafter in the small chapel and elevated himself to the noose – he would have had to have levitated. There was nothing to stand on and knock out from under him. The cops thought he stood on the back of a pew, but there is no way that was physically possible. This boy was strangled and then hung up, hoisted up, like a side of beef."

"What did the maid say?"

"I asked her if she was there when the little boy died in 1971. She said that it was her day off, but she never stopped praying for that little boy. She said his name was Bobby and he came to the rectory almost every day and when he left, sometimes he was crying. She said, 'That boy had lots of troubles. He was crying a lot.'"

"You have no doubt?"

"None. Father Ellison killed Bobby sure as Turtle is going to forget the biscuit you asked for. It was murder."

"The brother?"

"The scene of his death has completely changed, doesn't resemble the photographs taken at the time. What supposedly happened is that this kid, Dwayne, was riding his bike on the edge of a narrow country lane bounded by a steep drainage ditch on one side. This was a few weeks after his little brother hung himself. And… and he got a tire off into the ditch and crashed down the embankment and died of a massive head wound."

"Well, it could have happened that way, couldn't it?"

"The scene has changed. Now the ditch is lined with concrete, paved on the bottom and up both sides. Even the pecan tree that marked the site in the photographs has been cut down. The body was discovered about mid-morning on a Saturday, but the coroner put the time of death at about two a.m. The photographs, grainy black-and-whites, show a smooth, muddy surface. The photos show no evidence of there being a rock or other object for the kid to have struck his head on. There is no damage to the bike. The fall didn't even twist the handlebars."

"So what is a young kid doing riding his bike on a country road at two in the morning?"

"He wasn't going home. He lived two miles in the other direction, in a trailer park with his mother. And no one knows where he was coming from."

"No one?"

"I found the mother of the boys living in a mobile home park in Duval County, Texas. But she's not talking. She wanted to ask me questions, wanted to know what I was doing bothering her. I was honest. I said I was investigating the deaths of her sons. I asked her where Dwayne had been going on his bike at that hour on a Friday night. She shook her head and told me, 'Nobody knows. Maybe he was running away. He had never been right in the head, not since Bobby hung hisself.' I asked her why she thought Bobby killed himself."

"And?"

"You're not gonna believe what I tell you."

"Try me."

Wilcox reached into his briefcase and pulled some typed sheets out. "I was wired in every conversation I had. All the tapes were transcribed by my wife. It's all here for you. It's a pretty big file. Think I made at least a new boat trailer on this investigation. But here is what the lady said. I'm quoting directly. She said, 'Bobby killed hisself because of the bad things he was telling me 'bout the priest, Father at the church. Bobby didn't have no daddy because he run off with a young girl after Bobby was born. Bobby never even saw him and it don't seem Dwayne could remember him neither. So I was the daddy and momma and I took to Bobby with a yardstick and whipped his little butt till it looked like it was going to bleed. Did that three days in a row 'cause he was lying on the priest and saying the priest was pulling his pants down and making Bobby do things with the priest's pecker and that the priest tried to put his pecker inside Bobby in the back. And I knew he was lying and he jus' didn't wanna be no altar boy no more and I think he killed hisself because of the whipping I was giving him. And then... then when Bobby is dead, don't you know, Dwayne started trying to tell me Bobby was telling the truth about the

298

priest and that the priest was doing these things to Dwayne too. Right before he died, Dwayne said to me he was going to talk to that Father and tell him to stop or he was going to go to a teacher and tell the teacher. I couldn't whip Dwayne's butt. He was too big for that, but I whipped him with my mouth and told him if he told lies on the priest to a teacher, he would burn in hell, but first he would be out of my trailer. But God took Dwayne. Bobby was lost in heaven and Dwayne went to find him. They both went to Jesus."

I was silent. I had stopped eating. "Is this it? You got it all in the briefcase? Copies of photographs? Transcription of interviews?"

"Nope. This isn't all of it. You said I was gonna make enough for a new bass boat on this stuff. You gave me no budget and I have been spending your money like a drunk Indian. I even flew first class to Sarasota and rented a deluxe convertible automobile."

I nodded as if to say go on.

"Finding Father Ellison was hard. Seeing him was easy. He met me in the lobby of this old folks' home. He's a strange-looking guy. Lousy teeth. Straggly hair, mangy looking. Lots of dandruff. Chunks of it, like snowflakes. I posed as a former parishioner from Willow Springs. Told him I never went to church much but that there was something from that time that had stayed with me. The priest took me outside to the end of a veranda that overlooked a small inlet. We sat in chairs. His voice was not strong, so I pulled my chair close to his."

Wilcox reached into his briefcase again and said, "Here. I'll just read the pertinent part to you."

I sipped the now ice-cold coffee.

After clearing his throat a bit, Johnny Wilcox began to read. "It's me talking first, Renon. 'Father Ellison, when I lived in Willow Springs there were two little boys who died, brothers. One hung himself and the other fell off his bicycle. I've completed an investigation into these deaths, Father Ellison, and I am convinced you murdered both of these children.'"

"You don't beat around the bush, Johnny."

"In a deal like this with a man like this, there ain't no point in beating around the bush. Your best chance of getting anything at all is in a frontal assault."

"And what did you get?"

"I got this," Wilcox said, as he pulled another page of transcript from his briefcase.

"What Father Ellison said to me was, 'I'm an old man. I deserve to die in peace. I have not had any peace for a long time. Now I wait for death. I will say nothing about this to you or to anyone. What is done is done. Nothing can bring those boys back. Nothing can increase my suffering. You, Mr. Wilcox, you go in peace now.'"

"That was it?"

"That was all he said. Then he got up and slowly walked off the porch and down a long hallway. I saw his face and his eyes, and I heard his voice. If you listen to the tape of his voice, you will know Father Ellison murdered both Bobby and Dwayne. Probably he killed them because they were getting out of control – out of his control. A month after he said the funeral Mass for Dwayne, our Father Ellison was removed from Willow Springs. He left two corpses in Willow Springs, but who knows how many live victims he left there. The first place he went from there was a Catholic treatment center in the northeast. Then he was transferred to a treatment center run by an order of priests in New Mexico. After a couple of years in nut houses, he moved into a monastery on the plains in Kansas and finally he retired to this place in Florida. There's no doubt about it. Father Owen Dante Ellison murdered two of the boys he molested."

I was suddenly so sick I felt I was going to faint. I had vertigo, wanted to vomit. Johnny saw my distress. "Close your eyes, Ren. Breathe from your diaphragm. Slow, full breaths. Easy."

I leaned against the wall, weak to the point of fainting. Johnny came over to the chair next to me, put a napkin in ice water and placed it on my forehead. It was a few minutes before I could open my eyes. Everything seemed to have a blue-green tint.

I excused myself and kind of wobbled to the men's room, where I splashed water on my face. I felt an almost murderous rage and I knew who I wanted to kill. It was the man I had an appointment with in one hour.

Late morning
Diocesan Chancery, Thiberville

I walked straight into the bishop's office and found Monsignor Moroux sitting in the desk chair, staring out the window at the place he had once referred to as the bone yard. I softly said, "Monsignor?"

Startled, he turned abruptly. "Yes? Oh, Renon."

"I'm on my way to see Father Patterson, the priest-psychiatrist in Virginia, this weekend."

"Thank you," he said. A genuine expression of relief flooded his features. "Thank you, Renon."

Monsignor Moroux stood, motioned for me to join him as he walked toward the wall of big windows. "There's your friend," Moroux said, pointing to the old man with his dog.

I watched the fellow as he sat in the shade, his back resting against a wide oak. He was tossing a rubber ball onto graves. The ball bounced crazily off the tombs and rolled into one of the grass pathways between the rows of old burial sites. The dog followed the ball like radar, leaping over dead people and grabbing it in his mouth, returning to his master. Then they played the game again. Moroux said, "I wonder if that old fellow really is a priest. That's what they say. If he is, he's found the perfect congregation out there. Nobody can complain to him about anything."

I needed to get to the airport, but Moroux had called my office and asked to see me in person. "What is it you asked to see me about?"

"Renon, I want you to know I am confident you are not the source of those newspaper articles. I know you've had problems with the lawyers about this."

"Monsignor, I've told you that I've never even heard of the priests *The Courier* named."

"I'm afraid you are right about our lawyers needing to scapegoat someone because everything is going wrong. Between us, I am in agreement with you. It seems clear to me it's their fault things are out of control. By the way, send me a bill for your services to date."

I nodded as he continued, "Last night, at their monthly meeting, I had the diocesan financial advisory committee approve your contract with Dubois and the diocese as guarantor of Dubois's legal fees and all expenses of his defense without any cap. I got the bishop's signature too. I had a copy of the minutes of the meeting mailed to your office this morning. No one can threaten to fire you again. You are doing me a big favor in going to see this Father Patterson. It's what the canon lawyer for our papal nuncio wants. I hope it gets them off of my back."

It was now my place to take a turn. Driving over to the chancery, I had made a decision to take a leaf out of Johnny Wilcox's playbook, the frontal assault.

"Monsignor, the reason I came here today is that I am confident that I can prove in 1971 that Bobby and Dwayne Richard, altar boys in Willow Springs, were murdered by Father Owen Dante Ellison."

Moroux moved more quickly than I had ever seen him move, spinning away from me as if I were a wild animal about to devour him. He walked behind the ornate desk and put all that wood between us.

I moved to a chair and settled in, signaling that I was not about to leave until I had answers.

Moroux's mouth and eyes closed tightly. When he opened his eyes, I saw pain, as Jean-Paul Moroux surveyed the office until he found something to focus on besides me. He finally made an audible noise. "Ummm… ummm… ummm." It was the only sound he made. His mouth never opened.

I waited.

Moroux opened a desk drawer and retrieved a pack of cigarettes. He struck a match. His hands trembled as he aligned the flame with the cigarette. Shaking the fire off the match, he let the burnt stick fall to the thick carpeting.

I waited.

Moroux took two deep drags off the cigarette in silence, then extinguished the butt on a saucer under a demitasse coffee cup. He got up and went to the doorway, closing the door slowly, almost gently, but securely. Once he was back in the desk chair, he turned his focus on me again. "Ummm… ummm." He smiled inappropriately. "Ummm… I don't see how any purpose can be served by delving into things of the past. You see, we have this situation, Renon. This situation with Father Francis. It's uhh… uhh, where we must focus. Ummm… ummm, I don't see how anything I might say to you might make any difference. Ummm… Ummm… I don't see how anything you might know at this point could make any difference. Ummm…" Another inappropriate smile spread slowly across his face as he closed his eyes tight against what was in front of him.

"Monsignor, there were two boys murdered by a priest in this diocese and you were vicar general by that time. Reynolds had been installed as bishop by then too. You knew about it. You had to know. The bishop knew about it. He must have known. It was not just the sex crimes of priests against children that were covered up. The bishop, you, and other men in this building covered up two murders."

"No. It wasn't that way. We are priests. Matters of confession are private and confidential even under civil law. This applies to the confessions of all sinners in Holy Mother Church, including her priests. What one hears in confession can never be spoken anywhere, not in a court, not here today in this room. I have nothing more to say about this other than to offer my opinion that O. D. Ellison is a very sick, very old man. All of his faculties as a priest were removed long ago and he was given extensive treatment and then sent into the most complete isolation and finally into an old folks' home."

"I know where he was sent. I know where he is. My investigator visited him a few days ago in Florida. There is no statute of limitations on murder in this state. He can be brought to trial. These murders can be prosecuted."

"He is very old."

"The boys were very young."

"He is sick."

"He's guilty."

"Ummm… ummm… I implore you to think about this for a long time, before you drag that old man back here. What would be achieved?"

"Justice."

Monsignor Moroux sat in the desk chair, stood and seemed shaky, and fell back into the chair, his head in his hands. When I could see his features again, there was a redness around his eyes, a pallor in his face. He tried for another cigarette, but his tremors were too severe to handle the packet or matches.

Staring out at the cemetery, Moroux said, "Thank you for coming, Renon. Travel well."

"I'm leaving now, Monsignor, but I'm not forgetting. I will never forget that Father Owen Dante Ellison killed two brothers named Bobby and Dwayne. He deserves to be brought back to this legal jurisdiction in leg irons and handcuffs."

Moroux continued to stare at the big cemetery.

When I went out to my car, I spent some time double-checking the big briefcase Mo had packed for me. By the time I drove away and made the turn in front of the iron gates to the cemetery, Monsignor Moroux had left the chancery building. I slowed down and watched him as he walked the grass paths between the graves. I felt certain that what the monsignor and bishop had learned from O. D. Ellison was not information protected by confessional privilege recognized by the law, but straight-out admissions to murder. As Ellison was not an active priest, his file would not have been purged. Somewhere in the vault of the secret archives was a damning indictment of a murderer and his mentors.

Moroux had lost all composure in my presence at the mention that I had proof of the murders. In a matter of a moment, the monsignor's facade had fallen. I knew something deep within him, perhaps in a part of him he did not know existed, had been stabbed by a burning sword. I thought of what he had told me one night about how odd it was that we didn't worry over what God knew, but cared more about shameful actions that might be discovered by fellow humans. If I had my way, one day Ellison would pay and the world would know murders were covered up by chancery officials. I knew Moroux knew this and it was weighing heavily on his mind as he walked among the dead.

PART FIVE

IN GOD'S HOUSE

48

ICE STORM

Saturday morning, January 19, 1985
Washington DC

Snow fell all day and night on Friday. I knew it had snowed all night because I had stood at my hotel window all night, unable to sleep, my mind tormented by the murders of those two boys at the hands of that priest. By morning, the weather was so bad that President Reagan's second inauguration festivities were canceled.

When it was 8 a.m. in Thiberville, I phoned Julie.

"Morning, Sunshine."

"Hi, Ren. It's not sunshine here. Raining so much I think I saw an old guy with a long beard building a big boat around the corner, rounding up animals."

I laughed. "Sorry, I have little time this morning, Julie. I need you to do something for me, if you will."

"Talk to me."

"Can you go back into the secret archives again? I need ya to copy another file."

"They've all been... how'd ya say it... sanitized, right?"

"Not this one. It's not the file of an active priest. It's an old one. It's bad. Worse than Dubois."

"What can be worse than Dubois?"

"Murder."

There was a long silence. In a weak voice, Julie said, "What's the name?"

"Owen Dante Ellison. He was pastor in Willow Springs when it was part of the diocese."

"I'll get it tonight, Ren. You okay?"

"Yeah. You?"

"I guess. Take care."

"You too, Julie." I rang off. I wanted to say "I miss you" but the words did not come out.

The streets were deserted as the taxi navigated its way to Hope House. Father Matthew Patterson was waiting for me in the lobby. He was wearing a bright red sweatshirt over a blue polo, faded blue cords and hiking boots, and he had a pair of expensive sunglasses dangling on a cord around his neck. He looked more like a movie idol than a priest or doctor.

Father Patterson led me into his office, where a bearded man in an Irish fisherman's sweater and blue jeans sat with his cowboy boots propped up on the desk. On the wall behind the desk, centered over the credenza, was an enormous photograph of a golden retriever with a tattered paperback copy of *Alcoholics Anonymous*, the AA Big Book, in his mouth.

Father Patterson pointed to the picture. "That's my dog, Mozart. He loves to fetch the AA Big Book. It's the best use I've found for that book." As Matt Patterson gently lifted the fellow's cowboy boots from the surface of his desk, he said, "This guy is Desmond McDougall. I've never found a use for him. He works in the Vatican Embassy as a canon lawyer."

I recognized the name Desmond McDougall from the conversation I'd had with Monsignor Moroux. I was surprised to encounter him at Hope House. McDougall was built like a compact, muscled fullback. "Hi, Renon. I work with Matt on sensitive shit like this deal down in Thiberville, but we do different things. Sorry about having to meet in this head-shrinking joint. This place gives me the heebies, but I tell ya, if you could see where I work every day, it would creep you out worse than this – there's pictures of dead guys hanging all over the place."

Father Patterson motioned us to a round table in the corner of the room. Father Desmond McDougall carried a cup of coffee with him from the desk. "What the hell is wrong with this coffee? It tastes like hot brown water."

"That's because it is hot brown water. There's no caffeine in this building, no sugar, nothing like that. We can't have our patients getting buzzed on anything."

"Lovely place. Cheerful," Desmond said.

It quickly became obvious that our meeting had nothing to do with any discussion about Father Dubois or a possible medical evaluation of Dubois. McDougall took over as soon as we were seated, and the questions he asked did not even touch on my client's psychological condition, treatment regime, or his history as a pedophile.

"So, tell me about the situation in Louisiana. Has there been any publicity? Are there going to be trials?"

"On the criminal side, if I don't get a twenty-year sentence for Father Dubois in a plea bargain with the DA, there will be a trial. I'm pretty well locked out by the diocesan and insurance defense lawyers down there, but I think new cases are being filed almost weekly now – against Father Dubois and against other priests. I'm pretty sure there will be at least one civil trial, a case involving a family called Rachou."

Father Patterson fiddled with the sunglasses around his neck as Desmond McDougall scribbled notes.

"The plaintiff's attorney in the Rachou civil case is a lawyer named Kane Chaisson."

"Is he better than the Church and insurance lawyers down there?"

"The lawyers carrying water for the diocese are not even in Kane Chaisson's league. Chaisson's moving his Rachou case like a freight train."

Father Patterson poured coffee for the three of us and retrieved a small bowl from behind a volume on the bookshelf. "My private stash of sugar," he said. "Let me ask you this – at the moment it's all still sealed and secret, right? I mean, outside of the diocesan officials and a few lawyers, no one knows anything about this, right?"

"There has not been any publicity, right?" Desmond McDougall asked.

I pulled out the thick media section of my Dubois file, which included the previous day's articles from the New Orleans and Baton Rouge newspapers, and handed it to Father Patterson. "On the top are two front-page stories from yesterday – the two largest dailies in Louisiana. Underneath is a three-thousand-word story from the Wednesday edition of the Thiberville weekly, *The Courier*, that named two new priests besides Dubois as child molesters. That article quoted some victims' parents about meetings they had with priests and monsignors. It's hardly a secret anymore. All the local reporting has been in this weekly paper. You will see that the articles from the local daily, *The Thiberville Register*, that I have in the file do nothing but praise the diocese and bishop, and condemn *The Courier*. The big stories published in Baton Rouge and New Orleans may be running on the wire today."

Father Matt Patterson raised a hand in the air as if to ask me to hold any additional comments until he had read the newspaper articles. He and Desmond McDougall began perusing the pages of the media file, reading some of it carefully.

Once I was out of the flow, no longer responding to Desmond McDougall's rapid-fire questions, tiredness overwhelmed me. I was afraid I would fall asleep in the chair and wished the coffee had contained caffeine. I thought about how I could no longer sleep without sedating myself with alcohol.

Father Patterson may have sensed my predicament for he said, "It will take some time for us to digest this. You can walk around the facility if you wish."

I wandered around the ground floor and found a chapel. Instinctively, I started to enter the church to pray, but something stopped me from crossing the threshold. It was like I no longer knew how to pray, who to pray to, or what to pray for.

When I walked back into Father Patterson's office, both Patterson and McDougall were laughing as Desmond McDougall was finishing some story he had been telling. "So that little shit of a cardinal, the spaghetti sucker, says to me, 'The American Church must learn that God lives in Rome.'"

Turning his attention to me, McDougall said, "Next meeting will be at my place. We have espresso." He picked my media folder up off the table. "I gotta copy these articles and jam them down the throat of the lying son-of-a-bitch, Monsignor Jean-Paul Moroux. That bastard must have barnacles on his soul. Every report of his, even one I got last week, claims there has been nothing in the press about this."

Father Patterson said, "You represent Father Dubois, right? Not the diocese?"

"That's right. That's my only real concern. I've been declared persona non grata by the diocesan lawyers, insurance lawyers and their lay advisor. In the beginning, I was trying to work with them, but they saw everything I wanted to do as the wrong thing. Anyway, at first Dubois was my only concern. Now it's the children he's hurt."

"Tell me about the children."

"Right. I have been advocating since the first week I got into this that the diocese has an obligation to find the victims, all the victims, and offer them whatever they can to facilitate healing."

"Somebody objected to that idea?" Matt Patterson asked.

"Everybody objected to that idea."

Desmond McDougall was still writing notes as he spoke. "What's your greatest concern about the defense of Dubois?"

"Well, worst case has already happened, I suppose. The weekly paper has named other child-molesting priests in the diocese. I think that may have done me in. Until then, my plan had been to portray Dubois as a single, solitary, aberrant, deviant man – one of a kind – which is what I thought he was when I signed on to defend him. If he was alone – the only one – I believed I could get a decent plea bargain out of the DA."

"And now?"

"It's doubtful. The DA will want to make an example of Father Dubois. The judge will want to give him the maximum sentence possible, life without possibility of parole. They'll want to punish him on behalf of the other thirty-one or more—"

Matt Patterson interrupted, "What do you mean – the other thirty-one or more?"

I told him about Chaisson's subpoena request and for another two hours we talked about the situation in Thiberville. They elicited my detailed views about how I felt every aspect of this crisis should be handled. At last someone was listening to my plan.

Desmond McDougall picked up a phone and made a call. All he said was, "Where's the old man? I don't care if the old bastard's on the squash court. You get his royal ass in his office in one hour. I'm coming to see him."

Our meeting ended with McDougall asking, "How about we meet for dinner tonight? Seven o'clock?"

I nodded.

McDougall addressed Father Patterson. "Café Roma. Right, Matt?"

As we stood up, McDougall said, "Matt likes this bullshit place, Café Roma. The two old maids who own it always make a fuss over him."

"You'll like it, Renon," Matt Patterson said.

McDougall shrugged, "Hey, ya think I want to eat Italian? My job, my lot in life, is to deal with Italians all day long. I don't want to see anything that reminds me of my work when the day is done. I work for our papal nuncio in an institution stuck in a time machine – the dark ages."

49

A PRIESTS' PLACE

7 p.m., Saturday January 19, 1985
Café Roma, Washington DC

After spending most of the day at Hope House with Father Patterson and Father McDougall, we were on a first-name basis, and there was an ease I felt with them I'd not experienced with anyone associated with the Catholic Church the past five months. When I met Desmond and Matt at the restaurant, they had changed clothes since our meeting at Hope House, though neither wore a priest suit. However, many other diners in the huge restaurant were clothed as clerics.

"Lot of priests here," I said.

"Yeah, and Mafia too," Desmond said. "This place is about as festive as a Russian funeral. The Mafia modeled itself on the Church. They looked around Sicily and Italy and realized the Church was the most powerful, secretive organization in Italy, a cabal that could get away with anything. The Mafia is actually better run than the Church. The Church – the Mafia – it's the same food, same secrecy, same everything."

I laughed.

Desmond said, "What impressed me about you, Renon Chattelrault, why I wanted that Monsignor Moroux character in Thiberville to order you to come up here is this, quite frankly – it seemed clear that you are persona non grata with the bishop, vicar general and all those people down in Loooooosiana. The cliché is true. You can judge a man's character by knowing his enemies. The monsignor told me over the phone that he thought you were a loose cannon rolling on the deck, someone whom they had no control over. For the longest time, Moroux didn't even think you would ever call Matt or come up here."

"Yeah. I never could see a reason to come here. I don't want a priest treating a priest."

Desmond nodded. "I have been monitoring this business involving your client in Thiberville since they first paid over three million to buy the silence of victims and their families and lawyers. Reports from the diocese come across my desk. I knew the diocese, through Monsignor Moroux, were lying their asses off in reports filed with my boss, and obviously so. But I didn't know what they were lying about. For instance, in every report Moroux filed he said that no adverse publicity existed; there was no scandal to the Church. He said people down there were only interested in LSU football and duck hunting."

I laughed. "The part about football and duck hunting is not far off the truth. But obviously, there's been tons of adverse publicity."

Desmond said, "When a bishop through his vicar general lies to me in writing, they are lying to my boss. Who is the Pope's personal representative to this country. Which means they are lying to Rome, lying to the Pope."

The conversation paused as a round of drinks was delivered. Matt Patterson took over. "After our meeting this morning, Des and I decided to roll the dice and trust you. We need your help. Between us we know of hundreds of priests that are time-bombs waiting to explode like Father Francis Dubois, with the same consequences for the Church. I treat sexually dysfunctional priests. Bishops consult with Des about problem priests. From LA to Boston and everywhere in between, there are priests like Dubois, and complaints being made to their local dioceses."

"Are there any other lawsuits or criminal prosecutions?" I asked.

Des shook his head. "Not yet. But there could be hundreds, maybe thousands of cases one day. There is no policy to deal with the problem because the position of the American Church and the Vatican is that the problem simply does not exist. To develop a policy and put it in place would make good sense to most people, but not bishops, because to adopt policies would be an admission that the problem exists."

"Let me ask you," I said. "You really gonna jam all those newspaper articles down Monsignor Moroux's throat?"

"Or stick 'em up his ass? That jackass knows better than to lie to the Pope."

I laughed. "Funny, no? Moroux forced me to come up here against my will and all I've accomplished so far is I've put Moroux's ass in a sling."

"You worried about those people down there in Louisiana?"

"Naw. What can they do to me that they've not already tried?" I said. "Screw 'em."

"Well, Renon, when you start dealing with people higher up the hierarchy than a diocesan chancery, when you get to the National Conference of Catholic Bishops, and then all the way to the Vatican, you're treading in treacherous terrain where men have careers rather than vocations. Bishops will lie to popes to protect themselves, and popes will lie to the world to protect the Church." Desmond sipped his Bloody Mary and continued. "The truth here, like Matt said... the truth is, there are hundreds of other situations like the one with Father Dubois in Thiberville. It's just a matter of time before the whole Church blows itself up. And there are no policies in place to deal with any of this. The things you told us this morning about the criminal and civil issues are damned important."

Food was ordered, and before we finished the meal one of the old ladies who owned the restaurant sent over a second bottle of wine with her compliments. Desmond looked at the wine label approvingly. "Told you the old girls were hot for Matt."

Matt shook Desmond off and returned to the discussion. "I think Des knows all the canon law required to deal with these kinds of Dubois situations. And I believe I have sufficient resources to address the clinical issues regarding the injured children and the perpetrators. But we don't know anything about the civil law and criminal law issues."

"Aren't there Church lawyers here in DC?"

Desmond said, "They're mostly cocktail-party attorneys, and pompous, pious pricks, senior partners in corporate law firms. They are a lot more comfortable in golf clubhouses than courthouses."

"You think I know more than they do about what you call—"

"The civil and criminal factors of clergy abuse. Yes, from what we heard from you today, we think you know a lot more than any lawyer here knows. We want you to write down everything you told us today in detail – your ideas for a comprehensive way of dealing with one of these incidents. Okay?" Matt said.

"I'll dictate it for my secretary, Monique, tomorrow. She'll type it and mail it the fastest way possible, a copy to each of you."

Tiramisu was set on the table. "Who has the authority to do something about this?" I asked, pointing to Desmond. "Can your boss, the ambassador, or papal ambassador, whatever his title is – can he do something?"

"I met with my boss, our papal nuncio and ambassador, Archbishop Verriano, earlier today, after we saw you. Right now it doesn't seem to mean anything at all to him. He was very strong that the nunciature and Vatican had to rely on the reports filed by the bishop and archbishop in Louisiana. He was unimpressed even when I explained those reports were lies – that in forwarding those reports to Rome, the papal nuncio was lying to the Vatican, lying to the Pope," Desmond said.

Matt said, "To put it mildly, Archbishop Verriano doesn't see the urgency Des and I see."

Des laughed. "When I met with Verriano today, it was like I was torturing the old man. All he could say was, 'We must pray over this, my son. I will pray.' Hell, I can tell you, the only time that old bastard ever gets on his knees is to kiss some rich Catholic's ass."

As we walked toward the parking lot, Matt said, "I want to see Francis Dubois. Can you arrange this for me?"

"Sure. I'll have to talk with both the administrator and Dubois's physician at the Stalder Institute as I had Dubois sign a paper barring any visits or the release of information to anyone associated with the Church. I'll have your visit with Dubois cleared by the end of Monday."

50

THE PROTOCOL OF POWER

10:30 a.m., Monday January 21, 1985
Papal Nunciature, Washington DC

At 7:30 a.m., Father Desmond McDougall sat at his desk in the Vatican Embassy. Before pouring his first coffee of the day, he did what everyone in the building did each morning – he glanced at the calendar for the papal nuncio, Archbishop Carlo Verriano. It surprised Desmond to see his name listed on the ambassador's agenda for a conference at 10:30.

When Father McDougall entered the papal nuncio's office, the old man was sitting behind his desk, shuffling the papers in front of him. Desmond could tell he was not reading anything. Archbishop Verriano continued to look down at the paperwork, motioning with his right hand, making a kind of downward wave, for Father McDougall to have a seat. The papers that were props were pushed to one side and the old man laid his reading glasses on top of them.

"My son, I prayed over this today at Mass, asked the Holy Spirit for guidance."

Desmond nodded. "That's good."

"You do not understand. I prayed that the Holy Spirit would guide you in these matters. You understand how Holy Mother Church works, my son. We have doctrines, traditions, and we have protocol. One is as sacred as the other. It is not our position, those of us who work for the pontiff, the Holy See, in this building in the United States... it is not our position to question reports forwarded to the nunciature by our bishops in America. We are only to transmit their reports to Rome."

"But the bishop in Louisiana is lying. The archbishop too. I've told you this. I have documentary proof. They are lying to you and you represent the supreme pontiff in this country. The lies are designed to protect themselves, not Holy Mother Church. In protecting themselves, they could be precipitating a catastrophic crisis in the Church, bringing the greatest scandal to the Church in five hundred years."

"No!" Verriano shouted. He sipped his water in an attempt to dissipate his anger and restore his composure, then tried to regain control of the meeting. "We will do nothing here, Father McDougall. We will do nothing but what the protocol of our positions mandates. You will continue to receive the reports from Louisiana, review them, make copies and send them to the Congregation for the Doctrine of the Faith in Rome. Should Cardinal Kruger want more information, he will cable us."

Father Desmond McDougall shifted in his chair. "But... but, Archbishop... I discussed this matter with Cardinal Wolleski after the dinner for the Polish ambassador last month. We have talked a number of times since then. The cardinal is very interested and he's spent time with Father Patterson talking about the clinical factors surrounding the issue. He has requested I write a paper for him to carry to the Vatican. I am working on this paper now. It will be brief but comprehensive. I will outline the canon law issues, Father Patterson will outline the clinical issues, and the lawyer we met with over the weekend will contribute his thoughts on the civil and criminal issues. Cardinal Wolleski wants to take the document to his friend, the Holy Father. I will show you the final draft, if you wish, before delivering it to the cardinal."

"If such a paper is produced here and delivered to the pontiff outside of official protocol channels, I will be recalled as ambassador. Only God himself knows where they would post me next – some godforsaken place, I'm sure. My son, there is only one way for me to speak to you about this subject."

Papal Nuncio Verriano drained the glass of water that had

been sitting on his desk while Desmond McDougall awaited his final word.

"If you prepare any paper for Cardinal Wolleski or anyone else and cause such a document to be delivered to the pontiff in the Vatican, my son, that will be the last paper you ever prepare. Your career in the diplomatic corps of Holy Mother Church will be at an end. God will call you to a new and different kind of ministry. I will end your career myself. You understand me?"

"I understand you, Archbishop," replied Father Desmond McDougall. "But do you understand what will happen if more cases like this are reported in this country, in other countries, all over the world? The great potential for scandal to the Church that exists here? Do you understand what priests are doing sexually with boys and girls, with little children and adolescents? What devastating harm is being done to young people, and what this may mean to the Church?"

Archbishop Verriano repeated the same gesture with his right hand, this time motioning McDougall by waving him away, signaling him to take his leave from the office. "I have spoken. Do not let me hear of you speaking ill of an American bishop again or accusing a bishop of lying. You send something to Rome with Cardinal Wolleski or do anything else about this and… and God will call you to a new, different ministry. And I will be God's instrument."

51

AN IMPERFECT CONFESSION

Noon, Saturday January 26, 1985
Hay-Adams Hotel, Washington DC

Saturday morning, I had landed in Washington again. Matt Patterson was having brunch in my hotel suite. He said, "A good man, a retired cardinal, John Wolleski, will see us this afternoon. He's an old friend of the Pope's. I think maybe they were the only two Polish cardinals in their day. Des and I incorporated the stuff you sent us on the civil and criminal factors into our report. The cardinal is bringing our document to the Pope. Des is sending it out to bishops he's close to in the US. Your stuff is the only material that could get anyone's attention. Bishops don't give a damn about canon law and every diocese has its own canon lawyers. They sure don't care about psychiatric or psychological issues, and don't want to understand any of that. But they care about losing law cases, losing money, losing priests, and maybe bishops going to prison for not reporting crimes, and they care about scandal to the Church."

"Cardinal Wolleski is taking the document to the Pope?"

"That's right. He flies to Rome on the private jet of Callahan Industries several times a year. He says he goes to research a book. He really just goes to hang out with his friend, eat Polish food and play cards. Cardinal Wolleski's a good man. So good that I don't know how he ever got to be a cardinal."

"The Pope? Damn," I said.

"Right. Your bishop won't speak to you, but the Pope is going to hear you out."

"Can the Pope do something? Stop this stuff?"

"History provides the answer. The first papal edicts and decrees from Church councils against priests sodomizing boys were issued centuries ago – in the fourth century, I think. The sick sexual behavior in the priesthood involving the rape of children by priests is nothing new. Some popes have been appalled by clerics sodomizing young boys, raping young girls. Some popes tried to stop this behavior. Some popes enjoyed sodomizing boys and raping girls themselves."

5:45 p.m.
Basilica of the National Shrine of the Immaculate Conception,
Washington DC

Father Matthew Patterson and I stood before the twenty-foot-high bronze doors in the inner sanctum of Washington's vast Basilica of the National Shrine of the Immaculate Conception. Desmond was running late. Cardinal Wolleski had asked to see us before he celebrated 6 p.m. Mass.

Desmond joined us just as the doors were opening. "We're not going to have but five minutes. Let the old man take the lead."

Matt and I nodded.

Inside, we encountered Cardinal John Wolleski dressed in beautiful emerald vestments. The cardinal dismissed the priest who was with him by nodding to the door and motioned us to take chairs in front of him.

"And you are Renon Chattelrault?"

I nodded.

He extended his hand. I thought I was to kiss his ring. He read my mind. "Let's just shake hands, Renon."

I was amazed at how unhurried the cardinal was. I knew he had to be on the altar in a few minutes. He seemed to have some kind of internal clock that told him he was on schedule, that there was no rush.

"What I want to say to the three of you is this. This problem of priests sexually abusing children is not new and my personal belief is that it is far more widespread than any of us can imagine. The problem is as old as the Church itself. Why this has always existed in the Church is a question I have no answer to. I want to confess to you now, old as I am, that as long as I have been a priest, I have always known about men like this priest in Louisiana. A priest anywhere who says he has not known of men like this in our midst is not being truthful. He is lying before you and before God. There is no excuse for the manner in which I handled this problem as a priest, pastor, vicar, bishop, archbishop, or after they put these heavy robes on me. It was not until Matt explained things to me in clinical terms that I began to understand the behavior of these priests and the lifelong devastating consequences for the children. I did what all people in the hierarchy do – I hid behind morality, told myself it was a moral failing for a priest to sexually abuse children. It was denial, for I never wanted to see it as an incurable addiction. However, there is no excuse for my own conduct when I was confronted with these sins against God and these crimes against children. There is no excuse or explanation for what I've done and not done."

A cardinal of the Roman Catholic Church was confessing in my presence.

"Whether the Church can or will act to save children, to save the very soul of the Church, is something I don't know. Now I will go on the altar and pray that you will continue this work."

The deep drone of the basilica's organ started to sound through the stone walls.

"Do you have children?" the cardinal asked me.

I nodded.

"Please write their names on this paper."

I did and he placed the paper in a pocket inside his robe.

Turning to Desmond, Cardinal Wolleski asked, "Do you have the final draft of the document?"

"Yes." Des opened his briefcase and handed the cardinal a

sealed envelope. Wolleski placed the package in a worn satchel and snapped the bag shut.

"Tomorrow this old man flies to Rome. I ask for your prayers. I will keep you in mine."

The three of us stood, thinking the cardinal was going to the altar.

"Enjoy Rome," Matt said.

"I always enjoy my work in the library there. My research never ends but it's not as important as carrying your document to my friend. This is the first important work this old man has. had in many years. Renon was right when he wrote the Church must try to find every child damaged by one of our priests, every single victim no matter what age they may be now. Bishops will not want to do that. Bishops will want to ask people to pray. Praying over this would be sinful hypocrisy. This is something the Church created and the Church is bound by every civilized covenant that ever existed to heal the innocents it has injured. If the Church does not heal the children, then hellfire should rain down upon us."

Outside the stone-walled cathedral, dwarfed by its massive dome, the three of us stood in a tight circle. These were not the same men I had met only seven days ago. Last week they had both been relaxed, even joking at times. Now the obvious tension in Desmond's face was mirrored by concern in Matt's expression.

"You ran this by the old man, your boss, Verriano?" Matt asked.

"It was like the final judgment. He said he'll play God, remove me from the nunciature and shitcan my career if I send anything to Rome with Cardinal John Wolleski."

I said, "Des, you have no authority...?"

"Authority? Hell, I have orders. I have orders not to do what I just did," Desmond said.

I was confused. "Des, what is the deal? Obviously, I don't know something."

"The deal is this stuff is radioactive in the Church. Anything about clergy abuse is more closely guarded than they guarded the secrets shared by Our Lady of Fatima. In the sixties Pope John XXIII sent a document to every bishop in the world and instructed them to keep the document in the secret archives of their diocese and to never comment publicly on its existence."

"Jeez, what was in the document?" I asked.

"It was sixty-nine pages long. A lot was in there, but the nuts and bolts was the imposition of a strict secrecy on those priests processing cases of clergy sexual abuse in Diocesan Tribunals. Everyone aware of any case of clergy abuse was bound by the Church's highest degree of confidentiality, something called the Secret of the Holy Office."

"What was the penalty for speaking about this?"

"Excommunication. Only the Pope could lift the excommunication."

"Excommunicating priests, Des?"

"Yeah. And the priests in the tribunal were to inform the victim and his or her family members that they too would be excommunicated from the Church if they ever spoke about the clergy abuse to anyone."

Matt said, "Pretty severe, no?"

I shook my head in disbelief. "A child who was raped by a priest was to be told they would be excommunicated if they spoke to anyone. A policeman?"

"Yeah." Des shook his head too. "Even a therapist."

"It's a blueprint of obstruction of justice in every country in the world," I said.

"Right. Same as the Mafia," Matt said.

"How many people know about the existence of this document?"

"Not many have read it." Des held his hand up. "Including me, I can probably count those who've read the document on one hand, and last year we redacted the code of canon law and whether the new code supersedes Pope John XXIII 1962 edict is arguable.

But no one needs to read the document because everyone knows never to mention anything about clergy sex abuse to anyone. That's why my boss hammered me when I told him we were putting something in writing about this."

"What if someone in the Church is questioned under oath about a case of clergy abuse?"

Des spoke softly. "My friend, an oath to the Church is sacred. An oath to a civil court is secular. Means nothing."

"So, you're telling me under these guidelines any cleric to the rank of the Pope is supposed to lie if asked about clergy abuse?"

"Men of the cloth don't lie, Ren," Matt said. "We have something more clever than lying. It's called mental reservation."

"Mental reservation?"

Des took his turn. "This is beautiful. You're gonna love it, Ren. Mental reservation is a nuanced concept that can be employed to embargo the truth about a sex scandal involving a cleric. Though the concept has never been adopted formally or approved officially by the Church, it has been relied upon by some in the Church since it was first introduced in writings of moral theologians in the Middles Ages. Mental reservation is a form of 'moral lying' about matters that could bring scandal to the institution. With this, one can lie and at the same time tell the truth. The truth is told to God, mentally reserved for God only, and the lie is spoken for human ears."

I was stunned by what I'd just heard.

"You think maybe we ought to rethink this, Des?" Matt said, after a long pause.

"Nope. Wolleski can get to the Pope in Rome. The cardinal is one of a handful of people in the world with both access to the Pope and the trust of the Pope. The Vatican has to know the truth. Cardinal Kruger and others in Rome have been receiving the lies coming out of Louisiana. They've been told everything's under control in Louisiana. Rome has no idea how close Louisiana is to blowing up. The flames of a big fire down there could create a fire that could engulf the whole Church. If Louisiana goes, the whole damned country might go, every diocese, maybe every diocese on earth."

"You're gonna end your career to get this document to Rome?" I asked.

"Nope. That prick, the papal nuncio, is going to end my career."

PART SIX

CITADEL OF CATHOLICISM

52

AN OLD BRIDGE

Monday evening, January 28, 1985
Rome

An hour after arriving in Rome, Cardinal John Wolleski was walking toward Piazza Navona. He was offered a ride as he passed through the Porta di Sant'Anna at the Vatican, but the old man liked to walk. The night was dark and cold. The wind blew his shock of white hair in a direction different than his comb had set it.

Rome was a place he loved. He had arrived in the city in 1929, aged twenty-two and fresh from the US. He came with the bundle of money his father had handed him the previous Christmas Day, saying, "Go find your dream, Johnny." Before the year ended, his father's immigrant dreams had turned into a nightmare as America fell into a deep financial depression. But never once while John was in Rome did his father let on that the money John was spending was the last the Wolleski family had.

At the time he sailed to Europe, John Wolleski fancied that he would be a writer. He knew little about writers and less about writing. His notion was that it was preferable to be well traveled than well schooled. His travels began in Rome and ended there. He never got to Poland, the land of his father, or across the Mediterranean to Seville to see Juan Belmonte fight bulls; nor did he make it to Milan to see an opera at La Scala.

On that first trip to Rome long ago, he had visited an ice-cream stall on the edge of Piazza Navona. Isabella Rinaldi was seventeen when she handed the handsome American his first gelato. She served him an ice cream every day until she was twenty. Over that time, John Wolleski learned to speak Italian well enough to converse with Isabella's father. He read Italian books and taught Italians his own language, making enough money to live comfortably in a small pension. Each day he exchanged pleasantries with the girl's father, but he and Isabella never spoke beyond what was necessary for him to purchase his daily serving of strawberry ice cream.

One day Signor Rinaldi gave John a free bowl of ice cream and sat across from him, wiping his hands on his apron. In his own language, Isabella's father said, "I now work in this stall just like my father, and his father, and his father before him. We sell many things here. There is always a price. Everything has a price, no?"

John had nodded in agreement.

"But today I'll give you this ice cream for free. Do you know why I've done this?"

"No."

"It is so you can know we are friends. And so now you can ask me if you can go for a walk on a Sunday with my daughter, Isabella."

Fifty-five years later, as he headed toward the place where the ice-cream stall once stood in Piazza Navona, John stood on Ponte Sant'Angelo, spanning the Tiber River, reflecting on the distant past. He could still remember how flushed he'd felt when Signor Rinaldi had given him permission to take his daughter for a Sunday walk.

"Isabella's mother and her grandmother will walk with you, just far enough behind not to hear you two. But when Isabella returns home, they will ask her about everything you talked about."

"We will do this on this Sunday, in three days?" John Wolleski asked excitedly.

"No. You have not properly asked me yet. You have not asked Isabella. Maybe she will say no."

"May I...?"

The old man got up and slapped John on the back. "Of course. I was having fun."

As her father walked away, Isabella looked at John in a way he had only dreamed she might.

The Sundays ran on for months until suddenly, one Sunday, the two old women did not follow them when they left the house. John had slowed their gait, brought them to a snail's pace, waiting for the old women to catch up. When they reached the river, Isabella put her arm in his and whispered, "They are not coming."

"And why?" John asked.

"Because I told them I am going to kiss you today whether they follow or stay home."

And she did kiss him, right at the very same spot where he stopped on the Ponte Sant'Angelo fifty-five years later, the first spot he went to every time he arrived in Rome. He could never remember the kiss, hard as he tried, or whether it was one kiss or many kisses, but he never forgot the feelings that rushed through him.

It had been May 1931 when he and Isabella first embraced and kissed on the bridge. By June they had announced their plans to be married, and her grandmother had taken to her bed, swearing she would die if Isabella left Rome to go to America. John had vowed to the family that they would never leave. By then he had begun work as a clerk at the American Embassy. He had job security and a good salary by the standards of the city. He and Isabella would be able to have everything they needed, and be able to help the Rinaldi family as well. To show his good faith, he began to relieve her father on Saturday nights, working side by side with Isabella.

In the fall, Isabella fell sick with polio, and in less than a month she was dead. Her lungs stopped working properly, her legs became crippled, and her beautiful face aged. And then she was gone.

As the old man stood on the bridge, he wiped tears from his eyes.

*

Ristorante Rinaldi was full when Cardinal Wolleski walked in. Giovanni Rinaldi, the younger brother of Isabella, was now seventy, but he quickly stood up from his table in the rear of the elegant room. Seeing John Wolleski in the door, Giovanni rushed over to him. "Zio Johnny, your smile warms a cold night. Come off with the big coat. I have a little drink that will take the night air off you."

The closet where Giovanni hung the cardinal's coat and muffler was the space where the ice-cream stall had stood years ago. Giovanni hustled the old man into the kitchen, where a cheer went up as the double doors swung open. There were hugs, kisses, shouted greetings. This was John Wolleski's second family.

After Isabella's funeral, John Wolleski had entered the seminary in Rome and completed studies for ordination to the priesthood. He had baptized every Rinaldi born since he was ordained and as his stature grew in the Church so did the venue of the baptisms. The last dozen years or so the Rinaldi children had been christened at the Basilica di Santa Maria Maggiore, the most important church in Rome.

Before Isabella's father died, he had asked the newly promoted Cardinal Wolleski to take a ride with him, saying he had something he wanted to show him, and something they needed to talk about. They changed buses twice as they crossed the city. Then they climbed almost to the top of a steep hill. As they walked up the stone steps, old man Rinaldi paused a number of times to catch his breath. Cardinal Wolleski knew where they were going. He sometimes came here on Sunday afternoons when he was in Rome, to this hilltop cemetery where Isabella was laid to rest. Some Sundays he brought something with him, a small bouquet of flowers. Every Sunday, he took something away with him. When he walked away from her grave it was like she was with him on their Sunday walks long ago.

Both old man Rinaldi and the brand-new cardinal prayed at her gravesite, then John helped the old man off his knees. "I am going to die soon, I think. The doctors say a half year. Who knows?

I brought you here to ask you if will you do me the honor of saying my funeral Mass and putting me in the ground here?"

"I will do anything you wish, as I would do for my own father."

"Good. Now we know I will have a cardinal bury me. That might impress some."

Pointing to Isabella's grave, John Wolleski said, "It will not impress her and I almost envy you that you will be with her again."

"That's good you say that because I think it is right that you are with her when this life ends. The family has talked about this and it is odd that all of us have had the same idea for many years, something no one would say aloud to the others. We want you to know that this plot, to the right of hers, is a place that will never be taken by a Rinaldi. This place is for you. She walked on your right arm, no?"

John smiled. "But who will bury me? Who will say the prayer over me?"

"If you cannot get a holy man to do this, then let an Italian cardinal do it. God will forgive you."

By this cold January night in 1985, Isabella's father had been dead many years and over a half-century had passed since John Wolleski had first come to the Piazza Navona for an ice cream. Nevertheless, the cardinal still felt some of the spirit of his youth. As Giovanni Rinaldi started bringing plates of food to Cardinal Wolleski's table, he looked at the pictures on the wall, looking backward into the past. His favorite was a large picture of the girl he'd loved. In costume and make-up, she posed as Chaplin when he played the Little Tramp.

53

A FAMILY MEAL

Early evening, Tuesday January 29, 1985
Vatican City

The three Polish priests – Monsignor Jozef Majeski, Cardinal John Wolleski and the Holy Father – had a feast spread before them. Every time Cardinal Wolleski came to Rome, he brought boxes of provisions from a Polish deli in DC, better than anything Majeski and the pontiff could get out of Warsaw or Krakow.

The Pope delighted in these small, informal dinners in the papal apartment.

Cardinal Wolleski sat still, with the papers compiled by Renon Chattelrault, Father Matt and Father Desmond on the table in front of him. He read aloud from the document. "Based upon information known to the authors, it is certain that there are hundreds of priests guilty of sexually abusing children, and there are undoubtedly thousands of child victims. The authors believe that the offending priests may number in the thousands, and that their victims may number in the hundreds of thousands."

Monsignor Majeski was sampling three kinds of sausages and a potato salad, washing it down with swigs from a big brown bottle of Polish Warka beer. The Pope had not touched any of the food, though they were his favorite dishes, since Cardinal Wolleski had mentioned the estimated number of offending priests and child victims in the United States.

When Cardinal Wolleski's reading was finished and the last page turned face down on the table, he took a long drink of water.

The Holy Father seemed unsteady as he stood and slowly walked out of the room.

Monsignor Majeski turned to Cardinal Wolleski. "It's all right, John," Majeski said. "Whenever the Holy Father receives this kind of news, he always retreats to his chapel alone. It is not that he does not want to talk with you about this. First, he will talk with God. When he has finished praying, he will return to us."

The owner of the Polish Deli in DC always put extra things in the packages he made up for the Pope. Jozef liked the festive candles he found in the boxes, and he and Sister Margarita, the Polish nun who attended to the kitchen, had placed them in silver holders and set them on the long table. The candles had burned down to half their original height by the time the Pope returned to the room.

Jozef Majeski motioned for his friend to finish his meal. The pontiff waved his hand dismissively, indicating he did not intend to share in the feast. He walked over to Wolleski and put a hand on the cardinal's shoulder. "John, you are one of my oldest friends. This is not a job that facilitates making many friends. Every human encounter I have is formal; every word I utter must be spoken with care and with thought."

The Pope pointed to the hiking boots, khaki cargo pants and faded blue sweater he was wearing. "I rarely can even dress this way or be seen by anyone when I am dressed this way. Sometimes, at night, I wear these shoes I used to wear when I hiked in the mountains. These shoes are as close to the mountains as I get now, and these little dinners with you and a few other friends from the old days are the only real conversations I have."

"You should eat something," Jozef said. "You have that medicine to take and the doctor says always you should eat something first."

"Maybe I will eat something in a while, Jozef."

The Pope walked to one of the huge French windows and tried to open it. He struggled with the latch, looked at Jozef and shrugged. Jozef wiped his mouth, stood, walked over to the window, and effortlessly flung it open, admitting a gust of cold air that extinguished the candles.

Jozef said, "God gave you the right job, my friend. An engineer you are not."

Staring into the cold, dark night, the Pope spoke in a low voice. "There are things out there that we know about, and there are things out there we do not know about, and can never know about. There are good things, bad things too. But evil... tonight, we talk about evil. The evil we talk about is not out there. There is evil inside this Church."

The Pope turned back to them. "Historically, we all know there have been these same kinds of problems in the Church since the beginning. This kind of sin in the Church has never been eradicated. Even now I know there are complaints against some priests in places other than America – one who is in a high place in Mexico, who I know well and has personally professed his innocence to me. These things are investigated and handled in a manner that avoids scandal to the Church. But to my knowledge all complaints have always been only against one single priest. These things have been isolated incidents."

There was a long silence.

Cardinal Wolleski said, "Here we are not talking about complaints against one single priest. We're talking about complaints against hundreds of priests in one country, maybe thousands of priests, and thousands of innocent lives damaged or destroyed."

"Medieval," the Pope said. "What this paper describes is medieval, like something from before the time of the Reformation – immorality on an unimaginable scale."

"I believe the Church will suffer as it has let children suffer," Cardinal Wolleski said.

Jozef anticipated the pontiff's next request and walked over and latched the window against the cold.

"Was it this cold when we used to walk and sleep in the mountains, Jozef?"

"It was colder."

"We were young and hardy then, weren't we?" the Pope said.

"We were crazy then. Sane people do not leave a perfectly warm dormitory room to spend a weekend under the stars in freezing temperatures."

"It was the happiest I ever was, I think. I had a sense of wonder about everything in those mountains. Death and sadness had come to my life already. But the personal spirit of my being then, my youth, the innocence God created within me – those things were intact. Innocence had not been taken from me. Those are things no one should ever be able to take from any child. Christ himself spoke of this, of the evil of taking the innocence of a child."

The Pope sat down and nibbled on a piece of sausage. He drank two glasses of water. As he poured the second glass from the pitcher, his hand trembled and water spilled on the tablecloth.

"John, I know you would not bring this to me if you did not believe it was true. I do not want to believe it is true. We know the Church has had this kind of wickedness in its history… this same evil. But… but in the numbers you mention? It is as if this document you read for me is a report about a legion of sinners in North America – ordained priests."

John Wolleski nodded. Jozef picked up the Pope's plate and went to find Sister Margarita in the kitchen so that she could warm the meal.

"A man who would do this to a child is truly evil, John. But hundreds or maybe thousands of priests in one country? What is wrong in the American Church if this is true?"

"A lot is wrong," Wolleski said. "It may not be only the American Church."

"The priests in my country – your father's land – were men who had to have discipline against the occupation of the German army, and then the Russian army. It was rare that I ever heard reports or even rumors of things like this in our homeland. And as I have said, here, since I have been in Rome, I have heard a word here and there about accusations of this kind. Priests have been removed from ministries where they worked with children, I think. I know there are accusations investigated here. But since the 1960s, in accord with the dictates of John XXIII, we've handled these things to avoid scandal to the Church. These charges are investigated at the Congregation for the Doctrine of the Faith. No one has ever told me of any charges being proven true. I too have always wanted such things handled in a manner that no scandal would be created. Never has anyone suggested the magnitude of a problem like that of which you speak of tonight. It describes a hell we created for children God entrusted to our care."

The Pope thanked the nun who set his warmed plate before him and said, "When I was made a bishop an old friend gave me counsel. He said, 'Two things happen when a man is made a bishop. First, he never again hears the truth. Secondly, he never again has to speak the truth.' I speak truth. In some things I don't know that I've always heard the truth."

"These things are true," Wolleski said. "That I failed the Church in these matters is of little consequence because I always believed I was protecting the Church. I, like you and all bishops, was following the dictum of Pope John XXIII's directive about secrecy."

The Pope nodded wearily.

Cardinal Wolleski continued, "I don't think there is enough time for me to do the penance my sins mandate. In failing the children, I failed God."

The Pope took the papers on the table into his shaking hands.

The cardinal looked away and then back to the Pope, taking a big breath. "I avoided scandal to the Church. I placed the reputation of the Church, of myself, of the priests, above caring for the children. All bishops have always acted this way. We've been mandated to act this way."

The Pope stood again and began to pace slowly. "Yes, yes. John, I will pray every morning for the children."

"We must pray for the children, Your Holiness. And I pray you will act."

"Yes. I will pray for the children. Children always fill my heart. Those who have had their innocence taken from them through these evil acts of our priests will be on my mind every breath I take. And, yes, my friend, we will act. I will have something done before the pigeons are in the piazza in the morning. We will appoint someone to investigate and report to us."

John reached into his pocket. "I almost forgot this. I have the names of the three children of the lawyer who helped write this document. When you pray for all the children whose names we do not know, would you pray for his children as well?"

The pontiff nodded and Cardinal Wolleski handed the slip to Jozef.

"Now, Jozef, would you please get a message tonight over to Cardinal Marcello. I want to see him alone in my library at six in the morning and he is to tell no one of this appointment."

Jozef turned to Cardinal Wolleski. "You know the definition of a Vatican secret? It's something a cardinal only tells to one other cardinal at a time."

"You know who I mean," said the Pope.

"The German? Kruger?" asked Majewski.

"Yes," the Pope said. "Neither the German, nor his men, Paginini and Bertolini, must know. This is something the Holy See must do my way and not the German's way."

John Wolleski knew they were talking about the Rhinelander, Cardinal Hans Kruger, a strong man within the walls of the Vatican who had amassed the kind of power not seen in the Church for centuries.

The previous pope, John Paul I, had served only thirty-three days before being found dead in his bed. When he was Patriarch of Venice, Pope John Paul I had shown a keen interest in financial corruption in the Vatican Bank, a scandal that led to murders. Many believed the Pope was also murdered.

Some Vatican observers believed the election of the present pope was manipulated by powerful forces in the Curia who knew the Pope had no interest in financial matters, no involvement in ecclesiastical politics, and had never exhibited any interest or skill in administration. He was a spiritual man and his vision was outward toward the world, not inward into Vatican politics and finance.

A power vacuum was created when the Pope opted not to micromanage Vatican affairs and showed little interest in administrative matters. After several years of quiet, sophisticated political maneuvering, the German cardinal Hans Kruger forged a partnership with two Italian cardinals, Paginini and Bertolini. The power the Pope did not exercise, they took themselves.

54

THE POWER

Thursday January 31, 1985
Vatican City

Behind his back, among Vatican personnel, Cardinal Hans Kruger was known as The Fuhrer. His power was more feared than respected. This man was certain he would be pope one day. To that end, he took a keen interest in influencing the selection of new cardinals, men who would be eligible to attend the conclave and vote in the next papal election in the Sistine Chapel.

Kruger modeled himself on historical figures, taking different pages from a lot of lives. There were things he wanted sole credit for that were the product of the combined efforts of many, and he always arranged it so he appeared to stand alone when it suited him. When he had to do things that he believed would not reflect well upon him, he acted through straw men. The tallest straw man, the one Kruger most often used to act for him in untraceable ways, was actually only five feet tall in shoes. This was Cardinal Niccolo Paginini, who originally came from a small fishing village in Sicily.

Cardinal Hans Kruger was born to great wealth. His mother's family had large holdings in heavy industry plants along the Rhine near Cologne. His father also came from a prominent family on the Rhine; he had chosen a career in the military, graduating with honors from the Military Academy and rising to the rank of general charged with command of Panzer tank divisions. While German Field Marshall Erwin Rommel earned distinction heading the famed Afrika Korps, General Kruger prepared battle plans for Operation Barbarossa, the German invasion of the Soviet Union.

As an only child living with his mother and a number of servants on a large estate close to Koblenz in the Moselle River Valley, Hans had been indulged, given every thing he desired. The housemaids and other servants referred to him with deference from the time he was a toddler. From birth he was accustomed to having his way and being treated like royalty.

Those who tended to the livestock and animals, including a string of six majestic horses from Andalusia properly referred to as Pre-Pura Raza Española, addressed the boy as Master Hans.

As he exercised them in the indoor arena on the family land, he learned the art of using his seat, legs and feet to drive and direct the horses. He trained them not to walk or run, but to canter in three beats, to the right, left, in circles, serpentines, pirouettes. Working with the mounts required great patience and skill, especially for a child. He never tugged the reins with his hands, but intertwined the leather straps with the combed mane. It was a lesson in learning how to control great power without appearing to be doing anything at all.

When not riding, hiking or rowing on the river, Hans learned to play chess from both his parents and a butler. Before he was ten years old he was winning matches against everyone in the house as well as a professor who lived in the village. His understanding of the complex chess matches he never lost was far beyond that of a normal child and indicative of a well-developed, multifaceted intellect.

With no siblings – and no classmates either, because he was privately tutored in the family home – Hans never had anyone of his own age to talk to. He developed what would become a lifelong habit of never sharing his thoughts and feelings, engaging only in internal dialogues with himself.

His father was rarely at home after the war commenced, and Hans was only twelve years old when plans were being finalized for the invasion of the Soviet Union, things he knew nothing about as he busied himself riding horses, rowing on the river, developing the lifestyle of an outdoorsman. Over the radio he heard the propaganda disseminated by Goebbels about the war and the evils of Jewry, and when he accompanied his mother to Koblenz for a doctor's appointment or shopping trip he noticed the lines of raggedly dressed poor people queuing for bread and other morsels of food. He thought Goebbels was right about everything he said in the broadcasts. Like him, he felt great sorrow for the poor who lined the sidewalks of Koblenz, and he hated the bombers that flew overhead on their way to destroy factories along the Ruhr and the Rhine and in the other cities of the Reich.

In the summer of 1940, Hans was eagerly waiting the time when he would be eligible to join the Hitler Youth League. He was fascinated by the Führer, and was impatient to become one of his future Aryan supermen. Hans identified with the movement and wanted to be a part of it as soon as possible. He also talked often of his dream to serve in a tank battalion under his father's command when he was old enough to enlist. But his father, General Kruger, was never a believer in the Nazi Party. He refused to allow his only child to talk about joining the Youth League or enlisting in the military in his presence.

When Hitler issued secret orders to his Generals to prepare the attack on the Soviet Union, General Kruger, like most senior career officers, knew the war was lost. He decided to get his son as far out of harm's way as he could. Hans was sent to northern Italy, where the regional German commander was his father's closest friend. It was left to the commander to find a safe place for the child.

The place the commander found for Hans was a Catholic seminary in the hills north of Sienna. It was here that Hans lived and studied until it was safe to venture outside the walls. During the war, the monastery walls were invincible. The Vatican had entered a concordant with the Nazis. There was no chance Nazis would enter a seminary and search for a German to conscript or have reason to believe a German would be found in such a place.

Hans Kruger's path to his powerful post in the Vatican had been a straight line. As a teenager he had mastered Latin and three other languages, and had undertaken all the courses necessary for ordination as a Catholic priest. He became one of the youngest men in history to take holy orders. His education was informal. He was taught by monks rather than university professors.

While Hans was living in Tuscany, his mother and all her family perished in an Allied bombing raid on Cologne. His father ended up in a mass grave near Stalingrad. Hans was orphaned by the war, and the Roman Catholic Church became his only family, his life. Immediately after taking holy orders, Hans Kruger was assigned to the Vatican. His entire career had been spent within the walls of the Holy See. He studied and mastered the byzantine politics of the Church, became a cardinal at a young age, and by the mid-eighties ruled much of the Vatican hierarchy with an iron fist.

Cardinal John Wolleski was summoned to the offices of Cardinal Hans Kruger by a messenger. Wolleski was in the Vatican library, where he had commandeered a long rosewood table and stacked it with piles of books he had ordered for his research. The elderly cardinal pulled off his reading glasses, laid them on the pages of an open book, and followed the messenger. He thought it odd that he had not been given an appointment with Kruger but was being commanded to meet him at once.

Kruger did not appear like a man in his late fifties. His erect military bearing and lean, muscular frame was that of a much younger athlete. Though the cardinal was easily the most controversial figure in the Holy See, no one challenged his power.

Cardinal Wolleski walked into the grand office and found Cardinal Kruger standing near a bookshelf. "Thank you for coming, John."

John Wolleski was not given to phoniness of any kind. "It did not seem I had a choice."

"You know why I sent for you? Of course you know."

"You're going to have to tell me, Hans."

All politeness ceased as the veins in Kruger's face became pronounced. When he spoke English, it was with the German accent he had never lost. "John, I almost sent you to the infirmary first. To have your head checked. Do you realize what you have done in having the Holy Father involve himself in this situation in North America? Do you realize what a breach of protocol it was to discuss this with the Holy Father? Do you understand what you have done?"

Wolleski nodded that he did.

"There was no reason for you to bring this matter to the attention of the Holy Father. Everything should have been done to keep this from him. This is not the kind of news that we give the pontiff. He has more than enough on his plate. These things are for others. It is our business what happens in the Vatican, not the business of a retired American cardinal."

Cardinal Wolleski was impassive, unable to remember the last time anyone had used this kind of tone when addressing him.

"We have reports of this one situation that exists in North America. There is only one active case, John. It involves some priest in a province called Louisiana in the south of the United States. The diocese involved has reported several times to the papal nunciature in Washington and those reports were forwarded here to my office, where they belong. There is no problem mentioned in the reports by the bishop. Now you want the pontiff to rely on the writings of three hysterics."

"I have confidence that what they have written is true."

"There are two things you must know. These things are exclusively under the jurisdiction of my office, Cardinal Paginini and whomever else I choose to delegate to. This does not involve the Holy Father. It should have been my sole decision whether something like this merited the attention of the Holy Father."

"I want to say—"

Cardinal Kruger raised his hand. "You have said enough

346

already in your secret, private meeting with the pontiff. There is no problem in the United States. It is only one priest."

Cardinal Wolleski shook his head in disagreement.

Kruger continued, "The Holy Father's head is filled with enough odd notions. He's even talking about some kind of apology to the Jews. He doesn't need to be involved in this situation."

"Hans, why don't you meet with the Holy Father and tell him these things yourself? And tell him you think his idea about apologizing to the Jewish people is an odd notion."

"You know I cannot do that."

John Wolleski wanted to leave. He had a very low opinion of Kruger. During the war Wolleski had fought Nazism in Italy, helping smuggle Jews from Rome onto boats that would take them to Palestine; after the war he had watched as the Vatican assisted Nazi war criminals to escape Europe. He did not want to be fighting a man he considered a Nazi in the Vatican now.

"This thing is not the Holy Father's problem or the Vatican's problem," Kruger reiterated. "This is North America's problem, John."

"The Holy Father is concerned and he has acted. It is not for anyone, not even you, to question his actions."

"The Holy Father did not act of his own accord. He did this thing after you brought him a hysterical report from America. The American Church alone has to take care of the American Church."

"This is not about the American Church," Cardinal Wolleski said.

"This is only about the American Church."

"This is about children."

"American children. They are not the children of the Vatican," Cardinal Kruger said.

"This could become a huge problem. It is the Vatican and the pontiff's problem."

"In having our Holy Father appoint someone to monitor the situation in America, you have taken the hand of the Holy Father and pressed it in ink. You have placed Rome's fingerprints on this. It is not Rome's problem. No one is ever going to make this the Vatican's problem," Cardinal Kruger said.

"It is the Church's problem."

"The Vatican is the Church and this will never be the Vatican's problem."

55

THE VATICAN ACTS

Friday evening, February 1, 1985
Georgetown, Washington DC

The Ascot Grill, Desmond McDougall's choice for dinner, was very different from Café Roma. It was a new, trendy, upscale kind of place frequented by congressional staffers from Capitol Hill.

Matt met me in the bar and we went to a corner table. He told me about his afternoon with Francis Dubois at the Stalder Institute the day before. I chewed peanuts and washed them down with a vodka rocks, looking for an honest response to what I'd heard him say.

"Jesus, Matt... you hugged Francis Dubois?"

"Yes, Renon, I hugged him. Poor guy hung on to me for two minutes, crying. I think it's been a long time since he had a hug."

"Yeah – from an adult maybe."

"You can make a joke about it," Matt said. "The human touch is important to a dying person. You ever notice that even in the hospital where people lie dying, even the nurses hurry out of the room? No one wants to be near the dead or dying, much less have contact with them. And your client is dying psychologically and emotionally. His breathing is an involuntary reflex."

I nodded. "What did you talk about?"

"First, I gave him a battery of tests, ones I've developed myself over the years. I doubt the results will tell us anything, because the first test I graded indicates he was lying, trying to make the test score read in a sympathetic way. He really wants someone to feel sorry for him. I told him that he did not need

349

anyone to feel sorry for him because he felt sorry enough for himself."

"You said that?"

"Yes. I can be kind with these people when I believe kindness is what they need, and I can be brutal too. Psychotics don't have honesty in their repertoire."

"Do you think it's possible that Dubois has multiple personalities? Matt, I've seen him come across as two completely different people in the space of a week. I mean really different."

"Not a chance. When your whole life has been a lie, there is no reference to truth anymore. A sociopath, a psychopath, can morph, change colors like a chameleon. It's a life devoid of any real emotion."

"I think I've seen him when he was devoid of everything."

"But Dubois is not like others I've seen."

"How?"

"Sick, Renon. This guy is as sick as they come, maybe worse than anyone I have seen. And I thought I had seen them all."

"You want to treat him?"

"No, I don't. There's a place not far from here where he can get the best treatment, Hannover House. Maybe I can discuss moving him with the staff at Hannover, if you agree. My interest is pastoral. I want to be his priest. I believe I can help him experience some healing spiritually."

"Why?"

"In my mind I can make clinical judgments about people. In my heart, I can't judge anyone. God created us all, the monsters too, and the final judgment is God's, not mine."

"Let me ask you this – you think I have any chance of finding anybody in the country to testify that Dubois meets the requirements for legal insanity? That he did not know the difference between right and wrong at the time these offenses were committed?"

"I guess you can find someone to say just about anything. Do I think it's true that he did not know the difference between right and wrong? No, of course it's not true. I think Dubois may be playing the game with a short IQ. I don't think he's all that smart, but he is sane clinically and legally."

"You would be a priest to Dubois?"

"I will if he wants that. I know he will manipulate me every way he can. He did a lot of that yesterday. The one truth I am sure he spoke was when he said he believed he has had sex with hundreds of children. The man has destroyed hundreds of innocent lives. And, Renon, he has no remorse."

"It's a big problem for me, no?"

"How do you expect that will play in a courtroom? A Roman Catholic priest has raped hundreds of children and has no pangs of conscience, not the slightest remorse."

Des walked in, late as usual. After we were escorted to a table and seated, Des said, "Oh ye of little faith."

Matt shook his head in amusement. "Okay, tell us. What is it that has you so ebullient tonight?"

"Well, first thing is I may have saved my own Scotch-Irish ass. Don't think the papal nuncio, old Carlo Verriano, can sack me now. The Pope's on our side. Even Verriano can't screw with the Pope. Rome is getting with the program. There was an exchange of cables today. Cardinal Wolleski had to have had his meeting with the big guy. The Vatican will appoint a visitator."

"A what?" I asked.

"Ah, the spaghetti suckers in Rome still use that kind of archaic language. They even still use Latin when they issue communications on sensitive topics."

Matt appeared unmoved by the message that so delighted Desmond. "Who will this person be and what will his charge be?"

"The specific language will charge him with monitoring the clergy sex-abuse situation in the Diocese of Thiberville and other similar situations in the event they should arise elsewhere. He will also assist in managing all of those situations, and will report directly to the Vatican through the office of the papal nuncio. His reports will all come across my desk. I tell you, we're going to get a handle on this mess and clean it up before it explodes. Some kind of way, we're gonna stop this business, run some priests to jailhouses and hopefully save some kids."

"And what about those children who've already been victimized?" I said.

"I don't know," Desmond said, "but the Church has to do the right thing."

"Who have they appointed?" Matt asked.

"They want the recommendation to come from my boss, Archbishop Carlo Verriano. Ol' Carlo doesn't know one swinging dick in this whole country. So he leaned on me."

"And who have you picked?"

"In Baltimore, there is that auxiliary bishop doing nothing, just sitting around waiting for some old bishop to die and create an opening for him to take over a diocese."

"You're talking about Bishop Franklin?"

"That's the one. Garland Franklin. He's not only a canon lawyer, he's a civil lawyer, and his undergraduate work was in psychology. He ought to be able to understand what I'm saying about canon law, what Renon's saying about civil and criminal law, and he might even understand your screwy head-shrinking stuff. And he's nearby, in Baltimore. Perfect, no?"

"Perfect, Desmond," Matt said as he rolled his eyes.

"What? What's wrong with this?" Desmond said.

"Do you really believe anyone with ecclesiastical ambitions is going to want to get anywhere near this stuff? It will explode Franklin's career. Franklin will never be bishop of anything if he does the right thing. Worse, anyone you have appointed will be Rome's man all the way, Cardinal Kruger's stooge."

"The cable traffic today was with the office of Cardinal Antonio Marcello, the Pope's buddy. It was an end run around Cardinal Kruger. Kruger's out of the loop on this one."

Matt seemed impressed by that.

During the meal, Desmond and I drank a lot of wine. I even

mixed in a couple of vodkas, knowing the drinks would help me sleep when I got back to the hotel. I felt that a big step in the right direction had been made. *To hell with Monsignor Moroux, Bishop Reynolds, Jon Bendel, Joe Rossi, all of them*, I thought. They had nothing; we had the Pope. *Now the victims will get justice; the priests and the bishops will get what they deserve.*

The three of us were pretty drunk when we walked out of the Ascot Grill. Des insisted on driving me to my hotel, saying, "I have diplomatic immunity. I imagine it covers drunk-driving arrests."

Matt's car was in a lot across the street. As he unlocked his car, he heard what Des said, and shouted back at us. "You guys are like gasoline and fire."

It was late, after 2 a.m. Des parked the car near an empty grassy area. "Come with me." When we got out of the car, everything about him was different. He was as sober and serious as I'd ever seen him.

"Where are we, Des? What are we doing?"

"You'll see. I come out here every night. It's the holiest shrine I know, Ren."

We walked across the wet grass in the light mist.

He said, "I've been coming here every night since they unveiled this thing. There are always people here, no matter what time it is. Sometimes when I wake up early, I come over before dawn too. The time of day doesn't matter. There are always people here."

The Vietnam Veterans Memorial was an eerie sight at night. The long granite wall was barely visible in the mist. When we reached it, Des said, "Touch it. Go ahead. Touch it." I did. It was cold.

Des nodded toward a knoll with a statue I could not make out in the mist. There were fifteen or more people sitting on blankets and sleeping bags. One was playing a guitar.

"What do you do here? You come as a priest?"

"No. These people don't need a priest. They need someone to listen. That's all. Someone who remembers them, what they did, understands what happened to them. They're broken inside. They come here because it's the only proof they have of what they did, and the names on the wall did, damn near sixty thousand dead – it's the only proof their buddies ever lived."

The 200-foot wall, the listing of names, was overwhelming.

"I brought you here to see something, Ren."

"Yeah."

"These people believed, they really believed. They gave everything." Touching the wall, he said, "These boys gave their lives. They all gave everything – to some belief. It destroyed them. It wasn't the war that killed them inside. It was losing their belief. You understand."

I said nothing.

"You walk this wall, Ren. See your reflection in this wall. Think about your beliefs. I don't want you burned out like those boys on the knoll. I'm going up on the knoll to listen to those guys. I'll be back."

I walked along the wall in slow motion. Along the base of the wall were things that had been left by visitors. Des had mentioned that the things were collected at the end of each day; large warehouses were filled with the stuff, he'd said, and no one knew what to do with it.

I reached down and picked up a large teddy bear. A handwritten note was safety-pinned to its chest: "Bear, you know, man, we couldn't find you, man. We just had to bug outta there. The LZ was hot. We looked, man. Nobody found you. I love you, Bear. Willie."

I gently put the teddy bear back in place.

56

FALL FROM GRACE

Saturday February 2, 1985
Julie's Apartment

I flew back to Thiberville to take care of some of the backlog at my office that was crashing around Mo. Leaving long-term parking at the airport, I called Julie from my car phone. She asked me to come by her apartment for dinner. When I arrived, she apologized for not having cooked.

"So, we're ordering in pizza again, right?" I asked.

She nodded, poured beers, and clinked glasses. "I dropped my papers," she said.

"What?"

"I wrote the head of my order and advised I would be leaving."

My heart sank. We clinked glasses again. "Well, now, this... I guess this is good news. It's big news, for sure. When will you be leaving?"

"I don't know. It's up to me. Today I got my response. They will leave it to me to tell the diocese and to leave my job and the religious community when I am ready. I don't think it will be long."

"Did something push you over the edge?"

"No. It wasn't one thing. I just need to get out of here and get out of this religious life. I can't take it anymore. I've felt unclean inside for a long time."

Julie paused. Her voice was softer, quieter. "I promised you I would never lie to you, Renon. I said it on the day we met. But I've not been completely honest. The truth is, before this business with

Father Dubois came to a head, I had worked with Moroux on other cases like this. We manipulated families whose children had been sexually abused by our priests. They used me to work with the mothers and children. Few of the children's fathers gave me the time of day, but some of the kids' mothers wanted to pray all this away. I was as guilty as anyone who covered this stuff up, guilty as hell."

She started to cry. She looked away. I wanted to hold her, but didn't. I was more concerned about her pain than what she was saying.

"It's okay, Julie. We all do things. You don't have to talk about it."

"Let me, okay? It's important to me that… important that you know me. My job was to placate the families, take the criminal violation of their children to some kind of spiritual level, make their anger with the diocese go away, convince them the problem priest had been dealt with even when I was sure he was in the process of abusing more children in his new assignment. That's why I was in the meeting at the Old Bishop's House on the day I met you. Don't you see? I was like part of their team. They kept me close because they thought they might need me again – the good nun. If they had taken your advice and reached out to other victims of Dubois… if they had, they would have sent me to those families to convince them prayer was all they needed, not lawyers or police."

I leaned back in my chair and looked at Julie, shocked.

"I was complicit in the cover-up – up to my ass in this sickening, sinful, shameful stuff. What I did made me sick when I was doing it. It was like rotting inside."

Julie's face changed as she spoke and it was more than just an expression of deep pain and distress. There were now lines in what I'd always seen as smooth, flawless skin.

My head was moving toward a harsh judgment of her I knew I had no right to make, but my heart overrode my head. I cared so much about Julie that I only wanted to support her through her distress. That she was so visibly sick in facing the facts was part of her goodness, and I believed, given her spiritual soundness, and love of people, that maybe she had been more of a comfort to the children and mothers than she believed she had.

I took her hand, and her palm was wet with perspiration. Suddenly a truth deep within me surfaced. I was falling in love with Julie.

"When I met you, I gave you my card, asked you to call. Remember? Why did I do that? Because I'm a coward. I wanted to do something that was right for once, but lacked the courage to do it myself. So I wanted to give the personnel files to you and hope you had the courage to do the right thing. I didn't know if you would do the right thing, but I knew no one else in that room would. I knew I had never done the right thing." She was staring at the floor when she finished.

I touched her face, held her left cheek in my right hand and turned her face softly, making her downcast eyes look up at me. "You've done the right thing now, Julie. None of us who've come in contact with this stuff did the right thing in the beginning. This stuff has put a stain on our souls that we'll never scrub clean."

"Well, I have those fifteen other files for you. I have had them since I copied Dubois's file. Those priests are as sick as Francis Dubois. When you use the files, please tell them that they came from me. Use my name, will you? Tell them where they came from."

I nodded. "I'm going to miss you a lot."

"And I am going to miss you. More than you can imagine, I think." She took her hand back, kissed my cheek, and said, "You're a good person."

"Good people don't conspire to destroy evidence," I said.

We had a few more beers and talked about where she might go and what she might do. She was looking at doing what she had always wanted, relief work in Africa, and said, "I want to do the right thing with the rest of my life. Really help people."

"You had no choice here in Thiberville. What could you have done to change the way the bishop and Monsignor Moroux handled these things?"

"Maybe I could not have changed them, but I did not have to be a willing participant. When I was telling mothers that prayer and the Church could heal the wounds of their children and their own wounds, of course I knew that wasn't true. The kids and their families needed extensive therapy. But that's how the diocese paid off these families. They paid them with prayers."

"Look, don't go beating yourself up. I just heard a cardinal confess that he had done far worse things. Everyone associated with the Church has something to answer for. People who finally choose to do the right thing can be redeemed."

"Stealing some priests' files from the diocesan secret archives and giving them to you is hardly a redeeming act."

"It's a lot. In time, police and prosecutors will get those files."

"It won't matter who gets those files. Not many priests will do any prison time for sex crimes against children. We both know this. You told me that if Kane Chaisson had not brought so much pressure on the district attorney, who is scared of him, then Father Francis Dubois would have had another get-out-of-jail-free pass. Bishops are maybe bigger criminals than the child molesters. Covering-up crimes—"

"Julie, if it's okay with you, I really can't talk about this stuff anymore tonight. My days are filled with it, my nights too. I hardly sleep anymore. I have dialogues with myself all night about this stuff. Let's order pizza and talk about something else, okay?"

"Okay. What do you want to talk about?"

"Let's talk about where you're going."

"Africa?"

"My beautiful friend, I think you're going to be in trouble in Africa."

"Why?"

"I can't imagine they have pizza in Africa."

57

THE TRUE CHURCH

Sunday February 3, 1985
Baltimore, Maryland

It was late Sunday afternoon by the time I navigated my way across Baltimore to the rectory of Bishop Garland Franklin. If someone had gone to central casting looking for a man to play a handsome bishop or cardinal, the part would have gone to Garland Franklin. He needed no vestments, altar, pulpit, or other trappings to project the sense of authority he exuded.

For four hours, I briefed the bishop on the Thiberville situation. I returned on Monday for another three hours. Throughout both sessions, Bishop Franklin never let on what he was thinking or feeling. He never took a note, never asked a question, never said or did anything that could provide a clue about how he was receiving the information.

The books that lined the shelves of the bishop's study seemed to reveal a literate, well-rounded intellect. One wall was dominated by photographs depicting him with elderly women. There were photographs of the group at the matinee of a play, a flower show, an art museum, a waterfront shopping mall, a restaurant on the shore. He told me that was what he did on Saturday afternoons. Together with a school bus driver and a nurse, who both volunteered alongside him, he picked up these women from their urban public housing projects, places they were ordinarily too afraid to venture out of, and took them out for the afternoon. He said, "My mom passed away a bit too soon. Like any son, I wished I had spent more time with her, done more things with her. I found this opportunity to bring some joy to some elderly women and… the truth is, Renon, I think I get as much enjoyment from these outings as they do. I have probably seen more art, more plays and museums, and more state parks than I would have ever seen. And I've heard a lot of laughter where I'm not sure there was much before."

He was almost too good to be true.

When I motioned to a different kind of photograph, a picture of him as a tanned young man on a beach, holding a surf board, he broke into a wide smile. "Can you believe the kind of boards we had back then? It was more like floating than surfing. I was born sixteen miles south of the best stretch of water California has. I almost flunked out of school a couple times because I was riding waves instead of going to class. I don't tell many people this, but I still go back to California every year. Usually, I watch. But sometimes I still try. One good wave is all it takes. After that, the air you breathe is better, food tastes better, everything is better. I'm going back out there to get in the water again. Nothing is more humbling than the sea."

As our Monday meeting ended, the bishop walked me to my rental car behind the rectory, shook my hand and said, "I'll be coming to Louisiana soon, Renon. First, I have to make another trip, a short trip, on some Church business."

Wednesday February 6, 1985
Vatican City

Bishop Garland Franklin of Baltimore was seated in a well-appointed suite on the top floor of the most important building in Vatican City, an office some referred to as "the Eagle's Nest". Cardinal Hans Kruger entered the office wearing riding gear.

As Bishop Franklin stood to greet the cardinal, Kruger shifted a coin he had been holding in his right hand to his left. It was the last gift his father had given him and it was always in his pocket – a 5 Reichsmark coin minted in Potsdam in 1936.

"I am off to the countryside for an afternoon of riding. If I had been sure you would make it from the States today, we could have saddled a horse for you."

"I'm not a horseman, Your Eminence," the bishop said.

"With these mounts, it wouldn't matter. They can make you look and feel like you've been riding all your life. I have always loved riding. It takes me away from my work. The stable is only 47 kilometers outside the city, but it takes me far away."

Bishop Franklin had never met Cardinal Hans Kruger, and he had never heard a good thing about him, but, like everyone in the Church hierarchy, the bishop understood that the cardinal's power in Rome was nearly absolute. It was widely believed that Hans Kruger was only one funeral away from the papacy. The easy talk about horses and personal references surprised Bishop Franklin. Such small talk was not commonplace inside the walls of the most formal religious institution on earth, where conversations were usually guarded.

The bishop knew from the language of the summons that this meeting was to be private and confidential. From the timing, he surmised that the discussion was to be about the Vatican appointment he had received a week earlier.

The cardinal slipped the coin in his pocket and perused his bookshelves, tapping the bindings with the index finger of his right hand, making a kind of humming sound as he passed his fingers across the volumes that were crammed into the bookcases. Pulling a thick volume from the stack, the cardinal put it into Bishop Franklin's hands.

"Do you know this book, *Of an Order in Life*?"

"No, I don't, but obviously I recognize the names of many of the authors."

"I don't do a lot of reading, Bishop, but I read this book twice. It's a collection of writings – essays and meditations – by some great thinkers. Some Christian, some Muslim, several Jews, many without any spiritual or religious identity. Their subjects are duty, obligation, and loyalty. Some of the writings date to antiquity and the most recent is from just before the book was published in 1953. Keep it. If you read it, I believe you will be inspired. The things discussed in this book we no longer encounter much in the modern world, where there is little sense of duty and obligation and almost all loyalty is lost. These things guide my life. Without them, there can be no order. Without order, there is nothing."

Bishop Franklin thanked the cardinal and slipped the book into his briefcase. Also in Franklin's briefcase was his two-page Vatican appointment, and the set of papers that was becoming known as "the Wolleski Document".

Cardinal Kruger stood ramrod straight in front of the seated bishop. "I have read the document of your appointment by the Holy See, Bishop. I have read the document Cardinal Wolleski carried to Rome that provoked the hysteria that led to your appointment. I have no intention of attempting in the slightest degree to interfere with the terms of or the charges contained in your appointment. Considering the appointment was issued from the office of Cardinal Marcello at the insistence of the Holy Father himself, it would be inappropriate for me to even comment on the content of the appointment document, and I certainly will not criticize the appointment. The Holy Father's will shall stand."

Until that moment, it had not crossed Bishop Franklin's mind that the pontiff was involved in the matter or that the Holy Father had personally selected him from a roster of over four hundred American bishops. He would never know that the Pope had never heard of him and that a young priest at the nunciature named Desmond McDougall was the one who had chosen him.

Bishop Franklin selected his most enthusiastic tone. "I understand completely, Eminence."

Kruger took a key from his pocket and unlocked a side drawer in his desk. He pulled out the appointment papers and looked them over.

"And so, I see your appointment and charge is to monitor... assist in managing... and report to the Vatican through the office of the papal nuncio in Washington," the cardinal said.

"Yes. That is as I understand it."

"Let us now see if we understand this entire business in the same way."

The bishop nodded.

"The problem was surely exaggerated in the document Cardinal Wolleski carried to Rome. What you have is a document about one priest in some southern place in America that no one has heard of and… and statements of supposition that are baseless. These three men have sounded an alarm, rung the bells in the Vatican, about something they call… what?" Cardinal Kruger reached back in the drawer for the Wolleski document and flipped through the pages. "Yes, yes. Here it is. They refer to this as 'a crisis of clergy sexual abuse in the United States Catholic Church'. It is nonsense. It's the work of madmen."

The bishop nodded his head in agreement.

"Always remember in this meeting that I did not comment on the charge of your Vatican appointment. My comments were restricted to the document that caused your appointment."

"I understand, Your Eminence."

"So you will return to the United States. You will monitor this situation, and you will assist in managing the situation."

The bishop nodded again.

Cardinal Kruger pulled the coin out of his pocket, and turned it over and over in his fingers during a long silence.

"Report," Kruger said in a sharp tone. He continued in a loud voice, "Report what? What will you report from America? This is what I care about; this is why I asked you to come here."

The cardinal's tone threw Bishop Franklin a bit off balance. He did not move to answer the question about what he might report, for he believed the answer was going to be supplied by this powerful cardinal.

In a lower tone, but more commanding than any voice he had used since Bishop Franklin entered the room, the cardinal resumed. "Each report will of course be filed with the office of Cardinal Antonio Marcello as directed, routed through the office of the papal nuncio in Washington. Do just as your appointment requires."

"Yes. Those are the instructions in my appointment."

"And you will confidentially send a copy of each report to me. These matters are the responsibility of my office, my responsibility."

"As you wish."

"Each report will advise the Vatican, Cardinal Marcello, the Holy Father, his Polish pal Majeski, or anyone else who reads them… each report will tell the truth. I want the reports to tell the truth. Do you understand this, Bishop?"

"I do."

"And the truth, Bishop, is that these three men who wrote the document are engaged in hypothetical situations and hyperbolic rhetoric that has no relationship to reality. The truth is there is no problem in America worthy of Vatican attention. Do you understand this is the truth?"

Bishop Franklin nodded, but not nearly as strongly as he had earlier.

"These reports filed by you, over your signature, could be discovered in future years and if these reports contain untruths that point to a big problem existing in America, the Vatican could have problems. Do you understand this?"

"Yes."

"And finally, do you understand that if these men are right about what they wrote and a big problem develops, it's America's problem and the Vatican does not need to have knowledge of the extent of the problem, especially in the form of written reports from one of our bishops. None of your reports can contain language that could be used by anyone to impute direct knowledge about this problem to the Vatican."

Those remarks too only resulted in a slight nod from Bishop Franklin.

"These three men," Cardinal Kruger fumbled with the papers looking for names, "McDougall, Patterson, and Chattelrault, will discredit themselves, and this you will report. They must be discredited and you must report it. That will be an easy task as they discredit themselves in this hysterical document. Their statements are not the statements of serious men."

Bishop Franklin understood what he was being told to do. He swallowed hard.

"There are ways to bring this lawyer and these priests under control. Everyone involved – except our Holy Father – has a superior. These priests have superiors, I know. The lawyer works for a diocese."

Bishop Franklin's affirmative nod was a tired nod. Either jet lag or the intensity of the German cardinal had sapped all of his energy.

"I believe you understand about duty, obligation and loyalty to the Church, and I believe you will demonstrate those things. Now, I take my leave. The horses are saddled, awaiting some exercise. God go with you."

58

SACRED PLACES

Tuesday February 19, 1985
Washington DC

Mardi Gras morning I woke up in the Hay-Adams Hotel across from the White House. The Washington Post had a photograph of Lorne Greene reigning over the Sunday night Bacchus parade in New Orleans. I knew Kate was taking the kids to the city to see the parades. Her parents lived one block off the main parade route. From the weather reports, I imagined Kate and the kids would be bundled in warm clothing, standing somewhere along Saint Charles Avenue, waiting for the first parade of the day, Zulu.

I took a morning flight out of National Airport in Washington with Fathers McDougall and Patterson. Des had forwarded the Wolleski document to a number of bishops, many of whom had requested that we visit and consult with them. Today we were to begin our campaign. Over the coming weeks we planned to crisscross the country, moving to a different city every two or three days.

We quickly established the pattern that we would repeat in most dioceses we visited. The consultation began with a day-long meeting with a small group of diocesan clerics and officials – the bishop, his vicar general, the diocesan attorney, the canon lawyer who headed their diocesan tribunal, and a local psychiatrist or psychologist who consulted with the diocese regularly. We discussed cases involving specific, named clerics, who were euphemistically referred to as "problem priests", and we reviewed the relevant civil, criminal, clinical and canonical factors. The following day we addressed the entire diocese, hundreds of priests, in a rural retreat setting. Sometimes principals and administrators of the local Catholic school system were in the audience as well.

The anticipated one-week trip to three dioceses lasted nearly the whole forty-plus days of the Lenten season and extended to sixteen dioceses. In some places I had to play all three speaking roles as Matt and Des had pressing business to attend to in Washington.

It soon became a blur to me. As I moved from city to city, diocese to diocese, I began to wonder what our mission was. What was it Des, Matt and I believed we were doing? Was our mission to save children from the Church, or were we trying to save the Church from itself? In either case it was clear we were failing. Nothing was being accomplished. The child victims were never mentioned once by anyone except us.

Monday March 4, 1985

After one Monday session, I was chastised by Matt in our hotel suite over a performance I had given earlier that day during our presentation to an entire diocese of hundreds of priests in the chapel of a rural retreat house. During the question and answer session, a fat, young priest wearing thick glasses had approached the microphone.

"Mr. Chattelrault, you talked about millions that could be lost in civil cases. Exactly whose money are you talking about here? Should we do something to protect our pension funds? Protect the good priests?"

"What do you mean by good priests?" I said. "Who are the good priests? If the entire diocese is in this room as I was told they would be, then it is certain from my experience that there are men among us in this room who have sexually abused children. And it is also certain, to my mind, that everyone in this room knows exactly who the guilty priests are. One of the things I have learned is that priests who sexually abuse children and adolescents do not live in a vacuum. They live in communities like this one. Their lifestyles make others suspect them; there are complaints made against them; they are shuttled from one parish assignment to another. Everyone in their community knows who they are. No one contacts the police."

"But... but—"

"No, I'm talking here. Let me tell you – tell all of you – I know all of you have a penis and I know all of you can get an image of an erect penis in your mind. But none of you have children, and not one of you – none of you – can imagine what a parent feels when they are forced to picture an erect penis entering the vagina or rectum of their seven-year-old child, or their young teenager."

"But... but—"

"Father, if you were a good priest – indeed, if any of the men in this room were good priests – there would be no bad priests in this room; they would all be locked away in jails. If you were a good priest following the teachings and example of Christ, you would be consumed with empathy and sympathy for the young victims and their families. You would not care only about yourself and your money."

The fat fellow was red in the face. I picked up my file from the podium and stepped away from the microphone. With my file in my hand and in a voice loud enough to be heard in the last row without the aid of a microphone, I said, "A man who has reason to believe children are being sexually abused and does not contact the police is not a good priest. He's not even a good man."

I walked out of the room. Twenty minutes later Des and Matt found me seated at the wheel of our rental car. No one said anything as we returned to the hotel.

Once we were settled in the hotel suite, Matt opened up on me. "Renon, we can't have any more performances like your act this afternoon. If word gets around to other bishops about what you said—"

Interrupting him, I said, "Wha'? Wha' the fuck happens then? So, I don't get to talk to any more of these bastards? Fuck 'em. That piece of shit priest deserved what I said. They all did. I don't know the Bible, but I swear if it's really the Good Book as some say, then it would sanction the killing of adults who prey on children sexually and those who cover up their crimes."

Matt said, "You gotta understand, the concept of keeping the Church free from scandal is tattooed on these guys' souls." He laughed and slapped my arm. "Monsignor Moroux was telling the truth when he told Des you're a loose cannon."

"I'm not a loose cannon. I aim carefully."

Every night my hotel room looked the same. Legal pads filled with notes I had scribbled were stacked on the desk and spread on the bed. I'm not sure what I thought I'd learn by poring over these notes every night. I now knew of over four hundred priests who had sexually abused children. A clinical text I'd read claimed a forty-year-old pedophile in a position of trust could have as many as two hundred victims. I had visited less than 10 per cent of the dioceses in the country, and yet there could be as many as eighty thousand children who had been sexually abused over the years in these dioceses. It was unfathomable to me, and unimaginable that no one knew these secrets.

Six months earlier, I had been convinced that I faced absolute evil in the form of a single aberrant Catholic priest who had sexually defiled seventeen children, and a vicar general and bishop who had covered up his crimes. Now, the Church appeared to me as lethal and morally dead as any criminal enterprise on earth. Based on the evidence I had from the dioceses I'd visited, I believed there had to be five to ten thousand sex-abuser priests in the United States, which meant every single bishop must have been involved in covering up their crimes. And it was only logical to assume a similar situation existed in every other significantly Catholic country in the world.

Wednesday March 13, 1985
Williams Crossing, Virginia

Matt cooked dinner for me and Des. But first I had to play fetch with a tennis ball until Matt's dog, Mozart, lost interest and calmed down from the excitement of having visitors in the house.

I wasn't hungry. I picked at the food, paid more attention to the wine. "How many victims do you think there are?" I asked.

Matt said, "When you factor in the child's family members as victims – and family members are victims, collateral damage, and Catholic families are large – then you're probably looking at over a million in this country whose lives have been severely damaged or destroyed by people in whom they placed their faith and trust. Maybe a lot more."

"What in the world can we do about this?" I asked.

"Ask Des. He's our supreme optimist."

Des ignored the shot and enthusiastically offered, "Cardinal Laurence from Atlanta was at the nunciature for dinner last week. I brought him up to speed and he's a good guy who is with the program. He said he'd take this issue to the National Conference of Catholic Bishops in May. He wants a proposal from us, policies and procedures, a manual for the American bishops to adopt. I think he can take the bull by the horns."

Pouring another glass of wine, I said, "There's something I hate to bring up, fellows. But it has occurred to me that the three of us may be criminals now."

"What?" Matt asked.

"Every time we go into a diocese we learn the identities of more child molesters, heinous criminals. Do we report this to local police authorities? No. We just go to the airport without stopping at the police or prosecutor's office. There are laws in a lot of states that mandate that anyone possessing knowledge of a sex crime against a child report same or they are guilty of a crime for failure to report. I can't differentiate what we do from what the bishops do. We're part of the conspiracy to cover up these crimes."

There was a long silence. Matt's silence seemed like a stunned silence. Des was more stoic. "We're doing good work. Some priests have been removed to treatment facilities."

"What's the difference between moving a criminal cleric to a new parish and hiding him away in a distant treatment center? There's no difference," I said.

Matt asked, "Where would you put them, if not in a treatment facility?"

"Prison. I'd put them in prison. All of them belong in prison."

Des said, "I grant you, it's a tough place we're in, but we can't blow up the Church before we've placed it in a position to save children and save itself. Cardinal Laurence—"

"Do you think Cardinal Laurence or anyone else has any idea that there are thousands of priests having sex with minors and little children in this country?"

Matt said, "No. No one knows the whole truth. You probably are as close to the truth as anyone has ever been. Your briefcase holds the worst secrets of the American Church. We will prepare a proposal for Cardinal Laurence to present to the Conference of Bishops, a plan."

"What happens if the world comes to know what we know? What happens then?"

"If the world learns what we know now, the moral authority of the Church will be severely diminished, maybe destroyed," Des said.

"Will bishops understand that, in doing nothing, they're putting the Church's moral authority at risk?" I asked.

Des grumbled, "Bishops would never believe that anything could adversely impact the moral authority or the supreme power of the Church."

59

BOYS ON THE BAYOU

Friday March 22, 1985
Coteau

Matt was the ringleader. It was his decision that he and Des should travel to meet my family, see the land of Louisiana. When I told Kate they were coming down and asked if she could put them up in the guest cottage at Coteau, she suggested I stay at Coteau as well. Kate offered to swing by my town home and pick up some casual clothes for me. She said I could stay in the master suite in the big house with her and added, "Maybe we can even fool around."

The prospect of being back in Coteau with everyone had the effect of recharging me, shaking away some of the exhaustion that had dogged me day and night on the road. I had talked to Kate and the kids often over the past two months since I'd met Matt and Des, describing them as best I could.

We arrived at Thiberville airport Friday morning at ten. Sasha was standing in the baggage-claim area with Kate. When Kate told me Sasha couldn't go to school because of a tummy ache, she winked.

"It's all better now," Sasha said. She was not a shy kid. Rather than hiding behind Kate, she kept looking behind Matt. "My daddy said you had a dog, Mozart. Where's Mozart, mister?"

Matt bent down on one knee, face to face with her, eye level, and said, "You can call me Matt, okay? You're Sasha, right?"

"Un-huh. I mean, yes, sir."

"Un-huh's okay. It's good to call strangers who are grownups 'sir', but we're gonna be friends. I'm just Matt, and that guy with muscles hauling our bags off the conveyor belt – his name's Des."

"Where's Mozart?" Sasha said.

"Do you like airplane food?" Matt said.

"No way. When we go skiing, I bring my own food in my backpack."

"Well, maybe I'll get Mozart a backpack. See, Mozart doesn't like airplane food either. But he sent some gifts for you."

Matt reached into a carrier bag and pulled out two Cabbage Patch Dolls and two Care Bears. "I don't know what kinds of toys little girls like, but somebody told me these were the right things, and your dad told me you had a stuffed doll and stuffed animal collection that filled your room. Mozart got into this bag and put each one of the dolls in his mouth. He wanted to play fetch with them. I had to fuss at him. He decided it was a good idea to leave them in good shape for you."

"You're pretty funny for a priest and everything."

Desmond laughed and said, "Matt's stealing all my thunder here, Sasha. Your dad said you loved the movie, so I got you all the *Star Wars* figures. They're in my suitcase."

Sasha squealed, "This is really great. Jake and Shelby are gonna be soooo jealous."

"Oh, we didn't leave them out," Des said. "I brought them a couple of signed baseballs and a signed football from a collection I've had since I was a kid."

Kate kissed and hugged me, squeezed my hand. "It's good to see you," she said. Then she kissed Des and Matt on the cheek. "You guys are sweet to bring these gifts. It's not like Sasha's not spoiled enough."

Matt smiled. "Gifts are good. In my med-school years, I worked all summer every year at camps for underprivileged children who I don't think ever got gifts. I learned more from those children than I ever learned in school."

*

I found it was an official Chattelrault holiday when we arrived home in Coteau. Jake and Shelby had skipped out on school too. The visit of Matt and Des was a big thing for the whole family. The boys were in the swimming pool. It was a heated pool, partially covered, but I knew it had to be cold at this time of year. It didn't take twenty minutes for Des and Matt to borrow trunks from me and Shelby, and dive in and begin playing "Marco Polo". Soon everyone but Kate was in the pool. She was cooking in the kitchen, bringing out small portions of Cajun dishes poolside. We stayed in the pool long enough to get sunburned.

When Kate and I announced we were taking Matt and Des to a classic old country supper club with a Cajun band that evening, the children insisted on coming too. Kate and I offered the back seat of my car to the guys, but they opted to grab Sasha and climb into the back of Shelby's jeep, undaunted by the deafening music of the Rolling Stones pouring out of its huge speakers. We followed the jeep as it bounced along the winding country roads, crossing bridges over two muddy bayous lined with moss-covered oaks. Shelby suddenly swung left to take a shortcut across the sunbaked rows of an abandoned bean field, and all five in the jeep started laughing and shouting over the music as they bounced over plowed rows of dirt that were as solid as concrete. Matt and Des hung on to little Sasha as all in the jeep were convulsed in laugher. Kate shook her head and grinned. "So, these are the two guys you've been telling me are so brilliant. Riding anywhere with Shelby and Jake is not the brightest idea."

Inside the old, sagging, wooden dinner-dance place, Kate did the ordering from a menu of dishes foreign to Matt and Des. Soon we were tucking into the rice, chicken and andouille sausage of a classic jambalaya, and feasting on shrimp remoulade, marinated crab fingers, hush puppy fritters made from special cornflour, and a seafood gumbo with a bit of everything from the Gulf of Mexico in it.

Before we got to the pecan pie and praline ice cream, Des announced, "I don't know how to do what you call the Cajun two-step, Kate. I only learned one dance as a boy. But let's give it a go anyhow." Des took Kate to the floor and to the accompaniment of the old-timers' ensemble of accordion, guitar, fiddle and drum they danced one wild polka after another.

Most of the night, Matt sat at the far end of the table, talking with Jake and Shelby about their lives, interests, likes and dislikes. At Matt's side, Sasha had a stack of crayons and coloring sheets the waitress handed out. She worked as she always did, diligently, becoming frustrated as she could not consistently color within the lines. I watched Matt at times as he picked up colors and helped her, and I heard him say, "Now, Sasha, think about it. Who put these figures on these pages? Who made these lines? Do lines really matter? Of course not. You're an artist expressing yourself and we're gonna turn these sheets over to the blank side where there are no lines at all. Then you can draw any line with any color you want. And when you finish making these crayon renderings, if you allow me, I would love for you to give me two of them if you want to. I will frame one for my office wall, and the other I will hang at a low level in my den at home, low enough for Mozart to admire it."

Sasha smiled broadly. "Okay. Deal."

Just before closing time, Des said, "One more dance, Kate."

"No way. You've thrown my back out, Des."

Matt stood and offered his hand to Kate. "It sounds like a waltz. I think I can muddle through that without injuring you." Matt was a talented dancer and the two of them glided in circles small and large, smiling and laughing.

Des sat next to me, put an arm around me, and took a pull off a long-neck beer. "This is some life, some country, some culture you got down here, Ren. What a night! First time I danced with a woman all night and what happens? I'm jilted for a head-shrinker, Matt. Them's the breaks, eh son?"

When the kids were asleep upstairs in their rooms, Kate served cognac and coffee on a glass-topped table by the pool. Desmond was still marveling to me about the dreamlike landscape of south Louisiana, the richness of the food, and the fabulous sounds of the Cajun band he'd been dancing to.

At some point, I got up to check on the automatic pool sweeper. I was standing on the edge of the deep end, where the device was trapped in a corner. Together, Des and Matt snuck up behind me and pushed me into the pool, fully clothed. It was like ice water. When I surfaced, shouting, "That's not fair," Matt said, "You're right. Fair's fair." And he dove in headfirst with all of his clothes on, popping to the surface and calling out to Des, "Are we in this together or what?" Des walked to the shallow end and down the steps until he was over his head too.

Kate tried to escape. She ran, she shrieked, even showed a flash of anger, but we tossed her in too, blue jeans, sweatshirt and all.

We were out of the pool as quick as we were in it. Once we'd dried and changed, I built a big fire in the den, and we arranged ourselves comfortably around it and started to talk. Kate was interested in the guys, in why they became priests. Des said, "I never wanted to be a priest when I was growing up. I wanted to play professional hockey. Then in college I took a comparative religion course and became interested in the history of religions. I felt I wanted to be part of that life. I'd been baptized and raised in a Catholic family, so I chose that course, but I've never really thought of myself as a Catholic cleric. I'm a Christian who happens to be Catholic."

Matt said, "I was attracted to medicine, especially psychology. I believe a huge segment of society suffers some form of psychological condition or disorder and most are treatable, but these people go through life without any diagnosis or medical regime. The quality of life they have is less than it should be. The mission of the Church is supposed to be healing. I converted to Catholicism for that reason and within the Church I've been able to work with a lot of damaged priests. Some of them were restored, like alcoholics going into recovery; priests who have been able to return to church parishes and touch many lives in a positive way.

But I'm no saint of any kind. I just like giving whatever I have to help heal suffering wherever I find it."

"This shit's getting too serious," Des said. "I'd rather dance or swim."

We sat there sharing great memories and funny stories until the sun was almost in the sky.

Saturday March 23, 1985

When I stumbled into the kitchen Saturday morning, Kate told me Sasha had kidnapped Matt early. She'd banged on the door of the little house, handed him a packed backpack and together they had saddled up horses named Dreamer and Pretty One and ridden off into the surrounding countryside.

As I poured coffee, I looked out the window and saw Des tossing a football with Shelby and Jake.

"Our kids are gonna kill Matt and Des!"

"I don't think they came here to get rest," Kate said. "They're great guys."

I nodded, "I'm lucky they came into my life."

She hugged me tight. "They're lucky you came into their lives too."

Late in the afternoon, the horse-riders returned, walked and cooled down their mounts, groomed them and came up to the house where Kate had fired up a barbecue pit. It was a mild March night. Kate grilled blackened redfish and corn on the cob that she served with a side of crawfish étouffée and fried green tomatoes.

While Kate cooked, the kids pulled wood from a pile on the side of the cottage and built a big bonfire near the pond, encircling the woodpile with wooden rocking chairs they took from the porches of the cottage and big house. By the time we sat down to eat at the long table under one of the big oaks, the fire was blazing in the distance.

During the evening, Shelby, Matt, and Des must have told every joke they knew. Jake and Sasha did what they did best – squabbled interminably. Jake was talking about fishing in the pond.

"Well, here's the deal. Our pond is nine years old, so I know there's a six pound bass out there somewhere, a big one. Nobody ever caught anything bigger than two pounds. Dad says I can mount anything over four pounds. Tomorrow, will you help me catch the big one?"

"Has anyone ever seen the big one?" Matt asked.

Sasha said, "I see the big one every day when I feed the ducks. Sometimes I catch the big one on bacon and popcorn, but I always let it go. And I'll never tell Jake where it is."

Jake laughed, "Ya gotta understand – Sasha has an imagination that is... well, her whole mind is imagination. She lives in a dream world."

"Not true, Jake."

Kate jumped in, "Now look, you two, I told you already. None of this bickering while company is here."

"Okay," Sasha said. Turning to Matt, she asked, "Will you fish with me? See, I can't touch a gross worm and need someone to bait my hook."

Matt laughed, "Think I can do that."

When the fire burned down to embers, everyone was quiet. There were birds calling out in the night.

Shelby said, "Ya know, I've never seen one of those birds. They only sing at night. What kind of birds only sing at night?"

"Blind birds," Jake said.

Sunday March 24, 1985
Louisiana

Matt and Sasha put their fishing gear in a canoe and shoved off. Jake and Des loaded into a pirogue, a low-slung Cajun boat built to navigate waters only inches deep.

Kate and I were sitting in chairs that almost touched. She reached out and held my hand. I looked in her eyes, thinking about how we had been together in bed the past two nights, how much we obviously loved each other still. I knew she understood by my expression that I was asking her a question and she slowly shook her head side to side.

From where we sat, we could see the fishing rodeo on the pond. Jake was pulling in lots of small bass and releasing them. I think Des boated one. Matt was tied up, literally, spending all his time untangling Sasha's fishing line from low-hanging branches.

When Jake started hollering, Shelby came outside and joined Kate and me as we walked toward the pond.

"Matt's got the big one! He's got him!" Jake shouted. The closer we got the louder Jake shouted, "He's got him! He's got him! The big bass!"

Matt's fishing pole was bent to the breaking point. He reeled slowly. Finally, fearing the pole would snap, Matt laid it in the boat and pulled the line by hand. He landed the monster in the canoe and almost tipped it over.

Kate shouted, "I'll mount that one myself."

As we watched, Matt hauled Sasha's rusted old tricycle into the canoe. All of us remembered how Sasha's trike had mysteriously disappeared at the same time she was badgering us every day to buy her a two-wheeler with training wheels. We had believed the trike had been stolen, the only thing ever taken from our place.

There it was, all the evidence anyone needed. As Matt rowed toward land, Sasha sat in the front of the little boat, her arms crossed, her posture defiant. If she had not been caught red-handed, she was red-faced.

Shelby laughed. "Come on, kid, how'd you get that thing way out there? You gotta tell us now."

"I don't have to tell nobody nothing," Sasha said. "Whoever stole it, threw it in the pond. They musta been mean people, mean as you, Jake, mean as you, Shelby. Maybe it was you, Jake, or maybe it was you, Shelby."

*

Sunday afternoon, after everyone had given Matt and Des tight hugs and made them promise they would return to Coteau, the three of us set off in my car for a tour. First, I drove them down to Cypress Bay and through Dubois's former parish, Our Lady of the Seas. Then we toured Bayou Saint John and drove on to Thiberville, passing Bendel's office before stopping at Saint Stephen's Cathedral and its chancery. Inside the big church, I watched as the two men walked over to a side altar with a statue of the Holy Mother. They stood silently side by side for a few minutes before turning for the door.

Matt and I dropped Des off at Thiberville airport. He had an early-morning meeting scheduled for the next day at the papal nunciature in Washington. When he said goodbye, he added, "I really wish I could be going with you guys."

Matt and I were on our way to the center of the state, to Morgan's Hope, for a meeting with Iris and Willifred Dubois and their children and spouses of their children. I had set up the appointment earlier in the week, at Matt's request. "I want to see Iris Dubois," he'd said. "Dubois's whole family, Ren. I just want to sit with them. Listen. I know there's nothing I can do or say that can change anything. I can't be a comfort to them. But they will know someone understands their pain and cares about them. If they still pray, maybe we will pray together for healing all who are involved – the children, their families, Francis and the Dubois family. I know their pain will never end. I just want to sit with them, ya know."

60

DEMANDS AND PROPOSALS

Tuesday March 26, 1985
Jonathan Bendel's Law Office, Thiberville

Ricardo Ponce and Brent Thomas barged into Jon Bendel's office. Ponce glared at the diocesan lawyer and threw a copy of the motion to set each of their ten cases for trial onto his desk.

Brent Thomas was a nervous wreck. He knew if the families were advised that there would be a public court trial, five of the ten sets of parents would fold their hands and force Brent to dismiss their lawsuits, costing the young lawyers a million in fees.

Though they had argued over the weekend on the phone, Brent Thomas had not been able to hold Ricardo Ponce off any longer. Ponce had driven in from Florida Monday night.

Pointing to the legal papers he had slammed onto Bendel's desk, Ponce exploded. "We're gonna lift the seals on these ten lawsuits and file for trial dates. We'll have a press conference to discuss the 3.6 million dollars that covering up the crimes of Father Dubois has already cost the diocese, revealing the terms of the Halloween Settlement. The language of that compromise binds our clients to silence. But it does not gag me."

Jonathan Bendel knew his response would be a lie, but he was not sure what the lie would be. He did not want people to know millions had already been paid, especially lawyers who were filing new lawsuits and had no idea what the value of their claims was. Bendel also knew that Blassingame did not want to shell out six million more dollars of insurance money to settle the ten Ponce–Thomas cases. Blassingame's law associates and paralegals had been poring over the language of the insurance policies, devising arguments to the effect that the diocese was obligated to make a large contribution to the settlement of the new set of eleven lawsuits. And new lawsuits were being filed against Dubois and other priests weekly. Bendel didn't want Ricardo Ponce grandstanding like Kane Chaisson for television cameras.

"I need time, fellows," Bendel said.

"You've had a year to come up with our six million," Ponce said.

"Yes, and I need more time. I know you two guys need six hundred thousand for each case. Ten lawsuits, and that's six million, but that kind of money isn't lying around anywhere. The problem is pulling the money together. I have half of it, three million," Bendel lied. "But three million won't do you any good, I know. I understand you have to settle all the cases at one time."

Ponce almost spat as he spoke. "Kane Chaisson filed for the first available guaranteed trial date and that date is six months away. If we move to set ten cases on the trial calendar, we will probably have to wait more than a year to get into court. Another year, on top of the year we've already wasted."

Scrambling to find some running room, Bendel lied again as he probed the greed of these two young barristers. "One way to look at this is that I have three million together, so you guys already have a guaranteed million in fees, in the bank."

Ponce scoffed, "I don't have a million anything."

"We can arrange a line of credit for you. I sit on the board of Southern National Bank. I can call the president and we can pledge your fee in these cases against a line of credit. You could draw down, say, a half million or maybe three-quarters of a million in legal fees right now, today, use it as you wish."

Brent Thomas said, "It wouldn't be ethical for us to be drawing down any portion of our legal fees before our clients get their money."

Ricardo wanted to slap the piss out of Thomas, but he remained stone-faced.

The meeting ended with Ponce saying, "You do whatever it is you think you should do, Jon. I'm going back to Florida. I'll be sailing all week. The Monday after Easter, Brent will file the motion to set these ten cases for trial. We'll have a press conference about these ten pending cases and the Halloween Settlement. You have until then to finish business, not a minute more."

Wednesday March 27, 1985
Papal Nunciature, Washington DC

I had flown back to Washington with Matt on Monday night. The nunciature was closed for the week. Most of the Italian employees were in their home country on holiday. By mid-week, Matt and I were working with Desmond at the embassy, preparing the first draft of a manual of policies and procedures that Cardinal Laurence was to present to all four hundred members of the National Conference of Catholic Bishops.

Only the nuns who took care of the kitchen and cleaning were in the grand residence. Much to the consternation of Sister Theresa, the head honcho, we insisted on taking some of our meals in the kitchen rather than the formal dining room. Whenever we were asked about a menu, Des told them to prepare their favorite dishes. We had piles of Venetian ravioli, great bread, fabulous soups and a Tuscan bean casserole.

Sister Theresa blushed the first time we asked her to have the nuns join us for lunch in the formal dining room. Desmond placed her in the seat of honor, the big chair normally reserved for the papal nuncio. It took a while, but eventually the four nuns became pretty gregarious, except for the two who were shy about expressing themselves in English.

I asked them to tell us where their homes were, to tell us something about the places where they'd grown up. Sister Theresa said, "In our village near Montepulciano we have donkeys in the street and they are for no good, for nothing. No one uses the donkeys. They live and sleep in the street. They ate the grass so many times in the big park that the men put stones down."

"Why doesn't someone take the donkeys out of the village?" I asked.

"The donkeys are the only thing my village is known for. It's the donkey place. If you take the donkeys out of the village, it will be known for nothing. It will be no place."

I thought Sister Theresa would have a heart attack when she saw me dump vanilla ice cream into a glass and pour a Coke over it. All the little nuns giggled as I unsuccessfully attempted to have them taste this uniquely American drink. They even seemed to think the phrase "Coke float" was funny. Sister Theresa was the only one who became converted to Coke floats, and that wasn't the only bad habit we passed on to her. Des broke into the private stock of the papal nuncio and presented them all with Cuban cigars. They laughed uproariously and handed the stogies back, all except for Sister Theresa, who slipped hers beneath her nun's habit.

When I called to check in with my office in Thiberville, Mo told me that DA Sean Robinette was looking for me. There it was: the criminal case of the State of Louisiana versus Father Francis Dubois. It had been months since anything had happened with the civil lawsuits or the criminal prosecution. The Dubois matter had been like a bag of snakes resting in the corner of my mind. All these months, I knew it would never go away, but I was not about to kick the bag.

Des showed me to an empty office with a phone on the desk. Sean came on the line.

"There's some news this morning. Kane Chaisson's date for the trial of the Rachou case is set for Monday September 23. It's a first fixing. There's nothing going to stop the Rachou trial from going down on that date. I've been waiting for Chaisson to make his move. I want his trial first for a lot of reasons. I've cleared the date of Monday October 28, for our case, State versus Dubois."

I only said, "Okay, seeya," and rang off. I suspected Sean knew the truth. I had nothing to talk about. I had no defense for Dubois, none.

Sunday March 31, 1985
Baltimore

On Saturday, when the three of us had finished our work on the document we wanted Cardinal Laurence to present to the Conference of Bishops, Des had called Cardinal Laurence in Atlanta. He was advised to have Bishop Garland Franklin vet the document before presenting it to the cardinal. Des had had a large envelope messengered to Franklin's rectory and a meeting was set for Sunday afternoon. Matt drove the three of us to Baltimore.

In the year since Bishop Franklin had been appointed by the Vatican to monitor, assist in managing problems, and report to the Vatican on the clergy abuse situation, he had limited his interaction with Des, Matt and me, pretty much ignoring me entirely.

At the rectory, a short fat father pointed the way to Bishop Franklin's office. The bishop had a copy of our proposal in his hands. I wasn't in the chair before the bishop began beating up on our work. "I see some huge problems with the proposal. I called Cardinal Laurence last night and read one section to him about the theories of civil liability, the legal basis for finding a diocese or bishop liable to a plaintiff for damages awarded by a judge or jury. He concurs with me that he thinks that section is way too technical."

Bishop Franklin drank from his water glass, acting as if he was being tape-recorded. "There are also sections about canon law and passages about clinical factors that are too dense for the purposes of those who will read this proposal and vote on it."

Matt, ever the diplomat, said, "Your Excellency, we can make the document easier to read and understand. We will do a revision."

"That's fine," Bishop Franklin said. "Now, the second problem is the recommendations this proposal makes to the Conference of Bishops."

The bishop referred to a set of handwritten notes on his desk. "The idea of a long-term policy committee is a good one, but you need to drop the word 'planning' from the title and body of the discussion. The word implies that the Church is anticipating problems of this kind to arise in its midst."

The bishop put on glasses and pulled his handwritten notes off the table. It seemed he was finding his own handwriting indecipherable. He took his glasses off and scowled at all three of us.

"Establish central record-keeping for cases of clergy sex abuse? That's an idea whose time will never come. Strike this. I have some ideas about records I will mention shortly. And gentlemen, this Church is never going to practice full disclosure or transparency in these matters. We will not have press conferences about problems within the Church. The media will never cross the line into the Church's affairs. Giving the accused priest a canon lawyer and civil lawyer is a good idea, if those lawyers advise him to shut up and stay shut up. That didn't happen in Louisiana, did it? No, Mr. Chattelrault had his client talk, confess."

I said nothing in response to his shot at me because I did not trust what might come out of my mouth, and I wanted to hear the rest of his comments on our proposal.

"There are not ever going to be search-and-destroy teams in any diocese looking for victims of Catholic priests, and no one is ever going to advise a victim or a victim's parents that they can sue the Church or jail a priest. This is not going to happen. No use proposing it."

He again glanced at his notes. "Now, this intervention team is a good idea, and I understand the three of you are doing this on your own, informally, without any sponsor or support. That's commendable. However, if there's to be any mention of this at all in the document, the word 'crisis' will have to be struck from the title and body of the document. That word implies there is some kind of crisis presently; if the proposal were adopted, the bishops would then be acknowledging that a problem of crisis proportions existed. Instead it should imply that this is something the Church wishes to research in regard to the safety of children and the well-being of its priests."

Des was squirming in his chair.

Matt took the floor. "Bishop, we will discuss all the things you have shared with us, await a reading by Cardinal Laurence, and address them when the document is revised."

Bishop Franklin nodded, sipped his water and seemed satisfied that he had straightened us out, the unholy trio. His eyes got brighter and he smiled for the first time.

"Gentlemen, I think I have a one-shot solution to this problem. A kill shot. I was down in Louisiana and I learned a lot there. What caused them the biggest problem down there was the personnel records of the priests. It was badly mismanaged. We know our Church keeps detailed records of what we call 'delicts' in canon law – offenses priests commit – and the records are filed in the secret archives. These records can come back and bury us. Some files were sanitized in Louisiana, damaging information was removed and shredded, and that might have been illegal. It was close to the line, for sure."

The bishop looked hard at me and I imagined the revised history in the Thiberville diocese had me alone advocating the destruction of personnel files. Maybe they'd even told him I did the shredding of the documents.

The bishop excused himself and returned with a tall glass of something that appeared to be Gatorade. He offered us nothing.

"So what can be done to solve the problem of these records? We cannot destroy them. It's a violation of law to destroy them if they are under subpoena, but more important than that is the fact that the bishops and dioceses need these secret archives to evaluate priests. What we need to do is prepare a memorandum to all bishops in the United States advising them that the papal nunciature is available for central storage of any and all diocesan records. Verbally, we get the word to the bishops that we are referring only to files that may contain evidence of criminal conduct on the part of a priest."

Des shifted in his chair, clearing his throat. "What are you suggesting?"

"Documents on file at the papal nunciature are on the grounds of a foreign embassy. Because of diplomatic immunity, the records are immune from both civil and criminal subpoena. If no lawyer can access that information, then our problems will lessen to the point where it will be too much trouble for a district attorney to prosecute a priest criminally or for a plaintiff lawyer to pursue a diocese for damages with a civil suit."

Des's jaw clenched. "Bishop Franklin, you are suggesting using the diplomatic immunity status of the Vatican Embassy to obstruct justice in the United States. The diplomatic mission could be expelled from this country if it were proved we used our embassy to hide information in contravention of US laws. This would be illegal, unsound and immoral in my view."

"No American president or administration would ever have the balls to attack the Church. We have sixty to seventy million Catholics in this country and a lot of them vote. Anyone who attacked their Church would be signing his death warrant as a viable politician. Our power as a Church, our ability to influence the outcomes of major elections, is well documented."

Matt rose from his chair. "Your Excellency, I think this is the critical time for Rome and the American Church to act responsibly out of a sense of common decency, plain common sense. The decisions coming down from Cardinal Kruger that you and Archbishop Verriano are embracing are not only faithless decisions where the Church fails in its mission to heal innocents it has injured, but fateful decisions that are setting the Church on a collision course with the justice system, the press, and prosecutors. We are talking about the erosion of the moral authority of the Church – something that could bring on a never ceasing continuum of catastrophic consequences for the institution. No one is going to push the Church off the high moral ground. The Church is going to walk off the high ground, ceding the high ground to those who will be rightfully offended by the Church's actions." Matt paused for a moment, then concluded his speech. "Thank you for your time. I don't even want to be party to any more discussions that are grounded in what I see as the arrogance and ignorance of the Church, and its inability or unwillingness to do what is right."

As we were taking our leave, Franklin said, "They made it too easy in Louisiana. That's the only lesson of Louisiana. They threw money at them. A child who makes public allegations of this nature against any priest of mine in this diocese will have a slander suit slapped against him and his parents. These people don't want justice. They want money. We cannot give these aggressors what they want. No child can attack us with a lawyer. We're the Roman Catholic Church. If a child sues one of my priests, we will counter sue the child and his parents for libel and slander."

When Des, Matt and I reached the parking lot, Matt and I leaned against Matt's car. Matt spoke first. "Got to hand it to you, Des. I remember how excited you were that night at the Ascot Grill when you got Rome to appoint Bishop Franklin, how you told us that Franklin was a good guy—"

I finished the sentence. "A good guy who was with the program. Yeah, I thought so too."

Des laughed at us. "So, I fucked up. Well, fuck you both. Let's go to Matt's place, Café Roma, and get invisible on vodka. And fellows, I can promise one thing – Bishop Garland Franklin has seen the last of us and the last of our work. He will not see the final draft of the document we prepare for Cardinal Laurence and the Conference of Bishops. That asshole is going to end up in a world of hurt one day. If Rome is listening to him, the Vatican will destroy itself."

61

A LETTER

Sunday evening, March 31, 1985
Thiberville

It was night when I landed in Thiberville after my meeting with
Bishop Franklin. From the airport, I went straight to my office to
look through the piles of paper that had accumulated in my
absence. Paper-clipped to an envelope in the center of my desk
was a note from Mo with the words "Read this first, Ren!"

I pulled the letter from the envelope. It was written in pencil
on ruled notebook paper like the Big Chief tablets children used
in school. There were erasures in places where one word had
replaced another, but the misspelling of names had not been
corrected. I read the letter slowly.

To Bishop Reynolds, Mr. John Bendle, Mr. Rennon
Chattellralt

Dear Bishop Reynolds, Mr. Bendle, and Mr. Chattellralt,
I am writing this to you because you are the bishop, but I am
sending this too to Mr. Bendle and to Mr. Chattellralt because
they are the lawyers for your diocese and your priest. I don't
think our lawyer who is Mr. Thomas would let me write you
if he knew.

My boy is hurt bad. You knew this priest did bad things
with little boys and you sent him here anyway. Why?

What you did is the biggest sin I know. God can't forgive
you. I can't forgive you.

390

Before he was an altar boy for Father Nicky – our Will was different then. When little Will woke up, he would always smile. His little arms would stretch so he could hug whoever waked him up. He went to sleep at night the same way. His little arms would stretch to you for a hug. Now Will won't let us touch him.

A little while after Will became an altar boy he stopped eating good. He got so skinny we took him to a doctor. He couldn't find nothing wrong. Then Will stopped playing with the other children. He didn't want me or his Daddy hugging him anymore. He said it made him feel sick inside to be touched.

Now he sits in his room. We quit trying to send him to school. I even sent him to the doctors but he didn't even talk he just poured red paint on wooden puppets. He said everyone knows what happened with him and the priest. He's ashamed.

He is scared the priest is coming back here. At night we find him checking the locks on all the doors. One night we found him with one of his Daddy's guns. He was sitting by a window with the gun.

I am scared Will is dying. I think a lot of children around here are dying. And a bishop and his lawyers are doing nothing.

I am begging each one of you to come here to our house to see our little boy. I want you to come so you will know that Will and the other boys are not just some names on pieces of paper.

If you come, Bishop, don't wear your priest clothes because it would scare Will.

I think all of you are probably going to go to hell for your sins. If you do not do something about this I know you will go to hell. People who kill children go to hell.

I still go to the church. I fix the flowers. Will won't go in the building anymore. I pray all the time in our church that God will help my son to be the little boy he used to be.

Mrs. Weston Courville

The phone rang. It was Matt checking to see that I'd made the flight I'd dashed for in Washington earlier that evening. I read him the letter from Mrs. Weston Courville. Matt said, "You have to go there. I'll clear my schedule as soon as I can. I want to go with you."

"I'm not sure this is a good idea to see the Courvilles. There have been death threats from down there around Amalie. We could be walking into more than we bargained for," I said.

"The lady is begging someone to come to her home and see her little boy. Someone has to show her the respect of responding. I'll be with you. If anything happens, it will happen to both of us."

I took the letter to Julie that night and let her read it. When she finished, she laid it on her coffee table and said, "I'm going."

"Where?"

"To see that kid. I know you're going."

"That's what Matt just told me over the phone."

"She's begging. Someone has to respond."

"Matt said that too. Exactly."

Julie picked the letter up again. Both of her hands were trembling too much for her to hold it. Putting it back on the coffee table, she put her finger on a line and read, "'My boy is hurt bad. You knew this priest did bad things with little boys and you sent him here anyway.'"

She started to cry, holding her head in her hands. "She's right. I... I... I..."

Julie let me hold her. In a hoarse voice, she tried again, "I... I... I..."

Her whole body shivered and she pulled away from me. "I was here. I was here. Everyone knew. I knew. We all knew Francis Dubois raped boys. Everybody knew. I probably signed the assignment transfer documents, his personnel authorization for the assignment. I was personnel director. We all knew. We sent him there anyway."

I pulled her close and heard her whisper, "She's right. People are going to hell."

Once she was quiet, she stayed in my arms. Her breathing was all I heard and gradually it returned to a normal rhythm. At times I would feel her hands clutching my arms. I kissed her forehead. She smiled through her tears.

She stood and took my hand and pulled me off of the sofa. "Tonight I'm going to cook for you. Let's go in the kitchen. I've been planning this."

I laughed. "I kissed a nun who's a tease too. A sassy nun."

She nodded. "I was just about to start cooking pasta when you came in. I really can cook. It's not always pizza."

"But it's always Italian. You Italian?"

"Both sides. We were what they called 'art Italians' as opposed to 'food Italians'. We were in love with art. When other kids' moms were reading fairy tales or primer books, my mom was putting me to sleep every night with books that had no words, just pictures. She would explain the paintings, telling me about the artists who created them and the time period in which they were painted, putting the pictures in a historical context."

"That's amazing."

"It was good and bad. When I started school, I couldn't read *Run, Spot, Run!*, but I could discuss sculpture and paintings made five hundred years earlier. On my trips to Europe, I saw a lot of the paintings I had seen only in books. I was stunned by how big some of them were and how different the colors were. My house was filled with the best art my folks could afford. I am sure my mom's dream was that one of her kids would be a painter, but she got a lawyer, a college professor, and a nun."

I thought about what she must have been like as a kid, a cute kid.

Monday April 1, 1985
Thiberville

Jon Bendel got the Diocese of Thiberville to kick in a million dollars of its own funds to add to the five million Blassingame's insurance group contributed, and the convoluted negotiations ended. The ten Ponce settlements were sealed away in the same vault of the Clerk of Courts Office in Bayou Saint John that held the Halloween settlement. The total paid out to victims to date in the Thiberville diocese for the criminal actions of one priest was now nearly ten million dollars. The Rachou trial was still pending, and a slew of new lawsuits had been filed.

Holy Thursday, April 4, 1985
Saint Augustine Cemetery, Thiberville

It was the longest Mass of the year, the one where they blessed the oils and washed the feet of twelve men. What Joe Rossi referred to as "smells and bells". I walked behind Saint Stephen's Cathedral, into the Saint Augustine Cemetery, and found a cast-iron gazebo covering some graves. There was a park bench inside and I sat there, waiting for my appointment with Monsignor Moroux.

When Mass finished, priests started filing out. All of them were in their standard black attire. They carried garment bags. The lack of collegiality among them was curious. There was no small talk, in fact, no talk at all. Moroux saw me and came sauntering down the walk.

"You've found the best grave in the whole bone-yard."

"I see the names. These must be relatives of mine."

He nodded.

I wanted to finish fast and visit with my father at The Palms. I stood up. "Monsignor, the date for the criminal trial of Father Dubois has been set for October 28, which I think is about four weeks after the setting for the Chaisson civil trial."

"May I have a cigarette?" he said.

I handed him one and lit it for him. He looked hard at the end of the cigarette as if he did not trust that he had enough fire there to draw smoke. "Renon, sometimes it seems nothing gets communicated in this Church. Other times it seems too much is communicated. There have been some things said about you and some of it was said by me."

"I have no interest in what anyone in this Church may have said about me."

"Oh, I think you might. I've had some phone calls from people in dioceses around the country, seeking my opinion of you. You know my hands are tied in that regard. I cannot say something different from what your legal colleagues Jon Bendel and Tom Quinlan might say. Soooo, if you should hear I've said something about you that does not ring like an endorsement, I want you to understand the pinch I'm in. I do what I have to do, Renon."

"Similarly, Monsignor, should you hear that I've ever said I believe your negligence in supervising Father Dubois was so gross, willful and wanton as to constitute a serious crime on your part for which you should be imprisoned, and that you were absolutely uncaring about the welfare of the youngest Catholics in this diocese, innocent children, I want you to understand the pinch I'm in. I say what I have to say."

"Touché," he said. He wasn't even offended. "Are these other bishops following your advice?"

"Do you think they would fare better if they were following your example?"

I started walking. Moroux moved quickly to my side. "Whose side are you on?"

I stopped walking and faced Moroux. "In the beginning, I saw a lot of sides. It's narrowed down now, I think. Seems simple to me now."

"And?"

"It's children against criminals. There are just two sides. It's innocent children versus perverted priests, criminal bishops, and criminal vicars such as yourself. Whose side do you think I'm on?"

The Palms

My father was finishing lunch when I walked in. In an irritable tone, he said, "I waited, Ren. I waited for you. You said you'd be here for lunch."

The older he got the more crotchety he became, but I had learned to ignore it as the mood always passed in a moment.

"Sorry. But I believe I said I didn't think I would make lunch. It doesn't matter."

"Yes, it does matter. I have the fish and everything laid out for you in the kitchen and I'm going to cook it. I doubt you're eating anything but crap since you and Kate split up."

My father went into the kitchen, cooked me lunch and set it before me. "You want some tea, a wine, beer, soda, what?"

"Beer's good."

"That's good, 'cause I don't have any beer. I just said it. Pick another one." He smiled, chuckling at his humor.

"Why don't ya just tell me what you really have?"

"Nope. Gotta guess again, son."

"Root beer."

"Coke. Close enough."

I had seen a lot of the old man the past six months, especially around the time Kate and I separated. We had talked about many things, but he never mentioned the case of Father Dubois. Once when I was visiting with him on his back porch at The Palms, the *Thiberville Register* was lying on the bench next to him with front-page headlines about the case. From the condition of the paper, it was obvious he had read the article, yet he said nothing. I wanted to talk to him about it now.

When he sat at the table, I sipped the Coke and asked, "Can you explain to me how the Catholic Church can lie about important things, why their lies are believed?"

"They're lying about all this stuff with kids, huh? I figured they were. You want to know why they do it, how they can get away with it? Count the steeples, son."

"Is this some kind of riddle? I'm not good at riddles."

"Count the steeples. Out in the country around here every community of any size has a church. There used to be more churches than gas stations in this part of the country. When the towns around here were surveyed, laid out and plotted, they always dedicated land for a town hall, a park for the people, a cemetery to bury the dead and the best plot of land was reserved for a Catholic church, the real seat of power."

I mumbled, "The steeples…"

"When I was growing up here it was just like in Europe in the old days. The priest was not only the agent of God – you could only get to heaven through his good graces. He also knew everyone's secrets from the confessional. What kind of power is that? I think… I don't know, but I think the most important thing was that the priest was the only person in the community with an education. My father and his friends had hardly any education. They had a lot of land they farmed and they were plenty smart, but they had hardly any formal education. The power of the priest has always been absolute here and you know what absolute power breeds."

"But it's still your Church, right?"

"My faith has nothing to do with a priest, bishop or pope. Some of the worst men I've known were priests. When our construction company built the seminary for the old bishop, that bishop forced us to buy all the lumber from a good Catholic friend of his at a markup of almost twice the price I could have gotten from an honest lumber broker. I could tell stories like that for days, and worse stories too. A lot of the priests I've known were nasty characters."

"But you still support the Church."

"Not with money. My money goes to a non-denominational foreign-student mission at the college to help kids from poor countries. I do go to Mass every day. I like the rituals, and the time… taking that time every day to pray in a quiet, pretty place. But all this stuff about the priest and the kids – it makes you sick to think about it. I knew they'd been lying. I didn't know what their lies were, but I knew they were lying. They have never had to tell the truth."

"For a long time I've wanted to talk to you about my involvement."

"We don't have to talk about that. I figure you got your own reasons for what you are doing. They might be good reasons. They might be bad reasons. But they are your reasons. I suspect you are not a Catholic anymore and I don't care. Probably a lot of younger folks are going to stop going to Mass for a whole lot of reasons. Maybe it's the right thing for people to do."

"I worried, I really worried what you might be thinking or feeling about me representing Father Dubois."

"There's nothing to worry over, son. I'm proud of you. I love you. I just want you to be a good father to Shelby, Jake and Sasha, especially now that your marriage busted. As good as you can be. It's the only thing that matters. This business with the Church – it's terrible, but it seems to be all true. They let this man wear that collar and sexually go after little kids for all these years. Whatever happens to them ought to happen to them. You just do what's right."

I slowly shook my head. "The steeples... huh."

"That's it, son. They put a church in every hamlet. They sent in an educated priest, God's agent, keeper of all the secrets. That's how they got the power and held the power. But today lots of people are educated. Not so many will go into a box and tell a man their sins, not many pay attention to what they say about birth control or anything else. And no decent person is going to allow themselves to be lorded over by sanctimonious priests and bishops whose own sins are worse than their own."

It was like a weight lifted. The affirmation was the strongest I'd ever received from my father. That afternoon we played his favorite game, Horseshoes, until dark, and then I took him to dinner at an old seafood place he loved.

When the waitress put the salad before us, he bowed his head, made the sign of the cross and whispered a prayer of grace. Then he winked at me. "The rituals, son. I like the rituals."

62

RESURRECTION SUNDAY

Easter, April 7, 1985
The Palms

Kate pulled into the drive at The Palms just after lunchtime on Easter Sunday. Old Seamus Chattelrault was standing by the last palm tree. Sasha bolted out of the car, kissed him on the cheek, and exclaimed, "Gotta go see Rags, Grandman," then skipped off to see her grandpa's sheepdog.

The old man embraced Kate. "Ya know, I'm always sorry for your troubles, lass. The very idea of you and Ren divorcing makes me sad. You and my boy, Ren, got two of the best hearts I know. You gave your kids good hearts too. You always bringing Sasha by is something I appreciate. She's a dear one, like her mom. And Shelby and Jake pull up in that jeep for a root beer almost weekly, telling me they're just checking up on their Ol' Gent. They're good kids, all three of them."

Kate smiled. "We're all going to be okay. The kids are good kids. I tell ya, Seamus, either Shelby's a good boy or if he's doing bad things, he's too smart to get caught. Jake's too wild to care if he gets caught. But Sash... I could use some help there, I think."

"What's going on with my angel?"

"Right, she's an angel all right. Just yesterday I got a visit from a neighbor down the road in the country. Nice man named Maurice. He's got two girls about Sasha's age, the only kids she has to play with. I don't know their religion, but those little girls can only go in our swimming pool with their dresses on and only if the boys aren't home. They go to some church all the time. Couple times a week, all day Saturday. Maurice was really upset."

"With Sasha?"

"Worried about Sasha's salvation. He said that he's asked her to go to church with his family a lot of times and she's always said no. Yesterday morning, he said he told Sasha, 'Honey, if you don't go to church, you can't go to heaven.' You know what Sasha told him?"

The old man shook his head.

"Sasha said, 'It's okay. I wanta go to hell, so I can be with my daddy.'"

The old man laughed. "That belligerence is her Cajun blood talking, but the flair for the dramatic – that's her Irish blood."

He motioned for Kate to take a place on the bench and he sat next to her. "We're a confused bunch, cross-blooded – Irish and French. When I'm troubled I talk my father's French, and when I'm joshing I sound like my ancestors from Dublin. Ever tell you how my Irish people got mixed up with the Acadian descendants?"

She shook her head.

He winked. "You know your ancestors and my papa's people were French exiles run out of Acadie in Nova Scotia by the Brits. My mother's Irish people were immigrants who had been run to Connemara by the Brits before they immigrated to the United States. Both these peoples were on the run from the Brits. People on the run are different from people who have places. You're a music person – ya know why Cajuns and the Irish didn't produce great piano composers? You can't run with a piano on your back."

Kate smiled.

"Napoleon Bonaparte sold a slab of land cheap to Thomas Jefferson and what is now Louisiana was part of that parcel. Ten years later there was a war between America and Britain. A bunch of Irish immigrants signed on to fight the Brits, wanting to kill as many John Bulls as they could. They ended up in New Orleans with General Andrew Jackson's troops that were joined up by the pirate Jean Lafitte's cannoneer, a fellow named Dominique, and the Brits turned and ran back down the Mississippi."

The old man clapped his hands. "I can only imagine how it felt for those Irish guys to see Brits on the run. It must have been a great day. General Jackson let some Irish boys out of the army down here in south Louisiana and they took up with Cajun girls and stayed. When Ol' Andy Jackson got to be president, he rewarded some of his former Irish officers down here with huge tracts of useless land carved out of the Louisiana Purchase. But we made that bad land good. Growing sugar cane, trapping furry animals and all that was a lot easier than pulling potatoes out of the rocky ground back home. The Irish prospered here. Most of my Irish ancestors drank, whiskeyed away their land, gambled it away too. But they stayed on. That's how your kids got those good Cajun looks and those wild Irish hearts."

"I wish we had kept the Irish names like yours."

"Oh, I don't know." The old man laughed. "Those names can be twisted up. I was so mischievous as a boy, my mom rarely called me 'Seamus'. She used to call me 'Shameonus'."

Kate gave the ol' gent a half hug. "It's a lucky thing our children have your Irish genes, Seamus."

"Oh, I'd not be thanking the Almighty for that. I know Renon himself has the stuff of some ancestors on the ol' sod. The whole lot of them ended up doing prison time and fighting till their last breath against the British on the island. The two things they couldn't abide was wrongdoing and weak whiskey. Their spirit was strong but it consumed all the good in them. Sometimes we have to accept that things are as they are, what they are, and there's nothing we can do about those things. Ren never accepts anything, always believes he can change everything."

Kate stood, kissed Seamus's forehead, and said, "I know what you mean about Ren. The very thing that attracted me to him in the beginning was what made we want to get away from him in the end. That intensity."

The old man nodded knowingly.

"You enjoy Sasha, Seamus. I'll come by about dark and bring us all something to eat, okay?"

The old man stood. He put his arms on her shoulders. "I know you can't be with my boy, Katie. But don't ever be too far from him."

Kate nodded.

Seamus found Sasha and Rags sitting under a pecan tree. Sasha had worn the dog out playing chase and Rags was taking a nap.

Her grandpa struggled a little bit to get situated on the ground. "Whew, when you're my age, ya sit this low and you wonder if you'll ever get up again."

Sasha giggled. "Grandman, last year you told me something about this tree and I forgot what you told me."

"Hell... err, I mean heck."

"Hell's okay, Grandman. You can say 'hell'. But I sure don't want to go there."

"Oh, there's no such thing as hell, Sash. But what I was saying is I don't know what I told you about the tree. Probably, I told you to watch out for the pecan trees every year. They're the only trees around here the weather can't fool. A lot of trees, bushes and flowers get fooled every year by early warm weather – they get new growth and then a big freeze comes and ruins everything. You can trust a pecan tree. When a pecan tree sprouts new leaves, spring is finally here, and not a minute before."

"That's good. I like to talk to you, Grandman. I'll remember to trust pecan trees. But I don't know exactly what trust means so I sure don't know what I can trust."

"Trust is like believing in something. What you believe in. It means the same thing practically."

"I sure as hell, err heck, don't believe in or trust this Easter Bunny business any more. I can tell you that."

"Why, dear?"

"'Cause it doesn't make any sense. You know... you know... a bunny that brings dyed eggs and hides them in the flower beds around the house. Really!"

The old man smiled.

"Maybe an Easter Chicken, huh, Grandman? That would make more sense, huh? At least it would explain where the eggs come from. I betcha I'm gonna hear a lot of stuff in my life that won't make sense. Is that the stuff you can't believe – the stuff that makes no sense?"

"I think that's a good rule. If something doesn't make sense to you, then it makes no sense for you to believe in it, Sasha."

"Does hell make sense? You said there's no hell. I know a man who lives by our house. He talks about hell all the time."

"Hell makes no sense. Not if you believe in my God, Sasha. My God is all powerful and all loving and would never create a place like hell."

"You have your own God?"

"Sure. So do you. You ever look at the stars at night? Think of God like you think of the stars. They are all alike and all different too. There's billions of stars and billions of Gods, but they are the same, all one, all the same thing. God is like the stars. There's a God for everyone. And it's the same God. You will understand one day. This will make sense one day. "

"That's great. Now I have my own God, Grandman?"

"You sure do. At night when you are in bed, close your eyes and you can talk to your God in your head. It will be just you and your God. You can talk to your God during the day too, anytime you want."

"Will God answer me?"

"Sure. In a way. Maybe not with a voice you hear, but with signs you will see."

"Is God like a man... like an old, old man or something?"

"I don't think so, Sasha. I think God's probably more like a young woman. Something like you. I think girls are better than boys, Sash, and women are better than men. That's one of the things I think I learned in life. The most important thing that happens in the whole world is giving birth and nurturing young. It's only females who God lets do those important things. If God thought men were equal to women, they would be able to do those things too. My God is a woman."

"So, if girls are better than boys, that means I should be the boss of Jake and Shelby, right? Can I tell them Grandman made me the boss of them? I can, huh?"

The old man laughed. "No, Sash. It's not about like being the boss of anyone. But don't ever let anyone tell you that because you are a girl that you are not as good as any boy anywhere, because you are as good, probably better."

"It's true, Grandman, really true that nobody, not even bad people... nobody goes to hell?"

"There is no hell, Sasha. It's just a place preachers made up to scare people into getting them to act the way they want them to act. God is all loving and all powerful. No God with all the power in the universe who is all loving would allow anyone to spend eternity in this place some people call hell. When we die, the same thing happens to all of us. Don't ever be afraid of God sending you to hell. When your time is over here, your God is going to bring you to be with God forever. You will be with me again. Maybe in heaven we will sit under a pecan tree and wait for spring together. Maybe I will be young and strong enough to run with you and ol' Rags."

"But my friend's father said if we don't go to church, we go to hell."

"Sasha, do you know, there are people all over the world who never heard of any kind of church. They live in jungles and they live in peace. Don't you think they go to heaven?"

Sasha appeared to be thinking. "Sometimes I don't know what I can believe. I want to believe everything. But this hell thing makes me scared. The Easter Bunny having eggs makes no sense."

The old man said, "The deal about the Easter Bunny and eggs came to this country with people who came from Germany or maybe it was the Dutch. I don't know. It had something to do with the Catholic religion in one of those countries. It's something people have done over and over and when people do something over and over it's called a tradition."

"It's silly."

"Come on, now, you have to admit to your old grandfather that hunting eggs was a lot of fun when you were little. Now that you are grown up, going to school and everything, you should let your mom keep dying eggs for you, and hiding them... until... until the year she asks you to help paint the eggs. Deal?"

"Deal."

"You see, angel, there's all kinds of things in life you are going to run into that don't make sense... things like the Easter Bunny. And you are going to hear about some bad things like hell that make no sense. The trick in life is to believe in two things... things that make sense... and good things. Believe hard in the good things. Let others believe bad things if they want to. You believe in the good things."

The old man slowly got up and motioned Sasha to stay put. He walked into the house through a screened door on the porch. When he returned, he was carrying two wrapped packages. The little girl beamed and tore open the first, an antique wicker basket.

"This was my Easter basket when I was a little boy. My mother made it from palm fronds that fell in the drive out front. I guess this is why I want you to let your mom hide eggs for a few more years. I want you to hunt for them and then put them in your old grandpa's basket. Maybe one day, you'll give this basket to one of your kids, eh?"

Sasha gave the old man a tight hug. "Can I put Disco Duck in it during the day? He's my favorite stuffed animal. Disco Duck sleeps with me at night. I can carry him in the basket during the day."

The old man nodded as he took the second gift and began to slowly unwrap it himself. "This one is fragile, Sash. I want you to be careful with it." As the gift wrapping fell to the ground, a ball of tissue still covered the gift. He let her separate the layers of tissue.

A highly varnished wooden sculpture lay in Sasha's hands. It was a delicate, detailed carving of Christ rising, ascending intact, without wounds or other evidence of torture.

"This is rare, darling. It's very old and really rare. All Christian religions have lots of drawings, paintings, and sculptures of Jesus Christ suffering on the cross. It's rare to find something showing Jesus Christ rising from the dead with no wounds. Today, Easter, is called Resurrection Sunday in many places in the world. This is the day we remember Jesus rising from the dead. This is an important thing – that Jesus rose again."

"Unhuh," Sasha said.

"I want you to always remember that no matter how bad things might seem in life, you have the strength to rise again. Whenever you feel you've been knocked down, always remember you can rise again. Remember this. I hope you keep this statue with you always to remind you that he rose from the dead and we can rise from bad times."

"I will remember. And… and let's see… what else I gotta remember. I gotta remember to let Mom hide Easter eggs… and what… what else? Oh yeah, I remember. Remember there is no hell. And remember to believe in the good things. Remember to believe in things that make sense."

"And, sweetheart, remember the pecan tree will tell you when it's spring." The old man tussled her hair. "And remember your grandpa always has the chocolate ice cream you love. Want some?"

The two of them slowly walked toward the old house. The old man's arms were filled with gift wrapping and tissue. Sasha carried the old basket in one hand and the statue in the other.

63

A COUNTRY PLACE

Wednesday April 17, 1985
Amalie

Finding directions to the Courville farm took one stop at a gas station. As I was walking back to the car, the old Cajun in khakis followed me and said, "Hattie Courville's gettin' famous for those preserves and jelly. Be sure you buy some mayhaw jelly from her. It's the best."

The long, paved drive bordered a neatly mowed expanse of lawn. As we slowly approached the house, the lawn gave way to a small stand of oaks with circular flower beds planted at the base of the trees. The rambling single-story ranch home cut the property in two. Over the roofline one could see the tall tin roof of a barn. It was a working farm, with a pecan orchard on the north side of the house and a garden of a quarter acre or more that was fringed by a grove of fruit trees. Acres of rice fields lay to the south of the home.

We walked up the front steps and I pushed the bell. When Hattie Courville opened the door, I was surprised. She was tiny, in perfect physical shape, looked like a teenager with her shaggy brown hair falling unevenly over her ears. Her dark eyes were lively. She was wearing jogging shoes, a pair of blue shorts and a white polo shirt.

"Yes. Can I help you?" She looked behind me to where Julie and Matt stood. "Help ya'll?"

"Ma'am, my name is Renon Chattelrault."

Her eyes widened, and she blurted out, "It's you. Wait here."

Before I could say anything, she spun around and shut the door, leaving Julie, Matt and me staring at the wooden crucifix mounted on the door.

I turned to Julie and Matt and said, "Well, I think it's going pretty good so far." Mrs. Courville did not return to the door for ten or fifteen minutes. Julie and I stood still. Matt walked around inspecting the flowers. At one point Julie looked at me, smiled nervously, and punched my arm. "You've got us in a fine fix now, Ollie."

We heard them before we saw them. Pulling off the road and roaring down the long driveway was a caravan of three oversized, jacked-up pickup trucks. The first truck was spotless and it parked under the carport. The dirty trucks blocked off my Mercedes.

One of the biggest men I had ever seen jumped out of one of the trucks, shotgun in hand, and headed our way. The other men closed in from different directions.

I immediately started walking toward the armed man, lest he make a mistake about which one of us was Renon Chattelrault. I didn't want Matt killed in a case of mistaken identity. The huge man slammed a shell into the chamber. I opened my mouth to speak but it was too dry.

A second man caught up to the big guy. "Gimme a minute, Poppa." To me he said, "What the hell you doing on my property? You got no right—"

I stepped closer to the gun and the speaker. Reaching into my pocket, I pulled out the letter from Mrs. Courville and handed it over. "Your wife wrote me this letter and said she wanted me to come here. Behind me is a doctor who knows more about these things than any doctor around here, and a woman who may be able to help your son. The doctor is also a priest and the lady is a nun, but the bishop did not send them here and doesn't know they're here."

The fellow shouted, "Hattie. Hattie, honey, get out here."

When Hattie came out, man and wife walked back in the direction of the pickup trucks and my car. I could see the man was reading the pencil-written letter. I never looked at the huge man with the shotgun. I turned to see Matt with his arm around Julie, her head buried in his chest so she would not see whatever was going to happen.

When the Courvilles walked back to me, Hattie's husband said, "Poppa, I'm gonna try to do this Hattie's way rather than your way. I'll catch ya'll later at the store."

The roar of those big trucks leaving the Courville property sounded like a symphony to my ears. The Courvilles led us inside, to a well-appointed den, and Mr. Courville pointed out the places where each of us was to sit. He kept me isolated from Julie and Matt, whom he situated on a sofa.

Wes Courville spoke first. "So, we settled our case two days ago. They gave my boy six hundred thousand dollars. Our lawyers stole two hundred thousand dollars, taking a whole third as legal fees, for doing next to nothing. That's what they think Will's life is worth, a human life destroyed – four hundred thousand. No apology, nothing. Now that the case is finally over, you come knocking on our door."

It was the first I had heard about any settlement of the Ponce–Thomas cases. I did not want to get into that, but decided I had to. "Mr. Courville, I didn't know your suit was settled. None of the lawyers or anyone else with the diocese speaks to me anymore. I don't see these things the way the diocese and their lawyers do."

"Yeah? Well how do you see it?"

I thought about it for a moment and realized I had spoken the truth to Monsignor Moroux on Thursday. "I see it as children versus criminals. Obviously, the man I'm representing is a criminal. But the monsignors and the bishop are criminals too."

Wes Courville stirred in his chair and kind of leaned toward me, casting a glance at his wife. He took a long breath that escaped slowly as his eyes softened.

"What's gonna happen to them – the monsignors and the bishop?"

409

"Not a damned thing, Mr. Courville, not a damned thing, except that I think they're going straight to hell, if that's any consolation to you. I think your wife's right about that, but I think they will go to hell before they go to jail."

"Don't they belong in jail when they send priests to parishes and they know what the priest has done and they know what the priest is gonna do again?"

"Yes, a whole lot of bishops belong in jail, Mr. Courville, every bishop I know about. But this is not going to happen for a long time, maybe never."

"That's what I thought."

"Another thing your wife is right about, I think, is that the bishop, vicars and monsignors don't give a damn about Will. She sent me the letter and she sent it to the bishop and Mr. Bendel. I knew they were not coming here, but I believed I had to come here and Sister Julianne and Father Patterson wanted to come too."

Mr. Courville said, "The big man out in the yard with the shotgun is Poppa Vidros. You're lucky he didn't shoot you. He's determined to kill Father Dubois. If he gets a chance."

I nodded.

"What did you come here to do?" he said.

"I came to say two things. The priest, Father Dubois, is not going to get off. He may get a really long sentence, but I can personally assure you that the shortest possible sentence that man will get is twenty years, a sentence that will keep him locked up until Will is at least thirty years old. I wanted you to know that. I'm not there to get him off. No lawyer could get him off even if he wanted to."

Wes Courville nodded in relief. His wife sank back into the chair cushions. "That's good," she said, "but what's the other thing you want to say?"

It surprised me when I felt my throat closing, as I choked up. I looked away from the Courvilles a moment, then turned to them and said, "I am so sorry, so terribly sorry for what happened to your boy and your family. I just want to say that."

Wes Courville nodded.

"I think that's all I had to say."

Hattie Courville spoke up. "You don't know what it's like. I go to that church every day. I fix the altar flowers."

Wes said, "Only thing could get me back in that church would be somebody's funeral."

I nodded my understanding, momentarily wondering if even a funeral could get me back in a Catholic church.

Wes turned to Matt. "Doctor, you a doctor, a priest, or exactly what? And you wanna see my boy?"

Matt nodded. "Yes, sir, I am a priest, but I am also a psychiatrist. I live and work in Virginia, near Washington, DC. I want to see if I can help Will, but I don't think he ought to know I am a priest."

"Lord, no," Hattie said.

Matt continued, "I came here because I wanted to see your son and meet with you both. No one in the whole Church ever interacts with families of victims of priests. Lawyers are not part of the Church. Consequently, the Church really knows nothing. I know people in the Church who are more important than the bishop in Thiberville, and I believe they will be interested in whatever I learn here. I hope so, but they may be just like the bishop here. Julie is a nun in Thiberville. She cares as much as I do and she will be able to come here more often than I can, if you allow that. I will work with her. If you prefer that we leave, we will. But I do want to help your son."

Wes Courville stood, took his wife's hand. "We're going to go outside and talk."

The three of us had a clear view of the Courvilles through a big picture window. Wes had his hands jammed in his pockets, his shoulders were hunched. Hattie touched his arm, stroked his arm, looked at his face, and appeared to be pleading. Finally, they stopped talking and opened the door. Wes said, "Come with me, Matt. Don't say nothin' 'bout being a priest."

Hattie said, "Let me make some lemonade. My lemons were so big this year, they scared me. Everything I grow is organic but these things looked like they'd been injected with something. I may need to add a lot of sugar."

Julie got up and accompanied Hattie to the kitchen. Wes came back to the den alone. When Julie and Hattie brought the lemonade, we settled in and the four of us talked together about our lives. They wanted to know about my children. They talked about their grown daughters. They never mentioned Will. An hour passed. When Hattie went to the kitchen to refill my glass, she shouted, "Wes, come here quick. Julie, ya'll come too."

When we got to the kitchen, she was standing at the window with tears streaming down her face. She just pointed outside.

Matt and Will were perched in a tree house, sitting cross-legged. They were playing some version of a patty-cake game and Matt kept making mistakes. The child was shrieking in high-pitched laughter.

Hattie wrapped her arms around her husband. "He's laughing, Wes, he's laughing."

Another half-hour passed with the four of us in the den. At one point Hattie asked Wes, "Do you think I ought to offer—" She looked at me. "I'm sorry. I forgot the doctor's name."

"Matt. His name is Matt."

"Should I get them some lemonade?"

Wes shook his head. "Let 'em be."

When the door opened, Will rushed in, breathless. "Daddy, Mr. Matt don't believe I can ride horses bareback. Can I show him? On Blackhorse?"

"Go get Blackhorse, son. You show Mr. Matt how a country boy rides."

All of us went onto the covered patio and watched Will race around the corner toward a barn. It wasn't long before a beautiful black Tennessee Walker rounded the corner with barefoot Will standing on its back. The kid rode the horse across the yard. He lay down on its back and dropped the reins. Then he stood again and started doing 180-degree jumping turns while the horse was still moving. He'd spin in the air and come down square on the horse's broad back while the horse continued trotting.

I mentioned to Weston and Hattie Courville that my daughter, Sasha, had horses, and she'd never believe the riding exhibition I had just witnessed. Hattie said, "You bring your Sasha sometimes on Saturdays when Julie's coming. She and Will can ride together."

"I will bring her. I promise."

When the riding exhibition ended, we told Will goodbye, and Wes and Hattie walked us to the car. Wes shook Matt's hand and said, "Thank you so much for coming, Matt. This is the first time Will has been himself in a long time. You have a gift."

"I think Will has the gifts."

Hattie rushed back to the house and brought a box filled with jars of preserves to the car. "Ya'll split 'em up even, okay?"

As I put my car in gear, Wes knocked on my window. I lowered the glass. Wes leaned in and said, "I'm glad I didn't let Poppa shoot you."

"That's his name, really? Poppa?"

"Elray's his name. Always been called Poppa. I'm glad I didn't let Poppa kill ya."

"Me too."

That night at Julie's apartment we presented Matt with the fifteen files she had copied from the secret archives on her own, and the file on Father O. D. Ellison that I had requested she copy.

"Matt, just please look through the Ellison file on top of the stack. Tell us what you think," I said.

As Matt read, Julie put on a Pavarotti tape in the background, poured wine for us and spread out small sandwiches she had made. She and I had a cigarette on the balcony and sipped wine. She said, "Thank you for taking me to the Courville family. Maybe with this child I can help, make some amends for the children I failed."

I nodded.

She went inside and brought out the tray of sandwiches, offering me one. I laughed. "So, this is what I have to do to get something besides pizza here – invite a guest from far away?"

"Yeah," she laughed.

When Matt finished reading the Ellison file, he slammed the folder shut and stood up. "There it is. Murders. You have evidence of two murders right here in a diocesan file. Christ, it's in the vicar general's handwriting. Moroux's a shrewd guy. The way he couched everything in writing about Ellison, it would be possible for him to argue that this file does not say what it says, but it's clear enough to me."

"That's why I wanted you to read it," I said, "knowing nothing about it. I wanted to see if you saw murders in that file. I have my own file, prepared by a fine investigator who spoke with Ellison, saw crime scene photographs and visited the crime scene. My file erases any doubt. This priest sexually abused and murdered two boys. The Church has him stashed in a Florida rest home. They're literally getting away with murder, the murder of two kids."

"What are you going to do with this?" Matt asked.

"I don't know yet. I want to see him die in prison. I know that. What I'm wondering is how many other murdering priests are out there. When I first got the Dubois case, I did not think there could be another priest like him. I really believed Francis Dubois was the only Catholic priest ever who did these vile sexual things with young children. Turns out I was way wrong, no? We now know there are thousands of priests like Dubois around the United States, probably all over the world."

Matt nodded.

"When Johnny Wilcox, my investigator, turned his file on Owen Dante Ellison over to me, I was sure that he was the only Catholic priest in the world who had ever sexually abused and murdered his victims. I was as sure about that as I had been that Dubois was *sui generis*, one of kind. I was wrong about Dubois being the only sex abuser. Maybe I am wrong thinking Ellison is the only priest who ever killed children."

64

BLOODY SUNDAY

Wednesday May 15, 1985
Chicago

Bonded like brothers over four months of intense battle, Des, Matt and I marched through the hard stuff in a matched cadence. We talked the same language and could finish each other's sentences, reducing paragraphs to phrases, phrases to words.

The fog of war was fading and in the clear light we were beginning to see the horizon and beyond. The Louisiana delegation of the Catholic Church, their lawyers and their political fixer had fought me hard, tried to kill off the truth. Then the American Church had fought Des, tried to kill off the truth. But in the process, the Church hierarchy, bishops everywhere, were beginning to panic as they looked at the disaster down in Louisiana, realizing how close they were to having the same situations in their dioceses.

We had been embraced for a time by bishops and cardinals across the country. Together we had flown thousands of miles at the invitation of bishops, addressed large audiences of clerics in retreat houses all over the country, given legal, canonical and clinical advice day and night in person and over the phone, working to a state of complete exhaustion over and over.

Now our time had come. We had assembled a document that told the truth of the coming crisis and predicted the concomitant scandal we saw as inevitable in the United States and perhaps globally. Our document provided legal, canonical and clinical solutions to the massive quake rumbling under the foundation stones of the Vatican, heavy stones that had buried the sins and shame of the Church for centuries. It proffered advice on policies and procedures grounded in the teachings of the Catholic Church; its mission was to heal. We were sure no individual cardinal or bishop, no group of four hundred bishops attending the National Conference of Catholic Bishops, could or would ignore the contents of the 120-page document we had prepared for them.

We were going to win. We believed this in our hearts and minds. Children would be saved and the Church would at last have the opportunity to save itself from its own worst instincts. A light was going shine in the dark back-corridors of the Church. We knew we had won.

We were assembled in a suite in the Hilton Hotel at Chicago's O'Hare airport. Long ago I had lost count of the hotels where we huddled, discussed problems and planned strategy. We arrived Wednesday evening. Des didn't arrive until almost midnight.

When we ordered room service, Matt asked me, "Do you eat anything but cheeseburgers and fries, drink anything but Coke floats?"

Indignantly, I said, "Sure. Pizza."

As Des stole fries from my plate and washed them down with a beer, Matt perused the final copy of our document Des had carried with him. He had a stack of them in a big briefcase. I tossed my copy on a chair.

Matt said, "Des, you changed nothing. You ignored everything Bishop Franklin said."

Crunching my fries, his mouth full, Des grumbled, washed down the bite and said, "Well, you see, my friends, it appears you fellows, my esteemed colleagues, were right – His Excellency, Bishop Garland Franklin, is an asshole of the highest order. He was not a good guy, and he was not with the program. He's a Vatican agent and up to no good like the rest of them. But I may have worst news for you guys, if ya want it . . ."

"Shoot," I said.

"It seems Cardinal Laurence will not be with us tomorrow. He canceled. They're flying in an assassin."

Matt set the document down. "What?"

"Ever heard of Bishop Miguel Chistera?" Des said.

Matt shook his head.

Des said, "Nobody's heard of Bishop Miguel Chistera. No reason anyone should have heard of him. On paper he appears to be a nobody – an auxiliary bishop in a big diocese, a fifth wheel on a car."

"And?"

"I pulled his file yesterday after Cardinal Laurence called me and said he had other commitments and was sending Bishop Chistera in his place. Know where Chistera spent the last five years?"

Des had our attention. Both Matt and I were leaning in toward Des, waiting for him to supply the answer to the question he threw out.

"Bishop Miguel Chistera is fresh from five years in the Holy City. He wasn't singing in the Vatican choir. He was on the staff of Cardinal Hans Kruger. Chistera was one of the German's fair haired boys. Pretty high on Kruger's staff. I don't know why he was rotated stateside recently."

"So, this means exactly what?" I asked.

"Tomorrow, Ren, you're going to meet a proxy for the most powerful man in the Curia, a cut-out. Chistera will not be acting for himself or Cardinal Laurence, but acting for Cardinal Hans Kruger. Cardinal Hans Kruger wants to know what is in our document. No one in the Vatican hierarchy has seen it yet. Bishop Miguel Chistera will walk out of here with a copy and it will be in Kruger's hand as fast as a plane can fly from Chicago to Rome. I believe this Bishop Chistera will be Kruger's eyes and ears in our meeting tomorrow."

Thursday, May 16, 1985

We spent the entire day locked in the hotel suite with Bishop Miguel Chistera. We went through our document page by page, covering every phrase in detail. Bishop Chistera was cordial, appeared sincerely interested, and at the same time acted as an inquisitor, albeit in a relaxed manner. He attempted to pull every thought the three of us had from our minds as he scribbled notes on a legal pad.

Without having had Des's warning that this man was an agent of Cardinal Hans Kruger, I know both Matt and I would have been taken in by him. We would have been convinced Bishop Chistera was on our side as it was obvious from all he said. He actually told us the Bishops' Conference would have to act to adopt this document officially, and he was confident this would happen. He said this as he packed his briefcase and left the hotel suite, the briefcase in one hand, a garment bag in the other.

Des believed when Bishop Chistera walked out of the hotel room he was bound for a concourse of O'Hare Airport where he would board an overnight flight for Rome.

Sunday, May 19, 1985
Thiberville

I was in my townhouse in Thiberville on Sunday when I got the word. Des called in the late afternoon. "Bishop Chistera just got off the phone with me. He told me we are to shut down our operation immediately. This would be coming from Cardinal Kruger himself, I imagine. Bishop Chistera said he would not distribute copies of our document at the Bishops' Conference. He basically ordered me to destroy all drafts of the document and any notes we might have relating to information we obtained during visits to dioceses. He said the information is too sensitive to remain in existence in writing. And he said the Conference has been working on their own program that they're going to adopt."

"Fuck me!" I said.

"Me too, buddy. But we're not going to destroy anything."

"Damn straight," I said.

"Yeah. Well, fuck 'em, Ren. They're not going to get away with this," Des said.

"This is some rotten news. Damn."

"Right. Well, this is not all the cheery news I have. The good Bishop Garland Franklin filed a report with Cardinal Antonio Marcello in Rome. It came across my desk as it was routed through the nunciature."

"Okay."

"Listen to this bullshit, my friend. And I quote from Bishop Franklin's report, 'From my observations, Attorney Renon Chattelrault in Louisiana is a panicky young man who is trying to push the Church leadership into paying exorbitant legal fees to him for his legal advice. There is only one legal case involving a criminal prosecution and substantial sums of money in the entire United States. It is in this one case Chattelrault has some small minor involvement.'"

"Fuck Franklin," I said. "He wants to risk the diplomatic status of the Vatican state by hiding personnel records on Embassy grounds to obstruct justice, and he's talking crap about me. Des, keep a copy of that asshole's letter. I'm gonna tattoo it onto Franklin's ass one of these days."

"I throw nothing away. I'll get it to you. It's been a bloody Sunday, brother."

When I hung up the phone, I dialed Matt.

"Ren?"

"How did you know it was me?"

"Des talked to me earlier and said he was calling you right then. I knew you'd ring me and the answer is NO."

"No? No to what?"

"You cannot bring Poppa Vidros and his shotgun up here to Baltimore to snuff out Bishop Franklin or hit Bishop Chistera either."

"I hadn't thought that far yet."

"Things are worse than Des thinks, Renon. I just didn't have it

419

in me to tell him what kind of closed-door presentation the bishops are going to get tomorrow afternoon on the subject of clergy abuse. I've been told it will all be verbal, no documents, no paper trail, no proof it was ever discussed. If we destroy all our drafts and notes like the Vatican ordered, then it will be like this never existed."

"They're criminals. The whole lot of them."

"Yep. They ought to put the collective bunch in the dock and try them. But we have to stay focused on what we're trying to do."

"What do you mean? What we're trying to do is in the past tense. We're done."

"No way. I'm already fighting back."

"With what?"

"With our document. We're not going to destroy it. We're going to copy it and mail it to every cardinal, archbishop and bishop in the country and get it in the hands of the right cardinals in the Vatican too."

"Damn good idea. Put it in their laps."

"Ren, this document of ours is the smoking gun. That's why the Vatican wants it destroyed. It is documentary proof of what they knew and when they knew it. Our data, predictions, warnings and advice were known only to us, Bishop Franklin and the Bishop Chistera character, and Cardinal Kruger. Now when they receive their copy of our document in the mail, every bishop will know, and the Vatican will know. Some of the staff at Hope House are copying our document now. They're running off over five hundred copies. There will be a brief cover letter from me, giving a summary of the history of the genesis of the document and the urgency of the message it contains. On the cover page of the document I will credit the authors. Under my name and Des's name I will list our titles, degrees, whole pedigree. Under your name I'll put the words 'Panicky Young Man'."

The tension that seized my neck and back when Des called began to loosen. That Matt and Des were determined to fight on at what I could only imagine would be great cost to their careers was inspiring. These were the only priests I knew who cared about any of this.

The last thing Matt said was, "The bishops will never be able to deny that they knew the truth in 1985. They will continue to lie, but it will come out one day somehow that they had the truth in their hands. And this Bishop Chistera, Cardinal Kruger's agent, had the truth. Kruger had the truth. The Vatican had the truth in 1985. The Vatican appointed Bishop Franklin in writing this year too. One day all this will be known."

We had believed we were going to save thousands of children from having innocence ripped from their hearts and souls by removing thousands of perverted priests who would be dealt with justly and severely by the legal justice system. We felt the thousands of children who were dying inside as a result of having been victims of priests, discarded after degradation was inflicted, would be placed in extensive therapy regimes designed to restore some of the damage done to them by priests and Bishops.

We had been wrong. To state the truth of what had happened and couch same in military parlance, the three of us had been "walking point" for the Church, sent on a mission to seek and engage the enemy. We found the enemy. When we radioed the message, "We found the enemy and the enemy is us," the most powerful man in the Catholic Church, Cardinal Hans Kruger, got a fix on our coordinates, our exact location, and called a direct bombing strike on our position designed to obliterate us and all evidence of our work. The Church knew its real enemy. The enemy was truth.

65

THE RED MASS

Monday September 2, 1985
Thiberville

By early September, Shelby, Jake and Sasha were back in school after the summer holidays. I was back in my office trying to pick up the pieces of a lost law practice, fallen to ruin through my neglect over such a long time.

The mail brought an invitation, a standard invitation every lawyer in the diocese received each year, an invitation to attend the Red Mass at Saint Stephen's. The tradition of the Red Mass dated back to thirteenth-century Europe, when a Catholic Mass would mark the official start of term for civil courts. In Thiberville, celebrants, judges, and some attorneys donned the traditional red robes for the annual Mass, and everyone attended the public reception afterwards. This year, in a separate envelope was an invitation to a private lunch at the Old Bishop's House after the Red Mass. It had been issued by Monsignor Belair, the vicar of finance for the Diocese of Thiberville, and was accompanied by a handwritten note. "Please attend. Yours in Christ, Monsignor Buddy."

The summer had passed quietly. On the civil side, because the Rachou case was being handled by Kane Chaisson, I heard nothing. On the criminal side, I had convinced Hannover House in New Jersey to take Dubois from the Stalder Institute. The Hannover facility specialized in the treatment of serial sex offenders. Dubois would serve his prison sentence there, and receive medical treatment, conditional upon the diocese agreeing to pay all associated costs. DA Sean Robinette was amenable, saying only, "It's not where he serves, but how long he serves that matters to me."

Des had had me on the road to a number of dioceses throughout August. Most of the time, Matt was with us. The results were the same and no less frustrating.

Julie had spent the summer months learning to cook – with mixed results. Our friendship was like an accordion. At times, we were real close and saw each other a lot, and then several weeks would go by without contact. It was a curious relationship to me and the more I got to know her, the more fascinated I became with her simple approach to life and the goodness that came through in all she did and said. I had not ever known anyone like her.

When Julie went to see Will Courville on Saturdays, I often went with her. When Matt could get down to Louisiana, he joined us. Every week since Matt first met Lil' Will, he had his assistant buy a book that was right for Will's age and mail the book to Amalie. Sometimes Matt sent toys as well.

On weekends when he could not come to Amalie, Matt always called and spoke with Will and his parents. He was staying in close touch with Iris Dubois as well. Over time I realized that Matt extended himself to hundreds of people in all walks of life in places scattered across the country. All of them had been hurt badly by some deep injury inflicted by another or by a pathological condition that made them act out horrors and caused deep sadness in their families. Once Matt told me, "The families of these pedophile priests suffer as much as the families of the children, but in different ways."

Hattie and Weston Courville always insisted we bring Sasha to the Courville farm. She and Will rode horses together and played in his tree house. Sasha and Will seemed to spend all their time laughing. She and Will became fast friends. Sasha was smitten for the first time in her life by the dark, handsome kid with the great smile. We had some good times with Hattie and Wes Courville, and Lil' Will seemed ready to return to school in the fall, even if he would have to repeat a grade.

The most important parts of the summer were the two long holidays I spent with my children at a beach on the Gulf Coast. I was able to temporarily push all the things relating to Dubois and the Church from my mind and I felt I got to know my children again. I wondered if that time would one day seem as important to them as it did to me then.

Nothing could have dragged me to the Red Mass, but I did accept the invitation to the private lunch. In the dining room of the Old Bishop's House, Monsignor Moroux's domestic servants, Joe and Fanny, were filling water goblets as Moroux, Monsignor Buddy Belair, Sister Julianne, Jonathan Bendel, Thomas Quinlan, Lloyd Lecompte, and Joe Rossi were seated. It was the first time I had been in the Old Bishop's House since Bendel and his colleagues had stopped talking to me months before. All of us took the places we'd had at the first luncheon a year earlier.

It was odd being in that setting again and trying to ignore Julie, pretending we were still strangers. If everyone else in the room had secrets, Julie and I shared a secret too. We had a stack of fifteen personnel files that could blow the diocese apart.

The oddest thing about the luncheon was the presence of the ever absent Bishop Reynolds. I assumed he had celebrated the Red Mass at the cathedral. From the way he looked at me as I entered the dining room, I could not tell whether he was acknowledging me or even recognized me.

As salads were set down, Joe Rossi opened without any preliminaries. "Renon, we're gonna get the Chaisson case out of the way this month. The new cases coming in are easy. The lawyers in the new cases don't know about the amount of the settlements paid in the Ponce–Thomas cases. These guys have their hands out and are settling for chump change, whatever we want to pay. Jon paid one guy twenty-five grand last week, bought a claim for twenty-five. Chaisson's Rachou case is the only big one left. It cost this diocese a million dollars to get rid of the Ponce–Thomas cases. We can buy the Rachou suit out from under Chaisson too. Maybe Chaisson won't want to settle with us, but we can flash enough money at the Rachou family to choke a horse. They will make Kane Chaisson fold his hand. This can all be over in a couple weeks."

Bendel was more cautious in his approach. "Renon, you've done a magnificent job of representing the priest's interests. It's true not much of what you've done pleased me or those colleagues of mine who had interests that conflicted with Father Dubois's interests. But here, in front of these people, I want to extend an apology to you for things I may have said and done out of anger, things that might have offended you. Professionally and personally, I hold you in the highest regard. I ask you to please be open-minded today."

I believed what Rossi said was mostly the truth. I even suspected the diocese might have chipped in a million in cash to pile on top of the insurance money to settle the Ponce–Thomas suits. I knew everything Bendel had said was a lie.

Monsignor Moroux had a speaking part too. He cleared his throat, sipped water, wiped his lips with a napkin and turned to me, speaking in a low voice, softer than any voice I had heard him affect. "Well, Renon, it is not just about us at this table anymore. And it's not about the archbishop in New Orleans, or even Bishop Franklin in Baltimore, or those people you know in Washington at the papal nunciature. This is now about Rome and the Vatican."

I had heard the same thing from Des in an early-morning phone call from the Vatican Embassy a week ago. Rome had spoken.

The monsignor sipped tea from a goblet, patted his mouth again with a linen napkin and continued. "Bishop Franklin has informed me that Rome does not want a criminal trial of any Catholic priest on these kinds of charges. They will not abide that kind of publicity. Rome has said your criminal trial involving Father Francis will not happen."

It was my turn to talk and I passed. After an awkward silence, Thomas Quinlan emphasized the hopelessness of my situation. "You entered a plea of not guilty by reason of insanity. Could you inform us of the name or names of the expert witnesses you've retained who will testify on behalf of Father Dubois that he was legally insane at the time he committed these crimes?"

Quinlan, a seasoned pro, instinctively knew the weakness of my case. I had consulted fourteen psychiatrists and psychologists who had been previously accepted by courts as expert witnesses in cases where the defense was "not guilty by reason of insanity". Not a single one would testify that in their opinion Dubois was legally insane at the time he committed those crimes. I am certain Quinlan suspected that I had nothing, but he was not going to get that out of me. I ignored his question.

When I did speak, I looked directly at Monsignor Moroux on my left, ignoring everyone else in the room. "Monsignor, I've had this conversation too many times in too many settings not to know where we're heading. Let me get to the issue. Let's assume for the sake of this conversation that I do enter a guilty plea on behalf of Father Dubois this very afternoon, and Rome has its way and everybody in the Church is happy. Let's also assume that the DA helps me convince Judge Labat to allow the sentence to be served at Hannover House, a penal institution especially for serial sex offenders, a place where the best medical treatment in the country is afforded to prisoners, providing them the best chance to be rehabilitated and live the most productive life possible in prison and upon release."

I paused as Fanny and Joe entered and began serving the entree of shrimp creole. Fanny and Joe returned to the kitchen twice to get more plates and during that time no one spoke. When the serving was done, I resumed.

"Here is the issue. It's all about cost. The per-day cost of caring for a prisoner at Hannover House is expensive compared to a Louisiana prison, which would cost the diocese nothing. The

426

question is this: can I get a commitment from this diocese to pay all costs incurred for the medical care and imprisonment of Father Dubois at Hannover House?"

Moroux said, "I would not have the authority to answer that question. If you wait, I'll make a phone call."

As Monsignor Moroux left the room, headed in the direction of his office, Bendel said, "Then you're in agreement now?"

"I have not said anything like that. What I've said is I have the commitment from Hannover to hold Dubois during his incarceration and to have him treated. If I can get the commitment from the diocese to pay the costs at Hannover, I have another piece of the puzzle in place. All that would be left would be for DA Robinette and me to have a meeting of minds regarding the length of the sentence."

Moroux entered the room, pulled out his chair and took his seat. We were all looking at him. "Well, Renon, I am informed that the answer to your question is 'No'. There's no way this diocese will commit to pay any expenses related to Father Francis once he's convicted and placed in prison. The expense over his lifetime could be enormous. It could set a kind of precedent that would apply to other priests elsewhere."

"Wow," I said sarcastically, feigning a kind of innocence and naivety that fooled no one. Actually, I was wondering who Monsignor Moroux had consulted over the phone. His bishop was in the room. Except to bring his fork and wine glass to his mouth, the bishop had not moved, nor had he spoken.

I pushed away from the table a bit. "So, let me see if I have got this straight. The Vatican is ordering me not to bring this case to trial, and when I present an alternative to trial, the Church refuses to pay for that."

Rossi was lighting a cigar which he waved in my direction. "Now you get it, Renon. It's not just us talking. This is coming straight from the Vatican. The leader of all Catholics, our Pope, has weighed in on this. The Pope says no trial; there's no trial. We have no choice. Not even you have a choice anymore."

I looked at Rossi. "Joe, just tell the Pope I said no." I started walking to the door.

"Wait a minute!" Rossi shouted. "Wait one damned minute!"

Joe followed me outside, all the way to my car. When I got in the car, he went around, opened the door and sat in the passenger seat. I turned on the motor, reset the air conditioner and ejected a Ray Charles tape. Rossi was out of shape, overweight, and breathing hard from the exertion of chasing me down, almost gasping for breath. He looked straight ahead as he spoke.

"Renon, you got some big problems. Real big problems. And I don't think you know what they are."

"Well, Joe, somehow I feel confident you're going to tell me what they are."

"You know what moral turpitude means? From what I'm told, this is how someone gets disbarred. They commit an act of moral turpitude, like advising a man of God to destroy evidence under subpoena and assisting this man of God in destroying evidence, and telling him to lie if asked about it under oath."

"Bullshit, Rossi. Quinlan is the one who told Moroux to sanitize the personnel records, and Bendel seconded the motion. I might have been the chorus, but I wasn't singing lead. Any acts of moral turpitude were committed by archdiocesan and diocesan counsel."

"Suppose the good monsignor would not remember it that way? Suppose Quinlan and Bendel could not recall being present for such a discussion? Suppose there was only one witness at your disbarment proceeding? Suppose it was a Roman Catholic monsignor's word against the word of a young lawyer? What do you think the result would be?"

I put the car in gear and turned to Rossi. "I think Moroux would double-cross you and tell the truth under oath. That's what I think. Now, get the fuck outta my car."

Rossi opened the door. "I'm just talking supposes. Suppose this, suppose that."

Edinburgh City Libraries
Portobello Library
Tel: 0131 529 5558
portobello.library@edinburgh.gov.uk

Borrowed Items 16/06/2016 16:36
XXXXXXXX8544

Item Title	Due Date
Born to die	30/06/2016
Bring me home	30/06/2016
third sin	30/06/2016
* In God's house : one man'..	07/07/2016
* Paris spring	07/07/2016
* Heads or hearts.	07/07/2016

* Indicates items borrowed today
SATURDAY BOOKBUGS
EVERY WEEK AT 11.30 am
www.edinburgh.gov.uk/libraries

Edinburgh City Libraries

Portobello Library
Tel: 0131 529 5558
portobello.library@edinburgh.gov.uk

Borrowed Items 16/06/2016 16:36
XXXXXXX8544

Item Title	Due Date
Born to die	30/06/2016
Bring me home	30/06/2016
third sin	30/06/2016
* In God's house : one man's	07/07/2016
* Paris spring	07/07/2016
* Heads or hearts	07/07/2016

* Indicates items borrowed today
SATURDAY BOOKBUGS
EVERY WEEK AT 11.30 am
www.edinburgh.gov.uk/libraries

66

GOD'S WILL

5:30 p.m., Tuesday September 10, 1985
Thiberville

I was standing in the wide hall on the fourth floor of the Thiberville courthouse, waiting for DA Sean Robinette to arrive. We had been called by Judge Labat for a conference in his chambers after hours.

Sean approached with a slow gait, head down. His hair was uncombed, windblown, and his tie was hanging loose around his neck. His face was deeply lined, as if he had aged overnight. His voice was hoarse. "I lost a witness last night in my criminal case against your client. The Courville boy in Amalie used his father's gun and shot himself in the head. He was on life support for a short while. I'm just back from the funeral home. Fortunately, he was part of a sealed settlement and no one in the media got wind he was connected to the case, thank God."

I leaned against the marble wall.

"I visited with his parents at the funeral home. The child had asked them where they'd been last Wednesday night. They told him they met with me and the other parents about the trial. He was scared he would have to go in front of people and tell what happened. And then, at suppertime Sunday, he saw a newscast with old footage of you and Dubois getting in a police cruiser last year at Chaisson's. The boy apparently knew you – you came to his home, they said. Mr. Courville thinks the child realized you knew the priest and was scared you would bring the priest to his home. That's what they think, Ren. They heard a shot behind the house and found him in a corral with his horse. He was brain dead on arrival at the hospital in Bayou Saint John."

I hung my head, staring at my shoes, tasting the salt of my tears. I knew it would not have been any different had I held the gun and pulled the trigger myself. I had pushed things too far. My mind raced in reverse. Had I done what Rossi and the others wanted in the beginning, maybe Dubois would be dead now by suicide, but Lil' Will Courville would be riding Blackhorse bareback.

"There are a team of school-board psychologists from three areas down in Amalie now. They are worried about copycat suicides, more dead children."

Sean handed me a handkerchief. I wiped my tears.

"Come on, Ren, can't we stop this now? Enough is enough. We have a lot of kids whose lives have been destroyed. Now we have a dead little boy. Can't we shut this down now? You go in Labat's chambers and tell the judge you're giving me a guilty plea to a single life sentence. I can tell the families this tomorrow night, and maybe… maybe it will be the end at last. This child is dead, Ren, dead." He paused. "I can't remember the child's name."

"Will," I said. "His name was Will."

"The boy's mother told me they know this is your fault. I told her it was your fault. It is your fault. She said for me to tell you they never want to hear from you again, or the nun and priest you used to bring to their home."

"Gimme a few minutes, Sean. Will ya?"

He nodded.

"Tell the judge I'll be back. I need some time."

"Take all the time you need, Renon, but for Christ's sake, when you come back, do the right thing. There is only one right thing. Shut it down."

I made my way to the large magnolia tree outside the courthouse. Having attended too many funerals and buried too many friends and family members, I was no stranger to death. But no death had affected me like Will's. I was responsible. My decision to represent Father Francis Dubois as I had, to fight for Dubois against huge odds, to bring things to this point, had caused the death of a child. I walked around the courthouse square.

My sorrow over the loss of the little boy was only exceeded by the rage I felt against my client, Francis Dubois. By the time I reached the broad steps of the courthouse again, I knew what I had to do. My heart was wrecked by sorrow and, following my heart, I wanted to throw Dubois under the train, give him the fate he deserved. But my mind was locked in the law, my obligation to defend and assert the rights of my client. I knew I had no choice. My guts burned and churned.

Judge Eloi Labat had originally been appointed to fill a vacancy in the judiciary by a governor from north Louisiana who didn't know any lawyers in Thiberville. Sean Robinette had played a hand in the appointment as Labat was serving as one of his assistant prosecutors at the time. The judge owed a lot to the DA – everything. Over the next fifteen years, Judge Labat was re-elected over and over, something of a mystery to some members of the Bar. When he was on the bench it was like having an extra prosecutor in the courtroom – impartiality and fairness were as foreign to him as the Constitution and Criminal Code.

There was something called Louisiana Law and there was something called Labat's Law and they were not altogether the same thing. Though he looked like the cartoon character Foghorn Leghorn, with his shock of reddish grey hair and his huge wingtip shoes, Labat's head was filled with whirring razor blades that cut lawyers he did not like to pieces. And he did not like me.

We were the only ones on the fourth floor of the courthouse except for the janitorial crew. As we settled in his cramped chambers, the only sound was the banging of trash cans and the laughter of the cleaning crew.

"Renon, I've been talking to Sean about this for some time, and I figured it was time to include you in the discussions," Judge Labat said.

In any other jurisdiction, a lawyer would have been appalled to learn that a presiding judge had been having private conversations with a prosecutor about a pending case. But nothing Eloi Labat said could surprise any lawyer who had already appeared in his court.

"There are four things I want to discuss: the gag order I signed today, arrangements for the media during the trial, the way I will handle the testimony of the children, and the length of the trial."

"Your Honor, is this our pre-trial conference?" I asked.

"I've set aside this hour each Tuesday until the trial date. I think we'll be able to have seven of these meetings. There aren't going to be any last-minute histrionics in this case. We will iron out every detail in advance. Sean will meet with the parents of the child victims each Wednesday night. If there's anything that happens in one of our Tuesday meetings that the parents should know, Sean will be able to tell them on Wednesday."

Judge Labat and I had tangled enough times for both of our lifetimes. I really did not want to lock and load on him now. "Your Honor, while it is true that Sean's job as district attorney is to serve the people, and it is right for him to work closely with the victims, I'm not sure it's the court's role—"

"Mr. Chattelrault, the court will define its role in these proceedings for itself without your interference or influence."

Sean said, "Eloi, to get back to your agenda, specifically the media..."

The judge became animated. "The clerk of court told me he's had phone calls from foreign press, Houston, even New York. People want to make arrangements to rent space in the courthouse, install phones and some kind of machine. I don't want the foreign press making a circus out of my trial. I won't have it. Nobody's going to talk to them. Maybe they'll get bored and go back to where they belong."

I closed the legal pad that had been open on my lap. "Judge, I won't continue this unless and until we have a court reporter present to transcribe our comments."

The judge arched his eyebrows. "Mr. Chattelrault, this court has entered the gag order today." He picked up three legal sheets stapled together and handed them to me. "The original was filed with the clerk of court at four this afternoon. It is now the order of the court. Anyone who violates this order will be cited for contempt and jailed. No one will discuss this with the media, not our local people or the foreign press."

I couldn't believe this man. First, Judge Labat chose not to notice that I had said I would not go on with the meeting. And I thought it bizarre that he considered any press outside of Thiberville to be foreign media.

The judge continued. "I am awaiting three bids by video firms. What I have specified is the design and construction of a system where cameras will be installed in the small courtroom behind the big courtroom where we will be. Video monitors will be put in the large courtroom – one for me, one for the prosecution table, one for the defense table, plus a large monitor for the jury and two large monitors for the audience. The sound will be engineered so the dialogue of counsel and the court can be heard in the small courtroom as well as by all in the large courtroom."

"I'm lost," I said.

"Let's cut the crap, Mr. Chattelrault. I know your gamble is that if you force a trial, the district attorney will not be able to produce any witnesses, any of the child victims, because their parents will refuse to let them testify. Sean told me one of his potential witnesses committed suicide. I know you now believe no other parents will allow their children to testify. Well, you're not going to get away with your gamble. You're not going to play games with me, sir. I will not traumatize these children by having them face the defendant in court or testify before a room packed with strangers. When Sean calls a child to testify, the child will be escorted by a female bailiff with his two parents, his psychologist

433

and whomever else he may wish to have with him – escorted to the small courtroom. There he will take the stand and the female bailiff will administer the oath. The child will hear your questions and Sean's questions and the child's responses will be seen and heard by everyone in the big courtroom."

It was classic Labat, Labat's law. In less than five minutes he had vitiated two of my client's constitutionally guaranteed rights, freedom of speech and the right to meaningfully confront one's accuser. I braced myself and confronted the judge.

"Judge, you filed a gag order, but all this other stuff you're talking about is not documented. I don't want to go any further until you bring in a court reporter to record your comments and ours."

In one movement the judge both stiffened and smiled sardonically. "Mr. Chattelrault, you are right – this is the last meeting of this kind we will have. Nothing in the code requires that we have these conferences. Sean and I can plan this trial without your input if you are going to be obstinate. Sean tells me he believes once the jury is seated that he can put on his entire case for the state in five days, maybe as few as three days. We all pretty much know what Sean's witness list is – the child victims and an expert on the issue you raised in filing an insanity plea. Who will your witnesses be, Mr. Chattelrault, and how long do you expect it will take to put on the defense?"

"Your Honor, I expect my end of the case will take a long time, weeks and weeks. Maybe months."

The judge stood up, red-faced in apparent rage. "I... I... I know," he stammered. "This priest is going to prison for the rest of his life... and to hell after that. I know about this stuff. I... I... I know. I was an altar boy in my parish and the priest there..." The judge turned a purplish red color and walked out of his chambers.

My God, Judge Labat was abused by a priest, I thought.

Sean and I walked down the steps in silence. Under the old magnolia tree, we stood looking at each other. He said, "Renon, the things that make you great as a lawyer make you a prick of a human being. You and I – we'll never forget this day. It won't pass."

I got Julie on my car phone just as she came in from her afternoon run. When I told her about Will, she began crying so hard that I could not understand what she was saying. She eventually caught her breath, and said, "I want you to come over here. I don't think it's good for either of us to be alone."

"Thanks, but I think I need to be alone. I'm sorry."

I found myself driving on country roads, kind of heading for Coteau, my former home, a place where I had felt safe. As I meandered alongside a bayou, I passed horses in pastures and could see the scene at the Courvilles in my mind. I pictured the paddock, and the Tennessee Walker, Blackhorse, that Will had said a last goodbye to.

I did stop by Julie's. She was on the front porch, like she was waiting for me even though I had said I was not coming over. I motioned for her to get in the car.

It was dark when we got to the stadium. I had her climb behind me. She followed me to the top, my secret refuge. Trying to be lighthearted, she said, "Now, do we jump?"

I shook my head. "How did it come to this? Was I playing to my own ego as a lawyer – big case, a lot of exposure and all that crap? Did I lose sight of what matters? Hell, does anyone around this Church stuff have clean hands? I was working for a client who should be dead, and now the boy I wanted to save is gone."

She brushed my hair back. "Ren, there is nothing I can say…"

"There's no forgiveness for something like this."

Julie leaned closer to me. "God has his hands on you."

I knew she believed that.

We were sitting next to each other. I leaned against the railing. "I've never been this confused. I've never been so tired. I've never had any doubts – not about anything in my whole life. I know I've always had faith – a belief in God, in myself."

"You still have that faith, Ren."

"No, no. I don't... I don't think I have faith in anything anymore."

The dark clouds covering the night sky opened up, and burst above us. I thought the hard rain falling on my face would cover my tears, but she knew. I had now cried twice in front someone else.

"I can't tell Sasha. She's gonna want to know why she can't go see Will anymore. What do you tell a little kid, Julie? How do you tell her that her buddy killed himself with a gun? What do I say when she asks me why Will killed himself?"

67

ALL BETS OFF

Sunday September 22, 1985
Thiberville

I was sitting on the patio, scanning the sports page, looking at the college football scores and trying to figure out my balance sheet for the bets I'd made with my bookie. Julie had come over on her bike early and was making breakfast. As Julie set coffee down on the glass-topped table, the phone rang.

"Renon, Robert Blassingame. Please excuse this intrusion on your Sunday morning. I received your private phone number from Monsignor Moroux."

"Yes?"

"I'm here, in Thiberville, at the Hilton. The whole legal team arrived from New Orleans yesterday. We also have the two principal insurance company men here with us. Last week we worked out a whole myriad of offers for the Rachou family – lump sum settlements, even money for the two parents who are not entitled under the law in our view. Structured settlements that spread out payments for ten years, twenty years, thirty years."

"I understand."

"All the information was delivered in a package to Chaisson's office Friday with a request that he meet with us today at noon in Tom Quinlan's hotel suite to settle the case."

"And?"

"A half hour ago Chaisson had this message delivered here: 'There will be no meeting today. There will be no discussion of settlement. There will be a trial, Monday ten a.m. in Bayou Saint

John. My clients want a jury to assess their losses, not some insurance actuary."

I suppressed laughter. Kane Chaisson had been way ahead of these high-steppin' New Orleans lawyers from the first day. Now it seemed he was tying their intestines in knots. No one gets as dry in the mouth as an insurance defense lawyer on the eve of a big trial, for a big loss can cost his firm a lucrative client.

"So, why are you calling me, Bobby?" I asked, deliberately addressing him by his hated nickname.

"We all believe that you are the only one among us who has any rapport with Kane Chaisson. We need for you to intercede. To call Chaisson. Meet with him and bring him to us to discuss settlement. We gave him our research. The most money ever awarded an injured plaintiff in the history of Bayou Saint John is less than a quarter million dollars. The largest settlement paid in the Dubois cases was six hundred thousand. In cash, in one lump sum, we are prepared today to offer him three quarters of a million."

As accustomed as I was to the gall of these kinds of lawyers, I was still astounded that Blassingame would believe he could prevail upon me at the eleventh hour to assist him after all the water that had gone under the bridge between us. I asked him to hold. Placing the phone under a chair cushion, I started in on breakfast and began circling the last of the college football games I had wagered on.

Julie took a seat and felt the lump under the cushion. She pulled the phone from under her and looked at it with wide eyes and a smile. Covering the mouthpiece, she whispered, "Who?"

I whispered back, "Beelzebub."

I took up the phone and said, "I seem to remember you once saying you were going to destroy this Rachou kid and his parents. I think you said, 'The kid is going to put up or shut up.' You said you were going after 'mother, father and child'. Now, Bobby, it seems you got the game you wanted. The kid has stepped up."

I hung up.

I turned back to the sports pages and continued trying to sort out all the bets I had made on Friday with my bookie, Leo. I called him "the beggar" because of the manner he assumed on Tuesdays when he came to settle our account at my office. Leo always told me I was a bookie's dream, one who bet with his heart rather than his head.

PART SEVEN

THE BEGINNING OF THE END

68

JUDGMENT BEFORE GOD AND MAN

Monday September 23, 1985
Courtroom, Bayou Saint John

Diocesan lawyer Jon Bendel had told me that in a meeting among counsel it was decided that he alone would sit at counsel table in the courtroom. Instead of being surrounded by Blassingame and his cohorts, Bendel would have the bishop and Monsignors Moroux, Belair and Gaudet seated behind him. Counsel felt the presence of the high-ranking priests would influence the jury, create empathy for the diocese. And they didn't want all those New Orleans suits inside the court rail, giving off the scent that big insurance policies were available to pay the Rachou verdict.

Whatever the result of the civil trial, it was certain it would not be a secret. There were none of the gag orders or video links that Judge Labat was envisaging for the criminal trial of Dubois the following month. The judge in the Rachou trial had no beef with the media being there. Television news trucks surrounded the courthouse square in Bayou Saint John. Some had camped out there since the night before. Writers from around the country staked out places in the first row of the courtroom, placing down books, jackets and briefcases before wandering back out to the large columned porch across the front of the courthouse.

I had no role to play in the trial. The stipulation of liability had made it unnecessary for Dubois to be present or represented in the case. I was attending the trial in order to monitor the proceedings for Des and Matt. A ten-year-old child victim was bringing a bishop to court before a jury. It was historic, the first trial of its kind in the history of the Roman Catholic Church.

At about 9:30, Kane Chaisson stepped up to the microphone and cameras on the courthouse lawn. He ignored the reporters' shouted questions and launched into a prepared statement stressing the historical importance of the proceedings that were about to begin. He quoted the Bible about the value of innocence, and celebrated the fact that under the United States constitution a young child is equal to a bishop in the eyes of the law.

As Chaisson sauntered off, fussing with the middle button of his sport coat, Jon Bendel passed him, headed in the opposite direction, moving toward the microphones. Bendel addressed the media. "This is a very hard time for the bishop. From the beginning, all the bishop and diocese have ever wanted is for the right thing to be done. We are here this week for that very reason." With that weak statement, he turned and walked off, ignoring all questions.

The old courtroom had been closed to fresh air since air conditioning was invented. Choosing the jury took no time. Chaisson asked very few questions of the prospective jurors and this told me he had paid a small fortune to investigators to prepare dossiers on each one. He had their life histories in files in front of him. He used his challenges quickly. Jon Bendel was unsuccessful in trying to keep women off the jury as there were too many in the jury pool. By noon the jury had been selected and seated – seven women and five men.

Kane Chaisson's first witness was Monsignor Phillip Jules Gaudet, pastor of Saint Bernadette's in Bayou Saint John. As there was a stipulation of liability in place, Chaisson could not open the door wide on the diocesan actions in regard to Father Dubois, nor could he showcase any of the monsignor's bizarre views that he had elicited during Gaudet's deposition in January. The scope of inquiry was limited to establishing that the original complaint about Dubois's actions in Amalie had been received by him and that he had relayed those complaints to the diocesan chancery in a telephone conversation with Monsignor Moroux.

The Bendel–Blassingame strategy of having the diocese admit legal responsibility for the "losses" of the plaintiff – the Rachous – was holding. It was a strategy I had advocated from the beginning, not least because it meant that the only evidence to be heard by the jury would be that which pertained directly to the Rachous. Whatever egregious conduct the diocese had engaged in would be suppressed. The job of the jury was simply to determine the amount of money the Rachous deserved in compensation.

The parents of Donny Rachou followed Monsignor Gaudet to the witness stand. Neither of them was effective in advocating their cause. They both appeared to be very nervous before the court and I felt they were intimidated by the presence of the bishop and Monsignors Moroux, Bélair and Gaudet behind Jon Bendel's counsel table.

Donny's dad never made eye contact with anyone. His mother trembled and answered only "Yes" or "No" to Kane Chaisson's questions. At the end of her testimony, she broke down crying, and said, "I can't think about it. I can't think about what Father Dubois did to my son, but I think about it all the time. I can't stop thinking about it."

But the jury did not know what Father Dubois had done to her son. Those questions could not be asked of her for that would have been inadmissible hearsay, being only what she had heard her son say to her. At this point, the diocese was carrying the day. Several jurors fidgeted in their seats, one stared at the ceiling. All seemed bored. When the first day of trial ended, it seemed to me the trial would result in a small amount of money being awarded to the Rachou family. It was not Kane Chaisson's fault that his clients, simple country people, froze up in the courtroom setting. But the bottom line was the bastards were winning.

Tuesday morning, September 24, 1985
Courtroom, Bayou Saint John

The day started with ten-year-old Donny Rachou being escorted to the witness stand by Kane Chaisson. The contrast between Chaisson, a big man, and tiny Donny was dramatic. The bailiff placed the Bible on the railing. The child's little hand lay on the leather cover, and the bailiff recited the oath, ending with "Do you swear to tell the truth, the whole truth, so help you God?"

Donny responded in a surprisingly loud voice. "Yes, sir. Yes, sir. I want to."

"Donny, please tell the jury how you met Father Francis Dubois – explain how you knew him then, what he was to you?"

Donny turned to the jury. For a moment, I feared he was frozen as his parents were. Then he began in a steady voice. "I was little. Pre-school. Father Nicky – that's how we called him. He would come to our class sometimes. He always had a big jug of Kool-Aid and cookies. It was the kind of cookies you get in stores. He was so funny for us. Father Nicky had a bunch of puppets and a little box thing where he did puppet shows. The funniest puppet was a little dog that was always biting this fat lady's dress and pulling it off, but she had other dresses under. And he did magic tricks. He had lots of tricks. He could make a quarter disappear and then pull it out of your ear. He was so funny. That's how I got to know Father Nicky."

The child's composure was in stark contrast to that of his parents. The whole courtroom was riveted by his presence. When he was speaking, you could hear him in the last row.

"You came to know Father Nicky better, didn't you?"

Looking in the direction of Kane Chaisson, Donny said, "Yes, sir. When I was taking communion classes from him—"

"Excuse me for interrupting, Donny. But would you tell the jury what you did in the communion classes Father Nicky taught you? Tell us what you learned."

Turning to the jury as he had been instructed to do, young

445

Donny said, "Nothing. I didn't really do nothing. Father Nicky made me one of his helpers. He called us his special boys – the helpers. I helped. With the puppets and cookies and stuff like that."

"Tell us what you learned in communion class."

"Nothing. Father Nicky played with the puppets and did magic like he did when I was in pre-school. It was the same. We had parties."

"Did your parents know you were not being taught anything?"

Donny turned to look at Chaisson. "No, sir. Father Nicky had us promise we wouldn't never tell our mommas or papas that we just goofed off in communion classes. It was a secret."

"Did you become an altar boy?"

"That was the worsest mistake."

"Why?"

"I would have to go to his house one night every week. There were other boys that spent the night too. Can I say names?"

"No, Donny. Don't say any names of other boys. How many boys?"

"About four, I guess. Sometimes three or five. It was different sometimes."

"What happened when you spent the night at Father Nicky's? Tell the jury what happened."

The child did not look at the jury. For a long time he looked down at his shoes. When he lifted his head, he stared straight at Bishop Reynolds. "We did sins. I know now it was sins we did with Father Nicky. But not first. After school, Father Nicky first he gave us a lot of snacks. And he took pictures with this little camera that made the pictures in a minute. Then we all took a shower. In the same shower. All of us naked as jaybirds. He would soap us down there. He made us soap him down there too. And..." Donny's strong voice cracked and gave way to sobs. His mother rushed to him as the judge declared an early lunch recess.

69

A CHILD'S TRUTH

Tuesday afternoon, September 24, 1985
Courtroom, Bayou Saint John

Young Donny had his baseball hat in his hands when he climbed
back in the witness box to start the afternoon's testimony. He was
composed. So were the five female jurors who had been crying as
he was led out of the courtroom by his mother before lunch.

Resuming, Kane Chaisson said, "Donny, what did Father
Nicky tell you about him touching you – about him making you
do things to him?"

"He said about secrets. If we told anyone, we would die and
who we told would die too. He had guns. With bullets. All over the
place. By the bed."

"Did he touch you with the guns?"

"The guns were cold. And he said the hole where a bullet goes
in is a little hole, but where it comes out, it's big, big."

Kane Chaisson walked over to the witness stand. "Donny, I
know this is hard for you to talk about. It's hard for us to hear."

"Yes, sir." The child was staring at the priests seated behind Jon
Bendel. "Some men could have stopped all this."

Bishop Reynolds had a coughing spasm, downed a glass of
water, and coughed more. Kane Chaisson stood motionless,
watching the bishop until his coughing subsided.

"So, Father Nicky scared you with guns. Made you believe he
would kill you and your parents if you told them about what was
going on—"

"And pictures. He was always taking pictures of us doing

things to each other with no clothes. We was all scared who might see the pictures."

"Did he ever talk about whether this was right or wrong?"

"He said it wasn't wrong 'cause he was a priest. And he showed me a picture on his wall of Jesus eating something with a lot of men. He said this was the way holy men loved each other."

"How, Donny, how did they love each other? What did ya'll do in Father Nicky's house that was supposed to be a secret?"

Donny hung his head. The room was silent for three long minutes. In a soft, quivering voice, Donny said, "Everything, I guess. Father Nicky made us put our pee-pees in each other's mouths and sometimes he made us put our pee-pees in someone's behind, or they did it to us and stuff."

Kane Chaisson laid a hand on Donny's shoulder, and in a stage whisper he asked, "And with Father Nicky? What did you do with Father Nicky?"

"Father Nicky played with our pee-pees. He put his mouth down there too. He made us play with his pee-pee and make stuff come out of it on his stomach. Sometimes he grabbed it and made stuff come out on us. He put his in our mouths too."

"Did Father Nicky put his anywhere else?"

"In our behinds. Some of us. It hurt. It was too big."

"You? Did he do this to you?"

"Yes, sir."

Kane Chaisson could have ended the trial then and there, but for good measure he called Doctor Aaron Kennison, Donny's treating psychologist. Doctor Kennison gave the jury a textbook account of how the boy's devastating injuries had caused permanent damage from which Donny would never fully recover. He talked about how the injuries were made worse because they were inflicted by a Catholic priest, a father figure in the child's eyes, God's agent on earth.

The closing argument of Kane Chaisson was subdued. He simply reminded the jurors to replay in their minds the testimony of Donny Rachou. Jon Bendel seemed disconcerted as he mumbled to the jury about how money could not replace everything.

The crowd of spectators had not even finished filing out of the courtroom and into the hall when the bailiff boomed, "Jury's coming back. Court will come to order."

A mad scramble brought everyone back to the pews. The whole courtroom stood as the jury filed back in. The audience remained standing, waiting for the verdict. The judge had to bang the gavel and instruct everyone to be seated and remain silent while the verdict was read.

Moments later the verdict was announced. "One million, nine hundred thousand dollars." More than double Blassingame's highest offer on Sunday. The courtroom erupted in cheers. As Kane Chaisson made his way through the gate in the railing and into the mob of reporters, Jon Bendel led the bishop and monsignors out via a private side door. The Rachou family had left the building before the jury returned with its verdict.

70

A BIG TRICK BAG

Wednesday October 9, 1985
Thiberville

A fortnight after the Rachou trial, the morning mail brought a handwritten letter from Tom Quinlan's young law associate, James Ryburn, informing me he had left the firm and the law to work in a family farming operation in Mississippi. He said he had been sexually abused for four years by a parish priest when he was an altar boy. He wished me luck and encouraged me to keep pressing for an outreach plan to find victims of clergy abuse.

I set the letter down and answered the phone. It was Des, in the first of many calls I would receive from him that day. "Renon, they're screwing with you big time now."

"Who?"

"There's a meeting going on in the old man's office here. Archbishop Carlo Verriano, Bishop Garland Franklin and an idiot Church lawyer. They're all locked up in Verriano's office. I was specifically told by the old man that Bishop Franklin did not want me in the meeting."

"What's it about?"

"It's about you. Rome thinks they can do everything with a decree. Apparently the Vatican has decreed there will not be a criminal trial of Father Dubois. Rome has made this the papal nuncio's problem. I think everyone in the American Church and those that are watching in Rome are pretty pissed about all the media stories the Rachou case created. They don't want a highly publicized criminal trial of a priest on these kinds of charges."

"So what exactly are they doing in their meeting?"

"They're going to shut you down. Best I can figure out from my buddy who runs the message center is that the unholy trio in the papal nuncio's office are hooked up on a conference call to Archbishop Donnegan in New Orleans, his lawyer Quinlan, and Bishop Reynolds and Moroux and Bendel in Thiberville."

"Geez."

"Exactly. Geez. Your Coke-float-drinking buddy, Sister Theresa, is serving the meeting, spying on 'em for us. She can't really figure out the program. She tells me that the speakerphone is on in Verriano's office and it sounds like the others are on speakerphones too. She says too many people are talking English at the same time and she can't understand English well enough to know what they are saying."

"Keep me posted."

"You bet. Me and the little nun. We're on the case."

There were a half dozen other calls from Des during the day. The last call came after Sister Theresa had served sandwiches and soft drinks. As she was picking up the plates and preparing to bring in the coffee, she distinctly understood a consensus had been reached. It was half past one in the afternoon when the last call came in from Des.

"Ren, they got it. The geniuses have reached a decision," Des said.

"Yeah?"

"Right. They're gonna cut off your money. Sister Theresa is sure that is what they decided. She could not understand the guys on the phone, but she heard it loud and clear in the conversation between Franklin and Verriano. You're going to get the rug pulled out from under you. Guess the way they see it is: no money for the defense of Dubois, no public trial of Dubois, no media stories, no scandal to the Church. All this dies with the Rachou verdict. The crisis will be over. Think that's how they see it."

"When are they going to do this? Cut off my money for Dubois's defense?"

"My guess is soon. They have little patience when it comes to people like you disobeying them."

As we rang off, another light was blinking on the phone. Mo stuck her head round my door. "Mr. Bendel on line three, Renon."

"Jon, how are you?"

"Fine. Fine, Renon. Look, I just stopped over to have a coffee with the bishop and Monsignor Moroux. I was hoping you would walk over and have coffee with us."

"Sure, Jon. Be there in a minute."

Julie had not yet resigned from her position in Thiberville or her religious order. Sometimes I thought she was staying on just to be close to me, to support me until the Dubois business ended. I called her at her office. I said the call was urgent and got straight to her. She came on the line and I summarized what was going down. "This is it, Julie. Ever since Des rang first thing, Mo has been making copies of the fifteen personnel files you gave me. I am going to take the bishop, Moroux and Bendel copies of those files."

"You tell them the files came from me, Ren. By the time you get out of that meeting, my resignation from the diocese will be on the desk of Moroux's secretary. This is my cue to exit stage left."

"You sure you're okay with this?"

"Rock their world, Ren. See ya tonight."

"Later."

I walked into the bishop's office carrying two large briefcases. There were smiles all around. Even Bishop Reynolds smiled and seemed to recognize me. We sat in a rectangle around a coffee table. Bendel was alone on a small sofa, the bishop and Monsignor Moroux were in wingback chairs to either side, and I was seated opposite Bendel, across the coffee table. Only Bendel glanced at the briefcases I set down beside my chair.

"Renon, the bishop has something he needs to share with you," Bendel said.

Bishop Reynolds had a huge computer printout in his lap and he tried to hand it to me twice. I kept my hands in my lap, refusing to cooperate and accept the printout. Then he tried a third time, became flustered and dropped it on the floor with a dull thud.

"Ron," the bishop began, getting my name wrong as was his wont. "We have looked over the finances – you know, the money. We don't have enough. We just—"

"Let me cut to the chase, Renon," Bendel interrupted. "As I told you at lunch after the Red Mass, I deeply admire the job you've done for this priest. I know the bishop and the monsignor share my admiration. But... but this afternoon at five is the cut-off. All fees and expenses you have incurred through this date will be promptly paid or reimbursed. That's it. After today, there'll be no more money paid to you or anyone else for the defense of Father Dubois."

Moroux said, "We just do not have the money. We have obligations to charities and works of the diocese. These things provide needed services for thousands of people. The services cannot be sacrificed for one man. Also it could set sort of a precedent, couldn't it? We could find ourselves having to pay heavy costs for any accused priest."

I said a silent prayer of thanks for Des and Sister Theresa, my Coke-float-drinking buddy at the papal nunciature, being in my life. Without them, I would have been blind-sided, totally unprepared to respond. Instead, I'd had almost the whole day to prepare for this confrontation, to think it through.

"I hope you understand this," Bendel said. "We know it means there can be no trial, and we want you to know we'll help any way we can with the district attorney. We can use political pressure from the governor on Sean Robinette or whatever else Joe Rossi can put together. We will try to get you a plea agreement that is somewhere between what you want and what Robinette wants."

"Jon, I don't want any help with Sean Robinette. And I have no problem with the diocese withdrawing all funding for the defense of Father Dubois." Pointing to Bishop Reynolds, I said, "There are some things you must understand, Jon. I am going to need the bishop in court next Wednesday, October 16. My office will issue the subpoena in the morning."

Bendel abandoned his slouch and sat up straight. "For what?"

"Wednesday is motion day on the criminal docket. I am going to have to prove Father Dubois is indigent, without any funds, in order to get indigent defense funds released to us. The Indigent Defense Board won't furnish much money, but it'll be something. To prove that this priest is without funds, I will need the testimony of his bishop that the diocese will not provide money for his defense. While I am at it, I am going to also establish that the bishop and archbishop will not pay for his medical care during incarceration, though this is the only job he ever had, and the diocese knew of his illness as long ago as his seminary days and facilitated him acting out his illness, empowered the illness and enabled his criminal life. And, Jon, I'm going to send an engraved invitation to every media representative you saw around the courthouse in Bayou Saint John at the Rachou trial."

"What are you doing, Renon? Come on," Bendel said.

"The media will send a message to all fifty thousand priests in this country that if they have any kind of problem – addiction to alcohol or prescription drugs, depression, or any other issues – when they need help, their bishop or religious superior will cut bait on them."

I stood up.

"Joe Rossi is right, Renon. You're crazy," Bendel said.

"I'm telling you something right now that you better hear. By ten tomorrow morning, you will have a letter on my desk. The letter will either confirm what you just said, that there are no funds for Dubois's defense, or the letter will confirm that the diocese will underwrite any and all costs of Dubois's defense and any cost associated with his incarceration and medical care for the balance of his life. If you send the first letter, I issue the subpoena for Bishop Reynolds. If you send the second letter, the subpoena will not be necessary."

"What makes you think...?"

"Shut up, Jon. I know you guys have been plotting on the phone all day long with Archbishop Verriano, Bishop Franklin, legal counsel in DC and those guys in New Orleans."

I opened both briefcases and piled up the personnel files on the coffee table. If I had not been standing, I would not have been able to see Jon Bendel's face over the towering stack of documents.

"Wha... wha...?" Bendel stuttered.

"If you learn of another plan to screw me or my client over, you have exactly fifteen minutes to tell me – or the media will get these other fifteen priests' files, case studies of Thiberville priests who defiled children just as Dubois did. And on top you will see my sworn affidavit recounting the advice you and Tom Quinlan gave Monsignor Moroux to sanitize files and destroy evidence you knew had been subpoenaed – advice you gave in our meeting on September 3, 1984 in the bishop's office. My affidavit also covers the events of that same evening, when I witnessed the destruction of evidence in the shredding of damaging information contained in the personnel files. And a comparison of these original files on this table with the ones in the secret archives today will prove pages were removed, evidence was destroyed – because, Jon, these copies were made before Monsignor Moroux sanitized the personnel records, before the archbishop's legal counsel, Tom Quinlan, purchased the shredding apparatus and had it delivered to Monsignor Moroux."

To Jon Bendel, I said, "Read the file on top first. It's about one Father Owen Dante Ellison, a priest formerly of this diocese who murdered two boys he sexually abused, kids named Bobby and Dwayne Richard. The account of these murders is in the handwriting of Monsignor Moroux. It's written in a clever, disguised form, but there's no question about the murders."

I turned to Moroux. "You remember the murders, Monsignor, don't you?"

Facing Bendel again, I said, "I have more evidence of the murders than is in that file. I have my own investigator's report, including an interview with the priest who murdered those boys. The murders can easily be proved beyond reasonable doubt before any jury."

"We-ell... and exactly where did youuu get these files, Mr. Chattelrault?" Monsignor Moroux drawled.

"From the former personnel director of this diocese, Sister Julianne."

"Former?"

I turned my back on them and walked out of the room, leaving the empty briefcases open on the floor.

When I got to Julie's that night, she was cooling off after her daily run.

"Have they called you?" I asked.

"God, no. They are not going to call me, Ren. Now they know I am in cahoots with you. They might say they think you are crazy, but they're scared of you. They are not going to mess with anyone who is in cahoots with you."

"Is that what we're in? Cahoots?"

"That's it. Cahoots."

"Well, let's go out to dinner then and celebrate our cahoots."

"I'm sweaty. Let me shower. I want you to take me to a nice place. You ruined my career as an employee of the diocese, my vocation as a nun, and my plans to become a saint. You owe me."

"I do owe you, but—"

"But what?"

"What exactly is cahoots?"

"No worries. Cahoots is a good thing."

71

MAKING THE DEAL

Friday morning, October 18, 1985
Bendel's Law Office, Thiberville

Mo had buzzed me at my desk at 11:30.

"Renon, Mr. Bendel called and said it's an emergency. And he needs to see you right now. In fifteen minutes."

In fifteen minutes. I knew what that meant. The Vatican was making another move against Dubois and me, and Bendel was going to spill the beans in the hope that I wouldn't make the Ellison murders public. I was blackmailing the Roman Catholic Church and it was working.

Walking from the lobby of Bendel's office toward his private suite, I almost trembled from the cold. I wondered whether the air conditioning was set low or whether maybe I had spiked a fever. No meeting with Bendel could last long, so I shook off the freezing feeling.

Bendel's door was wide open. I closed it behind me and took a chair.

"Renon, I'll come right to it. About twenty minutes ago I received a telephone call from Archbishop Donnegan in New Orleans. It was a brief conversation. First, the archbishop asked me if I could get you under control."

I smiled.

"Renon, I told the archbishop that no one could control you."

"At last," I said. "At last, after all this time, there's something we agree on."

"The archbishop told me he knows where Father Dubois is

being treated. He said he called the place yesterday and the doctor told him you had left instructions that no information about Dubois could be given to anyone within the Church. He said you have expressly forbidden Dubois from having a visit with anyone in the Church."

"Jon, to say Dubois is in an emotionally fragile state would be a gross understatement. He's a real sick man – demented is not a strong enough word to describe him – but he's not stupid. He knows no one in the Church is on his side. He's terrified of having a confrontation with someone as powerful as an archbishop."

"Well, the archbishop was pretty pissed off about you trying to block him out, but he got around it through Bishop Franklin up in Baltimore, who knows a cardinal who has friends on the board of the institution housing Dubois. Bishop Franklin called this cardinal and calls were made to board members of the facility, and—"

I sat up straight. "And what?"

"The archbishop has been granted permission to make a pastoral visit with Dubois on Monday morning."

"A pastoral visit? What's that?"

"I'm not going to lie to you. I sure the hell don't want you publicizing whatever the hell is in that O. D. Ellison file, or getting any other priests indicted here with those personnel files. I've got my hands full. Here's what I understand will happen Monday when the archbishop meets with Dubois: the archbishop told me that he will explain to Father Dubois what his obligation is to the priesthood and the Church."

"You're telling me that an archbishop is going to enter an insane asylum and tell an insane priest that his obligation to the priesthood and to the Catholic Church – to prevent scandal to the Church, to spare Rome the embarrassment of a criminal trial of a priest – that his duty is to accept a life sentence? The archbishop and everyone else around this case knows damned well Dubois will kill himself as soon the archbishop leaves, as soon as Dubois knows he will serve a life sentence. The fucking archbishop knows this. Is there no limit to what these bastards will do?"

458

"I'm only telling you what the archbishop told me."

"The archbishop wants a Catholic priest to kill himself for the Pope?"

Sunday night, October 20, 1985
Chattelrault Law Office

Whatever success I had as a lawyer was due to my understanding that justice had little to do with the facts, less to do with the law, and everything to do with leverage. I was all too aware that the law was about raw power, perceived and real, and not some rational system of order codified by a congress of individuals.

Sean had walked in my office Sunday night and I had greeted him with a cold bottle of beer, saying, "I want you on my turf for once."

From the first day I had believed that Father Francis Dubois deserved to spend twenty years in prison and to be treated for his disease. I still believed this was the right outcome.

Now I was going to play a bluffing game with the best poker player I knew. I believed that if Sean Robinette tried to convince me that there was a single parent willing to expose their child to a public trial, Sean would be running a bluff. Will Courville's suicide had been more than enough to convince any responsible parent that they could not inflict the stress of public trial testimony on their own son without placing the child at risk. That was my obvious leverage.

I was so sure of this that I believed if I had wanted Francis Dubois to be a free man, I could have just straight out paid the price of poker to see Sean's whole hand, all of his cards, and find his hand was empty – that he did not have a single prosecution witness, that he had nothing.

"Sean, we both know you don't have a single witness."

"I have the Rachou kid. He's already testified."

"If you had been in the courtroom in Bayou Saint John, you

459

would know the Rachou parents would never let that child take the stand again. On top of that, you know Kane Chaisson won't do you any favors. He'd rather see you fall on your face than try to convince the Rachou parents to have their child go through another court trial. Kane Chaisson hates you as much as you hate him, Sean. Don't kid yourself that you have a witness in the Rachou boy. You and I both know you don't have a single victim who will testify. Let's get straight to it. You can't buy my hand with a bluff."

"I have Dubois's confession he gave in the deposition under oath at Kane Chaisson's office. It's admissible."

"Yeah, you're right, Sean. You can admit it. Maybe you want to look at this first."

I handed him a pharmacology report from a research physician at a leading university in the northeast. Then I handed him a second and a third pharmacology report from eminently qualified experts that tracked the language of the first report. I gave him a package containing the curriculum vitae of the three physician experts I was prepared to call on Dubois's behalf to negate the confession. Finally, I handed him the Thiberville jail infirmary record listing the drugs Doctor Sonnier administered to Dubois before the Chaisson deposition. All three doctors were prepared to testify that nothing anyone did or said under the influence of that substantial dose of the particular medication could be relied on by anyone for any reason.

"You think this will fly?" Sean said.

"I might have never proved he was legally insane when he sexually abused those children, but I can easily prove this narcotics business. We can argue all night. Let's just end this thing, Sean."

"How d'you feel about this, Ren? Really? How do you feel busting my balls to try to save a sick bastard from a life sentence he deserves? How you feel about that?"

"Not good, Sean, not good at all. Miserable, in fact. But I'm doing my job. I'm not trying to subvert justice. Give him twenty years. Twenty years is a long damned time. Let the kids grow up. Let him get medical help while imprisoned."

Sean had not taken a sip of his beer. He carefully set it on my desk, on top of a file folder. "Well, this whole thing is making me feel sick. I wanted to do the right thing, but it does not seem like the right thing's gonna happen here," Sean said.

"It's all we can do. Twenty years. And Dubois serves his sentence in the Hannover institution in New Jersey, where he can get medical help."

Sean nodded and started to leave my office without saying goodbye.

"I wanted to do the right thing," I said, "and I'm still trying to do the right thing. The kids should not be made to testify. Those children should have twenty years to work on healing, surviving what this monster Dubois has inflicted on them. And Dubois should receive intensive treatment while incarcerated so there's a chance he's different when he's released."

I walked over to my credenza, opened two doors on the bottom and pulled out a huge file bearing a title scrawled with a heavy black pen: "Father O. D. Ellison". As I walked toward Sean with the file in my hands, I said, "You want to right a wrong, Sean? Ya wanna see justice done? Read these files – a Diocesan file and Johnny Wilcox's investigative file. You know Wilcox from his days on the police force. He'll cooperate with your office any way you want. Sean, just read these files. This fucking priest killed two boys in Willow Springs when it was still in the Diocese of Thiberville. Willow Springs is still in your legal jurisdiction. There's no time limitations that run on murder. Put this fucker away. That would be some justice."

I laid the heavy files in Sean Robinette's hands.

Monday morning, October 21, 1985
Chattelrault Law Office

It was early, 8:30 in Louisiana, when Mo opened my door. "It's him on line four."

"Hello," I said.

"Good morning, Renon. This is Monsignor Moroux. It seems we have a problem."

"Yes?"

"We-ell, it seems our archbishop is in New Jersey this morning at the Stalder Institute to pay Father Francis a pastoral visit."

"Umhuh."

"We-ell, the situation we are faced with is... it seems Father Francis is no longer at the facility and no one there has any idea where he is."

I said nothing.

"Renon?"

"Yes, I'm here."

"The records show that Father Francis checked out AMA – against medical advice – at four fifteen Saturday afternoon. They only have a court order signed by you, the DA and Judge Labat authorizing his release into your custody. There is no indication of where Father Francis was taken by you."

"That's correct, Monsignor."

"We-ell, Renon, will you please tell me where Father Francis is?"

"He's in another secure, lock-down facility under a name other than his own and there are strict instructions that no one associated with the Roman Catholic Church is to have any access to him."

"Could you please hold? The archbishop is calling again."

"Okay."

About three minutes passed and Moroux came back on the line. "Renon, our archbishop wants you to know that he is not angry with you and—"

I cut Moroux off. "Monsignor, I really don't care what the archbishop feels or thinks about me. His opinion of me is no business of mine."

I could hear Moroux tearing open a pack of cigarettes, lighting one, inhaling and exhaling deeply.

"Renon, I'm trying to mediate a resolution to this problem. All the archbishop wants is a chance to pay a pastoral visit on Father Francis. He wants me to ask you where and when, with your permission, he may visit with Father Francis."

All weekend I knew this moment would come, that this question would be asked of me, and my answer had been formulated after a lot of thought on a southbound flight Sunday morning.

"Given what I know about the Catholic religion and Francis Dubois's life, I think, in the absence of a perfect act of contrition, Francis Dubois is going to spend eternity in hell. The archbishop can visit him there when he himself arrives."

72

A FAUX FINISH

Monday October 28, 1985
Thiberville Parish Courthouse

I had had Francis Dubois's eldest brother and two detectives accompany my client when he flew Philadelphia to Atlanta, avoiding Louisiana airports. They drove him from Atlanta to the Thiberville parish prison under the cover of darkness, much like the first time he had been brought home for a court appearance, more than a year before.

Matt had cleared his calendar for the week. "No one with the diocese is going to go near his prison cell after he's sentenced. I want to be there for him, for pastoral support. Can you arrange this with the jailer? I can spend the days with Francis and the evenings with you and your family, if that's okay?" Yet again I was amazed at Matt's capacity for kindness.

The night before the sentencing, I received a call from Des telling me Matt had a problem with his neck. He had been admitted to a hospital in Washington and surgery was planned for the next day.

This time we were in the large courtroom because there were so many media people present. It was standing room only. I looked over the courtroom. In the last row, against the wall, I saw Francis Dubois's parents, Iris and Willifred.

There would be no public trial of the priest. It was the result I wanted, the result the Vatican wanted.

To meet the expectations of the victims' parents, the press, and

464

the voters who had elected Sean, we had written a sentencing document that implied Dubois had no option but to serve his time at Hannover House in New Jersey, rather than in a prison operated by the Louisiana department of corrections. It stated that he would receive medical care at Hannover House, and would continue to take Depo-Provera.

In writing the plea agreement, however, Sean and I had unwittingly laid the foundations for a legal free-for-all that could conceivably play out to our disadvantage in the future. The truth was that, legally, Dubois had a choice. At that time no Louisiana judge had the authority to sentence a defendant to a New Jersey penal facility. Nor could a judge mandate that a prisoner receive medication of any kind, especially something as controversial as Depo-Provera, the drug the media erroneously referred to as chemical castration.

The court proceedings that ended the criminal prosecution of Father Francis Dubois took less than five minutes.

Sean Robinette, Francis Dubois and I stood in front of Judge Labat, very close to the bench. We all stuck to an agreed-upon script. Dubois entered the plea of guilty to a portion of the indictment. The judge asked Dubois whether he was taking injections of Depo-Provera and whether he intended to continue this medication. Dubois answered "Yes" to both questions. The judge asked Dubois whether he was presently under medical care and intended to remain under medical care, and again the response was affirmative.

Judge Eloi Labat then imposed a sentence of twenty years in prison without the possibility of suspension, pardon or parole. And the judge approved Hannover House as an appropriate site to serve the sentence.

After the sentencing, Dubois was returned to the Thiberville correctional facility, where he was housed in a comfortable single cell in the medical wing. There were no other prisoners in the clinic.

"Can you come to see me tomorrow, Renon?" Dubois asked.

"No, I'm sorry. Mo will come. I need some time to myself, some time to rest. I know the waiting was not easy for you, but the work I was doing down here was hard on me. I'm beat."

Feed & Seed Store, Amalie

Scheduled broadcasts on local television and radio stations were interrupted by the announcement of Dubois's sentence. After they heard the news, Elray "Poppa" Vidros and Tommy Wesley Rachou drove to the Feed & Seed store south of Amalie. When they walked in, Wiley Arceneaux nodded to a clerk to watch the counter and walked out the back door with Vidros and Rachou following him.

Poppa Vidros spit his whole chaw of tobacco against the trunk of an oak tree. "Dead and buried. That's where this Father Dubois should be. And this fucking priest gets a pass. Twenty years – twenty – and then what happens when he gets out of prison? He'll rape more kids."

Tommy Rachou said, "I don't think there was nothing the DA could do. There wasn't nobody I knew who was gonna let their son go into that courtroom to testify in Thiberville. My boy did it once in Bayou Saint John. I didn't want him to go through that again. There wasn't nothing anybody could do, I reckon."

"Where's the justice?" Vidros asked.

"The bishop wasn't even charged with nothing," said Wiley. "That's the thing that gets me. The priest only gets twenty years and the bishop's robes don't even get dirty."

Poppa Vidros growled, "You read all the shit that came out. The bishop knew all about that fucking priest when he sent him down here."

"He sent that priest here because he doesn't care what happens to our kids. We're a poor parish of dumb people. That's what he thinks about us," Tommy Rachou said.

Wiley said, "I know we're gonna talk about this again tomorrow morning. We're gonna talk about this for a long time, I guess, but we ain't gonna change nothing."

Tommy slapped the porch railing. "All I know is there's lots of people around the world who believe the Catholic Church is the one true Church of Jesus Christ. We know better. Hell, if Christ came back down here today, he'd be with the children and he would not go near those bastard clerics. If the world ever finds out what we know, they'll know different about the Church too."

After a long silence, Poppa spoke. "My sawed-off shotgun is still loaded since I first learned what that priest did. And – make book – it's gonna stay loaded till I unload it in his ass."

73

AFTERWARDS

Friday November 1, 1985
Thiberville

When the criminal case against Francis Dubois ended, I felt the loss of everything that ever mattered to me.

Kate had decided to move with our children to New Orleans to be closer to her aging parents. Whatever religious faith I had possessed had been killed off by the very institution I once believed in. The country place in Coteau that I loved so much would soon be empty and then sold. My children would be hours away from me. At my core, something told me I could no longer continue to work in the law or live in Thiberville, the place where my family had resided for generations.

The day after the Dubois case ended, I was completely exhausted, deeply depressed, and riddled with doubt about the role I had played. I was also ailing physically, running a fever so high that it scared Kate when she dropped in to see me at my town house. She insisted I move to the cottage in Coteau, where she could look in on me. A physician friend of ours came out to see us in the afternoon, examined me, and called for an ambulance.

Within hours, I was in the hospital and that night I underwent abdominal surgery as I was bleeding internally. When I was out of the recovery suite, the surgeon said he could not believe I had even been able to stand upright the past few months. I shrugged and honestly said, "I hurt sometimes, you know, bad. But I got through it with willpower during the day and whiskey at night." His caution was that I better make some changes in my life, reduce the stress. He said I'd had a really close call.

Kate stayed at the hospital while the children were in school. By the third day, the boss of the family, Sasha, was getting antsy, demanding to see her papa. The hospital floor I was on was off limits to children under twelve, so her mom brought her up through the stairwell, avoiding the nurses' station near the elevators. Sasha slowly walked into the room, looked at me, looked at her mom, then gave us her appraisal. "He looks okay to me."

"I think he looks great, Sash," Kate said.

Sasha touched my face. "He could stand a shave. Don't you think?"

Growling, I said, "You two are talking about me like I'm laid out in a casket. I won't have any more of this."

Sasha jumped on a chair and flew toward me.

"Noooooooooooo," I protested. A near catastrophe was averted when I caught her and set her on the side of the bed. She insisted on looking at the bandages, tubes, and IV hookups. Then she went back to the entrance area of the room, saying, "I brought you just the right thing."

She had brought her favorite stuffed animal, Disco Duck. She put him by my pillow. "Disco will make sure you do everything the doctors tell you to do. Except one thing. There is one thing you don't have to do. I'm telling you, Papa, it doesn't matter what they say about eating all your food. Ya know, I've been in this hospital. The Jell-o here tastes like plastic. You don't have to eat any."

"I'll remember that, but I think I'm going home in a few days."

"No worries, Papa. I'll let you have Disco at home too. All the way to... lemme see. How many days are there till Sunday?"

Monday November 4, 1985
Thiberville

One night when Julie was in the hospital room, she pulled a chair close to the bed. She appeared tentative, not herself. Like Sasha, Julie enjoyed touching my scruffy face. "I don't want anything to

469

happen to you," she said. She started to cry. "I can't lose you from my life."

I held her hand. "I know, Julie. We're in cahoots, whatever that is."

When the ten o'clock news came on, the lead story had footage of an old man in a black suit, handcuffed and shackled, being guided by deputies into the local jail. The voiceover from the reporter explained, "These pictures show former Thiberville diocesan priest Father O. D. Ellison being escorted into the jail this afternoon, where he was to be held on charges involving two murders. Though the district attorney's office has issued no statement, sources close to the investigation have told us that the priest confessed in the presence of the DA and his chief investigator in a Florida retirement home where he was living. The latest word is that Father Ellison has been moved to University Hospital after suffering a massive heart attack."

I switched off the TV. Neither Julie nor I spoke about the news story on Ellison. She told me she was beginning to pack up and would begin the drive to her parents' home in Virginia soon.

"This is it?" I asked. "Goodbye?"

"No, I will not say goodbye until you are well enough to come by the apartment for a meal. I'm going to cook something. No pizza. A real Italian meal."

"No pizza? It's a deal."

Early November, 1985
Coteau

When I was released from the hospital, Kate insisted I go back to the guest cottage in Coteau. She looked after me and I recovered well from the surgery, but my depression hung on. I didn't know if it was some kind of post-surgery reaction or a result of having depleted all my resources during the Dubois saga. There were periods when I could not sleep at all, and times when I could do nothing but sleep. Kate took the phone out of the cottage because she wanted me to rest, rather than try to practice law over the phone. I felt isolated, but in a way it was a comforting feeling.

Kate told me Des McDougall called her every day. It turned out our good friend Matt was also out of commission. He was still in hospital, having been admitted with a debilitating neck problem on the morning Dubois was sentenced. The next day he had undergone an anterior cervical fusion, a routine operation involving a bone graft. Apparently the donor site for the bone graft was his hip and an infection set in there. He was now in an isolation unit where no visitors were admitted. It was hard to think of that vibrant man in a hospital bed.

One afternoon when I could tell Kate was holding something from me, I pressed her. "I'm sorry, Ren," she said. "I didn't want to tell you, but last night Des told me they found Matt has some kind of cancer. I'm so sorry."

I lay in bed in the cottage, trying to remember the things that had happened since I first walked into the Old Bishop's House, a lunch that now seemed like it had taken place years ago rather than fourteen months earlier.

I tried to remember things. Rather than the memories rolling like a reel of film, they presented like a thousand snapshots scattered in the recesses of my mind. I saw different chancery buildings, faces of bishops, monsignors, and lawyers I'd encountered around the country. I saw pedophile priests, and families of priests, faces of child victims and their families. I couldn't remember which faces belonged in which places, and my memory had no audio. Things I'd said, things they'd said, were all lost. It was a memory of motion. I had been in almost constant motion. I could remember some stark, still images, but the journey was a blur.

All I knew for sure about my recent, extended journey was that I had failed. I had failed the thousands, probably hundreds of thousands, of little children whose names I would never know. The Church was not going to change until the crisis engulfed them and the fires of the scandal scarred the walls of the Vatican itself. It would take many years for Catholic victims to find the courage to stand up to the formidable, intimidating power of their Church.

In the afternoons, Kate would come out to the cottage with a list of people who had called to check on me, some of whom wanted to visit with me. My brother, Mo, Julie, Des and Sean called every day. Soon she gave me the phone back, and I was taking calls and taking walks around the pond, getting stronger and laughing again with Sasha, Jake and Shelby. Sasha was still fishing with her popcorn-bacon combo because she could not bear to touch a worm. I spent hours on the cottage porch, sitting in a rocking chair, watching her fish.

74

A LAST HOPE

Wednesday night, November 20, 1985
Coteau

I walked over to the wood pile and, mindful of my stitches, gingerly piled one log over another until I had the makings of a good fire. The wood had been soaked by a long afternoon downpour, which had also canceled Sasha's daily fishing rodeo. It took time for the logs to catch fire.

Sitting in a rocking chair by the fire on the banks of the pond, I cleared my head and focused on my last hope.

I thought about my last hope until the fire burned to ashes. Still I believed it was possible that in the end, all the pain, suffering and tragedy I felt I was partly responsible for would not be for nothing. I had a plan no one knew about except two physicians at Hannover House and the members of Francis Dubois's family.

Every pedophile priest I had met had said in one way or other that his actions were a matter of compulsion, not a choice. The medical volumes I had read on the subject, and the consultations I'd had with experts in the field, shed little light on the causes of the disorder. I began to wonder whether it might be possible to identify and treat people like Dubois before they started attacking children. Was the etiology founded in psychology, where the perpetrator had himself been a victim of sexual abuse, or had suffered some other trauma in his formative years? Or could such behavior be physiologically rooted – organic, perhaps genetic, even a part of one's chemical composition, something that could be diagnosed early on?

Francis Dubois was from a large family. One sibling, his brother Walt, was a self-confessed pedophile. I had made countless trips up to Morgan's Hope over the summer and during my many private conversations with Dubois's siblings it became clear that none of them were aware that Walt shared this trait with Francis. Each one of the other siblings assured me that they were heterosexual and had never been attracted to a child or acted out with a child.

I wanted to see if a series of physical and psychological tests might somehow turn up something that matched Walt to Francis, while at the same time set both of them apart from their siblings and parents. Dubois's parents and siblings agreed that, once the criminal case was resolved, they would all go to Hannover House, or any other sexual disorders clinic I directed them to, and submit to any such tests the doctors prescribed. Francis Dubois was aware of my plans.

My hope was that something positive would come from all of this, that something important would be learned that would make children safer from sexual predators. Soon Dubois would be incarcerated at Hannover and the testing could begin. This was my last hope.

Monday December 2, 1985
Chattelrault Law Office

As soon as I walked back into the office, Mo handed me a document whose embossed gold letterhead identified the writer as a Judge Garret Livingston, chief judge of an appeals court in New Orleans.

Judge Livingston's letter was brief:

Sir,
I have telephoned your office five times since Father Francis Dubois was sentenced on October 28. Your failure to return

*my calls amounts to disrespect bordering on insolence. I
expect you shall telephone me when you receive this.*

G. *Livingston*

"Mo, you know who this is?"

"No, but he sounded like a jackass on the telephone."

"Well, I think he is a jackass. I've never met him, but I've heard.
He's the most powerful judge in the state. He was once considered
for the US Supreme Court. Put in a call to the judge."

"Okay, Ren. Hey, don't be insolent."

When the judge came on the line, I offered reasons of health
for my failure to return his phone calls.

The judge said, "Okay. Let us understand. Henceforth, when I
make a call to you, your secretary will locate you. Even if you are
in surgery, she will locate you. There will be no more of this.
Understood?"

"Yes, sir."

The judge plowed on. "Father Dubois's family members are
friends of mine and I want to help. I have spoken with the bishop
in Thiberville, the archbishop in New Orleans, the Louisiana
secretary of the department of corrections, and I have talked to
the governor about moving Father Dubois out of that sheriff's jail
now and putting him in the best possible prison in the state. The
move will happen this week."

His contacting me was an astonishing breach in judicial ethics.
All I said was, "Yes, sir, I understand."

"Good. Goodbye, young man."

The truth was I did not understand the judge at all. From the
beginning, I had an ironclad agreement with Dubois that no third
party would ever be involved in his legal affairs. The idea of a man
in Judge Livingston's position involving himself in the affairs of a
notorious criminal, a pedophile, was beyond the reach of my
intellect or imagination.

Thiberville Jail

Dubois was stretched out on his bunk in his single cell in the medical wing, reading a book on bow hunting. The guard unlocked the door and let me in. Dubois snapped the book closed.

"Hi, Renon. You look great. Looks like you recovered from surgery well. You rested yet?"

"Think so."

"Mo has come by every day."

I handed him Judge Livingston's letter.

Dubois glanced at the letterhead and laid the stationery on his bunk. "Yeah. He's a very nice man. He wants to help. He's getting me moved to a prison by Baton Rouge that he believes is perfect for me. He's a close friend of the warden there."

"What are you talking about? What in the hell are you talking about? You're going to Hannover House. I fought like hell to get Hannover set up for you. You are going to get treated while you are incarcerated. There's no treatment in the Louisiana prison system. You know all of your family members have agreed to be examined, tested, and evaluated at Hannover. You agreed to this too. Hannover is your one chance to do something meaningful with your life. It's your only chance at redemption. I almost killed myself to get you this chance. I pushed things so far, so hard, that Will Courville committed suicide."

Dubois looked at me impassively, almost as if he had heard nothing. Then he said, "Renon, don't get so mad. Let me go to this place the judge has set up first, okay? Let me see how I like it there."

"Look, I can't make you go to Hannover. Francis, if you stay in the state system, the Depo-Provera injections will stop the first week. You will never receive any kind of treatment. You will always be the way you are."

"Don't feel that way, Renon. I will never forget what you did for me. There aren't many decisions that are mine to make. Where I serve my sentence is my choice, according to the plea agreement papers we signed."

476

"That's true, but Francis, why in the hell didn't you tell me about this judge being involved in your affairs before you were sentenced? We had a deal. No one was to be involved in your affairs but me. This judge has talked to everyone. He's talked to the governor."

"He's an important man."

"I know he's important. He's chief judge on an important court."

"I mean... the judge is important in the Church. He knows everyone in the Church, even people in the Vatican. He's a Knight of Malta."

I figured a Knight of Malta must be a member of an ancient Christian order, like the Knights of Columbus, but I sure as hell wasn't going to ask Dubois.

"How long has this Knight of Malta been involved in your affairs?"

"He was on the visitors' list at the Saint Martin Center in New Hampshire, and I put him on the list at the Stalder Institute. Every place I've been. We're old friends."

"Judges don't get involved in the affairs of a state prisoner. And they are not usually friends with people who have your lifestyle either."

"It is none of your business. It's my business. The judge is my friend," Dubois said with authority.

"Okay, Francis. I'm sure Mo will be here after Mass today."

In a very detached way, almost as if Francis knew this was the last conversation we would ever have, he said, "You take care of yourself, Renon."

"You belong in Hannover House, Francis."

Francis Dubois became more assertive. "Don't tell me where I belong. No one asked you to give up twenty years of your life. I belong in the most comfortable environment I can find. The judge is going to get me sent to the best prison for me. He's sure I'll like this prison."

I stood quietly, not knowing what I wanted to say to him. Now

I knew definitively that no good could ever come of this. Dubois and his family would not be tested. I felt like I had been a pawn in a game played by a pedophile and someone in the shadows whose presence I never even knew about, a powerful Catholic judge.

I had a flashback, remembering an all-night conversation in a New Orleans hotel on the same night I met Dubois's family. At once, I knew I should have listened to Joe Rossi long ago in that hotel room and pled Dubois to a life sentence; ended it all. Maybe Dubois might have killed himself, but Will Courville would be alive. Whatever damage and destruction I had inflicted on others, and whatever destruction I had visited on my own life had all been in vain.

I was certain this was the last time I would ever have to see Francis Dubois and I took a good look before I walked out of the jail cell. Dubois stared at me and slowly a smirk formed in the corners of his mouth, that same expression I first saw in the Saint Martin treatment center in Deerfield, the expression I had seen so many times. The expression that told me Francis Dominick Dubois knew something I didn't know. The last image I had of him was a half-smile beneath flat, dull eyes.

75

A CALL ON THE HEART

Tuesday January 7, 1986
Thiberville

I had resigned as Dubois's legal counsel the same day I said goodbye to him in the Thiberville jail.

According to a television news piece I saw a few days later, Dubois had been transferred to the Louisiana state department of corrections that same week and was now housed at Riverbend Prison near Baton Rouge.

The TV reporter mentioned that until recently the Riverbend facility had been a place that only housed juveniles and that a significant part of the population was still juveniles. *This is the prison the Knight of Malta, Judge Livingston, thought was perfect for his friend Francis,* I thought. *A place where the warden is a close friend of the judge. Dubois would be locked up with hundreds of juveniles.* The news made me sick in the same way I had been sick so many times during this saga.

During the first week of January, rain fell for four days in near freezing temperatures. The high humidity and frigid air settled the coldness in my bones. I rushed from the parking garage to my office. I wasn't out of my raincoat when Mo said, "I'm dialing Father McDougall right now."

I had last spoken with Des about Matt's medical condition on Sunday and knew things were not good. I sank into my chair and watched the lights on the phone.

Mo buzzed.

"Des?"

"Yeah, buddy, you okay?"

"Fine."

"Good, 'cause our comrade's in trouble. Barbara called from Hope House and asked that I phone you. He wants to see you. You have to get up here if you want to see him and tell him goodbye."

"My God, he's dying?"

"Yes."

"I'll clear things here and be there tomorrow," I said.

"Barb says if we want to see Matt, it better be tonight. They think he's going fast."

"Let me go, Des. I'll call. Mo will call. Somebody will call and let you know when I'll be there."

Washington DC

Washington's National Airport was deserted when I de-planed. Halfway down the concourse I saw Des coming toward me in his priest suit, carrying a big briefcase. We hugged and Des pulled me into a men's restroom.

"Get outta your clothes."

"What?"

Des opened his briefcase and pulled out some clothing. "It's a priest costume. Trick or treat, Ren. Tonight you're gonna be Father Chattelrault."

"What?"

"Come on. Get outta your clothes and put this on. No visitors except clergy can get into the hospital after nine. We're going in as priests."

I started laughing. "Look, I have brown shoes."

"What do priests know about fashion?"

We walked right past the security guards at the check-in point in the hospital lobby and rode an elevator to the eighth floor. A nurse led us to a small, empty room and gave us each something like a paper space suit, a see-through outfit that covered us from our shoes to our heads and masked our mouths and noses. She showed us the door of Matt's room and cautioned us, "Do not touch the patient." I was afraid to enter first. Following Des into the room, I heard Matt's labored breathing. It seemed he had lost 40 per cent of his body weight. We stood there in silence for a while. Then Matt opened his eyes. He looked at me and then turned to Des. He closed his eyes and tried to smile.

Matt spoke in a soft, scratchy voice. "I'm dreaming, right. Tell me Ren is not wearing a Roman collar."

"That's the program tonight," Des said.

I kind of laughed. "Yeah. I'm a good guy who is with the program. Weird, right?"

Matt opened his eyes wide. "Thanks for coming. I asked Barb to find you rascals. I'm dying and I wanted to tell you something before I cross over."

We both nodded.

"I'm not too sure of anything, but I'm pretty sure of one thing."

We nodded again.

"I love you guys."

Des bit his lip. I did not have that kind of control. I began to cry.

Matt put his hand on my arm. "It's okay, Ren. I'm okay. You'll be okay."

"It's not fair."

Matt turned to Des and asked him to crank the bed up a bit. Looking directly at me, Matt continued, "You're right, Ren. It's not fair. But what you don't understand is that it's not fair to you. You're being left behind."

I nodded.

"Remember me like I was with you guys in Louisiana..." He coughed and continued, "Eating jambalaya, crawfish, seafood gumbo."

I smiled and wiped my tears on the sleeve of the paper hospital suit.

Des spoke. "Is there something we can do for you?"

"Yes. I think some of the people on this floor think this room will be empty by sunrise. I think they're wrong. I never died before, but I feel too strong to die just yet. This is the best I've felt since the last surgery, whenever that was."

"What can we do?"

"Two things. Please. There are some nuns next to that big ugly red-brick church on 16th. They make big wooden rosaries. Could you pick one up for me? The feeling in my hands…"

Des said, "Sure. What else?"

"Would you come see me separately tomorrow?"

We nodded. A nurse came in. "Excuse me, Fathers. I think that's enough."

Des started out of the room behind the nurse. I took Matt's hand in my gloved hand. I leaned over the bed and touched his forehead softly with my other hand, stroking his hair back, remembering that he once told me about how important the human touch is to a dying person.

Matt's eyes smiled. "Pray for me, Father."

76

PRAYER AND PROMISES

Tuesday night, January 7, 1986
Washington DC

I called Julie at her parents' home in Virginia and told her what was going on with Matt. After talking with her, I reflected on my relationship with Matt. We had worked together so intensely for so many months in so many different locations on things so important to us. I tried to distill Matt to a single characteristic, his gentleness. I wished to have some of his gentleness.

Julie arrived at the hotel shortly after I'd phoned her.

"Hey," I said. "What are you doing here?"

"I felt I had to come. To be... for... well, hell, we're in cahoots, remember?"

I smiled. "I guess we are."

"What do you want to do?" she asked.

"Get a drink, a big tall drink. That's what I want. And then I want another drink."

She shook her head slowly from side to side. "Not now. Not this time. You're going to have to go through this. You're going to have to feel this."

She propped up the pillows on one of the beds and motioned for me to settle there. She took the other bed and we began to talk. We were still talking when the sun came up. We talked about Matt dying, Will Courville's suicide, my divorce from Kate and my separation from my children. For a long time I talked about the strong recommendations I had received from a couple of doctors that I should leave the stress of the legal profession.

"There can't be many things more stressful than a law practice," she said.

I nodded slowly. "But it's what I am, who I am. Without it..."

Wednesday January 8, 1986
Washington DC

At sunrise, Julie ordered room-service breakfast for us and commanded me to shower, shave and change into clean clothes. She was taking charge of me and I was comfortable being in her care.

"I want you to stay here with me until I fly home," I said.

"I can't. You know—"

"You can."

"No."

"Why?"

"Technically, I am still a nun."

"Technically, you're still a nun? Well, technically, I'm still a married man."

"Those technicalities are important, Ren. We may be in cahoots, but we can't be any more than that."

"I tell you what then, Julie. If that's the case, this being in cahoots is not all it's cracked up to be."

She reached up and wrapped her arms around me and pulled me close, holding me tightly. Then she stepped back and put a finger to her lips, signaling me not to speak. She whispered, "One day it will be right. One day. Be patient with me, with yourself. One day, Ren."

Then she was out of the door.

Des had a full day Wednesday, so we agreed I would pick up the rosary and visit Matt in the afternoon. This time I went to the hospital as myself without a priest costume, and I donned the paper space suit before entering his room.

Matt was delighted with the rosary. I told him how my father said the rosary in French and I confessed that I did not know the order of the prayers. Matt taught me. We prayed the rosary together. Then he asked me to have a seat.

I adjusted his bed so that we were face to face.

"Ren, you want to know what I prayed for?"

"Yeah."

"I prayed for a short remission, enough good health to last a week."

"You shoot low, Matt. I prayed for a miracle."

"Ren, I think… Heck, I don't know. I might have dreamed this. My assistant at Hope House, Barb, said I had some bizarre reactions to some of the medicines. She said I was hallucinating for a while. But I think I remember Cardinal Wolleski coming by sometime. I can't remember time anymore. I've been in here so long it doesn't feel like I was ever anywhere else."

Matt was suddenly short of breath. I waited for him to resume.

"I want you to call Cardinal Wolleski and check this out. I believe he was sitting right where you are now. You know he gets a ride to Rome every couple of months on a private jet. As I remember, he told me he would put me on the plane to Rome with him and open the Vatican doors I want opened, if I could get well enough to make the trip."

"Can you make a trip like that?"

"If I can go, Ren, will you go with me? I want only you to go with me."

I nodded.

"The cardinal can't take care of me. I think I'll have to have someone with me who can take care of me. Will you do that?"

"I'll do anything you want me to do. Is there anything else I can do for you?"

"Boy, I tell ya, this dying is some deal. Everyone wants to do things for you. Yes, there are some things I really want you to do for me."

"Okay."

"You sure?" Matt asked.

"Sure."

"Leave tomorrow. Go home," Matt said.

"Okay."

"Let's say our goodbyes. When I die, don't come back up here for the funeral. Spend the day of the funeral with your children. If I don't die soon and we can go to Rome, we'll go. Either way you must stop doing this work with the Church. The Church won't change until someone puts a gun to the head of every cardinal in Rome. This work is gonna kill you."

I nodded.

"One more thing," Matt said.

"Yes?"

"Your girl, Sasha, loves animals."

I nodded.

"When this is over. When I'm gone…"

I nodded again.

"Bring my dog Mozart to Sasha."

77

A CONFIDENCE AND A CONVERSATION

Friday March 14, 1986
Thiberville

I got my miracle. Matt rallied and was released from the hospital. We talked on the phone every day. He said his condition was complicated and hard to treat, but that he was responding well to experimental medications.

Most of Matt's calls came at night, but this Friday morning his call came early. "How do you feel about Roma?"

"You wanna go to Café Roma? I can come tomorrow."

"No. Italy. Cardinal Wolleski leaves Sunday evening. They'll have a bed on the plane for me. The plane will stay on the ground in Rome for as long as we need to be there, and then they will fly us directly back to Washington. Wolleski tells me he has my appointment set up with the cardinals I need to see at the Vatican."

"Which cardinals?"

"Kruger, Bertolini and Paginini. I wanna dump everything in their lap. Will ya work up the list of all the priests we have knowledge of – their names, their bishops' names, the dioceses they are in. The list ought to be over five hundred, maybe over six hundred by now."

"I already have that list done. Mo typed it months ago and kept updating it."

"I'm going to put a time bomb in their laps. I want the name of every priest, his bishop, and the approximate date complaints of child sex abuse were made against him."

"I have it," I said.

Saturday March 15, 1986
Williams Crossing, Virginia

I arrived in Williams Crossing Saturday afternoon. Matt was alone with Mozart in the den. He had experienced a drastic weight loss and his face had a strange pallor I had never seen in anyone else. He was sitting in a large leather chair with his feet on an ottoman. I made a fire in the fireplace and sat across from him.

"You look—"

Raising a hand, he signaled me to silence. "Please. In med school, I saw cadavers that looked better than me. Ren, only Barb here at Hope House knows what I'm about to tell you." Matt paused. "I'm dying of AIDS."

"How? How did—"

"I'm gay, Ren. I contracted HIV sexually."

I nodded like I understood, but I understood nothing. I never knew Matt Patterson was gay. I tried to digest the news, formulate an appropriate response.

"You okay, Ren?"

"No. Yeah. I don't know what to say."

There are a lot of moments in our lives that there is no way to prepare for, impossible to rehearse, but I had never experienced one like this.

"I don't think there's an appropriate response, Ren. Are you scared? You saw how cautious the nurses were with me. They were afraid to touch me, to let anyone touch me."

I knew I was scared I would not be able to adequately care for him.

Matt smiled and went on. "You needed to know this in case something happens on the trip. You need to know what to do."

"You're gonna tell me what I need to know, right?"

"Sure. There's not much. We'll have some pretty powerful dope with us and I'll teach you how to give an injection. If I get out of hand, you'll just knock me out."

"What if... what if... you know...?"

488

"What if I die on you in Rome? It won't matter to me anymore. Do what you think is right."

"Whoa! I have no idea what's right."

Matt laughed. "Toss me in the Tiber River. I don't care. Here's the thing that's important about when I die. I am not the first Catholic priest to die of AIDS. I've had patients die of AIDS in Hope House and there have been other priests who've died of AIDS. The cause of their deaths is just another secret the Church has hidden. The cause of my death is not going to be some dark secret. I don't want to lie about my death. I want you to prepare one of those lawyer papers I can sign, an affidavit. When I die, if the Church tries to hide the cause of my death, then give it to the press. I want the world to know that AIDS is not something that exists only among needle junkies in New York or young gay men in San Francisco. I want them to know this Catholic priest died of AIDS."

I nodded my assent. I was staying silent, sitting as an audience, allowing a dying man to have a full say. If he wanted to talk, I was going to listen.

Matt coughed, sipped some juice, and continued. "I am not ashamed to die of AIDS and I am not ashamed of how I contracted it. I'm not ashamed of how I have lived my life. I know I have lived a good life."

"If that's what you want, I'll prepare the affidavit tonight," I said.

"I am a man, a priest, and I am gay. I contracted this disease somewhere along the way. That's the truth and this thing called Holy Mother Church will have to deal with it, and so will all the Catholics who read about it."

I looked at Matt in amazement. His body was gone, but his mind and his will were unaffected.

I said, "I have the document you asked me to put together. It lists way over five hundred priests who have had complaints made against them. It covers over half the states. I listed the names of the priests and the bishops' names as well."

"Good, I will put that in Rome's lap. Then let them deny there is a massive problem, a crisis, now." He leaned back in the chair, perspiring heavily, breathing deeply. "I get so tired."

"Shouldn't you go to bed?"

He nodded weakly. "You will have to help me. Go to the counter and get some gloves out of the box and put a gown over yourself. I have sores on my legs, my left arm and my chest. Be careful not to touch the sores."

Moving Matt to his bedroom took some doing. As he stood at the edge of the bed, he fainted and fell into my arms. I could not believe how light he was. I picked him up and put him in bed the way I would Sasha, tucking him in. Mozart had been right behind us. He peered over the bed, watching Matt for a few minutes and then curled up on the floor next to him.

Monday March 17, 1986
Rome

Matt was strong when we checked into Hotel Hassler Monday morning. I joined him on the terrace. He joked about whether Des was celebrating Saint Patrick's Day back in the States. Then Matt pointed to carriages near the Spanish Steps. "We ought to take a carriage ride tonight on the way to the restaurant."

"I'm wiped out, jet-lagged, and you want to go out to dinner?"

"Cardinal Wolleski invited us. We're going."

"Okay. You're the boss."

"I studied here for a year, a long time ago, loved the city. I'm now seeing everything for the last time. I know this. It's a lucky thing to die this way."

"Lucky?"

"I think it's a fortunate thing to know you are dying, seeing everything for the last time."

"Do you?"

"I don't know, but you overlay any memories you may have of

490

the way it was at other times in your life. The vision becomes more textured, a bit blurry, and then clearer than you can imagine. The feelings of dying are rich feelings, intense."

I nodded, not in understanding, but rather in acknowledgment of what he said.

"Ancient places like Rome, old walls, old buildings, make us realize how inconsequential, how unimportant we are. What is our life measured against thousands of years? The things we do in life do count, but they don't matter. Everything counts, nothing matters."

"Everything counts, nothing matters?"

"That's it, Ren. Remember that."

The proprietor of Ristorante Rinaldi on Piazza Navona was waiting for us when we opened the door of the crowded restaurant. I gave Giovanni Rinaldi our names and he led us to a semi-private area at the rear of the big room. We passed a pianist, violinist and heavy-set, bearded singer. Cardinal Wolleski was waiting for us at the table, wearing a thick sweater. Giovanni hovered over us and took our drink orders.

Cardinal Wolleski turned to Matt. "Your meeting for tomorrow morning with cardinals Hans Kruger, Gregorio Bertolini and Niccolo Paginini is set for ten o'clock. My friend, Monsignor Josef Majeski, has arranged it. Meet him at the Porta Angelica."

The dinner at Ristorante Rinaldi was memorable. Matt led the old cardinal down memory lane. Wolleski told stories about smuggling Jews onto ships during the war. And he told us in great detail about his first years in Rome and his romance at the ice-cream stand with Isabella Rinaldi. It was a beautiful story. Twice he had us get up and walk with him to different corners of the restaurant, first to see the small coat closet that had once been the ice-cream stand, and then to show us a photograph of Isabella dressed as Charlie Chaplin.

The ruggedly handsome cardinal was stirring his coffee as he looked across the room at the photograph of the grinning girl. "To have loved, really loved, if only once, is a great gift. Only by loving deeply do we realize our humanity. Without love, there is no humanity. Part of the hardness you encounter in the Vatican, in the entire Church, is due to that. Too many men in the Church never loved deeply, never realized their humanity."

78

THE MESSENGER

Tuesday morning, March 18, 1986
Vatican City

Father Matthew Patterson wore a large topcoat. The color in his face was good. The heavy clothes masked his emaciated state. He had pulled himself together for what he knew was the final scene of the final act of his life. His step was steady as he made his way down the cobblestone walk with his escort, Monsignor Josef Majeski.

As they walked, Monsignor Majeski put his hand on Matt's shoulder. "I work with the Holy Father in the Papal Office. We would always grant any request of John Wolleski. And the men you asked to meet with – our cardinals Kruger, Bertolini and Paginini – they always grant any request of the Papal Office."

"Thank you," Matt said.

"It was only this morning that I told them the subject of this unusual meeting. The secretary to Cardinal Kruger telephoned me. The cardinal insisted on knowing what the meeting was to be about."

Matt nodded. They walked on in silence until they reached two heavy wooden doors. Monsignor Majeski rapped his fist on one door and took his leave.

The door was opened by an old man whose complexion was nearly the color of the crimson sash around his waist. Extending his hand, he said, "I am Cardinal Gregorio Bertolini, Father. Come in."

He led the way to some parlor seating in front of an oversized desk, where Matt was introduced to the small, rotund, and rather odd-looking Cardinal Paginini. The cardinal held his hand out for Matt to kiss his ring. Instead, Matt took a chair opposite him, and said, "Pleased to meet you, Your Eminence."

Cardinal Bertolini sat in the chair nearest Cardinal Paginini. "I am sorry to say it, but Niccolo – Cardinal Paginini – is not comfortable speaking English. He understands. He will listen."

"Are we waiting for Cardinal Kruger?"

"No!" blurted out Cardinal Paginini. "He not coming. Me no want be here too. Only because Monsignor Majeski I come here."

Clearing his throat, Cardinal Bertolini said, "Cardinal Kruger says you have no business with him. He will not be here."

"But I am here about something that is his business. It is the business of his office. He is responsible for this. He has all the authority. Only Cardinal Kruger can act—"

"We have all seen the paper you made that Cardinal Wolleski brought here last year. We do not need this meeting."

Matt reached into his briefcase, pulled out a thick document and set it on the coffee table.

Cardinal Paginini visibly recoiled and shouted, "No!"

"We have your document," Cardinal Bertolini said. "We don't want to hear any more about priests in America."

Matt leaned forward and picked up the document in his hands. "This is not about priests in America." He dropped the document in Bertolini's lap. "This is about bishops in America."

Cardinal Paginini attempted to fake a laugh. "One year ago you make Wolleski tell priests in America having sex with children. You have no proof. One priest only. Now you come tell bishops have sex with American children. You crazy?"

Matt looked both of them in the eye, one at a time, staring them down in silence. Then he spoke. "Yes, some bishops in America do have sex with children. That is true. I did not come to tell you that."

"What you come for, you?" Cardinal Paginini said.

"To tell you that bishops in America have thousands of priests having sex with children. The bishops know who these criminals are. The bishops protect the criminal priests. Your bishops, bishops appointed by the Pope. Some bishops may be breaking American law by protecting criminals. If the Vatican does not do something about the bishops in America there will be the biggest scandal in this Church in five hundred years."

"That is an alarming statement," Cardinal Bertolini said. "The document you sent to the Pope with Cardinal Wolleski last year, and the document you wanted presented at America's National Conference of Catholic Bishops – those documents were alarming too. But, Father Patterson, you have only one case involving one priest in all of America. One priest?"

Pointing to the document, Matt said, "There are the names of over five hundred American priests in this document. Each one has had complaints about the sexual abuse of children made against him. The names of the bishops of these priests are also in this document. It's not one priest. It is thousands of priests. Every bishop."

Cardinal Paginini took the document from the lap of Cardinal Bertolini, walked around the table, opened Matt's briefcase and deposited the document in the case, snapping it shut. Then he wiped one hand against the other as if knocking dirt from his palms. He walked out of the room and slammed the door behind him.

Cardinal Bertolini said, "We are not authorized by Cardinal Kruger to receive any papers from you. It was his specific instruction that you leave the Vatican carrying every paper you brought through the gates. The Vatican has no use for any information from you, Father. Do you understand me?"

Matt nodded. He stood, opened his briefcase, removed the document, and tossed it onto the cardinal's desk. Turning his back on Cardinal Bertolini, he exited the chamber and walked down the hall toward the stairwell that would lead him back to the Porta Angelica.

79

FINAL RITES

Tuesday evening, March 18, 1986
Rome – Washington DC

The light was fading when the plane lifted off, bound for Washington. I put Matt to bed and asked him to sleep. He was restless and wanted to talk. I could hardly hear him. He whispered, "Cardinal Paginini is a buffoon. He said it was of no importance to the Vatican. Bertolini was the same."

Matt started coughing. Soon things got worse than I could have imagined. I gave my first injection of morphine. His fever spiked and never broke.

It was a dark, moonless night without turbulence. The sound of the engines was like a whisper. As we approached the coast of the United States, the co-pilot, whom I had bothered repeatedly through the night with questions about how much flight time was left, came to the cabin and told me we would be on the ground at National Airport in DC in forty-five minutes.

I asked him to call an ambulance to meet the flight and alert George Washington Hospital that patient Matthew Patterson was returning in rough shape.

I turned back to Matt. He was holding the big wooden rosary in his hands and mumbling. I looked at my instruction sheet, realized enough time had passed, and gave him a second shot of morphine. It took effect immediately. The heavy breathing was replaced by shallow, soundless breaths. I knew what was happening.

The co-pilot came back into the cabin again. "We're going into our approach for National. Put the straps on the bed, and buckle your belt. How's your friend?"

"My friend is dying."

Friday, March 21, 1986
George Washington Hospital, Washington DC

Matt was conscious, but quiet. For the first time since we landed Tuesday night he was not fighting. Except for a few hours spent at a nearby hotel, I had been with him since we touched down. The floor nurses had given up on trying to keep me out of his room.

When he was offloaded from the plane, I thought he wouldn't survive the ambulance ride to the hospital. The medical attendants seemed to be of the same opinion. But he had fought for his life the past two days, tenaciously defying death. Des had come to the hospital two and three times a day. We tried to talk Matt into letting go. But he fought.

When Des walked in Friday, Matt smiled and asked hoarsely, "Did you bring the medal?"

Des nodded and gave the box to Matt, who dropped it on the sheet. "My hands don't work anymore," he whispered. "You give it."

Des turned to me and said, "Matt wants to give you this medal. It's a Celtic cross. He knows your mom's people were Irish and…"

I put the medal around my neck and Des helped to secure the clasp.

At that moment, Matt had some sort of seizure. Instinctively, I slid my arms under him. Des got on his other side. Together we held him in our arms, feeling his life drain from him.

Des said, "He's going now."

As I stood there, I felt some of Matthew Patterson's life-force leave his body and enter my own.

I was so dazed I walked into a post in the lobby of the hospital. Des took my arm. "Come with me, Ren. He wouldn't want us split up at a time like this."

"I gotta go home. Matt told me to go home when he was gone," I said.

"Come with me. We'll go to the sorry-ass Italian place he loved so much. When I tell the old ladies at Café Roma Matt passed away, they'll give us a private room and wine too."

"Fuck, we're not going to get maudlin."

"I got lots of Irish in me. You too. We were born maudlin. Let's go raise a glass to absent friends, have a drink for our troubles."

"Greatest man I ever knew, Des. He loved everybody, judged nobody." In a kidding way, I lightly punched Des's arm. "Hell, he even loved you."

Des put his arm around me and walked me to his car.

Café Roma

The old ladies did give us a private room. It was clear that anything we consumed would be on the house. Once we were alone with a bucket of ice and a bottle of Scandinavian vodka, Des said, "If you thought I was really finished before… well I am really, really fucking finished now."

"Yeah?"

"Right. That old prick Verriano, our esteemed papal nuncio, had a meeting in his office today with the new bishop they have chosen to take over the Thiberville diocese from that incompetent, Bishop Reynolds. Bishop Garland Franklin was in the meeting to brief the new bishop on the situation down in Loooooosiannna."

"Franklin?"

"Right. I was excluded from the meeting. When Sister Theresa told me what was going down, I barged through the door, polite as can be."

"You barged politely?"

"Well, ya know I got some rough edges, but I told the new Bishop of Thiberville that if he wanted to learn any truth about Thiberville, he should immediately meet with Renon Chattelrault off of Church property as soon as he got down there. Told him you knew everything, had no reason to lie, never lied."

"And?"

"The fucker Franklin said, 'We have discussed Chattelrault. I've explained that it was Chattelrault who created all the problems in Thiberville. He committed legal malpractice. Instead of having his client assert his constitutional right not to testify, he had his client admit his crimes in sworn testimony, telling the truth, opening Pandora's box. Chattelrault either stole or had someone steal confidential personnel files from the secret archives of the diocese. He's written a document with you' – he pointed to me – 'and with that priest who everyone knows is dying of AIDS, a document filled with lies claiming there are thousands of priests sexually abusing children. And Chattelrault has talked to the press about this confidential matter. Chattelrault did all these things for one reason – to scare the American Church into hiring him, paying him exorbitant legal fees. Renon Chattelrault is an incompetent lawyer who should be disbarred, a criminal extortionist, and enemy of Holy Mother Church.'"

"What?"

"I hit the fucker, Ren. Flat out nailed his fucking ass. Knocked him over a chair. Broke his eyeglasses, drew blood on his face. I gave him a shot at me. Think I said, 'You talk big, you bastard. Get your ass up off the floor and finish this now, you fucker.'"

I dropped a cube of ice into each of our glasses, filled them with vodka and raised mine to Des. We clinked glasses. I said, "To you, to Matt – the best there ever was."

"One day they're gonna get what's coming to them and a lot of victims are going to get justice."

We clicked glasses again. "To truth, the power of truth," Des said.

"To lies, the power of lies," I said. "The lies seem to be winning out now."

"Have faith, Ren, in the truth, in what's right," Des said.

We drank past legal closing time. The old ladies set food and

499

wine on the table from time to time. By the end, we were laughing about the great times we'd had with Matt down in Louisiana.

Des would be on the altar for the funeral in two or three days. Word was already out that Matt had died of AIDS and, fearing the story would be broken by the media, the archbishop had pre-emptively informed *The Washington Post*, portraying himself as supporting Matt throughout his illness as if he were his own father. The Church was going to pull out all stops and give Matt a funeral mass in the same cathedral where John F. Kennedy's final rites were held, a church appropriately named Saint Matthew's. I knew I would not attend.

Saturday morning, March 22, 1986
Hay-Adams Hotel, Washington DC

After attempting to shower off my hangover, I ordered some breakfast from room service and asked the concierge to have all the newspapers delivered to my suite.

A story about Father Matthew Patterson's death and the cause of his death was spread across half the front page of *The Washington Post*. In the piece, an archbishop was quoted as saying he was like a father to Matt at the end. This was the same archbishop who had tormented Matt in the hospital, forcing him to sign a document saying he had lied to the prelate about his medical condition. The archbishop feared he would not be made a cardinal if it became known in the Vatican that a priest in his diocese had died of AIDS. The Church couldn't run from Matt's death, couldn't toss his body in a dumpster on his death. So they pretended to embrace him in death when they shunned him at the end of his life, one of the biggest lies they had told to date.

I glanced at the story in *The New York Times* before calling Julie in Arlington, Virginia.

She answered the phone and I said, "Hey, kid."

"I saw it on the news last night, read the story in the morning newspaper. I thought you were at the Four Seasons in Georgetown. I called all night and this morning. Where are you?"

"Now I'm at the Hay-Adams Hotel. Last night Des and I got drunked up."

"I can imagine. I'm on my way."

"Thanks."

Monday morning, March 24, 1986
Rhode Island Avenue NW, Washington DC

It was chilly when the funeral hearse pulled up in front of the Cathedral of Saint Matthew the Apostle. Hundreds of priests in matching green vestments, Desmond McDougall among them, flanked both sides of the long aisle. The line stretched to the big double doors at the main entrance, where the archbishop waited to receive the coffin at the top of the steps.

Julie and I were dressed in sweaters, warm coats, gloves and wool scarves she had bought for us. We stood across the street from the cathedral in a crowd of other onlookers.

There was trouble trying to remove the casket from the hearse as there were so many television cameras and still photographers crowding the back end of the carriage, vying for an image for the evening news or the morning newspapers.

Organ music drifted out of the cathedral, a faint melody we heard from our position. When they began carrying the coffin up the steps, the bells of the great church began ringing. I stood soldier-straight even though inside I felt like I was collapsing. Tears rolled down my cheeks. I was silent. Julie had both of her arms wrapped around me.

When the archbishop received the casket and turned to lead the procession to the altar, I took Julie's gloved hand and we walked down the street. At the corner, as we waited for a traffic light to change, I said, "I gotta go get a puppy named Mozart and bring him to a little girl in Louisiana."

PART EIGHT

NO DIRECTION HOME

1989

THREE YEARS LATER

80

LEAVING THIBERVILLE

Friday October 13, 1989
Thiberville

In the three years after the Dubois criminal case ended, Kate and the children moved to New Orleans, Julie left Thiberville, and Matt died. I was kind of lost. Doctors didn't want me subjecting myself to the stress of practicing law, and I'd lost interest in being a lawyer. For that whole period, I felt like I had just been sleep-walking through life. It was no longer fair to my clients or to me to continue to play the part of a lawyer. This morning was the first morning of my life when I did not know where I would be going after today. I knew there was nothing left for me in Thiberville.

I was in my office, wearing one of Matt Patterson's sweatshirts. The sweatshirt had arrived in a package shipped by Barbara from Hope House a week after Matt's funeral. She included the note, "Matt wanted you to have this – his favorite." It was his legacy to me.

Mo too would, reluctantly, have to be moving on. She and I had been packing up my office and were just about finished. I was in the process of closing my law practice. By the end of the month, my professional life would be over. Mo and I were alone in the office, putting away files, listening to the Rolling Stones. As she boxed the law books I had sold cheap to a young lawyer just starting out, I truthfully told her, "I never much cared for those books. There are no pictures, ya know."

Our old family country home in Coteau had stood empty since Kate had moved to New Orleans. When I thought about Coteau and the wonderful times our family had there, I found myself drifting into a melancholy state. I tried to never think about it. I had listed it for sale several years earlier. A mutual friend had told me Kate planned to marry a good man in New Orleans. She was moving on with her life and I was now making plans to leave Thiberville.

Matt had been dead for almost four years. Desmond McDougall had essentially been fired from his former position at the papal nunciature. He continued to tell the truth about the Church, testifying on behalf of victims who had filed lawsuits against the Church. I was proud of him and happy that he was so effective. Recently I had seen him on a national talk show on a Sunday morning. "It's simple," he'd said. "When it becomes known that a priest has sexually abused a child, there are only three forces in play: a bishop, a prosecutor, and the press. If one of those three does the right thing, does their job, the right thing will happen. All too often none of them does their job, and then the priest abuses another child, and another and another. We need responsive and responsible bishops, prosecutors and journalists. One wonders how they can all duck their responsibility to these children, but they have done so consistently in some places."

The Christmas after Matt's funeral, Des sent me one of those tourist photographs in a cardboard holder with the logo of Café Roma written above the picture. It was a picture of Matt, Des and me laughing. I'd kept it on my desk. Now, I picked it up and looked at it for a long time before handing it to Mo to put in a storage box.

Julie was in Africa, working for a private relief organization. She moved around a lot and her letters took a long time to get to me. Sometimes I would receive a batch of three or four in the same week. I responded to her through her parents' address in Arlington, as they were able to get parcels to her via her employer. On her rare visits to the States, she called and we talked for hours. I always traveled to meet her in New York on her way home. In Africa, she had found what she had been looking for all of her life.

Just as I asked Mo, "You want to tape me inside a box and stick me in storage too?" the phone rang. She picked it up and slammed it down a few seconds later.

"Renon, my friend Sally says the Old Bishop's House is on fire. Let's go see."

We walked out of the office into the outer bands of a late-season hurricane due to come onshore during the night. The sky already had a strange look as layers of clouds raced along a low course, holding to the contours of the earth. The wind was gusting.

It was only four blocks to the Old Bishop's House. Firefighters were dousing the spire and steep roof of the nearby cathedral and adjacent chancery building with gallons of water, trying to protect them from the flames and sparks that were shooting out of the Old Bishop's House. Other hoses were aimed at the house.

The fire chief, Wayne Doucet, a client of mine, stood on the sidewalk in front of the house, walkie-talkie to his ear. He saw me and motioned that I could approach him, nodding to the policeman to let me cross under the crime scene tape.

"Look at this," the chief said, pointing to the ground in front of him.

I pressed against the waist-high iron fence and looked at the lawn. There were fifty or more carved African masks scattered near the fence line.

"A neighbor across the street said she noticed smoke, looked closer and saw someone throwing these things out of an attic window. There has to be somebody in there."

"Are you going in after him?"

"No. The staircase is gone and we think he's on an upper floor. There's nothing left up there now. Not enough oxygen to support life. And it's too dangerous."

The walkie-talkie cackled. The fire chief listened.

"A fire officer in the back says he thinks he saw someone downstairs. Now they don't see him. Maybe a smoke shadow. Smoke does strange things."

The wind was kicking up and water from the fire hoses was blowing on us. I had no protective gear and became drenched. Some of the smoke was no longer rising straight up in a plume.

It was blowing down the boulevard just above ground level.

"Man in the hall! Man in the hall!" The chief shouted into his walkie-talkie. He grabbed something that looked like a scuba-diving outfit, strapped it to his body and ran up the front walk toward the house. Two of his men followed.

For an instant, I clearly saw the man in the house. He was standing in the center of the entrance hall, surrounded by flames. He was still, his arms at his side.

As the chief reached the porch swing on the front gallery, a beam fell in, blocking the entrance to the house. The second falling beam caught the chief on the shoulder and knocked him to the porch floor. Two of his men pulled him to safety as the porch collapsed. A loud rush of air came from the back of the house and blew out some of the front wall, causing part of the structure to fall in on itself.

When the paramedics had finished looking at him and bandaging his shoulder, Chief Doucet walked up to me. "Did you see him?" he asked.

"Yeah, I did. I saw him," I said.

"Did you recognize him?"

"Yeah. It's Monsignor Jean-Paul Moroux."

"What the hell do you think he's doing in there? Why didn't he get out?"

I shrugged and shook my head. I couldn't take my eyes off the place where Moroux had been standing. The smoke obscured my vision as I strained, trying to see Moroux again.

Doucet said, "When I got up on the porch, I could see him real good."

"Yeah?" I said, staring hard, still looking for Moroux.

"He was smiling."

The fire chief walked away.

Minutes later, the Old Bishop's House was reduced to a pile of charred rubble. I looked at the ground. Moroux had saved the masks but made no attempt to save himself.

I walked inside the gate. I picked up two masks, one for me and one for Julie.

81

A FIREWIND

Friday October 13, 1989
Thiberville

The truth had been heavy. The truth had been contained in
cartons sealed, taped tight, and addressed to the police department
in Thiberville, the district attorney's office, and the office of
diocesan and insurance legal counsel. Monsignor Jean-Paul
Moroux had borrowed a utility van from the diocesan maintenance
department the day before. He had spent all night copying
thousands of pages and packing a number of identical boxes with
the fifteen personnel files Renon Chattelrault had deposited in the
bishop's office three years earlier – the last time Moroux and
Chattelrault had met.

Added to the incriminating material contained in the personnel
files was a 174-page affidavit, notarized by an attorney in Jean-
Paul's hometown in neighboring Acadia Parish. The attorney had
not bothered to read the affidavit, but only verified that Moroux
had signed it in his presence, attesting to the truth of the contents
of all of the documents.

Moroux had typed the long, sworn affidavit over the past
month in evenings during sober intervals. It detailed what Moroux
knew about every diocesan priest who had violated his vow of
celibacy during Moroux's tenure as vicar general, whether the acts
involved very young boys and girls, teenagers, or adult males and
females; it included information on priests who had impregnated
women. Moroux even mentioned his drunken encounters with
undercover vice cops when he was a young priest.

When Moroux finished offloading the cartons at the post office, he was wringing wet with perspiration. He returned the van to the maintenance warehouse, and drove away in his car. With all four windows down, the breeze chilled his wet clothing and skin. He drove until he reached his childhood home, the farm in Acadia Parish. He slowed as he passed the house where he had spent the first fifteen years of his life before he entered the seminary.

When he returned to the Old Bishop's House, he phoned his secretary, Lydia, to inform her that he would not be in his office until the afternoon. He climbed the steps to the attic and began working with a wood burner, scorching deep lines into a wooden African mask.

The fire had started in the attic when Jean-Paul Moroux set his woodburning tool on a stack of color photographs. The flames quickly began sucking oxygen out of the air, hurting Moroux's lungs. As he pulled masks off the wall and tossed them through an open window, his sleeve caught fire and charred the flesh of his arm.

Carrying his favorite mask under his good arm, Moroux walked downstairs to the ground floor. He made his way to the kitchen. Behind him, he could hear the fire snaking down the stairs. The old cypress boards sounded like they were breaking apart. He set the mask on a counter and drank a glass of cold water. Out the back window, he could see the cemetery and wondered for a moment what his funeral would be like, whether he would leave a corpse or only ashes. He wanted to sleep in the cool earth of the Saint Augustine Cemetery.

He walked into the center hall, holding the mask under his arm. He was mesmerized by the flames crawling down the stairs, coming closer. His brain rapid-fired images – his younger self lying prostrate in the cathedral as he received holy orders; as a six-year-old, crying on a riverbank as he watched the first fish he ever caught die; his mother in a coffin with rouge smeared on her cheeks, even though she had never worn make-up in her life; a young African man sitting with James Baldwin outside Les Deux Magots in Paris, eyeing Moroux flirtatiously; and a snapshot from his recurring dream of brightly dressed Africans on a red-dirt road bordered by lush green fields.

For a moment he thought of the huge packages he had deposited in the mail that morning, material sent to lawyers, the police, and a prosecutor's office. In making that mailing, he had broken a sacred vow by intentionally acting to bring scandal to the Church. He had been prepared to live with the consequences. He would now die with the consequences.

He stood rooted in the hallway, fascinated by the flames, how quickly they spread around the room, randomly attaching themselves to objects. He felt water from a fire hose, just some spray. There was no air left to breathe. He lifted the mask and peered through the eyeholes for his last look at this world. As he squinted at the flames coming closer, he hummed the song his mother used to sing in the kitchen when she baked. He had not felt this way since he was a boy. He was happy.

82

A LAST GOODBYE

Saturday October 14, 1989
Coteau

The hurricane came through during the night, knocking down trees and power lines. When daylight came, only the hospitals and government buildings with generators had power. I drove out to the country to see if there was damage at the Coteau house. I unlocked the gate, left my car on the road and waded through standing water to the house that had been our home for years. The force of the night winds had pulled some shutter stays out of the walls. Now the shutters were swinging free, banging against brick walls.

The front porch light was swaying in the breeze. I righted the old rocking chair and had a seat. The place was in poor condition, in danger of falling into ruins. For the first time, I wondered if I had kept it this way intentionally so it would never sell. When the house was gone, everything would be gone. If I no longer had my family, my profession, or my faith, I still had this place. It was all that was left.

I resolved then, while sitting in the rocker, that I would fix it up, sell it, and let it go. It was no more than a symbol of a time, and my whole life seemed to be made up of symbols and remembrances. For the first time since Kate and the kids moved away, I let myself into the house and wandered through the empty rooms. It smelled damp and dusty. Sasha had forgotten some stuffed animals in her bedroom closet, or maybe she left them there on purpose. Jake's old snake-hunting gun was propped in a corner of his room, rusted from him leaving it in the gazebo for a winter when he was a kid. Some torn rock-star posters dangled from the wall in Shelby's room. In my study, a tree branch had cracked a leaded glass window.

The grand piano was the only piece of furniture left in the house. Kate had insisted I sell it as no one ever played it. I had been unable to bring myself to sell anything that had belonged to us. Her clarinet was on the piano bench. It was not something she would have forgotten or overlooked. I picked it up and walked back onto the front porch.

I sat in the rocking chair holding the clarinet in both hands, looking over the land around the house. The grass had turned to weeds that were now waist high. I could not see the pond. I blew a note on the clarinet and was startled by the response. The ducks on the pond started quacking. I couldn't see them through the tall grass, but I could hear them coming to the bank. The ducks were still here, waiting for Sasha to feed them again.

PART NINE

THE RETURN OF IT ALL

1995-2002

83

A SECOND ACT

Monday December 18, 1995
Frankfurt, Germany

When winter came to Frankfurt in December of 1995, I had been in Europe for six years. It was ten years since Francis Dubois had been sentenced to a twenty-year term and I was trying to put the past in the past. Kate had remarried, but she stayed in close touch, as did our children. When my dad got sick, Kate and the children had visited him often, though it was only me there at the very end when he asked a home healthcare lady to put a sponge to his dry lips. The last words my old gent ever spoke were, 'Thank you.'" Now, whenever Kate called, she always ended every phone call with: "You have our love. Take care of yourself."

An essay I once read stated that the place we consider home, the locale where we are most comfortable, the place we long for when we are absent, is not necessarily the place where we are born and reared, but rather the place where we encountered the most significant emotional experiences of our life. For sailors, it might be the open sea, for pilots, the night sky.

For me, it had always been Frankfurt, Germany. Especially the old quarter of Sachsenhausen, along the River Main, where I had lived for nearly two years with Kate and young Shelby, long ago. I was in the army then. It was that time in life we all have, that time before anything bad has happened.

Three months earlier, in September 1995, a headline in the International Herald Tribune had caught my eye: "Cardinal John

Wolleski, 88, Dies in Rome". The short notice said the cardinal had passed away in a Vatican apartment and would be buried in Rome later that week. Arriving in Rome a few days later, I went straight to Ristorante Rinaldi on Piazza Navona. Old Giovanni Rinaldi was there, but he did not remember me. He told me where the Mass would be the next morning and gave me the address of the cemetery. Giovanni motioned for me to take a seat anywhere I wished. I chose a small table that gave me a view of Isabella in her Charlie Chaplin costume.

The cemetery was on a hill with tall trees, cedars. There were only three men at the freshly dug grave when I arrived: two laborers in khakis and a nervous older man in a baggy blue suit. The old man was smoking a short, unfiltered cigarette and constantly pulling on his long, fat nose. Unconsciously, he tossed the lit cigarette butt into the trench. Realizing what he had done, he cursed, and one of the laborers jumped into the hole, retrieved the cigarette, took a hit off it, stubbed it out and stuck it in his pocket. The name on the headstone next to Cardinal Wolleski's plot read "Isabella Rinaldi". I made a mental note to one day tell someone the story of the cardinal and the ice-cream girl.

The funeral cortège slowly made its way up the hill. At the graveside, the priest offered prayers and remarks in both Italian and English. When the service was over, the priest greeted the mourners. I took the last place in line and extended my hand as I reached him. "Father, you described the cardinal well."

"He was a good man," he said. "I am Jozef Majeski."

"Renon Chattelrault. A long time ago I worked on a document for the cardinal with two priests in the United States, Fathers McDougall and Patterson."

"Yes, of course. I remember. I know who you are. John thought highly of you. Once he gave me the names of your children on a piece of paper. The paper remains on the altar in the Holy Father's private chapel."

I reached in my pocket, pulled out a card and carefully printed two words on the back of the card, handing it to him. "Will you put this on the altar of the Pope's private chapel?"

He nodded as he looked down at the words I had written: "Will Courville."

It was a freezing Monday night in December and I was staring out at the snowy Frankfurt streets when the phone rang. It was Kate, calling to tell me that Francis Dubois had been released from prison ten years early.

"You're serious?"

"Yeah, Ren. He was released without any supervision. The media in Louisiana is saturated with the story of his early release. The biggest and worst story was a wire story originating with the *Houston Chronicle* that ran in the New Orleans newspaper. It quoted prisoners at the Riverbend facility saying Francis Dubois ran the prison when he was there because of the influence an important judge had over the warden. According to the *Chronicle*, Dubois had his own office where he scheduled prison activities, and he was allowed to pick his own assistants, always choosing the youngest-looking kids on the juvenile wing. Apparently, he spent a couple of years of his sentence, when he was supposed to be in a state penitentiary, living as a trustee in the jail of Morgan's Hope, his hometown. He was free to come and go as he pleased at Morgan's Hope, only required to make a ten p.m. bed-check."

I waited to hear more.

Kate told me the new district attorney in Thiberville was outraged, offering interviews to any media outlet that would talk to him. The Louisiana state Senate convened a special panel to investigate the circumstances surrounding the early release of the most notorious criminal in Louisiana history. She said one of the United States senators issued a statement about the obvious miscarriage of justice.

I could only imagine what impact the news had had on the people of Amalie – Dubois's victims, their families and friends, the entire community.

Kate closed by saying, "I don't know how this could possibly involve you, Ren, but I have a bad feeling. I knew you'd want to know. All hell's broken loose over his early release and the stories about the special treatment this judge got for him while he was incarcerated."

I thanked her for calling and asked her to give my love to the kids. When we hung up, I made a mental note to research Judge Livingston and find out what a Knight of Malta was.

84

THE MANHUNT

Noon, Wednesday December 20, 1995
Feed & Seed Store, Amalie

Poppa Vidros, Wiley Arceneaux and Tommy Wesley Rachou were having coffee on the front porch of Wiley Arceneaux's Feed & Seed store.

The noise and smoke from the tires on Randy Falgout's truck startled the group. Falgout spun the truck off the blacktop onto the oyster-shell parking lot and nearly rammed into the side of the building. Throwing the door open and jumping from the cab of the truck, he screamed, "They seen him. The fucker. Dubois's Suburban was seen by an old trapper early this morning. Going in the direction of his camp at South Pass. The fuck has come back here. This time he ain't leaving."

"I got three guns," Poppa shouted.

"I got two shotguns inside the store," Wiley said.

"Get 'em," Randy shouted. "Give me one."

In less than a minute, the men were locked and loaded, in a two-truck caravan, headed for the wild marsh.

The old trapper had been right about seeing Father Dubois's old black Chevrolet Suburban on the South Pass Road. When he was released from prison, Dubois had gone back to Morgan's Hope, where one of his brothers had kept his car on blocks with the fluids drained for ten years. For reasons known only to him, Francis Dubois was returning to the scene of some of his most heinous crimes.

South Pass Marsh, Louisiana

Poppa Vidros was waving his arm out of the driver's side, motioning Randy Falgout to slow down and pull over onto the shell surface of an oilfield installation, a web of pipes painted silver contained within a high fence. Once the men had got down from their vehicles, Poppa said, "That's his truck. Up there by the boathouse. His camp is just the other side of the boathouse. We walk it from here."

"The fucker has guns too," Randy said.

The men checked the ammo in their shotguns and started walking on the soggy grass, being as quiet as they could.

Francis Dubois was on his knees in the small utility room at his fishing camp. It had a hot-water heater, a sink and shelving. With a crowbar in his hands, he pulled at the hard cypress planking. In his haste to leave the area years earlier, when he cleaned out the church rectory, he had forgotten about the camp. The weatherproof safe he had installed under the floorboards contained something he needed and some things he never wanted anyone to find.

The four men huddled behind the boathouse. They spoke in whispers. It was decided that Wiley Arceneaux would cover the back of the camp while the others approached from the front.

The first thing Dubois heard was the sound of Poppa's heavy boots on the front porch of the camp. The old structure shook for a moment. Poppa kicked the door open. A gust of wind blew in, shaking a camouflage jumpsuit hanging in the corner of the front room. Mistaking the suit for a man, Poppa unloaded a round of buckshot into the clothing.

Dubois flew out the back door of the utility room, surprising Wiley Arceneaux as he hit him with the crowbar, knocking him out. Dubois dove into the freezing water of the canal so fast he failed to close his mouth. He tasted the icy, muddy water as he plunged to the bottom and swam through the grassy reeds. He was only ten yards from the camp, but in the cover of the marsh he could have been ten miles away.

Rushing through the camp, Poppa, Randy and Tommy Wesley found Wiley unconscious and bleeding in the mud near the boathouse.

"Tommy, you get Wiley to the hospital. Randy and I can take care of the fuck our ownselves," Poppa said.

As Tommy Wesley Rachou was picking up Wiley out of the mud, he said, "We got to call the cops."

"Fuck the cops," Poppa said. "They had their chance. No fucking cops. Tell the ER nurse Wiley slipped in a boathouse."

Dubois had made a lot of ground by the time Randy and Poppa returned from helping load Wiley into Tommy's truck. Dubois had stripped off everything but his jockey shorts. He buried his clothing in the soft silt. The waterlogged, mud-caked clothing would have slowed him down.

He shivered in the freezing, brackish marsh water, colder than he'd ever felt in his life. Dubois mimicked the motion of a water snake, slithering on his belly on the surface of the slimy mud, beneath the cover of the tall grass. Aware he was making a trail, he doubled back and created a false trail to the east, another to the west. Then he entered a cut, a narrow slit through the marsh dug out for the mudboats used by gaugers taking pipeline readings. Dubois was all too aware that these ditches were known as alligator runs.

Randy Falgout, a master mechanic with boat engines, found Dubois's mudboat in the boathouse and managed to get its motor to turn over. The vertical exhaust pipe spewed enough smoke to fill the tin shed. Poppa and Randy were being overcome by fumes as Poppa struggled with the chain on the double doors. Exasperated, Poppa blew the doors open with a shotgun blast.

Hearing the motor and the gun, Dubois knew what was coming. As he heard the boat running up the cut, he twisted, lying on one side. Then he slid out of the small canal and back into the dense marsh grass, leaving as small a print as possible in the muddy bank, hurriedly righting the reeds he had disturbed. The mud was as cold as the water.

Dubois decided he would lie there until dark. As the hours passed, Dubois did not notice the mosquitoes that covered him, sucking blood from his flesh. He began to feel colder and weaker. Aware that his breathing was slowing and his mind was getting cloudy, he took his pulse. The slow heart rate he counted told him his body temperature was falling fast.

A small mound to his right appeared to be an alligator nest. He knew if that was the case, the big female would return soon and attack anything that appeared threatening to her hatchlings. He knew he would either be riddled with shotgun wounds, torn to shreds by an alligator, or frozen into a stiff carcass before the night was over. Not wanting to disturb the grass more than necessary, he began to inch away from the nest, finding it increasingly difficult to move. His limbs acted erratically, out of sync with his mind. The loss of coordination scared him as much as his slow pulse. He stopped and listened for the boat motor.

He knew his boat engine well and could tell it was not in gear but was idling in the cut twenty or thirty feet away. The engine noise drowned out the voices of those in the mudboat. He had not even looked at Wiley Arceneaux when he hit him with the crowbar. He had no idea who was hunting him or how many there were. He only knew they had guns. All he had was his knowledge of the terrain, his survival instincts, and his ability to blend in with the savage environment. With each attempt to move his limbs, Dubois lost more control. The freezing temperatures were conquering his naked body. Every moment the sun dropped lower in the sky, it seemed the temperature dropped another degree or two.

When dark fell, Poppa and Randy were already back in Dubois's camp. Tommy had returned with news that Wiley had come to in the truck and was getting X-rays at the hospital. They sat in the dark front room, their flashlights turned off. There was no moon and the low cloud-cover made it impossible to see one another in the blackness. They spoke in whispers.

"He's gotta come back here," Tommy said.

"Don't go betting on that," Randy said.

"You really think the fucker could stay the night out in that marsh?" Poppa asked. "Something is gonna kill him tonight. No one can survive out there. It's gonna freeze over solid tonight. Let the fucker freeze. Hope he hits a nest of water moccasins and dies of snake bites. Let a gator roll him and bury him in the mud in the bottom of a canal, bury him in the mud until he's rotten enough for that gator to want to eat him. Fuck him."

The three men stayed the night in the rickety camp. As dawn approached, Poppa said, "What the fuck ya think he was doing here?"

Randy Falgout walked through the rooms, using his flashlight to guide him. "There's a bunch of marks on the floor back in the room where the hot-water tank is."

The group gathered round the gouge marks in the cypress planking. Poppa addressed the situation as he addressed every situation. He blasted the boards loose with his shotgun.

When the dust and splinters settled, Randy got to his knees and reached down into an iron box beneath the floor. Its top had been torn loose when the floor was shot to pieces. Poppa held a flashlight as Randy pulled out a stack of plastic Ziploc bags filled with cash. Then he began to pull up baggies containing something altogether different – graphic photos of the men's sons engaged in sex with the priest and each other.

At the sight of the photographs, Tommy Wesley Rachou went outside and began vomiting. Big Poppa Vidros started crying, sobbing. Randy just looked down and muttered, "Holy Mother of Christ."

Tommy came back in, wiping his mouth on the sleeve of his coat. "Should the pictures go to the police?"

"Too late," Randy said, as he put a flame to the pile of photographs on the rear porch.

"The money?" Poppa asked.

"You take it, Poppa," Randy said. "Give it to the coach over at the school for the new baseball field and the leaks in the gym."

When the sun was up, the men began speaking in normal tones. Tommy said, "How long we gonna wait?"

"I'm done," Poppa said. "Let's go. Dubois's dead. He froze, or something got him in the marsh last night. Nobody coulda made it out there last night. He's gotta be dead by now."

When darkness had fallen over the marsh and Dubois could no longer hear the boat motor, he got back in the alligator track and made his way to the big canal. By the time he reached the canal he was so cold that he was losing all feeling. He swam away from the direction of the camp, only able to stroke in slow motion as his body began to shut down. When he was clear of the camp, he began to walk upright on the muddy bank, sliding into the water over and over, crawling out on his belly, using his hands like claws, digging into the soft mud, fighting to survive.

He knew there was a small Shell Oil Company fuel depot a mile away. It would be closed at this hour and no one would return until mid-morning. If he could make it that far, Dubois knew he could break in, clean up and find overalls and boots, something to wear. Though his mind was cloudy, his ability to think foggy, he believed there might be a boat to steal at the Shell depot. He knew the maze of canals that crisscrossed this marsh like he knew the back of his hand. He would make a large circle, cross under the bridge, and return to the vicinity of his camp in the morning. If the men who were hunting him were gone, he'd retrieve his spare key from under his vehicle, make sure his wallet was still in the console, and then drive along the ridge road that ran through the marsh. That would get him into Texas, where he could buy clothes, get ointment for his skin, and go to his brother Bobby's farm in Flatwoods.

As he clawed his way from the canal and slumped onto the bank, Dubois gave himself a reality check. His plans were no more than the last fantasy of a freezing, dying man. If he did not get up soon, he would expire right there. He rolled over onto his stomach, got to all fours and collapsed face down in the icy mud.

When Wiley, Tommy and Papa got back to the Feed & Seed store, they turned on all the gas space heaters, brewed coffee and made a pact never to tell anyone that they had caused the death of the monster. Poppa said, "I just wish I could have unloaded my shotgun in that bastard, hit him just hard enough in the right place... ya know, watched him die slow like."

85

WHITE AND BLACK

Christmas Eve, 2001
Frankfurt

The first time Julie and I made love was just after the Old Bishop's House burned down in 1989. I met her in New York when she was on her way out of Africa for a home visit in Virginia. When I walked her to her hotel room the first night, she took my hand and pulled me through the door. She kissed me while unbuttoning my shirt. Her dress somehow slipped and fell to the floor. I started to speak. She shushed me. It was a long time before we fell asleep.

I was awake sometime before dawn. I walked to the window fronting the street. There had been many nights in countless hotel rooms when I had stood and stared out of windows, looking outward, sometimes seeing nothing. This time my back was to the window. I was looking at her as she shifted and the blanket slid down her back. I quietly walked over to the bed and gently pulled the covers over her shoulders. In her sleep, she made a soft, murmuring sound. I slouched in a chair and watched her sleep, and soon found myself breathing in her rhythm.

Over the next twelve years, Julie and I spent as much time as we could together in Europe, in between her African assignments. In 2001, we spent Christmas together in Frankfurt. It had snowed every day since she arrived. Julie loved spending her days in the Christmas Market that spread across the city center, and standing on the footbridge over the River Main at night, watching the flakes fall to the water through the orange glow of the street lamps.

When Julie was away, I worked on writing, an endeavor I had

begun in the same city so many years before. When I had first lived in Frankfurt, in an attic apartment with Kate and young Shelby, I wrote stories that I made up. Now I worked at writing the truth.

When Julie was with me, she was my life. Spending days with Julie, wrapped in winter wear, evenings passed close together under a warm down comforter, I felt I was in the present for the first time in over sixteen years. At last the past was past.

When the phone rang at 5:30 a.m. on Christmas Eve, it startled us. In the blackness, Julie groped for the receiver, knocking it off the table. She fell out of bed reaching for it. I switched on a lamp. Julie was sitting cross-legged on the floor, wearing a full sweatsuit and heavy socks. She spoke into the phone, listened a moment and handed it to me, saying, "It's Kate."

Before I had the phone to my ear, Julie was back under the covers and tucked in tight, falling asleep again.

"Everybody's all right?"

"Everyone's fine, Ren. I'm so sorry to call at this hour. But the news was just on here and I felt you would want to know this. Dubois is in the Thiberville jail again."

"For what?"

"Here in New Orleans, the television news opened tonight with footage of him exiting a police unit in Thiberville, wearing handcuffs and leg chains, looking like an old man. He has some high-priced lawyer from here, who a TV reporter claims is close to that judge that fixed things for him when he was in prison before. Dubois's lawyer waived extradition from Mississippi, where he's apparently been living for a long time."

"What's he charged with in Thiberville?"

"He's being held here on a rape involving a boy that the new Thiberville DA says happened in 1983. The victim only came forward when a furor erupted recently over news that Dubois had injured a three-year-old somewhere on the Mississippi coast and only got probation. The new victim in Thiberville supposedly experienced a recovered memory in therapy."

"Un-huh," was all I could muster as I tried to wake up and comprehend what Kate was telling me.

"There's going to be some kind of court hearing in Thiberville about whether Dubois can be held in prison and tried for this crime committed in 1983. The charge is aggravated rape – supposedly Dubois used a gun to threaten the kid. It's the court hearing I'm calling you about."

"Court hearing?"

"Right. The reporter said the only witness would be you."

"Court hearing about what?"

"Dubois's attorney says Dubois was granted immunity in a plea agreement you negotiated with Sean Robinette back in 1985. He says it granted Dubois immunity for all crimes committed prior to '85, so this 1983 charge must be dismissed. Ya know Sean Robinette died, and Dubois cannot be made to testify, so you are the only available witness to testify to the meaning of the language in that 1985 plea document."

"Did they say when the court hearing would be?"

"The new DA is trying to get the plea agreement declared void. He'll have to go to the Supreme Court in New Orleans, according to the reporter. He's arguing that because Dubois got no medical treatment while incarcerated, he violated his side of the plea agreement. Which means the state is not bound to grant him immunity for crimes he committed before his 1985 sentencing date."

"Okay. It will take months then for those bullshit arguments to be denied by the courts."

"Hope it's okay to have called about this."

"Sure. I think I understand what's going on. Whatever you think about Dubois's past, in terms of the law it's all bullshit. They threw in the gun to make it an aggravated crime because time limitations don't run on such crimes. They're just trying to figure out a way to lock him up forever. The DA is grandstanding, playing for the cheap seats. Under the plea agreement he has immunity for any crime committed before

October 28, 1985. They just want to go to any lengths to lock him up forever."

"Not a bad idea," Kate said.

"Right."

"You have our love. Take care."

After switching off the light, I lay for a time, staring into the blackness. Knowing I would be unable to sleep, I dressed in the warmest clothes I had and wrote Julie a note telling her I had gone out to an all-night coffee bar.

The snow had stopped. It was probably too cold to snow now. I walked two blocks to the house where I had lived with Kate and Shelby over thirty years earlier, a much simpler time. Back then, as an army clerk, I sometimes had to be at work at seven in the morning. In winter, it was too cold to stand around and wait for a streetcar, so I used to walk to work in the pre-dawn darkness. I decided to walk in that trace now, to follow the exact same path down the steep hill, under the railroad trestle, along the wide snowy avenue to the river. It was here in that first spring we lived in Frankfurt, on the grassy area along the River Main, that Shelby learned to walk.

As I approached the building where I once worked, I detoured, veering off to the Hauptbahnhof, a cavernous train station made of stone, steel and glass. I walked out to the end of a deserted platform. It was like being on the end of a jetty in an ocean with the whole world behind me. Only the blackness of night was before me.

The last chapter in the Francis Dominick Dubois saga was about to play out. I thought I knew how it would end. One way or another, I would be the one to end it. Once again the past was the present.

86

DENIAL IN DARKNESS

Wednesday January 16, 2002
Vatican City

The Pope was dying. It was obvious to everyone in Vatican City. Most were surprised he had lasted as long as he had; some believed he would be too ill to participate in the Easter liturgy in the spring. His health was so poor that the Pope found himself considering something no other pontiff had entertained, a resignation of his office. But in the past he had always rallied, at least enough to make it through public appearances.

Behind the great facade of Saint Peter's Basilica, in the dimly lit back corridors where the power of the Church resided, the German cardinal, Hans Kruger, continued to amass and consolidate his power. He had almost everything he had lusted for during his career.

In a move that went unnoticed by many Vatican observers, Cardinal Kruger had pushed aside a colleague and persuaded the Pope to sign a document putting him in sole charge of the ritual nine days of mourning that would follow the Pope's death. More importantly, the position gave him full command of the conclave that would elect the Pope's successor.

The German had firmly positioned himself to become the next supreme pontiff of the Roman Catholic Church, an event he believed would happen sooner rather than later. Vatican politics were a matter of simple mathematics. There were over a hundred cardinals who were eligible to vote in a conclave to elect the new pope, and only three had been in a conclave before. Ninety-eight per cent of the cardinals eligible to cast a ballot had been appointed during the reign of the current pope – during years when Cardinal Hans Kruger had wielded considerable influence over everything in the Holy See, including which prelates were promoted to cardinals. Many of these cardinals owed their positions, prestige and power to the German cardinal. Kruger planned to call in his favors from these cardinals during the conclave, once a few favorites – like the Italian cardinal from Milan – had made a respectable showing on early ballots.

When he was in better health, the Pope had told Monsignor Majeski and others in his "Polish Mafia" that he prayed he would not be succeeded by the German. By the time Cardinal Kruger pushed the paper to the Pope that gave him full charge of the funeral and election of his successor, the Pope was affixing his trembling signature to almost anything.

87

GHOSTS ON THE BAYOU

Thursday April 11, 2002
Thiberville

The hearing to decide on the meaning of the 1985 plea agreement in the case of the State of Louisiana versus Francis D. Dubois was to be held in the Thiberville courtroom. The lower court judge ruled that I could be forced to testify even though I had originally served as Dubois's defense counsel.

I was home again. This time I was to be in court as a witness, not as a lawyer.

The original plea agreement that was signed by Dubois, DA Robinette and me contained language that was standard, granting the defendant immunity for all crimes committed prior to the date of the agreement – October 28, 1985.

But it also contained troublesome language that was arguably open to interpretation. There were paragraphs relating to Dubois serving his sentence at Hannover House in New Jersey, and a paragraph about Dubois continuing medical treatment, including taking the drug Depo-Provera. Neither of those things had happened. Dubois had not served his sentence at Hannover, and he had ceased taking Depo-Provera when he entered Louisiana's Riverbend prison.

The new DA was going to argue that Dubois did not honor the plea agreement, thus rendering the contract between Dubois and the State of Louisiana void. This would clear the way for Dubois to be prosecuted on the new rape charge and to serve the rest of his life in a Louisiana prison. If the judge found that the provisions relating to Hannover and Depo-Provera were optional for Dubois, he would not have violated the contract. The immunity provision would hold, and Dubois would go free.

Former district attorney Sean Robinette was dead, and Francis Dubois was under indictment and had a Fifth Amendment constitutional privilege not to give testimony in the case. The only other signatory to the original plea agreement was me. It would be a one-witness affair.

I knew Dubois had to be tired of jails and that the only way he could avoid incarceration in the future would be if he left no live witnesses to testify against him. I knew that some pedophiles routinely killed their child victims and other pedophiles gradually escalated their criminal behavior to murder. On the long flight back to Louisiana, that was all I could think about. If I testified truthfully, I could be freeing Dubois to rape and murder children. I was obsessed by that possibility as I paced the aisles of the plane. It would be the toughest test I would ever face. Father Owen Dante Ellison had murdered young Bobby and Dwayne Richard in Willow Springs. In my mind there was a real possibility that if my testimony freed Francis Dubois, I would be handing him a license to kill children.

The upcoming hearing was a front-page story in *The Thiberville Register* when I arrived in Thiberville and registered at the Hilton Hotel. The national media was far more interested in the explosive stories about Cardinal Bernard Law and his covering up of clergy abuse in Boston, but a few journalists had tracked me down at my hotel and asked for my take on the scheduled hearing.

Within forty-eight hours the number of calls escalated. A few were from journalists. Some were from people I knew well, others from people I had never heard of. Some of the callers were victims of Dubois, now adults. Some people left anonymous messages. The plea was always the same: make sure you keep this animal behind bars where he cannot hurt any more children.

Only Kate and our children did not express an opinion to me about how I should testify. They called me every day. They all offered to come to Thiberville and lend support, but I did not want any of them to be near this Dubois business again.

A few days before the hearing, a candlelight vigil was held on the steps of the Thiberville courthouse, attended by victims of sexual abuse and their supporters. A local television station closed its news broadcast with film footage of the gathering – a violinist played "Amazing Grace" in the background while a lady shouted through a bullhorn, "Renon Chattelrault made a back-room deal in 1985 out of view of everyone. In that back room, Chattelrault drew up an agreement that attempted to discount, dismiss and disenfranchise every child victim of sex abuse."

When I switched off the television, the phone rang. Hoping it was a friend, I picked it up and said nothing. Then I heard Julie's voice.

"Hey, Ren. I'm here. In your hotel. In reception."

"Wha...? But you're meant to be in Africa—"

"Never mind that, Ren. What's your room number?"

The knock came within the minute. I opened the door and she threw her arms around me in a tight hug. Once we were settled in chairs by the window, overlooking the nothingness that was suburban Thiberville, she went right to it.

"I can't believe this is happening again."

"It could be worse. At least no one's threatened to kill me this time around. Not yet."

"Could your testimony actually keep him locked up? Do you have that power?"

"Maybe. I wouldn't have to tell a big lie. It would only amount to a little lie, a one-word lie."

"What word?"

"'Yes.' I just have to say 'Yes' when the DA asks me if his interpretation of the plea agreement reflects the intent of those who signed the document back in '85."

"What are you going to do?"

"I don't know. I don't know what the right thing is. A long time ago I always knew what the right thing was. People used to talk to me back then about serving the common good. I didn't know what that was. Now, I'm sure the way to serve the common good is to do all I can to lock Dubois up forever. But I don't know if that's the right thing to do. If I lie, I do think he might end up locked in prison forever. But I'd have to lie. In court."

She touched my cheek. "You okay? You look so tired."

"That old nightmare I've told you about where my face is on fire – it comes almost every time I close my eyes now, so I hardly sleep."

"God, this has gone on so long."

"Right," I said. "Remember the first day I met you on the swing at the Old Bishop's House? Eighteen years ago this dominated my life. Tonight it's dominating my life again. It will never end."

"It will end, Ren. Everything ends. I just ended something. I quit my work in Africa. I came here to ask you to marry me."

I laughed. "You can't ask me to marry you. I've proposed twice a year for ten years. You have to accept my proposal."

"Okay, okay. I will marry you, Renon Chattelrault. Yes!"

Friday April 12, 2002
Thiberville

The next day Julie and I arranged to have lunch with my old secretary, Mo, at a small restaurant near the cathedral. While Mo was at noon Mass, Julie and I took a short walking tour. The former chancery building – Julie's old workplace – had been converted into a storage facility for Catholic school textbooks. Through the rounded glass wall on the front of the building, we could see that the bronze busts of the dead popes were still in place.

The fountain in front of the chancery had been vandalized and was out of order. The small angel had been broken from its pedestal, and the basin of the fountain was dry, with a layer of dust covering decaying leaves. The lot where the Old Bishop's House once stood was cleared of everything but two partially burned trees and the brick steps that once led to the front porch where I first met Julie. In the cemetery, we sat in the iron gazebo and I pointed out where the old bum used to play fetch with his dog.

By the time Mo joined us in the café, I was feeling melancholy. Was it possible that I missed the people and places of eighteen years ago, as bad as that time had been? Missed the role I'd had, the sense of purpose? Locked in my thoughts, I recalled something Matt had said in Rome, something about the need to understand how insignificant we are, how everything counts but nothing matters.

The Old Bishop's House and chancery no longer existed, the fountain was in ruins. These were places where I had stood up for what I believed mattered, at a time of monumental importance in my life. I had sacrificed so much in a vain attempt to achieve the impossible. Now, most of those people and places were gone, and I too was gone from Thiberville. The things I had done so long ago probably did not matter at all, maybe they did not even count.

Events had come full circle. The ragged remnants of the first historic case involving Father Francis Dominick Dubois and the Thiberville diocese were going to be adjudicated in the same courthouse where Dubois had been sentenced seventeen years earlier. Once again we were facing a court hearing that would determine whether Dubois would serve a life sentence. This mattered to the victims of Dubois and the people of the Thiberville diocese, but it hardly mattered to anyone else. The scandal was spreading from America to other countries like Canada, Australia, and Ireland and lay on the horizon in Europe and Latin America, and Thiberville was now just a footnote in the far greater crisis that was engulfing the Catholic Church. Even the National Conference of Catholic Bishops was now admitting that thousands of priests stood accused of sexually abusing children, and that victims of these priests numbered in the many thousands. The economic losses were no longer measured in millions, but billions, and new lawsuits were being filed almost daily around the country.

Mo snapped me back into the moment as the waiter laid menus in front of us. "Bet you want those crawfish enchiladas and jambalaya. I can't count the times I went to noon Mass and brought back enchiladas and jambalaya to the office for you."

I laughed. "We all worship in different ways, eh, Mo! Is Pablo Sanchez still in the kitchen here?"

"Yep, he's still the only real Mexican chef in the whole town."

"Then, yeah, I'll have some of his jambalaya and enchiladas."

"Does it feel like you never left?" Mo said.

"It feels more like I was never here."

When I returned to the hotel room, the light was blinking on the phone. The automated voice announced I had nine messages. I lay on the bed and listened to them all, smiling, then laughing. They were all from Joe Rossi. His first message said, "I knew you'd be in the Hilton. Too easy to shoot ya at a Holiday Inn." Then, "Lookit, I'm here too 'cause there's no place in this pissant town where anybody could have any kind of privacy."

When I knocked on room 1124, Rossi flung the door open. He looked seventy to a hundred pounds lighter than eighteen years ago, and his clothes hung on him like a clown suit. He was an old man now, in his early eighties, and so frail I'm not sure I would have recognized him. He no longer had any strands of hair to comb over, and he was wearing thick glasses with weird blue frames.

"Goddamn son, where ya been? I miss ya. Look, I brought my own whiskey. Hotel whiskey is watered down, ya know. I got three kinds. Whatcha want? We can pretend it's a reunion, fooking New Year's Eve."

"I don't drink anymore, Joe."

"Me neither. I don't drink no more or no less."

"I really don't drink, Joe."

"Well, that's good. Take a Coke or something."

We sat at the table by the window and Rossi said, "You know, I knew you was in town here. Everybody knows, huh? I used to tell ya you was crazy. You weren't no kind of crazy, son. You was right down the line 'bout everything about the Church."

He looked different, but he was the same guy.

"Lookit, Renon, you're smarter than every piece of shit lawyer in this part of the world. I know I fucked up on the diocese deal. We shoulda listened to you. I think in the end it cost the diocese and insurance companies almost thirty million bucks for Dubois and the other perverted priests. The sum-bitches lost everything but the echo off the chimes at the cathedral. Bunch of priests had suits filed against them, millions were paid out. Only one besides Dubois was ever arrested, an old priest, and he died before he could be tried in court. The new DA, the local newspaper, everybody stopped investigating this stuff. Sometimes I think even the Catholics around here don't care what priests do to children, what crimes bishops cover up, how their donations are used to pay hush money."

I smiled. "It doesn't matter, Joe. It really doesn't."

"Shit, son, and now you're back here. There's no end to this shit, is there?"

"I really don't want to talk about it."

"Well, this Dubois guy's like elephant shit. He's everywhere. I want ya to know, I ain't talking to ya today 'bout that hearing Monday. You do what ya think is right. I was always wrong, talking that shit about the common good, son."

"I dunno, Joe. Sometimes I think I should have locked up Dubois in prison the day I met him. Thrown the key away. Things woulda turned out better for lots of people."

"No, son, you're wrong. Without the Dubois deal, it woulda been a helluva long time before any of this stuff woulda come out about the Church. Now it's all over the damned world, every bishop been hiding these criminal priests. You done right down the line. I fucked up bringing in Bendel. Hell, the whole Church fucked up, blew itself to bits. How can anyone believe in the Church anymore? I don't, that's sure."

"How is Bendel? He must be getting up there in age now."

"Shit, son, ya never heard 'bout what happened to ol' Jon? Shit. He got dementia or something. He had married that Tammy woman who was his papoon way back then. One day ol' Jon brings this whore to his damn house. He introduces her to Tammy, his wife. He thinks his wife is his mother. His kids got him locked up in some place in Texas for crazy rich people. He just soon be dead. Ya know, everybody else is dead but you and me, son."

"What ya mean, Joe?"

"Well, first that crazy little monsignor barbecued himself."

I first nodded, then shook my head. Joe had a way of saying things.

"Then Bishop Reynolds died. The newspaper said natural causes. I heard it was frostbite of the nose – ya know, from being so close to ice cubes all those years. The son-of-a-bitch was the poster boy for bad bishops, don't ya think?"

I laughed.

"And those young buck lawyers that made millions – couldn't handle the money. One wrecked some kind of fancy Italian car into a tree on the Bayou Saint John highway, all liquored up. The other one? Heard he got drunk and fell off his sailboat down in Florida. The bitch he was with did not know how to turn the boat around and go back to fish him out of the ocean."

"What about Quinlan, Blassingame and those guys?"

"God took 'em all. Wonder where he put 'em. And I know you musta heard about your old friend, Sean Robinette. Died one night while he was sleeping. It's just us from those days."

"And Dubois?"

"Fuck Dubois, son. I told ya long time ago he ain't no kind of human being."

"You were right about that, Joe."

Rossi put down his bourbon and Coke. "I just wanted to see ya one last time. Ya know. Tell ya I'm sorry and shit like that, ya know."

"I know."

"Ren, you know I'm named in a big indictment with the governor and some of my friends."

"I read something about it."

"Son, I got that short little shithead lawyer, Wiley Darby, outta Shreveport. A fucking Yankee on top of everything else. He's got wiry, dirty-looking dishwater hair knotted on his head. It's Audubon hair – oughta been on a mule's ass. Paid him yacht money. Even he don't know how I'm gonna beat the Feds."

"Ya gonna beat 'em, Joe."

"Damn straight, son. Trial is set for next spring. I got cancer all over – less than three months to live."

Rossi paused, looked straight at me. "Don't worry, son. I'm ready. I done lots of good things in my life, but I only let people know 'bout the bad things. I'm gonna go through the pearly gates. When the time comes, my estate lawyer will find ya wherever you are. I'm leaving you some oil and gas royalty that's gonna last till hell freezes."

Joe Rossi was dying. I couldn't believe it. People like Joe never died.

"You're a good boy, son. You did some brave things. Somebody oughta give ya something, even if it's only me."

I thought I saw tears welling in his eyes as he walked me to the door. When I stepped into the hall, Joe looked at me and shrugged his shoulders, saying, "I guess this is it."

I reached for Joe, hugged him tight. "I love ya, Joe."

"I know, kid, I love ya too. Wish you'd been my son."

I nodded as tears filled my eyes.

88

AND JESUS WEPT

Wednesday morning, April 17, 2002
Vatican City

"POPE SUMMONS AMERICAN CARDINALS TO ROME". The headline topped the front pages of every newspaper in the world. It was unprecedented for a pontiff to summon all the cardinals from one country to discuss the issue of clergy sex abuse, a subject until now mentioned only in whispers in the halls of the Vatican. The sense was that the Vatican would finally act. Devout Catholics believed their pope would reach out to all of the broken children, and that he would severely chastise the cardinals and bishops implicated in the scandal.

A week before the two-day conference with the American cardinals, Cardinal Hans Kruger hosted a small meeting with the two other senior cardinals in his cabal. They convened in a salon adjoining Cardinal Kruger's office. Cardinals Gregorio Bertolini and Niccolo Paginini arrived together. All three men bitterly disagreed with the Holy Father's decision to bring the American cardinals to Rome. "What a disaster," complained Cardinal Kruger, "to walk the problem of clergy abuse through the front door of the Vatican when we have kept it from coming in the back door."

None of them had been consulted by the pontiff before he issued the summons. Their power was almost absolute at their level in the Curia and down through the ranks, but they had exerted little influence over the Pope in recent years.

The cardinals sat in large chairs in Kruger's parlor. The

meeting was conducted in the native tongue of the two Italian cardinals. Cardinal Kruger fingered a coin in his hand, turning it over and over. "We have let the bishops, clergy and laity drift for too long in America," began Cardinal Kruger. "The laity live outside of the Church's teaching on birth control and other matters. They make their own rules, their own religion, and still claim to be Catholics. The seminaries produce perverts, too many homosexuals. Bishops ordain inherently disordered men, homosexuals, who are looking for warm bodies on the altars. We cannot change these things today. But we must hold the line today."

"Yes," Cardinal Paginini said. "And so what can be done? Two billion dollars lost."

"This thing happened in a country that has gone mad with liberalism. It's the lack of morality in America that is the root of this. Even their President Clinton was a pervert. The collapse of morality has touched everything. It has even infected the priesthood."

"And what would you do, Hans?"

"We must issue a decree, something to state that no homosexuals will be admitted to seminaries, ordained, or allowed to be priests. We must enforce the decree. We must make people focus on the American culture where this was born. It is that culture that caused this."

The aged Cardinal Bertolini twisted his hands in his lap. "I am told that the Boston cardinal, Bernard Law, wants to quit. I hear he has a letter of resignation for the Holy Father and he is coming to Rome ahead of the others. To give the letter."

Niccolo Paginini laughed. "Is he Irish? He must be Irish. They have the same lack of fortitude as Mexicans. He cannot be allowed to resign. If Cardinal Bernard Law resigns in Boston, he will be giving a great victory to the enemies of the Church. This victory must be denied."

"You are right, Niccolo," replied Kruger. "Very right. And, my friend, there is another reason this Cardinal Law cannot be allowed to resign. If the press and the attorneys can force a cardinal in Boston to quit, they will believe they can do this in Los Angeles and all over the country. We could lose bishops all over America. Maybe we would have no bishops left in America. Now the aggressors against the Church in America have the scent of a cardinal's blood. Once they taste meat, their appetite will never be satisfied."

Cardinal Bertolini said, "One of our best Catholic friends in Boston, the powerful politician, called me Sunday afternoon. He said all he hears are rumors but he suspects there are criminal investigations going on and he thinks the wise thing would be for Cardinal Law to resign and leave Boston. If this happened, our friend said he did not think the prosecutors running criminal investigations would make any attempt to make a criminal case against the cardinal. Resigning in disgrace would be enough punishment. Even if it is just rumors, sounds like Law does need to resign. Our friend in politics said no matter what the truth is, things are bad in Boston and the cardinal must resign for the good of the American Church."

Cardinal Kruger shifted in his chair, then stood and walked to the window, keeping his back to the others. He quickly processed what he had just heard. Turning back to the Italian cardinals, he said, "We cannot have a cardinal named as a criminal. If he must resign, it becomes very important how we treat him. Every bishop in America will be watching us to see what support the cardinal in Boston is given from the Vatican. We must prepare the most prestigious post for Bernard Law, bring him to Rome, and place him in a higher position than he held as Archbishop of Boston. The message to the hundreds of bishops in the United States will be clear, no? All will understand that if forces in America seek to destroy one of our bishops, we will not only protect the bishop and keep him in his post, but if he must resign we will elevate him, give him a better life."

Paginini asked, "What would you do with this Cardinal Law?"

"Make him Archpriest of Basilica Santa Maria Maggiore. The

archpriest of the basilica is dying now. It is the most important church in the Catholic world outside of Saint Peter's. It will be for Cardinal Law, and he will have the villa, its stipend, appointments to Vatican commissions. Let him come back to Rome like a conquering Caesar. Send a message to every bishop in America – they fight our enemies and we will reward them."

The old man, Cardinal Bertolini said, "Many years ago, we..." pointing to Cardinal Paginini, "the two of us had that document thrown at us by the dying priest from Washington. I would not take it. He threw it on my desk. I gave the document to you, Hans. The priest said his papers named hundreds of priests in America and the bishops who supported the criminals. It was true?"

Kruger pocketed the coin. "Yes, yes, it was true." Picking up a paper from a side table, Kruger said, "This fax came from Maryland, from Bishop Franklin. At my request, he attempted to gather information about how many American dioceses are like the Boston diocese. And about how many of those dioceses are having reports of their problems appear in the press. You don't have to read his report. The problem is everywhere, in all of America. Almost every American bishop has this same problem Cardinal Law has in Boston, to one degree or another. In many places the bishops have been able to influence the press and state prosecutors, minimizing the scandal to the Church. In other places, the scandal is almost as bad as Boston."

"That's no good," Cardinal Paginini said. "Is anything good?"

"What is good is that this plague in the Church has not yet spread to every country. But there are serious problems in places – Canada, Australia and Ireland. There are indications in Europe and Latin America that the plague is taking root there too. Until now, this problem has never been identified as a problem for the Vatican."

Cardinal Paginini shook his head and groaned. "That was yesterday. This is today. Now our Holy Father is making this the Vatican's problem."

Cardinal Kruger looked directly at Cardinal Paginini. "I

cannot even get an appointment with the Holy Father. The man is very sick. He can hardly hold his head up and his limbs move erratically. He's sick, but he's not stupid. How can he do such a stupid thing?"

Cardinal Bertolini slapped his hands on the arms of his chair. "What is important is the laity. If seventy million Catholics in America remain loyal to the Church, we win. Catholics are bound to the Church – they are bound from birth, from baptism. They believe in their Church. They believe their salvation can only come through the sacraments of the Church. We must make any attack on a bishop or cardinal look like an attack on all Catholics. Catholics believe this Church is their Church."

Cardinal Paginini chortled. "Yes, but we know – we do know, don't we? We are the Church. The three men in this room."

89

THE FIRST PLACE

Saturday evening, April 20, 2002
Thiberville

At sundown, I was stretched out on the bed in my hotel room, holding the subpoena for my court appearance in my hand. As I stared at the ceiling, I covered the same ground over and over in my mind. What was I supposed to do in court? Lie? Tell the truth?

Julie was scrunched in a chair, bare feet on the cushion, working a crossword puzzle. It felt good to have her so close.

A knock pulled me out of my trance, and opening the door gave me a shock. Sasha, Jake and Shelby stood in the hall, grinning.

Jake had driven in from Austin, Shelby had flown from Los Angeles, and they'd picked up Sasha, who was living in Thiberville again, attending the university. Kate had orchestrated the visit. She knew I did not want her or the children around Thiberville now, but she'd set this up as a 24-hour visit, knowing they would distract me.

They were really excited to see Julie, having spent a lot of time with her in Europe over the past decade. Sasha gave her a big hug and said, "When are you going to marry this man so I don't have to worry about spending my life taking care of him?"

Jake said, "Yeah, Julie. He tells us nothing. When you gonna take him off of our hands?"

Shelby was smiling. "Come on, guys. Go easy. Be nice to the lady."

Julie laughed. "What you gonna pay me when I take him off your hands, Sasha?"

"You better work cheap," Sasha said.

The children insisted Julie join us and protested loudly when she refused. "You guys go on without me tonight. Just this one time. I'll never refuse another invitation. But I know what you mean to your dad. He has me here and I'll be with him a long time now. Maybe he'll tell you we're getting married. Tonight, he needs to be with you guys."

They had arranged a private dining room at one of my favorite restaurants so we would not be bothered by anyone. I had little appetite, but I laughed more than I had in months. Jake played his role as the family comic and he and Sasha reprised some of their better bickering routines from childhood.

Back outside, Sasha pointed to the old stadium and said, "They're going to demolish that old stadium and make a green area, plant trees, set out benches and stuff."

"The old stadium?" I said.

"It's coming down next month. They're going to explode it or implode it, or whatever you call it. Nobody ever paid any attention to it before they announced they were going to blow it up. Now there are art students sketching it every day and some kooks are passing around a petition and planning a demonstration to save it. Who gives a hoot about an old stadium?"

"Let me show you something," I said.

When I crawled through the hole in the fence, they followed. I led them to the top of the old press box and all the way to the top of the light standard.

"You've been here before," Shelby said.

"When I was a kid, I snuck out of the house and came here all the time. I thought of it as my hideout. But I was never hiding from anything or anyone. It was more like I came up here to dream. I even came here sometimes when I was a lawyer and we lived out in Coteau. This has always been one of my favorite places. When I was growing up, it was the most special place I knew. I never told anyone about coming here."

"Does Mom know about this place?" Sasha asked.

"No. Just you guys and one other person. No one ever knew. Until now. Tonight."

Sasha, Shelby, and I were seated on the platform. Jake was standing. He said, "It would have been really something to watch a football game from here."

"Never did that."

"Look," Jake said, "you know we're all here because we want to be with you this weekend. And there's something I want to ask you."

Shelby said, "We love you, Papa, and we're proud of you."

Sasha said, "Me too. And Jake too, but, ya know, Jake doesn't say 'I love you'."

Jake laughed. "I love you, Sasha-Belle, even if you are spoiled rotten. If there's reincarnation, I wanna come back as you."

I asked them, "You know, all this stuff with Francis Dubois supposedly ended eighteen years ago. You guys were young. What do you remember most from that time?"

"I guess I remember you were on TV all the time. Not much else," Sasha said.

Shelby said, "Of everything, I think I most remember the weeks at the beach after you and Mom separated, and how you took us back to the beach a couple months later."

"Me too," Sasha said.

Jake said, "I don't remember much. But I want to ask you something."

I knew what Jake wanted to ask me, but I said to them all, "How you guys like it up here?"

Shelby said, "It's strange how everything looks so different in the dark. The dark does strange things. I can see you up here as a kid."

"When I was a kid, I couldn't come here in daylight because the campus security police would have caught me. So, I always came at night. There were times I wished it would have stayed dark longer, that the night would have lasted longer. It was my

547

secret world. In life, there are only a few places you will ever go that will become part of you, of who and what you are. For me, this was the first place."

"Ya think anyone else ever came up here?" Jake asked.

"Naw."

"Then you put this here," Jake said, fingering some remnants of cloth tied to a crossbar.

I smiled. "Those are two of my ties. I always hated ties."

Sasha, always the brassiest of the bunch, bluntly broached the subject no one had addressed yet. "Mom told me that if you lie in court Tuesday, the Dubois guy will probably spend the rest of his life in prison. He will never be around another little kid again. And she said if you tell the truth, this guy will be let out of jail. Is that how it is?"

"Not exactly, but close," I said.

Jake said, "That's what I want to ask you. What are you going to do in court Tuesday?"

Shelby said, "I wish you weren't making us go home tomorrow. We all wanted to be in court with you. Can I ask you something? You're a writer. Are you gonna write a book about this stuff?"

"I'm not sure anyone would want to believe the truth. It's a terrible truth that goes back about eighteen hundred years. The Catholic Church has always been a haven for perverted priests like Dubois, and they've covered up their crimes all the way up to the popes. Ya think people are ready to read such a terrible truth?"

Shelby said, "Yes, I do. But that doesn't matter. I think you're still carrying all of this inside of you. And you need to write this for yourself."

Sasha raised her hand like she was in class, wanting to talk. I nodded at her.

"Look, Dad, the deal is... the deal is... I mean if you write about this... if ya do, can you do something for me... please?"

"What?"

"Leave out the part about me sinking my trike in the pond so I could get a two-wheeler – leave that part out, okay?"

Jake laughed, "Confessing now, are you?"

Shelby mussed Sasha's hair. "Tell us how you got that thing out in the middle of the pond. You couldn't have possibly done it alone."

"Nope. You're right. I had a co-conspirator. I told the yard guy, old Mule, that Momma wanted things on the bottom of the pond so aquatic plants would grow as food for the fish. He was so strong he just flung the trike way out to the deep part."

Shelby turned to me. "Really. Please. Let us go to court with you. We all want to stand by you. I don't think many people understand what really happened, what you were really trying to do for the children, and what price you've paid."

I shook my head. "I really have to do this alone. I hope you will honor that."

Jake said, "In court... you gonna tell the truth or lie?"

"I was kinda thinking I should do the right thing. I just gotta figure out what that is."

90

AMONG THE RUINS

Monday evening, April 22, 2002
Rome

The air was cool as Cardinal Kruger strolled through Rome, dressed in civilian clothes. No one recognized him. Actually, few outside of the Vatican had ever heard of him. He was deep in thought. When he passed the Swiss Guards at the Vatican City gate, he looked back at the Basilica of Saint Peter's. He could almost see a horrible monster looming outside in the dark, waiting to enter the Vatican in the morning, alongside the American cardinals.

Kruger had spent the afternoon reading summaries his staff had cobbled together from the internet, a sampling of recently published news articles in several languages, most of them emanating from America. The press apparently got their information from the lawyers who were suing the Church. Fortunately, the lawyers seemed to know nothing beyond the facts of the individual cases they were handling. Cardinal Kruger was relieved to find the media knew but a fraction of the story and was not even close to discerning the real truth. Together with various cardinals around the world, Kruger had publicly denied that clergy sex abuse was a widespread problem, saying the situation had been exaggerated by those enemies of the Church who owned major media outlets. He was unperturbed when many Jewish publishers and media moguls took offense at his remarks.

The cardinal mulled over possible responses to the worldwide storm he sensed was on the horizon. He had been confidentially informed by Bishop Garland Franklin that the situation on the west coast of America was far worse than what had been exposed on the east coast. Some were predicting the cost of settlements in Los Angeles and San Diego could approach a billion dollars. Contingency plans were being drawn up for certain dioceses to sell off their assets and even file for bankruptcy. As he strode along the pavements, Kruger shook his head in dismay. He could not believe the American problem was going to become the Vatican's problem in the morning.

That the media was fixated on new, breaking cases involving pedophile priests, new lawsuits being filed and the financial fallout from the claims was a lucky thing, Kruger thought. Until now, with the exception of Cardinal Bernard Law in Boston, the media had not shone a light on members of the Church hierarchy and their failings.

Kruger knew of scores of potentially explosive examples that were lying in plain view yet were somehow invisible to major media. Seven years earlier a cardinal in Vienna had resigned for having sex with young males and the Vatican had not even investigated the case. Thousands of pornographic images had been found on computers in a seminary in Austria. On Kruger's desk right now were complaints alleging the worst kind of abuse by an extremely prominent priest, the founder and lead figure of one of the richest, most influential and conservative religious orders, headquartered in Mexico – a valued friend of the pontiff, and an untouchable inside the Vatican.

For twenty years, it had been Cardinal Kruger's responsibility to deal with these matters, and he had dealt with them by doing his duty to Holy Mother Church as he understood it. In accordance with Church law, the 1962 dictates of Pope John XXIII, and the oath he'd taken to do all in his power to avoid scandal to the Church, he had either ignored or rejected the mountain of complaints. This would not reflect well upon him were it to become public knowledge. He knew that. Whatever chance he had to succeed the pontiff and sit on the throne of Saint Peter would be lost. But who would find out?

Though he was not a bookish man, Kruger knew his Church history. He knew he was by no means the first who'd had to face these problems. He doubted he would be the last. For nearly 1700 years the Church had weathered this storm. Cardinal Hans Kruger would not be the one to allow the Vatican defenses to be breached. As far back as the fourth century, shortly before Emperor Constantine formally recognized the Church, a document issued out of the Church Council of Elvira in Spain had stated that priests who had sex with young boys were to be deprived of communion even on their death beds. So widespread was the problem that for six hundred years the penitential rule books compiled by medieval monks included details of penances for clerics who committed sodomy with young boys – penance that was to be commensurate with rank, with high-ranking bishops facing the harshest punishment. There had been further public condemnations of clerical debauchery in the eleventh-century *Book of Gomorrah,* in the influential twelfth-century *Decree of Gratian,* and again in 1215, at the great Fourth Lateran Council. It was no secret that the depraved sex lives of priests had contributed to the worst crisis the Church ever faced, the Protestant Reformation of the sixteenth century. But Luther, Zwingli and Calvin had been wrong to see a connection between celibacy and the perverted sexual conduct of priests.

Cardinal Kruger knew all this, but for the last two decades he had felt confident that no journalists or editors in the secular press would ever do the hard work to discover, translate and interpret the documents drafted in Latin that provided the proof of how deep-seated a problem it was. Now, however, the Pope was inviting just that kind of scrutiny by summoning the American cardinals to Rome, involving the Vatican in the scandal.

Cardinal Kruger had walked a long way by the time he reached the Forum. He stood quietly, looking down on ruins which once represented the bastion of an empire that was supposed to last forever. The few remaining columns and fallen stones were now a wasteland, a home for hundreds of feral cats.

Far behind him, across the Tiber River, was the formidable Tuscan colonnade, the pillars of the Piazza San Pietro that circled the plaza in front of Saint Peter's Basilica and Vatican City. The Roman Catholic Church was one of the most powerful empires to ever exist on earth and it too was supposed to last forever. The Catholic Church, the one, true apostolic Church ordained by Jesus Christ, had survived for two thousand years and claimed a legion of over a billion followers. It was now under attack.

For a moment, Cardinal Kruger considered the obvious parallels between the two empires. If the true extent of the sins of the Church were ever to be known, Kruger knew the foundation of the Church, the pillars that supported it, its moral authority, could weaken, crack and crumble like the ruins of the Forum.

Kruger began to think like the future pontiff he was sure he would soon become. In his mind he did a quick rundown of the many attempts and failures of previous popes to deal with this problem, not least the constitution, *Romani Pontifices*, issued by Pope Pius V in 1561, and his *Horrendum* of the following year, which also addressed the "sin against nature that incurs God's wrath".

In seeking to enforce secrecy about the true state of its internal affairs, the Church had two powerful tools at its disposal – excommunication from the Church, and the less drastic, more nuanced *mentalis restrictio*, or "mental reservation". Kruger knew he would have to use these weapons judiciously. Mental reservation, a sort of moral lying as defined by moral theologians in the Middle Ages, was particularly powerful. Though the concept had never been approved officially by the Church, through the ages many had relied on it. To avoid bringing scandal to the Church, one could lie and at the same time tell the truth. The truth was told to God, mentally reserved for God only, and the lie was spoken for human ears.

The ultimate procedural manual for dealing with cases

involving clergy sex abuse had been developed just a few decades
ago, by Pope John XXIII in 1962. This was a model Kruger
respected and intended to reinforce. The American Church clearly
needed reminding. Pope John XXIII had sent the sixty-nine-page
document to every bishop. He instructed them to keep the
document in the secret archives of their diocese and to never
comment publicly on its existence. The instruction also imposed
a strict secrecy on those priests processing cases of clergy sexual
abuse in diocesan tribunals. The 1962 edict mandated that
everyone aware of such cases was bound by the Church's highest
degree of confidentiality, the "Secret of the Holy Office".

A recent document written by a high-ranking canon law
scholar in Rome, released in an official Vatican publication,
stated that under no circumstances was a bishop ever permitted
to report crimes committed by priests to secular police authorities.
The document went further, advising bishops never to divulge
information about a priest who had sexually abused children,
because to do so would injure the good reputation of the priest.
Kruger had read the reprint of this document on the front page
of *The Sunday New York Times* and wondered why this correct
interpretation of canon law was newsworthy in America. A sin
against the Church was the worst sin, and to substitute secular
law for Church law, or to injure the reputation of a priest and
bring scandal to the institution, were sins against Holy Mother
Church.

Cardinal Kruger decided he would issue a letter to every
bishop in the world reminding them of the threat of
excommunication contained in the document issued by Pope
John XXIII, a pope who had already been beatified and was slated
to be canonized as a saint of the Church. No one should speak of
these things outside of official Church channels. He would decree
this.

As the cardinal turned up his collar against a strong wind that
carried the cries of cats from the Forum, his concerns were not
institutional, but personal. As a child, Hans Kruger had hundreds

of toy soldiers. The army games he played were serious ones, pitted against his father, General Kruger of the Third Reich. His father had taught him the technique of the feint, where a commander would intentionally expose a large section of his force to the enemy, sacrificing them and allowing them to be cut to pieces so that the most valuable elements of the army could retreat safely, hidden from enemy fire.

It was a sound strategy, one that Kruger remembered well. The only element of the Church that was now exposed to its enemies was the legion of pedophile priests who acted out of a dark pathology or illness. The damage being done to the Church in America seemed likely to continue, and would probably spread to other countries. But it seemed most of the bishops and other members of the Church hierarchy, including the Curia in the Vatican, might remain insulated from the scandal. Kruger had engaged in chess matches all of his life and well understood the tactic of sacrificing pawns to protect bishops.

The cardinal turned away from the ruins of the Forum and walked back toward Vatican City. He directed his thoughts to the Pope's failing health. The Vatican had finally issued public statements about the pontiff's medical condition and the world knew his demise was imminent.

The successor to the present pope would have to be strong – strong enough to stand up to the enemies of the Church, strong enough to deflect criticism away from the bishops, the cardinals and the pope himself, and to direct it instead at individual sick priests. He knew he was such a man and that he could and would be the next pope. He had the votes of the College of Cardinals tallied in his head.

Cardinal Hans Kruger knew history. He knew why the Roman Empire collapsed. As supreme pontiff, he would not make the mistakes of the Roman emperors.

91

SO HELP ME GOD

10 a.m., Tuesday April 23, 2002
Thiberville Parish Courthouse

Morning came fast. As I picked up my change on the dresser, I held the light-copper-colored tin medallion the turbaned taxi driver had handed to me in Boston eighteen years ago. I had carried the medal in my pocket every day. I clutched it tightly in my left hand and slipped it into an empty pocket.

As I started for the door, Julie picked up my tie off of the bed and handed it to me. I laid it back on the bed and shook my head.

Julie had a plan. The day before, we had returned my rental car and kept the one she'd picked up in New Orleans, a Volkswagen Beetle that she referred to as our "getaway car". We would leave the Thiberville courthouse immediately after the hearing and drive the short distance to a friend's secluded weekend home in the Atchafalaya Basin. We would spend a week there resting before returning to Europe.

When we were checking out at the desk in the lobby, the clerk handed me a package. It was about the size of an 8x10 photo frame, wrapped in brown paper and neatly tied with string. I admired the bow, and looked at the printed lettering. It made me smile to see how my name was written. Her handwriting was still as bad as mine.

As Julie drove toward the courthouse, I gingerly untied the string and pulled back the tape to open the wrapping. Sasha had painted the old stadium at night. She had signed it, and on the back she'd written "The First Place".

The courthouse hall was crowded with victims of Francis Dubois who were now adults, and their families and friends. I recognized the giant Poppa Vidros, the guy who held the shotgun on me in the Courville's front yard. He was leaning against the wall near a bank of elevators, talking with two smaller men.

I looked away from Poppa Vidros, but my stomach tightened. I had walked through a metal detector on the ground floor, so I did not think the big man could have got to this floor with a gun. But I was sure somewhere on the street there was a jacked-up pickup truck and in the truck was a loaded gun.

Most of the media was still congregated downstairs, where the new DA was holding court before television cameras.

When Mo stepped off the elevator and started walking toward me, I crossed over to her. She took both of my hands and squeezed tight, smiling nervously.

"You really didn't have to come."

"I want to be here, Ren. I want to see this end for you. The last time we went through this, people wanted to kill you. I want to be with you... ya know," she lightly punched me, "in case someone blows you to kingdom come."

"That's not funny."

"Oh come on now, you love gallows humor."

"Not as much as I used to." I glanced back to the elevators at the far end of the hall. Poppa Vidros was not in view anymore.

Mo and Julie walked into the courtroom with me just before ten. It was packed, but it seemed not many wanted to sit too close. We made our way to the empty second row. Francis Dominick Dubois was seated at the counsel table, his back to me. The orange jail jumpsuit was oversized. His cuffed hands were in his lap, and I heard the shackles on his ankles when he turned his head around to speak to one of his lawyers. That unnerving smirk was fixed on his face.

"All rise." The bailiff opened the door and the judge entered. It was Judge Thomas Weir, the most scholarly of the judges in the district. I knew he would render the right decision, based on the evidence he heard.

The new, young DA spoke out of turn before the judge was ready for him to proceed. "Your Honor, we call Renon Chattelrault and announce our intention to qualify him as a hostile witness to allow us to cross-examine him."

As the judge pounded his gavel I rose from the second row and walked through the wooden swing-gate and inside the railing.

Judge Weir said, "I want all counsel in my chambers. We will stand in recess for fifteen minutes."

The lawyers and court personnel walked out with the judge, leaving me alone inside the rail with two court bailiffs and Francis Dubois. With my back to the angry stares of the crowded courtroom, I stood to the side of Dubois. He looked up at me. "Hi Renon."

I pulled out a chair and sat next to him. He looked like an old man, the way his father looked when I had met him. He was unshaven, sweating, his hair matted flat on his head.

"I didn't do this, Renon," he said, as his chains rattled a bit. "You know I didn't do this. Why would I have lied and withheld one name?"

"I know. The man claims it's recovered memory under hypnosis, and he said you forced him with a gun. I know it isn't true. Francis, I'm tired of seeing you in courtrooms. You need real medical help. You need to find some peace, live in peace."

"I don't have any money to get medical help. I don't have insurance. And nothing has ever helped me. If the judge lets me out of jail, I am going to my brother Bobby's farm in Flatwoods, Texas. Ya know, by Beaumont. Nobody can find me there either. I will get some peace."

We were interrupted by the lawyers filing back in and I walked to the witness stand and took my place.

"So help me God," I mumbled, completing my oath.

From the elevated witness stand, I could see that every seat in the courtroom was filled. Whenever I averted my gaze from the hate-filled glares of Dubois's victims and their families, my eyes would fall upon Francis Dubois himself, his expression fixed in a smirk. Finally, I noticed Julie in the second row, a face I could focus on. She looked composed, amazingly serene.

As the only witness, I was in a position to not only play God, but to be God. I held the ultimate power over the life of Francis Dubois. I had the power to assist the DA in condemning him to life in prison. I held the power to give Dubois his freedom.

The new young district attorney had been a college basketball star. He was so tall that when he stood before me on the witness stand, he blocked out my view of anyone but him. He fumbled with the plea agreement, had me authenticate it as the true document and introduced it in evidence.

I was not listening as the DA went through the motions of marking the agreement as an exhibit, allowing the judge to read it and handing it to the court reporter to be filed in the record. The noise of their voices was blocked by the blood pumping through my arteries, eliminating all sound but the sound of my interior dialogue.

I had to lie. The district attorney's interpretation of the plea documents was skewed, but if I agreed with his reading of them, Dubois would remain in jail awaiting trial on the 1983 rape charge. I knew a local jury would convict Dubois and a judge would sentence him to life in prison without the possibility of parole or probation. There would never be another child injured by him, never be another Will Courville.

All I had ever wanted to do when I worked with Des and Matt was save children from sexual abuse by priests. Now, at last, I had the power to protect children from the worst kind of sexual predator. I had to lie about the document. It was the only way children would ever be protected from Dubois.

As the DA moved back to the counsel table, I could see Julie again. I looked into her eyes and saw the goodness that defined her being, and asked myself what Julie would do if she was in my place that morning. Would she swear to tell the truth and then proceed to lie under oath?

The United States' justice system is based on the precept that witnesses who come before the court will testify truthfully. From the moment the District Attorney asked his first question, the truth came out almost as an involuntary reflex, against my will.

"Do you recognize this document?"

"Yes."

"Is this your signature?"

"Yes."

"Is it not a fact that the language of the agreement is to the effect that your former client agreed he would receive medical treatment during his period of incarceration?"

Again, I could not stop the truth from spilling out. "No. I think the document is clear that this is an option, and not a requirement."

As I heard myself testifying about the true meaning of the document that Dubois, Sean and I signed in the fall of 1985, so many years ago, I knew what the consequences would be. I knew that by nightfall Judge Weir would enter an order enforcing the plea agreement and all of its provisions, including the grant of immunity for crimes Dubois committed prior to 1985. Francis Dominick Dubois was again going to be a free man.

The judge called for a recess to consider my testimony and formulate a ruling. I sat still on the witness stand while everyone filed out of the courtroom. When only the two bailiffs, Dubois and I remained in the courtroom, the bailiffs flanked Dubois and walked him toward a side door.

As Dubois passed the witness stand, he said, "I knew you would get me out of this."

He looked back one last time with that same expression that had unnerved me since the day I met him. I sat paralyzed on the witness stand, alone in the courtroom, unable to will myself to leave.

Slowly, I pulled myself to a standing position. In the back of my throat, I tasted bile.

When I walked out into the hall, I realized an electrical storm had knocked out all but the emergency lights. There was more light coming from the narrow windows than the dim fixtures. I squinted, trying to find Julie in the crowd. I knew the judge would soon be returning to the bench to enter an order freeing the prisoner and I wanted to be on the road before that happened.

As I slowly navigated my way through the crowd, I was blocked by the immense presence of Poppa Vidros. He gave me a hard look, then gazed at the rain outside the window. He sucked hard on his cigarette.

The big man said, "Is the judge going to free him?"

I nodded.

"You know where he's gonna go?"

I nodded again. "Flatwoods, Texas. He will be going to a farm owned by his brother Bobby Dubois. Flatwoods is somewhere around Beaumont."

Poppa Vidros dropped his cigarette and mashed it with his big boot. With his hands jammed in the pockets of his raincoat, he turned slowly and worked his way through the crowd to the elevator.

Julie drove our getaway car from the courthouse on wet roads to the outskirts of Thiberville, turning onto the Interstate, bound for our hideaway in the Atchafalaya Swamp. I felt empty. The news broke on the car radio that the judge had quashed the indictment pending against Francis Dubois and he was to be released from the parish jail with immediate effect.

Friday morning, April 26, 2002
Atchafalaya Basin, Louisiana

Three days before we were to leave Louisiana, the biggest news story of the Dubois saga broke. First, the Associated Press put a condensed news item on the wire, two abbreviated paragraphs noting that the infamous serial sex abuser, former Catholic priest Francis Dubois, had been murdered in a small town in east Texas.

The next morning the Baton Rouge newspaper carried a full account on its front page. In the center of the article was a photograph of the front of Lizzie Johnson Primary School. In the lower left hand corner was a mug shot of Francis Dominick Dubois taken when he was last booked in the Thiberville Parish Correctional Facility. In the tight head shot, he appeared to be unshaven, sweating, his hair matted flat on his head, and his expression was the same smirk I had seen so many times since I first met him in Deerfield, New Hampshire, eighteen years earlier.

Dubois had been seen at the Lizzie Johnson Primary School in Flatwoods, Texas. He had been leaning against a chain-link fence, watching second- and third-graders play in the schoolyard during recess. Shortly after the bell rang and everyone returned to their classrooms, several teachers had reported hearing three explosive noises in quick succession. Rushing outside, they saw a dirty white pickup truck in the distance, speeding away down the Farm to Market Road that ran alongside the school. Beyond the description of the truck being white and dirty, they could offer no further details.

It was only when they turned to go back into the school that they saw the corpse. The shotgunned body of Francis Dominick Dubois was still almost erect, the traumatized teachers reported, its bloodied mass of flesh embedded in the chain-link fence. What was left of his skull dangled from the spikes on the top of the fence.

I crumpled the newsprint and tossed it in a wastepaper basket. For a long time I was still. Then I retrieved the article, walked onto the deck of the house that overlooked the wide Atchafalaya River, and put a lighter to the newspaper. The burning paper rose a few inches into the air. Dubois's face was consumed in flames as the newsprint disintegrated into ashes.

92

A LITTLE CHURCH

Saturday April 27, 2002
Amalie

On the morning we left the swamp house to make our evening flight to Europe, I was still tired. As we reached the Interstate, I realized Julie had turned away from New Orleans and was headed due south. "We're going to Amalie," she said.

"Amalie?"

"It's important, Ren."

Amalie was the last place I wanted to see. It was the one place I hoped I'd never remember. I leaned back against the headrest.

"Okay," I said. "Okay."

Rows of sugar cane stood low in the fields along the road. We passed the smokestack named Catherine.

As we approached the front door of the church of Our Lady of the Seas, I realized I had never been inside. I was taken by its beauty. Along the center aisle, the pews had elaborate carvings depicting scenes of life around Amalie and family names of the area. We walked to the communion rail and looked at the rose-colored leaded glass windows on the back wall of the sanctuary. To our left was a small altar with a statue of the Blessed Virgin.

Julie nodded to the side altar where the statue stood. When I saw the woman kneeling there, arranging flowers, my heart almost stopped.

I walked over, reached down and touched her shoulder. She stood and turned to face me.

"Renon?"

"Hattie."

Her lip quivered.

"Hattie, I am… uh…"

She threw her arms around me, hugging the breath out of me, holding me tight. "Oh God, Renon. It's so, so good to see you."

"I… I'm… sorry. Sorry, Hattie. So sorry."

"It was God's will. Not your will. Our little boy is with God. Wes and I know… We know… nothing is your fault, Renon. We forgave you a long time ago."

She pulled back and looked at me, taking a handkerchief to her tears. "We didn't know where you were. There's been no number for you in Thiberville for years. Julie had left the diocese. Matt had passed. Wes wanted to call too. We knew this was killing you. God, how hard I've prayed for you. When Julie called me yesterday, I was so happy."

I shook my head. "It was my fault."

"Nothing can be changed. You have our forgiveness."

I nodded.

"Do you want to tell him goodbye?"

She took a handful of summer lilies from a vase on the altar. "I brought these from the garden today."

She carried the flowers in one hand and took my hand in the other, walking me to the center aisle. When she reached Julie, she hugged and kissed her. "He loved you so much. Come with us. Renon wants to visit."

On the way to the cemetery, Hattie kidded me about how my hair had turned gray. She said Wes's hair was falling out. She told us Wes had gone off to Baton Rouge for some kind of equipment auction and he would be really sorry he did not get to see us.

My head was throbbing, my throat was raw and my body ached.

Hattie handed me the flowers and pointed the way. "They had a place next to the little girl, Amalie, who the town was named after, and everyone wanted him there. He's on the other side of the statue."

I walked to the grave alone. Will's marker had an image of a horse on it, his name, and the dates. I placed the flowers at the base of the headstone. I really prayed. I had not prayed that way since the day I'd said the rosary with Matt – Will's buddy – in the hospital in Washington.

I struggled with the clasp on the chain around my neck and pulled off the Celtic cross. In a whisper I said, "Mr. Matt gave this to me." Then I dug a tiny hole and buried the cross next to the grave marker.

I prayed for Will, his family, Matt, my family, for Julie. And for the first time in my life, I prayed for myself, prayed that I could accept the gift of forgiveness I had received. And I prayed I would find a way to forgive myself.

Julie lightly touched my hair. I looked up at her. She reached for my hand.

AUTHOR'S NOTE

First, I acknowledge the ones whose names I will never know, those children around the world who had God's greatest gift, innocence, ripped out of their hearts; those who survived and those who did not survive, and their families. These strangers to me are the ones who kept me at the task of writing this novel every day for many years, for they deserve the truth as terrible as the truth is. When I tired of doing this work, as happened many times, my thoughts always turned to the victims and their families. They are the real heroes in a story that otherwise is without heroes.

Anthony Cheetham, my publisher at Head of Zeus in London, is one for whom I cannot compose enough words of praise, for Anthony was the first publisher to recognize the importance of this story. He unhesitatingly took the risks to bring the novel to the world. He generously supplied me with everything an author could ask for in terms of the support and guidance of the staff at Head of Zeus, including Nicolas Cheetham, Mathilda Imlah and everyone else who works with Anthony Cheetham.

The special acknowledgment, the greatest debt I owe, is to a lady who has my undying gratitude, Laura Palmer, Editorial Director at Head of Zeus, the very best in the business. Laura provided me with phenomenally brilliant editorial advice regarding the novel manuscript, advice that was unerring. Similarly overwhelming was incredible work accomplished by copyeditor Lucy Ridout to whom I also owe a great debt. These two consummate professionals demonstrated characteristics a writer could only dream of having access to at the final critical stage when their work is being shaped for the market.

My agent David Godwin, and Heather Godwin, and Anna Watkins at David Godwin Associates in London came into my life like unexpected gifts I could never reciprocate. David was the first person in the publishing business to recognize the value of the novel. David and Heather Godwin, partners in everything, worked hands-on with the manuscript, devoting days that turned to weeks and months to shape this novel for presentation to publishers. They were right in every call they made.

The Dean of American editors whose career spans nearly half a century at Knopf, one with a career as distinguished as any in the history of American literature, Ash Green, encouraged and supported me from the time I had the earliest drafts of this story written.

My wife, Melony, edited many versions of the manuscript, and steadfastly believed in the value of the story. There are no words poetic enough to express my feelings about all she contributed to this novel and my life.

Father Thomas Patrick Doyle has become a historic figure and deservedly so. I've often read that Tom possesses great courage, but he possesses much more than courage. Courage is something we rely upon to confront and conquer fear. Tom Doyle is truly without fear, the only fearless person I ever encountered. Upon recognizing the potential scale of the crisis that might confront the Church and grow to scandalous proportions, and realizing the damage and destruction being done to minors and children, he immediately and unhesitatingly took actions that he knew would destroy his career in the Church as he sided with the child victims and the truth. He has never left the side of the victims or the truth. My debt to him is immeasurable.

When the history of the crisis and scandal is finally written it will be recounted and remembered that once there was a man called Michael to whom millions owe a debt. Fr. Michael Peterson's phenomenal comprehension of every aspect of the many issues and his unbounded compassion for all concerned, his humanity, and tireless work until his death amounted to a monumental contribution. Sometimes I think I can still hear his voice calling to the hierarchy of the Church to embrace common decency and common sense, for he believed that no man of God should require policies, procedures, intervention teams or any bureaucratic devices to simply do the right thing and act to protect God's greatest gift, innocence, that is only embodied in children. My memories of Michael never faded when doing this work.

The world owes a debt to Scott Anthony Gastal that I acknowledge on behalf of those who know of him and those who do not. He was a young child in 1985 when he was the first victim of clergy abuse to ever go into a courtroom trial against a bishop and diocese before a judge and jury and make the impervious prelate and the monsignors who surrounded him accountable for the grave injuries he suffered, changing history in the process. Without the brave, honest, strong testimony of this child, the crisis and scandal would not have ignited in the way it did 27 years ago.

Psychologist Dr Lyle Lecorgne imbued young Scott Gastal with the confidence to tell his truth before a court in the first historic trial against a bishop and diocese. Not only did his very presence have a soothing effect on the young boy, Dr Lecorgne's trial testimony should be engraved in stone in the Piazza San Pietro in front of Saint Peter's Basilica in Rome as a permanent monument to the damage done to innocent children at the hands of criminal priests whose crimes were covered up by those in the Church hierarchy all the way to the highest levels inside the Vatican.

There would never have been justice for child victims if the crisis and scandal had not been lawyer driven by a large number of outstanding American attorneys with Jeff Anderson of Minnesota heading the list and joined by many of his colleagues like Michael Pfau, Mitchell Garabedian and a legion of other courageous lawyers who fought fierce battles on behalf of victims to reveal the hidden crimes, sin and shame of the church.

I first met Helen Malmgren and David Gelber when they

produced a special hour of *CBS 60 Minutes II* that was presented by journalist Ed Bradley on the eve of the first Bishops' Conference to discuss clergy abuse in June 2002. The groundbreaking broadcast was awarded an Emmy. Helen remained in contact with me over the years, and was passionately motivated to see the story I told in the broadcast placed between the covers of a book in the form of a novel. She worked without either compensation or credit in revisions of this novel and was a tireless editor and tough taskmaster when she worked with the text.

Dr Eamonn O'Neill, a prominent international journalist and lecturer who resides in Scotland, and Michael Powell of *The New York Times* (formally New York Bureau Chief for *The Washington Post*) and Helen Malmgren of CBS asked the hard, probing, difficult questions in long interview sessions with me that were of monumental importance in helping me focus on the issues that matter, the truths that needed to be represented in the novel.

Leslie Schilling was not only one of the first to read the manuscript, she went the whole distance by my side, and was always there when I needed assistance regarding research or computer technology and gave her unwavering support to the project during its long time in the making.

I feel a debt of gratitude to some writers, as well as others with literary backgrounds, and a few friends and family members who generously gave of themselves, expending enormous time and energy reading various versions of the manuscript and commenting on same, including Helen Malmgren, Allen Josephs, Jesse Graham, Thomas E. Guilbeau, Edward Leblanc, Tom Turley, Vincent and Helen Grosso, my brother Johnny, my sister Camille, Carl Wooton, Jack Cooper, Joe Riehl, John Hemingway, Scott Crompton, Tom Gowen, Robert F. Smallwood, Ron Gomez, and especially Robin Kelley O'Connor who was the first to read the earliest draft and urged me to push on to the end through countless revisions to the final draft regardless of the number of years it might take.

My former wife, Janis, and our children, Todd, Chad and

Jeanné, lived through a very dark period in my life, a time that I am sure changed all of us in significant ways; a time when the sadness in our lives was eclipsed by a feeling of solidarity. I will never know what scars this time inflicted upon them, but I have the memory of how they loved and supported me in that time and daily reminders of how they love and support me now, love and support I hope I return in significant ways.

In the time I worked on the book, some people shared confidences with me and they know who they are and will read the result of their trust and honesty in the pages of this work and know how deeply I feel indebted to them.

Dr Sidney Dupuy is a gifted and gentle healer who knows what he contributed that can never be adequately expressed or repaid.

While working on this novel, I kept close company with some of the novels and stories by Ernest Gaines, William Faulkner, Eudora Welty, Carson McCullers, Tennessee Williams, Truman Capote, the singularly wonderful work by Nell Harper Lee and novels by other southern writers. The prose of these southern American voices is so compelling as to be convincing, and these distinct, strong southern voices were inspiring to me.